SUMMER OF THE SEALS

SUMMER OF THE SEALS

JOHN-MARK ROBERTS

Copyright © 2023 by John-Mark Roberts

All rights reserved. No part of this book may be reproduced in any manner whatsoever without written permission except in the case of brief quotations embodied in critical articles and reviews.

First Printing, 2023

My heartfelt gratitude to my treasured circle of family and friends, especially my wife Lynn, for support and tolerance of my many eccentricities. Finest-kind.

Thanks is not enough to my son Tim Roberts for navigating me through the modern literary world to bring this work to life. My son Rob Roberts has always acted as a sounding board and invaluable contributor on everything Maine as he makes it understandably his home as did I.

This book is dedicated to my dear friends and their ancestors from the island of Malaga. May we move forward remembering the injustices in hopes that never again will it be repeated or forgotten.

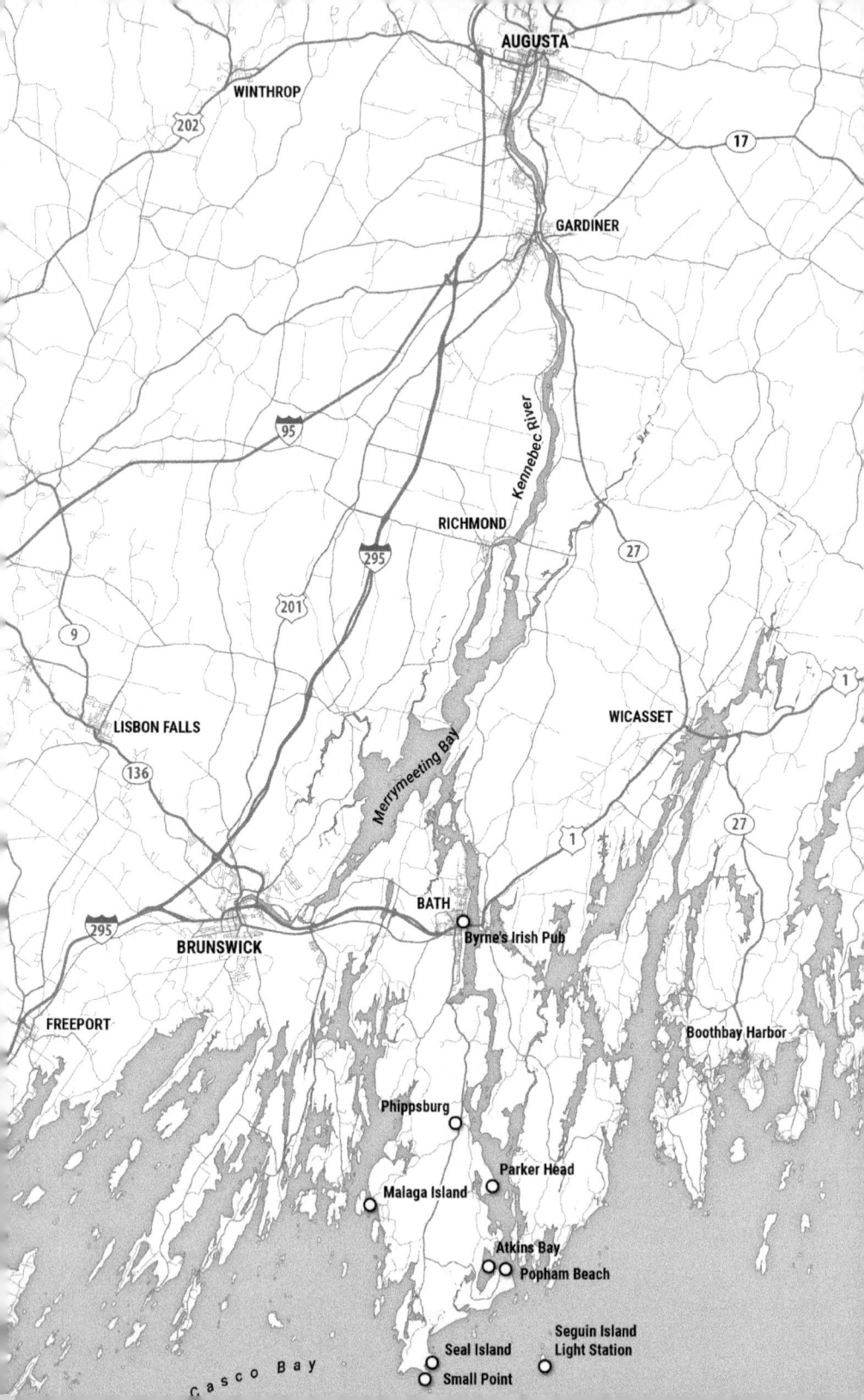

The man with the gray-white hair and stubbly gray-white beard wiped his hands on the old rag he brought out from his plaid shirt pocket underneath the chest waders. The glow from the kerosene lantern placed on the prow of the weathered boat moored to the dock flickered in the darkness. He surveyed the skyline. Dawn was still an hour or so from breaking. The old nets still had to be loaded. He straightened his worn and stiff back and replaced the rag.

A noise from the water caused him to peer out into the blackness. It was a blow of air and the accompanying snorting of something familiar catching a breath. He did not have to look further to know what it was. Gazing into the black he simply imagined the eyes he knew were looking at him. Large round eyes; they would be brown and wide. The man laughed a short, curt moment.

A younger woman appeared out of the gloom to join him at his task. Without a word she bent and started gathering the heavy nets. The man could just make out her somewhat wild, black hair in the flicker of the lantern. They worked for ten minutes before he spoke.

"Want to tell me what they want?" he ventured.

The silence spoke volumes.

"We'll talk on the boat, later, A-yuh," he consigned.

I

The afternoon Boston traffic was the way Boston afternoon traffic always was. Not backed-up or jammed as it sometimes could be, but nerve wracking and filled with seasoned aggressive drivers avoiding the tourists and out-of-towners that clogged the system. Throw-in commercial trucks, 18 wheelers, and school and Massachusetts Bay Transportation Authority busses and the scene was set for the drive home that only true Bostonians could suffer with New England fortitude.

A very sensible silver SUV, driven by a very sensible business lady in a very sensible business suit and skirt, negotiated the madness with practiced skill. On the front doors of the vehicle were magnetic signs in very businesslike letters stating 'Boston Maritime Insurers, LLC'. Under that was the expected phone and FAX numbers as well the website. Turning off of Route 1, after passing over the Mystic River Bridge, car and occupant wound through smaller streets in Chelsea until arriving at a very sensible gated community of elegant upper-middle-class condominiums.

As she got out of the SUV, the driver gathered purse and keys and empty travel coffee cup with the company logo affixed and a papers satchel also with the company logo affixed. She juggled the things and used a leg to shut the door and press the fob button to lock it. Striding to the mailbox on the small front porch, she waved an elbow at the lady two houses down that she had never bothered to meet but who got home the same time as she every work day. Just a fumble with the front door keys, the mail under her chin, and she was home.

After dumping her armload onto a small dining room table, she rifled through the junk ads and civic political pamphlets, tossed a bill aside as important, and then stared oddly at the letter remaining.

Hand-written, in rather shaky blue ink, the name 'Marie Mac-Leer' stared back.

"That's my name, alright" she said out loud.

Her gaze saw her address, equally almost scrawled, but when she read the return address she felt a cold shock pass up her spine. She put the letter down, unopened and on its face, and called out the usual phrases.

"I'm home! If anybody cares! Just your mother and the bread-winner, that's all!"

Two sets of muffled steps started down the well carpeted stairs. Marie's thoughts about the letter and anything from work that had concerned her on the way home had disappeared as two heads and then two forms bounded towards her.

"Sorry, Mom!" the girl smiled. "Reading on the internet!"

"Watching an old Film Noir flick!" the boy suggested. He was wearing an old gray fedora and put on a Hollywood detective accent. "C'mere, Toots!" he mimicked as he joined the girl in hugging their mother.

"And what have you two out-of-schoolers been doing all day, the same?" Marie tried to scold after the embrace.

"Aw, just the first day, Mom!" the girl reasoned. "At least I'm learning something; somebody else I know can't say the same thing."

"Not true, Doll-face!" her brother continued the act. "I know how to refer to a 'gun' as a Rosco, a Gat, a Heater, a Rod, a..."

"Enough!" his mother chuckled. "What's for dinner?"

As the two siblings were putting plates and silverware and casserole dishes into the dishwasher, their mother smiled as she watched them. Seated at the dinner table, glass of sparkling water in her hand, Marie allowed herself to be very proud.

There was her daughter Janet, or Jan as she preferred. Dark brown hair pulled back in a pony tail, her rather athletic arms reaching to dispense the crockery (the long hours of soccer and lacrosse mom had paid- off), she was turning into just what Marie had been herself. Her academics were only slightly shadowed by her brother and she seemed level, funny, reasonably but not overly popular, and suited for her life so far.

And there was Jonathon; not Jon so he and his fraternal twin would be the 'Jan and Jon' or 'Jon and Jan' of their younger days. He had put the fedora away for the moment to show his somewhat unkempt brown hair but Marie curled a smile at the thought of the closet full of hats upstairs that the boy had collected over the years. Each one was to match a different mood or comic whim. He was her jester; her smart, not-so-athletic, sometimes sardonic little man. Now he was on the verge of becoming a grown-up man.

At fourteen, both of Marie's twins had graduated Middle School and were on, in the fall, to High School. Many mothers may have worried over this. Many should be worried. But Marie was confident in a lot of things that she herself had done that would set this up to be a golden time for her children.

There was nothing miraculous these days in 2012 in a single mother rearing adjusted kids. Even in a greater metropolitan area like Boston, the community and the schools were poised to help in wondrous ways. But Marie had hedged the bet.

Jan and Jonathon's father had started a very, very successful business that insured both smalltime maritime companies and ships and fishing boats but also highly sought-after import and export firms here in Boston and also abroad. The company had kept the family service style approach that resulted in repeat and loyal customers and the fourteen-year old business was now nearing the net worth where incorporation seemed likely. Not that all the funds were liquid; but the business had provided a comfy without being spoiled life for the twins.

The old twinge of pain returned. Marie smiled through it as she always had. It was she who had worked so hard for her kids. It was she who had sacrificed her life to provide for them.

As she gazed at the two young people in the kitchen, now arguing over who had done more in the preparation and presentation and post erasure of the recent meal, she recognized the unmistakably sharp set features that their father had left them. High, Irish cheekbones, the almost too-good-looking noses, brown near-black hair, the Dark Irish angular chins; they were going to be pretty adults. And with all that add Marie's own natural wholesomeness and equally Irish-Italian-American beauty and the results might prove dangerous.

She had some pride about the looks her Costello side of the family, on her Dad's side, had betrothed her. From Sicily and then Ireland and then America the Great, the family had enjoyed tough but fair years on Boston's waterfront. Her mother was Italian-American, as well. Her people had migrated from the small islands almost in Greek waters to the Tampa Florida area where they fought with those same Greeks, now immigrants, in the tough sponge harvesting industry. Her mother's father had died young in a tragic diving accident of suspicious circumstances and his young bride had been sent away to friends of the family in Boston for 'a better life'.

She was proud of her heritage. Her father met her mother through local parish ties on the waterfront where cultures collided or melted. The two had borrowed from her mother's family in Florida enough to buy an old, established small grocery business of renown and continued to provide the very mixed, blended, comfortable sort of place that was quintessentially Bostonian.

Growing up, Marie had learned numerous phrases in numerous Bostonian dialects. There were Portuguese, Irish, Italian (Calabresse, Sicilian, Venetian) and Greek as well.

Her father's grocery even carried kosher products with pride. Marie's collection of Yiddish terms was a constant source of amusement to such clientele when she was but a child and working in the store.

Her parents had scraped enough money to give her, the only child, a warm, loving home and then had sent her to college as the first in the family to do so.

Business had been her major. She hoped to return to her family's small but respectable neighborhood grocery business and expand it in modern ways.

And then she met Manny.

Mannanan MacLeer, no middle name; he explained it was a moniker Americanized from an old Irish Sea-God. She had laughed then on the first time they met and would be laughing with him constantly for many happy years to come.

She had told herself over and over again that she had fallen in love on that same night.

Perhaps bewitched, her own Irish blood told her. But the thing was he seemed to have eyes for only her. She had of course seen him on campus, what girl hadn't. His wild dark eyes and handsome features filled the twitter of all the girls' dorms and gatherings. Each rash young woman had flirted and promised her girlfriends she would have this rogue under her wiles before long, but it never happened.

At an after-the-football game affair at an unremembered Sorority

House he had simply materialized before her with no drinks offered and no tired come-on line prepared. With one hand in his jeans pocket he took her hand with the other and smiled and caught her in his eyes and said words she would always remember.

"I'm Mannanan, Manny for short. I've been waiting to meet you..."

Marie looked at the letter laying face-down on the table. She didn't have to look again at the return address. She knew what it read. She knew where it was.

Manny and Marie, (how funny that sounded together) had been inseparable from that first night. They had talked, laughed some more, walked, and each day that passed only saw them apart when their classes forced it. The next semester that was mostly rectified.

They went to mass together. Manny admitted to not being as devout as he should have been, but he matched Marie's fervor. They got to know the campus priest and he them. They listened to his guidance as they made plans.

Marie's father had been the last of his people in America. His father had died before Marie was born. His mother followed just as Marie had turned one. Her father was immediately taken and impressed with the dark young Irish-American who asked permission to 'court' his daughter. Marie's mother was equally smitten. Her somewhat strange and sometimes mysterious relatives in Florida approved from afar.

During the second semester break Manny announced that he was driving Marie to meet what family he had.

He told her as much as he could about his relations. On the drive to Maine he explained that he came from a convoluted mixture of fishermen and investors. As they turned off I-95 and proceeded through ever increasingly smaller towns they eventually left old Route 1 and headed down a peninsular and several more small roads until they passed down a dirt lane under the spruce trees that had begun to cast lengthening shadows in the growing afternoon.

The place they stopped bore the address that was now scrawled on the unopened letter on the table.

"Enough of this" Marie said softly to herself. The kids had gone back upstairs and she took the letter, walked to her favorite overstuffed arm chair in front of the dark TV screen and sat down. She ripped the letter opened swiftly. It was not easy to make out the writing, but she managed. The message was short and as to the point as the person she remembered who had obviously sent it. The scrawled signature below confirmed her thoughts.

She closed her eyes, took in several long cleansing breaths then reread the letter. Putting the thing back into its envelope she stood up and walked over to her satchel that was now beside the front door. Placing it into one of the folds, she willed herself not to think about it again tonight.

It didn't work.

The following morning Marie had breakfast alone and left a note reminding her offspring of the things they had talked about the night before. Even though they were on summer break, she expected them both to get out into the light of the gated community. Sufficient grass was expensively manicured in areas to allow Jan to kick the soccer ball to her ever-increasingly bored brother.

The drive into town almost went by in a daze. Except for the semi that crossed over into her lane a few feet in front of her, Marie robotically drove and had disturbing thoughts galloping in her head like wild horses about to break free of restraining reigns. By the time she reached her reserved parking place in the newly refurbished old brick building that housed her business she was near panic.

She told herself that she was probably too short with her receptionist/secretary who had been a constant bastion of female strength and friendship since, well since. Marie knew that all too soon she would be answering the poised questions from her indispensable mother/sister/employee.

The morning's work on her computer seemed to drag on. Nothing was pressing, everything was ship-shape, to coin a well used phrase in the office. All she had to really do was go over some old policies that were up for renewal, put her electronic signature on the orders and send out these and copies of some pending overseas transactions to their lawyers. Each time her secretary Barb walked in Marie smiled and ducked the scrutiny. Finally at 10 o'clock she could take it no longer. She opened her door and told Barb to hold all other calls as she was making an important one.

Taking the letter from yesterday out of the satchel, she numbly opened it and found the telephone number scratched there. As she heard the phone ringing on the other end her thoughts raced. She had a brief sense of relief when nobody answered and by the 12th or so ring she practiced a calm message that she was prepared to leave on the answering machine that never picked up. By the 15th and 16th she wondered why she had not hung-up already.

"Hull-oo."

The silence of her pause seemed forever.

"This is Marie" she answered the male voice.

"Right-nice of you to call. Wicked-nice. Got ma letter, eh?"

"I did" she replied. The thick Maine accent was just as she had remembered.

"Well, no use mincing words, Marie. Here goes..."

An hour after the phone conversation Marie was still locked in a stare out over the parking lot of her building and to the docks beyond Border Street. The only words she had spoken since the call was to tell Barb she was having a quiet lunch and didn't want to be disturbed.

'That was a good word' she thought. 'Disturbed'...

The voice on the phone belonged to Manny's uncle on his father's side. She had been introduced after having to walk down to the water's edge with Manny warning of slippery rocks. 'Fin', short for

Finley Roin, was just coming out of a wooden shack-like structure that smelled like fermenting fish. Turns out it was. His main sustenance came from supplying the local lobstermen with 'the best, perfectly ripe bait on the Down East coast'.

The three had walked back up to an almost hidden white house of monstrous proportions. It loomed in the growing darkness like something out of a gothic novel. Once inside, however, it became a most hospitable place.

Over a, what else, lobster chowder supper, Manny further divulged that old Fin had practically raised him. Manny's father and mother had been out of his life since early teenager years. Marie had sheepishly asked, "They're...gone?"

The silence didn't answer her question but she pried no more. Fin filled-in a few more details saying he had a daughter who was out fishing and would be gone for several days. The conversation ended with a warm smile from Fin as he proclaimed "A-yuh. That's all of us left here. All the others are...elsewhere."

Fin had a cozy room for Marie and he and Manny sat up late into the night talking quietly downstairs. As the house had at least three floors, Marie though she might have trouble sleeping in such a strange place but she awoke the next morning surprisingly rested and in a great mood. Fin was gone, off to do what he did best, but Manny drove her all around the area and showed her the absolute beauty of the coast. They made it back to Boston before nightfall.

Not much was ever said again, at the time, about Manny's past. Marie felt it was painful for him and he seemed to take to her father and mother as ones he never had.

When the wedding was announced, an invitation was sent to Fin but neither Manny nor Marie was surprised when he didn't show.

What did show up was quite unexpected, at least from Marie's point of view.

After the ceremony college friends and Marie's parents had a small but heartfelt reception and everything seemed fine until Marie was reading the cards and envelopes containing wishes and some hard-gotten cash for the newlyweds. Marie read aloud 'MacLeer' on a very expensive looking parchment folded into a pouch and sealed with wax and a fancy stamp.

Manny's face went as stony as the rocks in Maine and he quietly took the thing from Marie and whispered "Later, Dear" in a voice Marie had never heard him use before.

The two honeymooned on Cape Cod in a modest honeymooners' getaway and Marie gave no thought in her bliss to the strange sealed parcel. It was several weeks in fact before Manny brought up the subject. They had found a place they could afford near campus as they each only had a semester left. Manny was working when he could in Marie's family store and only accepting the most meager wages. Life was good and everything lay ahead of them.

Manny had cleared away the dishes from dinner then gone to his side of the old dresser they shared. He returned with the package.

Sitting down at the card table they used he looked at Marie very seriously.

"Honey, I need to explain," he started. For the first time she could remember, he did not engage her eyes when he spoke.

"I told you my family was fishermen and investors. In the old days fishing was everything. But slowly ship building took hold on the coast. The ships needed backing and insurance and money. My family had some. It's a long story, but let me just say over the years we got our hands into a lot of things. The money grew. During the Great Depression we did better than some think we should have. Small towns harbor ill will. So for years we have tried to play it down. Most folks have forgotten what we had. The bank is so tied-up in old money and family secrets and deals made long ago that will never be brought to light. This...this is more than a wedding gift."

He showed her the contents. The abundant cash in large

denominations she could count, if given some time, but the gold and silver coins she had no way of placing a price on.

"I have to ask you before I take this back. I am expected to continue to make money like the family has. There are far-flung, shall we say, distant relatives here and in the old country. They might one day ask for...assistance. We, you and I, could start a business that would insure our children never have to want for anything. We can be happy. But I have always felt that this...money thing has a terrible price attached. It scares me."

Marie had been silent for a long period before she began to ask the obvious questions. No, the money was not 'dirty'. No, there was nothing illegal involved. Never would there be a nefarious or evil thing expected, just...strings attached, as Manny put it.

It took several days for Marie to talk things through with her new husband before he bowed to her wish and they began to plan a company. They indulged things to each other as married persons should do. An unplanned trip to see her distant relations in Florida brought a new level to their new marriage and partnership. They collectively decided on a course of action.

Sitting in the present, she shook her head at the consequences.

In the first year of business, ties to local and Irish shipping firms and local boats alike poured-in. Many of these came from Manny's family's 'contacts'. They had the cold hard cash to back the ventures. They were able to modernize her family's business on the side and sell it for a hefty profit for her ailing father. All the while life was like a wonderful dream to Marie. Manny was the dutiful business partner, husband, lover and father to their twins when they were born. He was a rock of strength when both Marie's parents passed. Never was there a mention of things 'owed' his family.

Until, that is, the twins had just turned four.

Manny had told Marie that he had to make a trip to Ireland. Some business opportunities needed his attention, he had said. He had promised that if things worked out he would arrange for her and the kids to come to the old country to see their collective heritages. He would be away for just a few weeks.

Marie had a strange foreboding about the trip but played the proper role as business partner and wife. They were able to hire help for the twins and had a nice place near their offices. Marie could take on more of the roles of the boss of the operation. She liked that. But she worried that she had read something in Manny's eyes that spoke of trouble.

After about three weeks Manny's daily phone calls fell to twice a week. He explained that he was out in remote areas of the west coast where phones were still a luxury. One day after waiting almost a week Marie calmly asked the love of her life what he was hiding from her.

He was quiet for a moment then spoke in that alien voice she heard only twice before. He had decided that his dealings there were about to get…complex. He would not involve his wife or his children in whatever it was Marie could not get him to explain about further. The conversation ended with both of them in tears and Manny pledging to find a way through this.

And then there was nothing.

For the next heart-wrenching few weeks Marie poured over their business books trying to find something that hinted of the secrecy. She personally contacted shipping firm CEOs and anybody she could think to make a connection as to what was going on.

In blind panic she had tried to track him down through his clients but nobody seemed to know anything except for what little time they had spent with him in actual business. She could not even trace the last place he may have been seen other than somewhere on the upper west coast near Galway, which was the last port where he had secured shipping contracts.

She fearfully left her children in Barb's care and flew to Shannon and then Galway as soon as she could push a passport through. It was almost a month before she got there and she didn't even know where to start. She filed missing person notices in several port cities and had to endure the sly looks and questions as to whether or not Mr. MacLeer might *want* to go missing. Several stations of the 'Guarda', or police, were sympathetic but no leads presented themselves. Marie finally went home to two children whose father had vanished and to a broken life she did not know if she could live.

So many thoughts haunted her. This had something to do with his family. Had he fallen in with Irish criminals or smugglers? Was he the victim of foul deeds? Or had he just met someone there who meant more to him, at least for now, than a wife and two small kids?

The rest she had forced out of her mind forever, or at least as far as she could. It took months before she stopped crying at night, when the business was closed and the twins were asleep. She never made up stories about where their father was. She wasn't cold or elusive but simply told them Daddy had gone away to the old country and she did not know when to expect him back. Over the years, she told them as much as she knew, as she felt their ages appropriate enough. And then they just stopped asking. That's how strong of a mother she had willed herself to be.

And she never filed to declare him dead.

So, when this letter arrived from Maine she had dreaded what that had meant. Was Manny actually dead? Did he want to come back? Had the family knowledge of him? She had thought over the years to contact Fin and question him, but she always backed down for no real reason except pride. Or perhaps, Manny had asked Fin not to say anything.

But in the conversation with Fin none of that was the reason for the call. Except a small part about 'family' that had made a chill run up her spine again.

"Marie," Fin had drawled, "I'm in a pickle here. Wicked-hard pickle. I've been put in charge of two distant cousins, both about fourteen, I think. Much like what I've done before. You know. I wouldn't have called only I remembered your two would be about that age now. You were very regular with your Christmas cards for a few years. I understand why you stopped. I heard things. Didn't like 'em, but that's water under the bridge. I suppose you can guess how crazy this seems, but I'm thinking you and the kids might come up and visit an old man. I don't know squat, pardon the French, about no fourteen year-olds these days! Don't give me an answer now, just stew on it awhile. The cousins get here next week. You don't owe me nothing but I'm asking that you at least think about it. That's all."

And that was all. Marie had sat stunned ever since.

She finished the day somehow and decided to go home a little early. Barb could run everything, anyway. The drive was another blur. The kids were indeed outside somewhere when she got home and she changed into some jeans and a tee shirt and poured a glass of wine.

When Jan bounded in she had a big smile and blurted out "Hey, you're home early! Great! Uh-oh, what's wrong?"

Jonathon followed and turned his Red Sox hat around backwards. He pretended to smoke a pipe. "Tally-ho, Watson! The game's afoot!"

"Can't a body relax with a glass of wine after a hard day?" Marie almost laughed.

"Sure," Jan said seriously. "So what's really up?"

"Go get something cool to drink and we'll talk," her mother said. "It's about...family."

With the twins attentively on the edge of their seats on the couch, Marie reminded them of just who Fin Roin was to them and then read the letter. She calmly described the phone conversation and even tried to inject some humor with attempting to mimic the accent. Then she was quiet and allowed it all to sink in.

Expectedly, Jan was the first to speak.

"Thanks for being so cool, Mom," she said seriously. "I mean, most mothers in this position would have thrown the letter away and never said anything about it. Nice to know you think more of us than that."

Jonathon was wearing a pith helmet now and Marie had long ago ceased to question his motives for choice of headgear until he spoke.

"Good to do some archeology work on the very un-trunked family tree!"

"I just wanted to let you guys in on everything. We are pretty much all we have, you know?"

The twins nodded.

"Anyway, just to get this out into the open before I call Fin back tonight and decline his most odd request..."

"What?!" Jonathon interjected. "We're going, right?"

"Now son, you can't expect me to drag the three of us up to a sketchy old house in Maine to stay with an old coot I don't know to do I can't fathom what?"

"Right, Brain!" Jan agreed. "Haven't you seen any Steven King movies? This is his backyard, right? Nice family, comes to visit, expects no problems...and the axe-murders begin?"

"No-way!" Jonathon pressed. "We have finally got a chance to connect with anything about Dad and our past. I want to see something different besides the same old summer routine of spoiled kids and texting and who saw who at the mall holding hands with who..."

"Whom..." Jan started to correct.

"C'mon!" her brother continued. "Sis, can't you see what this could be? You can't tell me that all this time you haven't thought about where our people came from and what might be more fun than the stupid camps in New Hampshire, sorry Mom, and just always wondering?!"

There was a silence in the room before Jonathon resumed his case.

"I know you guys think I want to play Ghost Busters or Scooby-Doo or Charlie Chan, but I'm serious here."

Jan and her mother laughed together. Jonathon smiled as well.

"I mean it," he said, straight-faced again. "At least talk about it?"

The ensuing pensive look on his mother's face made her son pounce again.

"You know you need to get away," he tried. "When was the last vacation we had together? Disney two years ago, that's when. That was fun but all we did was spend money and ride rides and get sunburned and we're not kids anymore Mom…"

"I know that" she conceded with a pang of maternal regret.

Jan jumped in. "You can't really be thinking about this? Right, Mom? How do we know what this 'great uncle' is all about?"

"I don't think" Marie stated, "That for an instance I think he's anything more than what I saw on meeting him once. I get that feeling. He is what he is and what's more your father loved him, I could tell. He raised him, you know that. But I do have to have a few more particulars from him. Jan, you think this is wise at all? I mean down deep. Are you not the slightest bit interested in this?"

Jan looked down to the carpet. She waited a few long seconds before she spoke.

"I don't want you to get hurt Mom. Any more than you already have been."

Marie felt the cold shock of just how grown-up her little girl really was.

"Honey…" she started.

"Really, Mom," Jan said, looking straight into her mother's eyes. "Does this guy know anything about what happened to Dad? And what's it going to do, drag out stuff for you now? Is it going to help or hurt?"

"I'll call him again tonight, no right now," Marie said. "You two find something to do, and don't even think of listening in, right?"

"OK" they both agreed.

Marie needed to finish her glass and refill it before going into her home office and dialing the number again. Another torturous number of rings and the voice answered again in the same way.

"Hu-loo?"

"Fin," Marie started. "I've got some questions."

"Sure you would."

"Who are these kids coming to stay with you?"

"From up north," Fin stated. "Need some direction. Not much more I can say. I have been asked to broaden their horizons. They are like my people; you know what I mean."

"Fin," Marie faltered.

"Say what you want to say, Missy, I already guessed it…"

"Do you know anything about Manny?" she tried.

There was a pause that Marie felt was justified.

"I haven't heard a thing, not since he called me about the twins being born. That's the Gospel. Haven't seen hide nor hair, neither. I tried to find out when I heard. I know it's hard, wicked-hard. We could talk if you come up."

Marie now paused the conversation.

Picking back up the thread the two talked for another fifteen minutes before hanging up and Marie had already made her decision when the line went silent.

Before speaking to the twins she stepped into the downstairs bathroom and composed herself. She caught her reflection in the mirror and stared as if looking at a stranger. Her brown-blonde hair shook freely about her shoulders and she liked the way she looked. She used to wear it longer and it took on streaks of light when she went on summer holidays to spend strange times with her family in Florida. Only, there were worn lines beginning to show around her blue-gray eyes. Creases that were not apparent to others suggested that she smiled for everyone except herself.

Her daughter had made sly reference over the past few years that she should try to date. Several opportunities had arisen and she had even agreed to meet a man she had met through a friend for lunch. It had been so awkward and embarrassing, to her at least, that she had given up the idea entirely. All she could see, even now, was her husband's face, his eyes, hear his voice. What spell did he have on her? She choked back the old tears and went to tell her children what she had decided.

2

The sensible silver SUV with the advertisement for Boston Maritime Insurers on the doors made its way north along I-95. A woman in sunglasses drove while a young boy in the front passenger seat looked intently at everything passing by. A girl sat behind him bent over a tablet device and surfed the internet on various subjects as they passed.

Not quite a week had passed since the first conversation the lady behind the wheel had had with the person they were going to see. All the arrangements had been made for the home owners association to watch the house, the cat was quartered with Marie's secretary and best friend, and the people in her office had their marching orders, as if such trusted friends needed her direct supervision, and as Jan had so aptly observed anything else could be handled via the Ethernet.

Besides the toll stops at every border plus some and several rest stops the group made good time and the morning was still young when the vehicle made the cross over the bridge from New Hampshire into Maine. Only a few minutes later, the boy whistled in amazement.

"Wow," he breathed. "Look at all the trees! Everything's so...wide open and green!"

"No billboards," his sister stated. "State law. All signs have to be under a certain height."

"Why don't you get your head up and look at something!" her mother chided playfully.

"I'm seeing it," Jan protested. "I'm just getting a history lesson in the progress. Did you know that Maine leads the nation in production of three things?"

"Lobsters" her mother suggested.

"Right. What else?"

With no more guesses, she filled-in the blanks.

"Blueberries..." and that got nods from the two in the front seat. "And toothpicks."

That drew chuckles. "All the wood." Marie surmised.

"Maine used to be part of Massachusetts," Jan continued. "And it's also where prohibition started. That's weird. Seems it had to do with how much rum was imported through here. Portland had so many warehouses and a real problem with urchin children getting blind drunk every day. Made the politicians listen to the temperance groups."

"Just remember," her mother warned. "Your father taught me straight-away that Mainers are fiercely proud of their independence from Mass and have some particularly savory names for those of us from home. Be careful and not too proud."

"Proud of what?" Jonathon reasoned. "I'd love to trace family roots and find out we come from the salty old seafarers and crazy characters always associated with this state."

"You are," Marie sighed. "And I'm afraid you're going to get more of a dose of Down East color and story than is good for you."

"Where did that term come from?" Jonathon asked.

"Well?" Marie referred to the back seat.

"It seems," Jan mused, "That it comes from the sailing days where one had to sail *up* or north almost to Canada before tacking back *down east* to get to the ports."

"Oh," her brother said. "Cool."

"I want some answers, too," Jan offered. "You both know for years I've been researching our family names. Mom, your side is so much easier than Dad's. I mean, I've searched everywhere in records for 'Mac Leer' and only found a few mentioned right here in Maine. Nothing specific, mind you. But going back to Ireland and Scotland the spelling doesn't match."

"You remember," Marie reminded, "When I took you guys to New York the first time? To Ellis Island?"

"Yeah," Jonathon recounted. "The officials changed so many names; if they couldn't spell it or if they took a fancy to make it sound more American they did."

"Also," Marie noted, "Remember that the Irish didn't have a written language when the English took over. Subsequently, Irish spelling and grammar relied on the Anglicization of the words. Family names were just as easily misspelled and there are numerous families with different ways to spell their name."

"The only place I can find something is about something you told us a long time ago when you said Dad made fun and said he was named after an Irish Sea god."

Marie nodded, keeping her eyes on the road despite the much-reduced traffic here than they had seen in the other New England states.

"In Irish mythology, there is a 'Mannanan *MacLir*...L-i-r. Jan continued. "He's sort of the Irish Poseidon or Neptune. He changes his shape into sea creatures and rides a chariot or horses across the waves. He's quite the lady's man, too. Only he tricks most of them."

"Nice!" Jonathon exclaimed.

"Your father wasn't like that," Marie said quietly.

"I know, I know," Jan said. "I'm just saying. And this...great uncle that we're going to meet. His name doesn't register either. If you're doing the whole name-spelling-change thing, then you have to consider the Irish word *roin* or *roane* which is the word for 'seal', depending where in the country you are dialectically speaking of sealing an answer, to coin a pun."

She smiled at her joke, but her mother tensed her fingers on the steering wheel and was visibly jolted.

"What's the matter, Mom?" her son asked.

"Nothing," she said after a brief pause. "It's nothing. That actually makes sense because where we're going there are a lot of seals this time of year."

"Really?" Jonathon said excitedly.

Jan even looked up from her tablet.

"In spring time the seals come to the river where your Dad grew up" Marie explained. "They have their babies and stay the whole summer. I saw some when I was here before."

"They come there to mate, too" Jan remarked, finding the article now on her device.

Her mother flushed but said nothing as she tried to tell herself that she and the twins had had 'the talk' many years ago. There was no reason to keep thinking they were small children still, even if she wanted them to be.

As the family travelled through Portland, they decided quickly that it was a city that needed further investigation if they ever had the time. The whole modern civic idea seemed to be melded instead into the rich history. Moreover, the city had a real feel about it much like Boston but on an obviously smaller scale. The modern hospital that stood out on the hill side was flanked by older houses, a spectacular cathedral with spires reaching into the slightly overcast sky, and a watchtower that the internet said was once used to look for approaching ships. Missing was the water, or at least the bay or ocean, but the 295 took them over vast expanses on back bays and mud flats. As the highway turned to take them away from the city sights, a very old looking baked bean factory puffed its brick chimneys and reminded all passers-by that tradition was alive and well in Portland, Maine.

The next few smaller towns were punctuated more by the views of the Casco Bay than by anything else. Boats could now be seen; not so many commercial but pleasure craft either lazily sailing or putting along. Nearing Freeport, Marie had to quell a request from her daughter about stopping at the numerous outlet stores and of course the famous outdoors outfitter that was ubiquitous to the town. Jonathon seemed relieved at this. His natural curiosity was growing by the minute. His hat choice-of-the-day was a gray button-down bill driving or country hat. It looked a bit large on him but his mother supposed he thought himself well topped for coastal New England exploration. What did interest him here was the very large model of the Earth that spun just off the highway and signaled the flagship store of a very famous map and now GPS manufacturer.

The silver SUV's own GPS began to signal that the rather bland ride of interstate was nearing an end. A long exit ramp took them into the outskirts of Brunswick. Jan announced, in her role of historian, that this was a mill town of textiles and wood products that had until recently been home to a U.S. Navy airfield. The base had closed, as had the mills numerous years before, and speculation was the rule as to how the area would survive. Somehow, it seemed Maine towns and people always survived.

As their satellite-guide placed them on Route 1, Marie remembered coming through here with Manny and him explaining to her that Maine had gone through a remarkably similar history economically as Ireland. Mills and tanneries and factories had closed with the outsourcing of American business. No one could expect a business to pay a seasoned, skilled, union waged worker what the business would pay a worker overseas. Or could they? Some Maine businesses had stuck to their guns, but even now had difficulty in the current market.

Add to that state of affairs, with the closing of the mills, etc, the young people had no work. Everyone not in the beleaguered fishing industry or tree harvesting business couldn't wait to leave the state after high school or college to find gainful employment. Maine was the 'grayest' state in the union, with more people of ever increasing advanced age.

Again, just as Ireland (and many other places as well) the fishing industry was taking hit after hit as rising fuel costs and government imposed regulations made the way of life not so appealing, if hard work and low wages ever had been, to Maine's youthful population.

The only difference, Marie mused aloud, was that Ireland had invested strongly in software production and thereby gained a momentum that lasted until just a few years ago and was called 'The Celtic Tiger'. As a businesswoman who had a lot of dealings in the old country, she knew all too well and things had changed there, again.

Maine had not.

But still, Marie had a hunch, the inhabitants of a place where the weather could be the most immanent and serious battle for life would find a way to survive; and do it 'their way'.

Remembering something Manny had showed her, Marie turned off on the New Meadows exit and came into Bath on the old State Road. She wanted to show her son and daughter a whimsical place just off the road on the left. She remembered it fondly as a house trailer with a large green alien figure affixed to the roof. The marsh around the property had been decorated with the most bizarre, weird, and somewhat scary figures and signs and painted cut-outs; all summed up by the self-proclaimed title of 'Looney Lagoon'. Unfortunately, the stuff was gone. Marie told herself something must have happened to the architect of the jumble and so passed another Maine tradition.

Another surprise lay in a traffic round-a-bout just up the road that Marie didn't remember. However, just past this, adjacent to a filling station of the 60's variety still stood an odd statue of sorts that seemed to be made out of old scrap metal parts. It resembled a giraffe, maybe a dragon; whatever, it was known locally and on the tourists' brochure of Maine oddities as simply 'The Thing'.

Rejoining Route 1 again ever so briefly, the SUV turned onto state road 209 and headed south. Both Jan and Jonathon gazed at the bridge in Bath that they did not cross and Jan remarked that she would like to investigate the town.

"We should have time," her mother mused. "This is the thriving metropolis compared to where we're going."

Indeed, the road led them out of Bath and down a peninsular. Jan followed on her tablet. It seemed the entire area was called Phippsburg. There were many outlying sections and a small 'center' that contained a few municipal buildings, a school, a library and an old church.

"It seems," she announced, "That the area was named for a William Phipps, who among other things found a fortune in Spanish gold."

"My kinda guy!" Jonathon decreed.

"We're actually going nearer to Popham," their mother said.

"You remember that," Jan stated to her brother. "I did a report on it a few years ago since Mom had told us it was near where Dad was from."

"Oh, yeah," he replied. "Ruffled a few Boston feathers in the class because the colony that landed here was before Plymouth."

"And they built the first ship in the New World just so they could get back!" Jan added.

"Uh-oh" she said suddenly. "Not a good sign; I'm losing my signal!"

"The GPS still works," her mother said. "I would not be surprised if service was sketchy out here. Might not be so bad, after all."

"Right!" Jan disagreed.

The car turned off of 209 and continued through an area called Parker Head down smaller and smaller paths, just as Marie had remembered, and eventually onto a hard dirt road that ended before they plunged into Atkins Bay.

Ahead of them an older 70's model Chevy truck sat with untold pieces of nautical fishing apparatus jammed into the bed. Off to the right, under very old trees, the side of a house could be seen. It was clapboard and appeared to have been painted many, many times right over the preexisting coats. Yellow or maybe just faded white, it had three stories and numerous dormer windows along with the thick-paned old-fashioned weighted sliding type.

"Well" Marie almost sighed, both to herself and to her children, "Here we go."

The three stepped stiffly out of the car and stretched like cats after a nap. They looked around, gathered in the sights of light through the branches and smells of old nets, not so fresh fish, and the sea.

Marie was just about to get up the courage to go around and knock on a door when a creaking sound from down near the water surprised them all. A wooden door of rustic antique appearance opened in a structure that seemed to be made of old logs and planks. A white haired head appeared and presently the entire man started shuffling slowly and stiffly towards them.

He smiled as he labored in walking. The smile was genuine and broad. It creased the weathered face that was somewhat shaven. Old faded coveralls over a red plaid shirt completed the almost epitomic figure of a Maine waterman.

Marie broke the silence.

"How are you, Fin?" she said somewhat softy.

"Good...you?" he lilted back. "I was afraid you might have changed your minds. I am very, very glad to see you three!"

He looked at the twins with a wink and an even wider smile. When he stood in front of Marie, he seemed unsure as to what to do next. He reached back and scratched the back of his white head.

Marie surprised him by gently giving him a hug. He kept his hand on the back of his head and seemed embarrassed. When Marie stood back he laughed a short bark.

"My, my," he beamed. "You couldn't have told me and I'd have believed ya, but Missy you have gotten more pretty than my old memory can recollect. And you two,"

He turned to smile at the twins.

"Finest-kind, I do declare!" He noticed their puzzled look. "That means you're all right!"

"It's a warm day," he said looking up. "Let's get your gear and go into the house. Bet I can find some lemonade if I try..."

Seated around a very heavy and very old kitchen table, the four sipped their drinks and Jonathon went into his detective role in surveying his surroundings.

He heard the conversation but let his eyes pour over the rather meager things in the kitchen. Everything seemed old, as he imagined it would be, and yet he was surprised to not see a micro wave or even a phone nearby. The stove at least seemed to be electric but from the 50's or early 60's if he had to guess. The refrigerator was equally antique although functional as the ice in his glass indicated. However, he had been amazed when his great uncle had gotten the ice out of a strange silver tray from the freezer that had a handle that cracked the cubes loose. His mother had noticed both he and his sister's looks and explained that this was how it was done before ice makers.

The very glass he was drinking from had a pattern of gold-looking swirls that he had seen in shops when his mother took them antiquing. And the oddest thing he observed was that there were no pictures to be found except for a current calendar hanging on a nail that had old scenes of by-gone days and read Bath Savings and Loan.

The kitchen utensils also looked out of date. He was actually surprised to not find a wood burning stove or fireplace. And yet, the place seemed cozy and welcoming.

Jan was not so much busy checking out her surroundings as she was her host. As her mom and he talked lightly about the trip down, she studied his face. She couldn't decide if she wanted to see what her father's relatives might look like or if she was simply struck by how different this man was compared to anybody she knew.

His smile was warm, she agreed. There didn't seem to be any sinister or axe-murderer traits readily apparent, but that was the way it always was in the beginning of the stories. After the horrific deeds the news would ask the neighbors who would all say 'But he was the quietest, most gentle old man! We never guessed!' And then he was looking right at her.

"Jan is it?" he asked. "So you are the historian?"

She realized her mother had been telling about their trip down.

"Uh, well, I just read what there is on the internet. But I am interested."

Her great uncle shook his head but kept smiling.

"Don't suppose it would come as a shock to you, but I don't know nothing about computers and such. Oh, I hear about them. Most of the lobstermen nowadays use some sort of new fangled gizmos. But we don't use 'em, and we do just fine…better than anybody else, for that matter!"

"Your daughter and you?" Marie ventured.

"Oh, yeah, I am getting old!" Fin remembered. "My daughter and I have been fishing partners for as long as she could stand in a boat. My daughter Shere, you call her...short for Sharon. Ah-yuh, wouldn't have no other partner."

"Are you a lobsterman?" Jonathon asked.

"Good Lord, no!" Fin continued. "Mind ya, I wouldn't have a living without them, but neither would they without me!"

He winked at Jan and moved his old face closer to Jonathon's.

"Ya see, son, I fish for the bait used in the lobster pots. Not many folks outside of here know that it's not just any bait that gets the best results. Oh, no-sir-ee! See, a lobster likes his fish, well, well-seasoned. Just the right amount of time out of the water; just so ripe. In other words, they have to be a right-might smelly. But not rotten! That's where we come in. The shack I was working in when you drove up, that's where I age my fish. I have a certain way of doing it. It's been in the family for years and it's a secret. Nobody does it anymore the way we do. And if you're a lobsterman who wants to make money, you buy from us! But I'm particular as to who I sell to. Old ways, old friends, old ties. Understand? Maybe not, but I hope I have time to show you, if you're willing to see."

"I sure am!" Jonathon blurted. "I'm fascinated by what my family used to do!"

"Right-smart young fella!" Fin said sideways to Marie. "We'll talk and see!"

"Fin," Marie asked, "Where is Shere? I didn't spend much time with her, well, the last time I was here."

"She'll be here later on tonight. She's gone in the boat. Might be too late, come to think of it, before you folks turn in. But you'll see her tomorrow, for sure."

"And the boy and girl? Cousins, I guess you'd say?"

"They'll be here tomorrow as well. We'll all have a time getting to know one another. Eh, Marie, you and I'll talk about that later, maybe?"

Marie nodded.

"Fine, fine," he agreed. "So, now I need to show you folks around the house and then around the grounds. It'll be low tide in an hour and I wouldn't say no to some help gathering mussels for supper tonight!"

The tour of the house was further interesting in that it was huge. Downstairs there was a spacious formal dining room, seemingly unused, and a parlor with an equally unused piano and just the sort of furnishings one might expect in this near museum. Yet, everything seemed tidy and not dusty at all. Jonathon was intrigued with the electrical wiring. It was exterior on the walls and ran in a pair of wires into a wall switch with a button-like device to turn on or off. There was a bathroom with a claw tub and sink and toilet and two more rooms with closed doors that Fin said were his and Shere's. A third bedroom had the door slightly ajar.

"That was Manny's room," Fin announced. "I opened it. Just in case, you know, anybody wanted to go in there. Not much, but I left it, you know."

This peaked attention with all three of the newcomers but for three different reasons.

Upstairs on the next floor there were four large bedrooms and a centrally located bathroom much like the one downstairs. Two of the bedrooms were situated to share the brick chimney that passed through the house. The beds and chairs looked comfortable if not again very old.

"I'll let you folks decide who sleeps where, doesn't matter to me. You see, Jonathon, these old houses, in summer it helps to sleep up higher with the windows open to catch the breeze. In winter, it's best downstairs and we shut up the top floors." Fin explained. "Let's see the third floor and you decide for yourselves."

The third floor had six bedrooms that had been added with the dormer extensions. The walls in the hall and in the rooms were somewhat elegantly papered in brocaded patterns that had not peeled nor faded much.

"I like this!" Jan exclaimed. "Can we stay up here, Mom?"

"Why not," her mother shrugged. "Only the one bathroom, remember?"

It too was in the center of the floor.

Jan went into one of the rooms and pushed back the heavy curtains on the dormer window. A wonderful view of the bay greeted her.

"Ya see," Fin mentioned, "In the old days families had to have lots of children. They were cheaper for workers than hiring somebody else!"

"We'll stay up here," Marie stated, smiling. She had past-by the rooms where she and Manny had stayed on the second floor and decided she did not want to stay there.

"Better tell ya, "Fin conceded, "There's only the one phone downstairs in the parlor. Local calls only. I figured you folks to have the new type with ya, only the service is not so good, I'm told."

'Great' Jan thought to herself. 'Another part of the Steven King story…cut off from the outside world…'

"Oh, and Shere and me don't have much use for the television," Fin added, "But we got a set in Manny's room. He liked it. Just local, but news and so forth. Three channels, I think, can't remember."

"Great Uncle…" Jonathon started.

"You call me Fin, OK?"

"OK, Fin…where does that go?"

Jonathon referred to a small staircase, not carpeted like the others, in relative shadow against the far wall of the floor.

"Oh, that," Fin offered. "That goes up to the attic and out to the widow's walk. Know what that is?"

Jan played her role and answered for all of them.

"It's a sort of balcony where women would look out to sea for their men to return?"

"Wicked-sharp, you are, little lady!" Fin smiled. "Only it's not safe up there anymore. Just as good a view here!"

"Alright," he continued. "Let's haul your gear aloft and then get into something you can get a little muddy. Tides right for mussels! That is, if you've a mind to?"

"Sounds like fun," Marie agreed.

They started downstairs with Fin in the lead followed by Marie. Just before Jan reached the second stair her brother caught her elbow and she held back a bit.

"Notice anything strange?" he whispered.

"Everything," she whispered back.

"No, not just old," he continued. "*No pictures!* None! I mean not of people. There are a few ships and some old seascapes, but not a single old photo or painting of relatives or boat workers or graduating classes or social clubs or church picnics...nothing!"

He smirked and moved past her. She considered his shamus observation and filed it away in her ever-growing mental journal of things that should have caused the good young family to flee before the massacre happened.

The tour of the grounds started with the fish house Fin had talked about. It was indeed rustic and old and smelly. But the smell was not completely unpleasant. It reminded Marie of the fish market in Boston, at least the area where she bought rather high grade tuna. The oily scent was similar.

Opening the door, Fin confirmed her thoughts when he explained that herring were very oily fish that if left on the wooden shelves in relative coolness would slowly leak the oil. It saturated the wooden shelves and long after the fish was 'cured' the next batch would gain from the oil of the last.

Only Jonathon ventured to step inside with Fin. When they

came out, the two smiled together and Fin made Jonathon promise to keep the family secret.

"You can tell these two," Fin suggested, "As long as they promise too."

"Sure," Jan offered, thinking to herself that the last thing she might be tortured for was such a secret for aging small fish.

Marie nodded as well with a slight smile.

"There's a small spring in there," Jonathon almost whispered. "It trickles out and down into the bay and keeps the fish at a constant temperature."

"Ah-yuh!" Fin said proudly.

He led the group down to the water's edge and onto a small dock that was constructed of piles driven into the rocky shoreline with the planks linked together and floating up and down with the tide. The planks were secured to shore and were on rings on the piles to allow for freedom.

"This is new," Fin stated. "Did this in the 90's. The old dock was solid but well beaten down. Miss it, though..."

At the end of the dock, the three newcomers had a chance to catch the true beauty of Atkins Bay. Fin further explained that it was the near ending point for the Kennebec River which ran all the way up almost to Canada and was one of the highways that tamed Maine. He tested the twins' history by recounting how Benedict Arnold had moved his troops up the river to attack the English in Canada before he was deemed a traitor. The natives had named the waterway 'river with no rapids' and it had been, here at its lower end, so important to the ship building industry up in Bath. Navy ships were still being built and launched out into the Gulf of Maine and then into the Atlantic.

Whatever the history, Marie and her children stood near stupefied at the spectacular vista. The rock wall on the opposite side showed watermarks that it was indeed almost low tide and the tides here were close to twelve feet in difference.

"What's that?" Jan suddenly asked, pointing out into the bay at a few dark specks on the water.

"Lobster trap buoys," Jonathon offered.

"No, not that, the dark spots." she corrected.

Marie strained to see as well.

Fin only smiled slowly.

"Welcoming committee," he said slowly. "Look closer."

"Seals!" Jan almost shouted. "I can see their eyes!"

"Oh, yes," her mother agreed. "Must be six or more."

"I need binoculars," Jonathon said, cupping his hands in pretending he had a pair.

"Plenty of time for that," Fin said. "I have a telescope or two lying around, if you want them. Anyway, they're just curious and want to say hello, I think.

"They're cute!" Jan decided.

"They're just staring at us!" Jonathon noted with amusement.

"Not everybody around here thinks they're so cute," Fin sighed. "Some lobstermen say they raid traps. Every year there's a few shootings that nobody can blame anybody for."

"That's terrible!" Jan said, aghast.

"Truth is, they are not trap raiders but they are not cuddly little teddy bears, either." Fin proclaimed.

"What's going on out there?" Jonathon interrupted.

The bobbing heads of the seal group had disappeared quickly as one, as if spooked. Three larger seal heads appeared in their place. They stared for a moment and then seemed to begin to slowly move closer to the dock.

"Let's go," Fin said as equally suddenly. The smile had left his weathered face. "Time to see to supper in the house."

"What about the mussels?" Jonathon asked.

"We'll try them later," Fin returned, almost herding the three off the dock. "I got some clams yesterday and I just realized we'd better eat them tonight while they're fresh. C'mon, now..."

They all followed but Jan took one last look over her shoulder at the three heads and six large eyes that stared intently at their departure. The larger of the heads snorted as if displeased, but she put it down to a natural breathing pattern.

After a meal of rich, thick clam chowder with creamy butter and soft potatoes, Fin asked the twins if they wanted to watch TV.

"Not tonight," Jan stated. "I think I'll go upstairs and start a journal on my tablet. You know, like a diary of the trip or something."

"Yeah," Jonathon added, "I'm sort of tired and I have an old DVD on mine I want to finish."

"Ok," their mother said strangely. "I'll be up to check on you two soon, OK?"

The twins told Fin good night and in a few short instants Marie was alone with him. He got up from the table and put the bowls in the sink. Then he reached up into a cabinet overhead and brought out a bottle of something black. He found two small glasses in a cupboard and turned to Marie.

"Join me in the parlor, Missy?" he asked. He poured two measures.

They went into the parlor and Fin turned on an old floor lamp. The two settled in, Marie on the red velvet sofa and Fin across from her in a faded gold armchair. After sipping their drinks, it seemed an awkward time before Marie finally spoke.

"I really had a tough time coming here," she admitted.

Fin just nodded.

"I didn't know how I would react. I still don't know what the next few days will hold."

"Let's start," Fin suggested, "With what you want to tell me about what happened when Manny went away. Then I'll tell you what I can remember about him growing up. I think it might do the both of us some good. You see, he came to me much like the two who will be here tomorrow. His parents, who I knew pretty well since his father was my brother, they had up and decided they couldn't care for him. So I took him in. Now he's gone. I don't know if I can do this again. I can't help but get attached. You know?"

Marie sipped her drink and realized the tears would be here soon but she wanted to talk.

Jan woke up for the second time since she had gone to bed. The first time it was her mother who had looked in on her. Jan couldn't see her face in the doorway, but she guessed she had been crying and talking to Fin. Saying goodnight, she had closed the door and Jan had drifted back off to sleep with her tablet on the bedside as a nightlight.

This time, she thought she was dreaming because she heard the sound of a small outboard motor from somewhere out beyond her open window. She looked at her tablet and realized she must had imagined the sound because it was past midnight and surely not even the hardened Mainers would be braving the rocks of the bay at this dark hour.

But the sound persisted for a few moments and then abruptly cut-off. Sliding from underneath the just-slightly musty coverlet and sheet, she padded softly to the open dormer window and peered out into the darkness over the bay. She had chosen this room for this very scenery.

The moon was just peeking out from across the water on the rooflines of the wooden houses there. Without really seeing, her keen sense of hearing filled in the picture below.

A boat had drifted up to the dock where she and her family had been earlier this afternoon. She could hear the bumping sounds and sloshing of water. Then the dock creaked with the weight of somebody or some bodies disembarking from that boat and heading towards the shore.

Now there was a terse silence that followed and seemed to last forever. Jan could not see if the person or persons were coming towards the house but she guessed it. Where else would they go?

Suddenly an opening door sounded below Jan's window and to the left on the ground floor. As she strained to see through the darkness, a very slight light from inside the house bathed three shapes in momentary illumination.

A figure with long, dark, almost bushy hair held the door as two other ones entered.

The chill that ran up Jan's back was because of the attire of the three. The one holding the door was wearing a dark robe-like thing and the other two had the same garb, only with hoods hiding their features.

'That's it,' Jan told herself as she jumped back in bed. 'So it's not only axe-murderers but witches or druids or devil worshipers. Great.'

She lay awake trying to decide how to wake up her brother and mother and convince them of what she saw and what she suspected was the beginning to their demise. Yet, something soft and lightly assuring filled her mind and she drifted back to sleep. A sound like the tinkling of a wind chime...

3

Sequin Island and its Lighthouse sat just three miles from Atkins Bay and Popham Beach and the mouth of the Kennebec River. It was Maine's tallest and second oldest Light Station, being commissioned by President George Washington. Tourists were able to visit the rocky, thin strip of island by boat. In the summer, 'friends' of the Sequin Light actually stayed on the island and besides giving tours and fixing up the constantly battered structures, there were undergraduate students involved in marine biology projects under the supervision of resident experts. Sea bird nesting patterns, numbers, and returning animals were studied. Seal population and number of offspring were also an ongoing study of great interest.

One of the undergrads named Kim, a tall girl with an almond shaped oriental face and black hair pulled back in a bun, had just stepped out of the two storied Light Station structure into the morning sun and found her teacher who was watching seagulls through a large set of binoculars.

"Dave, it happened again last night!"

"Not again!" the professor looked at his pupil with a frown. He stopped gazing and ran his fingers through his balding, wispy hair that was blown about by the constant wind.

"Same place and everything?" he asked.

"Yup," Kim nodded, "On the little island in Seal Cove. All the cameras were working perfectly last night when I turned in. Now, not a one of them are showing anything. Completely dead."

"We can't afford to be going over there two or three times a month, much less replacing expensive gear. Bet we'll find the same thing; cameras lens smashed. I thought this year we had a chance since we lashed the bloody things to the rocks," the leader said, shaking his head.

"It's got to be vandals," Kim stated.

"Well, yeah," her teacher agreed. "Only we can't catch them on camera. How they avoid being seen, I don't know. Just the seals there. And why would anybody bother to go out at night and wreck our gear? It's on protected land, for God's sake."

"Just to get at us?" Kim ventured.

"I can't figure why, but it's been the same every spring and summer for the six years I've been placing the cameras there. My predecessors told me not to bother, that nothing anybody has ever left out there got back in one piece."

"Got to be vandals," Kim repeated.

"You think?" Dave chuckled at his student. "Certainly wasn't the seals, now was it?"

The sounds of sea birds and the streaming sunlight woke the occupant of the room with a start. She lay there for a moment trying to collect her thoughts.

'Yep,' Jan told herself. 'You're playing right into the plot of the horror story. You fell asleep just when you should have been rousing your family and throwing luggage out the window and tearing out of here as fast as the car will take us. If it starts. Probably been monkeyed with. So today starts it...car won't start, phone won't work, and I bet I know who's for supper. I wonder how it feels to be *in* the chowder.'

The door to her room opened slowly.

"Hey, sleepy-head!" her mother cooed. "Coming downstairs for breakfast soon?"

"Mom," Jan started. "'I have to tell you something! Last night I woke up after midnight and I heard a boat and then I saw three figures in dark robes come into the house!"

She realized it sounded like a child's nightmare.

"So you did!" her mother smiled. "Already met them. They're downstairs and so is your brother and we're waiting on you!"

She closed the door and headed off back down the hall.

'And they've already cast a spell on my mother!' Jan told herself. She resigned to find a way to get them all out of this as she dressed and headed for the bathroom.

Downstairs, she saw Jonathon munching on thick toast slathered in butter and some blue viscous concoction. Her mother was seated at the table as well and was smiling and sipping coffee and talking to Fin. Then she saw the others at the table.

"Jan!" her mother announced, "Glad you could grace us! I've got some relatives for you to meet!"

The long thick hair from her vision last night belonged to a lady seated next to Fin. She was looking down at seemingly nothing on the table and an untouched piece of thick bread lay on a saucer before her. When she looked up and caught Jan's eyes, her face neither brightened nor changed at all. A distant gaze looked into Jan's eyes and yet somehow beyond.

"This is your cousin Shere," her mother was saying. "She came in last night in the boat and that's what you heard, dear."

Jan could not tell much more about the face that briefly met her eyes except that it would have to be called ruggedly pretty. The cheek bones were high and a bit gaunt and the lines shallow and fine. The nose was highly arched but graceful. Except for the need for grooming in the eyebrow department, Jan had decided she would put the description down in her journal as 'hauntingly beautiful'.

Shere was wearing a man's green plaid work shirt and as such Jan could not discern any other features. But she expected a hidden, muscular, working form that was also very feminine even if well hidden. The hair was rich and full and black and again somewhat unkempt. It fell down her shoulders and well over the back of her chair.

"And here's your other cousins," Jan heard her mother saying.

Not noticing that there were two people seated next to her brother, Jan now regarded them with interest.

"This is Hunter," her mother introduced the male of the two.

"Hi," Jan said automatically. The youth was older than she and Jonathon, but not by more than a year or so, she decided. He had large brown eyes and fine features as well. The lean and long face regarded Jan and one dark eyebrow rose as he spoke.

"Hello," he stated through barely parted thin lips that began to curl in a sly smile. The voice was deeper than Jan had expected.

His hair was dark brown and somewhat long for the current fashion. He wore it pulled back and fashioned into a pony tail.

'Was that a flirt?' Jan thought quickly as she turned to gaze at the female beside him.

"I'm Celia," the girl said in the same closed-lipped way, only with a much warmer slight smile.

Jan sat down on the far side of Jonathon who seemed a bit too intent on his breakfast. She realized the blue stuff was blueberry jam.

"Want some?" he asked her, without looking up.

She knew her brother too well. As such, she had to look past the still staring Hunter to assess why Jonathon was avoiding looking at the girl there.

Celia appeared to be the same age as they. However, she bore a larger frame than Jan that spoke of athleticism as well. She was still smiling lightly and began talking softly to Jan's mother.

"Your daughter is very pretty," she said.

"Thank you!" Marie beamed. "What do you say, Jan?"

"Oh, so are you!" Jan blushed. She had not expected to be taken aback so quickly. It disarmed her somewhat. She studied her cousins' features again.

Her hair was long and the same color as her brother's, Jan figured. Dark brown and sleek and parted in the middle, it came to just below her shoulder blades and turned up slightly at the ends. The face was similar to Hunter's in that it was long and slim. The same eyes, only in a softened doe-like appearance, glinted with what Jan guessed was intelligence. Her posture was what Jan's mother always strived to teach her daughter. Ramrod straight back and squared shoulders, she seemed confident but a little shy as Marie asked her about school.

"They were home-schooled," Shere spoke for the first time that Jan had heard. The voice was a bit curt and throaty and mysterious. Jan quickly assessed that she didn't speak often.

Celia looked down at this remark but Hunter took up the thread.

"We had different members of the family teaching us," he offered, speaking first to Marie and then looking back at Jan.

Marie sensed she had pressed too far too soon and went back to trying to talk to Shere but only got responses from Fin on the weather outlook and other chit-chat.

It struck Jan as strange that both Celia and Hunter were wearing odd fitting outfits. They both wore jeans and Hunter had on a plaid shirt that seemed too big for him. In contrast, Celia had on a Red Sox tee shirt that was much too tight, as far as Jan was concerned. The darting looks from her brother were understandable given the teenage male psyche and the fact that her attire left very little to the imagination. This included what Jan had decided without a doubt was the main reason for her brother's nervousness in that Celia's lack of brassiere was much too obvious.

As her mother was attempting to gain some information on what might be a suitable first day's adventure, Jan saw an opportunity.

"Can we go shopping?" she ventured.

Jonathon sounded like a balloon with a leak. He looked at his mother and made a face that he had perfected from Harpo Marx; puffed cheeks, stuck-out tongue and crossed eyes.

Fin laughed out loud. Celia put a hand to her mouth and stifled a chuckle. Marie shook her head at her son. Shere and Hunter sat stock still without apparent recognition of the gesture.

Jan caught her mother's eyes and in a much-practiced manner indicated her newly introduced cousins. It didn't take long for Marie to catch on.

"Hey, not a bad idea," she said. "We need to pick up some things and I'll bet shopping would let the young people here have a chance to get to know each other better."

"Couldn't hurt," Fin mused. "I can tell ya where to go, but count me and Shere out. Got work to do. Would you mind?"

"A pleasure!" Marie said.

Jan had placed some scrambled eggs onto her plate and half a piece of the thick bread and started to eat with the thought of why her cousins were dressed the way they were. Did they not bring suitable clothes? Then the thought struck her that maybe they didn't have such luxuries. She felt ashamed as she considered that anybody who was coming to live with Fin might not have much.

Then she spied some shapes hanging from hooks in the outer room beyond the kitchen; what Fin called 'the mud room'. Here boots and dirty shoes and coats were to be left. The shapes were familiar to her from the scene she had seen enacted last night.

"Are those capes?" she pointed a fork and asked to anyone listening. Her mother tried to stare at her but Jan averted her gaze.

"Sure-enough something like it," Fin said slowly. "We call 'em oilskins. Shere brought the kids in last night by boat. Them skins keep out the fog and damp."

"Oh," Jan remarked, looking back to her food. A quick look shot to her mother received the 'there, I told you so' face.

Jan chewed but thought to herself 'And why not come in by car or bus or train. Oh, sure, it's perfectly normal to arrive by boat in capes in the middle of the night. Sure it is.'

After breakfast Jonathon and Jan went back upstairs to clean up and get ready for the shopping trip. Fin was clearing away dishes and silverware as Shere addressed the two youths who remained seated at the table.

"You can go up and wait until we call you," she said rather flatly.

When they had left, without a word, Shere touched Marie's arms nervously and almost whispered to her.

"Take this," she said as she placed some folded money into Marie's hand. "They need things. Clothes that fit. Several outfits; play and work. And the girl…she needs…girl things. Woman things, you know?"

"I think I know," Marie said slowly. She glanced at the money and realized there were at least four hundred-dollar bills there.

"Hey, this is much more than they need!" she started.

"I don't know how much girl stuff costs. I don't know much about girls…"

Marie realized this was very embarrassing for her.

"I'll take care of it," she promised, smiling.

Shere simply turned and was gone back into the house somewhere.

"Did Shere give you money?" Fin asked, drying his hands on a kitchen towel.

"More than enough," Marie answered.

"Well, you can go shopping in Bath but the big stores are in Cooks Corner or Topsham," he suggested.

"I'll look at my GPS and let Jan pick out where we go. It's easier that way."

Fin laughed a small laugh and moved back into the house as well.

Jan sat in the back seat of the silver SUV between her cousins Hunter and Celia. Jonathon got his coveted 'shotgun' place up front and he had convinced his mother, prior to leaving Fin's, to take off the magnetic signs on the doors that announced to everyone that they from Mass. Marie watched the GPS prompts as the car skirted the town of Bath and headed back towards the interstate.

With much fanfare and declaration, Jan had decided to avoid the popular national discount store near Cooks Corner, a cross roads in Brunswick, and opted instead for the rival store in Topsham ('h' silent, as she had learned) with the large red bull's-eye as a logo.

Pulling into the parking lot, Hunter and Celia remained silent but they had been intently watching the traffic and scenery that they had been through. Indeed, Celia's eyes were even more doe-like and wide with apparent wonder and Jan was herself amazed at the whole scene.

"Do you have large stores where you're from?" she tried.

"No," Hunter said flatly. "Just small ones. More like 'general stores', I think you call them."

"Where are you from?" Jonathon asked as his mother found a suitable parking place. He purposely avoided the glare that he felt sure was headed towards him from his mother.

Celia started to speak but Hunter cut her off sharply.

"Up north," he offered, "In Canada. You probably wouldn't know the place. On the coast. Small towns."

Jan noted the plurality of his statement; 'towns'. She had the growing feeling that the two had no real place to call home. That both bothered and intrigued her. A gypsy life was both romantic and sad, as she had read about.

Entering the store, Marie instructed the youths to pair up as per gender and go about their ways unobstructed by an adult presence. She told her twins to help their cousins find garments for work, fun, somewhat dressy, and beach attire. They were to meet back in the health and beauty section in no more than an hour.

As the two pair scurried off, Marie set about the task of shopping for necessities for Celia that might otherwise be uncomfortably done. She also had some things in mind from the food section if she expected to have anything to eat that didn't include shellfish, crustaceans, fish or chowder.

Jonathon and Hunter perused the aisles first for shirts. Hunter had no real idea of what he wanted, and when Jonathon suggested first this or that logo or print Hunter looked puzzled and asked him why it mattered what was on the shirt.

"Well," Jonathon replied, "It sort of says who you are; what you stand for or like. It's popular to identify with a band, a life style like surfing or fishing, or a brand of some product you like. Like this..."

He showed Hunter a Guinness logo on a green shirt.

"You ever tried that stuff?" Hunter turned up his nose.

"No," Jonathon sort of stammered, "But everybody in Boston raves about it."

"Nasty," Hunter proclaimed. "All beer and ales stink."

"So what do you like?" Jonathon tried again. "What do you want people to know about you?"

"I'm strong!" Hunter smiled. "And I'm handsome!"

"And modest," Jonathon said sideways. He was grateful that his cousin didn't seem to notice the remark.

"Ok, how about this?" Jonathon suggested a shirt with The Hulk on it.

"I'm not green!" Hunter shot back. "Ok, here's me!"

He picked up a shimmering black shirt that was obviously meant to be skin tight.

"It's a start," Jonathon mused, putting it into their cart and moving on to the solid color polo shirts and khaki pants. He was all too aware that if he didn't make a Beau Brummell young man-about-town out of his cousin that his mother would take over and that was a fate worse than teenage death.

Jan was having a rather delicate time with Celia. She had decided that first and foremost the undergarments were to be found. While Jan was trying to have a serious and quiet conversation with her cousin about how bras should fit and what the taboo signs were, which were all-too present with Celia, when one didn't exist. Instead, Celia let out a short bark of a laugh and held aloft a pair of frilly pink thong panties.

"Who wears these?" Celia giggled.

"Lots of people," Jan hushed and put the thing back on the shelf. "But we'll find something more practical, if you like. But first, about the bras..."

"They hurt," Celia said seriously, "Too tight."

"Yes, yes," Jan breathed, "I get that. You have to try these on to get the right fit."

"You'll come with me?" she almost pleaded.

This was not what Jan had thought about when she suggested shopping. The thought of the two of them in a small dressing room and Celia, well, undressed was more than she had figured on in the line of being a newly-met cousin. But then the thought returned about the stark fact that Celia had no clue about this and Jan was somewhat shamed at her distain.

"Ok," she reassured. "Let's get several sizes and colors and do this first. Then on to other clothes."

As Jan started to put things in the cart, Celia suddenly caught her by the elbow. When Jan turned, Celia had her long face uncomfortably close.

"Thank you," she whispered, and Jan could just discern a slight tear in the large brown eyes. "I've never had a...a...friend like this."

"No worries," Jan brushed off. "Let's get going, Ok?"

Marie was pleased with her children when she surveyed their carts. Jonathon had outfitted Hunter with some presentable modest clothes befitting a young gentleman. Some of the other choices gave her a slight pang of regret but there was nothing too outlandish. Most of what Hunter had chosen for himself was black and tight. Even the swimsuit was not of the surfer-loose variety but more form fitting. She put it down to youthful male bravado.

Jan had outdone herself in choosing and guiding Celia's ensemble. Tasteful and pastel summer colored blouses and not-too-short-shorts complimented matching Capri's or clam-diggers. A coral pink one-piece bathing suit seemed a sensible selection and Marie thought that Celia would certainly fill it out with her curves without being too revealing in a two piece.

Her daughter got close to Marie's ear.

"Did you get some razors?" she whispered.

Marie nodded slightly.

"Good," Jan nodded back. "We got work to do!"

With that, Marie paraded the lot over to the deodorant aisle. The ride to the store had made it plain that Hunter and Celia were 'sans scent', or rather, had a scent of their own that was not roses. It was more of a cross between the outgoing tide and Fin's fish fermenting house. She masterfully chose her ploy to avoid embarrassment, but immediately figured it would not matter.

"Jonathon, Jan," she announced, "Pick out your favorite."

"But Mom I brought..." Jonathon started but caught his mother's 'evil eye' as he was wont to put it.

Jan caught on and went about letting Celia sniff certain ones for signs of acceptance. Jonathon was doing the same with Hunter and it was uncanny that both would turn up their noses in distain over the smells.

Finally Jan suggested "This is what I use."

"Oh," Celia frowned. "I'm sorry. I didn't know. You smell so good." Jan tried and failed not to blush.

"Let's find one for you that's a little bit different," she tried.

"Do you really like this stuff?" Hunter was asking Jonathon.

"Doesn't matter," Jonathon shrugged. "The girls do."

"Really?" Hunter asked as he cracked his closed lipped curl of a smile, "They do?"

"So I'm told," Jonathon offered back.

"Which one?" Hunter almost demanded.

"Beats me," Jonathon admitted.

Celia overheard and stepped very close to Jonathon. She closed her eyes and inhaled deeply.

"What do you use?" she said, opening her eyes and failing to catch Jonathon's averted ones.

He pointed numbly at a product.

"You smell so good," she said much more uncomfortably than Jonathon would have wanted.

Hunter pointed to a product that's label showed a toned male model being touched by two attentive female ones. The idea of the effect suggested was cheesy-ly emblazoned purposefully in the name of the thing.

"I want that," he said definitively.

"Who doesn't?" Jonathon shrugged in his best Woody Allen accent.

"No, the stuff!" Hunter pressed.

"Oh," and Jonathon showed him the dizzying array of products that promised to attract the other gender. Finally he chose one, not for its fragrance as much for the macho name.

While the two males were deciding which deodorant had a better marketing scheme, Jan wandered across the aisle to the stationary section. She wasn't even aware that Celia had followed until after she had picked up a blank journal. Jan had decided that with the sketchy signals from her device she had better physically jot some notes down if anybody was ever going to know what befell her family after the tragic events that were certainly about to unfold.

Celia seemed transfixed and stroked her lithe hands over a medium-small sea-green colored bound book of blank pages. Then she eyed almost childlike the arrays of colored pencils.

"Do you draw?" Jan asked offhandedly.

Celia shot back an almost embarrassed look.

"I like to write," she said quietly. "I have stories in my head. My...I mean, I have heard stories. They were told to me. They are important. And I can draw pictures."

"That's great!" Jan encouraged. "I'm sure you can buy these. Maybe we can share stories? Are they from our family?"

Celia nodded secretly as if someone should overhear.

Marie insisted pleasantly that Hunter and Celia should pay for their purchases after she gave them ample bills. It was a bit awkward, but both seemed to enjoy what was apparently a novel experience. All this seemed more and more puzzling to Marie and her children but none spoke of it tactfully. They each filed it away in their own fashion. Jonathon felt like he was on a case. Jan still was wary of sinister possibilities. Marie simply felt sorry for the two.

The trip back to Parkers Head was rather uneventful except for the almost twitter that Celia kept up with Jan in near whispers about the things she had bought. Hunter merely stared out the window and seemed to take in everything he saw with interest and gusto.

Piling out of the SUV, the four youths rushed past a waiting Fin and disappeared into the house with their treasures.

"Went well, did it, Dear?" he asked casually to Marie. She shrugged her shoulders and brushed a few strands of hair out of her eyes.

"Tell me something," she started quietly. "They, I mean Hunter and Celia, they don't get out much, do they?"

"Wasn't much different with Manny," Fin almost sighed. "Queer lot, our northern family. They don't put down much roots. To say they was Canadian is almost a lie. They spend time in Newfoundland and Nova Scotia, St. Lawrence River, to be sure. Some of them spend time down here as well. Acadia, you may know it as Bar Harbor or such. They don't spend too much time in one place."

"Why?" Marie implored.

Fin looked at her with a hard yet soulful face.

"We have to talk about that, I fear," he said flatly.

She felt the old bristle of hairs up her neck.

"We'll talk later?" she suggested.

Fin only nodded oddly. Then he straightened up and smiled.

"Got company," he announced plainly. "Call the kids. Might be interesting."

A boat motored slowly up to Fin's dock. It was old and yet new in the obvious repairs that had been made to keep it seaworthy. Marie walked to the house and called the twins to come down. She was grateful to see the response included Hunter and Celia.

As the waiting party presented itself on the dock a rather shocked person finished bringing the craft to mooring alongside the boards.

The figure working the motor was a young man with rusty hair and a youthful wispy red beard. He brought the craft to rest with a practiced ease that spoke of years at the task. He addressed Fin warmly.

"How are you?" he remarked lightly.

"Good, you?" Fin shot back.

"Who's all this lot?" the youth queried.

"Family," Fin explained. Marie noted that words were not minced nor wasted in this vicinity.

"Better looking than you," the youth joked.

"They don't have to deal with the likes of yours!" Fin answered back.

"The name's Joe Sanders," the youth remarked to Marie and the group behind her. "They call me 'Red'. I can't for the life of me figure out why."

A warm smile broke over his ruddy face.

"I'm a neighbor of this crazy old man," he continued. "My father's still trying to make a living catching lobsters. My older brother is his stern-man. I get to come over here and collect the perfumed fish required for such a refined enterprise. Lucky me, huh?"

"Come off that scow and meet the folks!" Fin pretended to order.

Red skillfully stepped off the boat and lashed it to the dock in a ballet-precision move. He extended a hand to Marie.

"Good to meet you Miss," he offered, doffing his Red Sox green hat with the other.

"Marie MacLeer," Fin announced, "And her children, Jonathon and Jan."

Red looked at both youths and smiled.

"Cousins from away as well," Fin continued, "Hunter and Celia."

Red looked them over with a slightly different gaze but smiled just as warmly.

"Good to make your acquaintance," he managed.

Jan tried to sum this newcomer up. He was older than her by maybe a year or two and bore the traits of the hard working folks hereabouts. She didn't know why, but she liked him almost immediately.

"Jan and Jonathon are what, fourteen going on fifteen?" Fin mused.

"I'm just turned sixteen," Red admitted. "Sorry, but I had to repeat a grade."

"Fine thing!" Fin fumed. "Not right, I still say!"

"How's that?" Marie asked nonchalant.

Red smiled wider.

"I have family in 'The County'. Do you know what that is?"

Jonathon spoke up.

"Yeah, it's the biggest county in Maine; Aroostook. Covers almost all the northern part of the state!"

"That's it," Red nodded. "My uncle up there had both his kids, my cousins; take sick two year ago and right at potato harvesting time. So I went up there to help with getting the crop in. See, up there they have a break from school so the kids can work the fields. They don't have that down here. So, I lost out and had to repeat a grade. Doesn't matter, we got the crop in."

"I didn't know Maine was so famous for potatoes," Jan admitted. "I don't recall seeing them in the stores next to Idaho spuds."

Red and Fin chuckled.

"Oh, you can eat some of them, alright," Red said. "There's plenty in the stores. But the majority of them go to other uses. 'Industrial' is what we call them. They go into everything from drugs to thickening agents in candies and processed food and lubricating stuff for factories; heck, they go all over the USA."

"I was interested more in Aroostook for what the cryptozoologists say about it," Jonathon admitted. "They say that with all the unexplored spaces up there if there is a species of animal we haven't seen in North America it would be there."

"Don't doubt it," Red agreed. "There are logging roads up there that go through places they say nobody has set foot on the ground around it. Except maybe for the natives. Only folks have flown over it and took pictures. I don't know."

"Bigfoot up there?" Jan almost laughed.

"Might be!" Jonathon shot back. "Don't count things out until you see for yourself!"

"Anyway," Fin proclaimed, "We got some work to do this afternoon. Hunter, Celia, I would appreciate some help."

"Say Fin," Red interjected. "I got to go into Bath. Got parts for the boat winch waiting. Maybe I could give the new folks a tour?"

"Not in that scow!" Fin indicated the boat tied to the dock.

"No, I could use Dad's lobster boat." Red suggested. "They won't be going out until tomorrow morning early."

"Tell you what I'll do," Fin suggested. "I know the cost of fuel. You take these folks on a tour and the fish today is on me."

"Deal!" Red agreed. "That's a bargain my Dad will thank you for!"

"Alright, take this load and be back soon," Fin said.

"Back in a flash!" Red stated and set about his task.

An hour and a half later Red was motoring his father's boat 'Sally Anne' up Atkins bay with some first time passengers. Marie and Jan snapped picture after picture on their cell phones of the twenty or more seals that chose to laze in the sun on a rocky spit of black stone in the bay. They were especially intrigued as to how the sun dried the animals' coat into a soft gray or brown instead of sleek dark as seen in the water. The occupants of the rock only cast a nonchalant look at the boat passing by. Most of them. Several seemed more...interested.

Jonathon, however, noted with his detective eye that of the other seals swimming around the little island, presumably waiting for a place in the sun, one rather large head seemed to follow their movement with keen interest. He put this down to a dominant male in the colony and from what had been done by man both in the past and in the present who could blame a sense of trepidation from such a once pressured species.

Red continued to play tour guide and pointed out landmarks as they passed. Lee Island was now home to expensive dwellings as was the far side of the river. Little Goat Island was so named because sailors of old would leave their goats there to avoid quarantine in

Bath. The sight of Squirrel Point light was another photo favorite. The slanting-towards-the-river boathouse was novel to say the least. He showed them Fiddler's Reach, 'reach' being a name for a stretch of the river where commerce was and could be conducted. Just before Doubling Point, where indeed the river seemed to turn back on itself, there were two small lighthouses that were used for navigation as well as the Doubling Point Light in its' own right.

At this juncture, a modern shipyard came into view. As the boat approached, the newcomers were awed by the sight of a Navy ship being constructed that looked like something more akin to an Imperial Star Cruiser from Star Wars than a modern vessel. After passing under the old railroad bridge of Route 1 and then the more modern, much taller roadway one Red called out the fine city of Bath.

They pulled up to the municipal docks, a small but functional landing, and Red tried to get his passengers to imagine a time when all along this waterfront ships were moored that had been built here and had travelled all over the east coast down into the Caribbean Islands and even abroad to parts all over the globe.

Now, a small town lay up the hill.

Tying up the boat, Red informed his charges that he had some parts to pick up just a few businesses down the street and suggested a walking excursion for the three up and to the left onto Centre Street. That and Front Street dead ahead would suffice to show them the local flair to the town now and he would find them shortly.

Marie and her two in tow wandered up to the corner of Centre and Front and began to look around.

Jonathon just had to step into the grand old city hall and they were all amused that prominently on display under glass was the old town newspaper that appeared on today's date from years gone by. The advertisements were especially interesting.

Marie decided she had to have a coffee from a corner café and the twins found some pastries to entice them. A slow walk down the hill had Jonathon staring through the window at some vintage guitars in a shop. Jan spied a confectioner across the street and the next twenty minutes were spent in glorious selection of made-on-the-spot chocolates in dizzying shapes and flavors. One specialty was an all chocolate depiction of a lobster boiled dinner.

Back on the street with a bag of sinful sweets, Marie couldn't pass up the inviting sight of an Irish Pub across the street. It just seemed to be so local and welcoming. She ducked in just to catch the sights of the numerous signs displayed. Her favorites were 'Shut Up and Drink Your Beer' and a Maine license plate over a musicians' area declaring 'Himself'.

Moving up again to Front Street, the trio sauntered leisurely past intriguing antiques and a small boutique where both Marie and Jan found some summer tops. Jonathon had forged ahead into a store that promised as its' logo 'A Maine Adventure' and had found a camouflaged baseball hat when he was joined by the females in his party. The place was a discount center and when investigated, Marie found some scarves that were from another time era and all three enjoyed the downstairs. The twins first noted that the floor there was not only sloped but wavy. Marie explained that it was due to frost heave, where the changing temperatures made buildings subject to Mother Nature.

Up into the sunlight again, the three were joined by Red who continued the tour down the street. He made reference to many businesses that had come and gone in the long history of this town. A drug store was a hold-over from days-gone-by. Jonathon asked for but was stymied by his mother in the wish for a particular local tee-shirt that showed a Navy vessel being built and the slogan 'Bath; A Little Drinking Town With A Ship Building Problem'.

Passing a few banks, which Red reminded the tourists had been around since the glory days of Yankee sailing (and Marie remembered as somewhat secretive in Fin's suggestion on old money) they could not resist entering a small antique shop. Pleasantly welcomed, Marie was beginning to realize that a local trait was in the female-on-female greeting of 'Dear' after any bit of conversation involving an older person to a younger... as in 'How are you, De-ah?'

The shop held many treasures both eclectic and not necessarily local but in keeping with the Maine theme. Jan found something disturbingly unique.

She brought the item to her mother and whispered, she didn't know why, "I have to have this. Do you know what this is?"

Marie studied the figurine for a moment and then wondered to herself how this could possibly be up for sale in today's day and age.

"I'll ask," she told her daughter. "Is this legal?"

The question was posed to the middle-aged lady sitting behind the counter. She took the figure from Marie and smiled as she looked it over.

"Yes it is," she said over her half-glasses. "Do you know what this is?"

"I think I do, but please go on," Marie asked.

"These little seals were made by the American Natives here in Maine." The shop owner continued. "Despite the laws so rightfully against seal harvesting, the Natives are allowed, like in other parts of the country, to continue their way of life and that includes seal hunting. So, they take the hides and make all sorts of things out of them. Many turn up in little models like this. The stamp on the bottom allows me to sell it. They did. So can I."

Marie turned the item over in her hands. It was a depiction of a seal, in real seal fur, with tiny black dots for eyes and cut monofilament fishing line for whiskers.

"You sure about this?" she asked her daughter. Jan nodded slowly.

"OK" Marie said. "Might serve to show how this should not be done."

"I agree," the shopkeeper said, "Just a part of Americana, like scrimshaw."

Marie paid the small price and gave the bag to Jan. It left an uncomfortable feeling in the pit of her stomach. She knew exactly why, but kept it to herself for the moment.

The return trip was punctuated by some dazzling scenes of bald eagles plying their trade. Red made a comment that they were not so regal as they enjoyed a good scavenging as well as the next buzzard. But the afternoon was still a picture-perfect slice of Maine early summer.

Red swung wide of Fin's place to show his eager onlookers the end of the bay. An old brick fort lorded silently over the exit of the great river into the Gulf of Maine. Several islands could be viewed in the distance. The one with the lighthouse Red commented further on.

"Sequin Light," he said rather proudly. "George Washington signed for it. Saved many a brave soul back in the day. Look there!"

He pointed to a two storied structure situated on the sandy beach on the very edge of land.

"Lifesaving station," he explained. "Before the Coast Guard. Imagine a bunch of volunteers getting into a long-boat in a wicked-bad storm and rowing out to try to save some schooner and crew from certain drowning in the grips of freezing water and towering waves. That there's the definition of a neighbor!"

The three in the boat nodded in solemn agreement.

"Anyway," Red lightened, "Look at this beach. We're lucky to have it. Great tourist trap. No offence, but you guys need to spend some time there while the weather's allowing. Maybe tomorrow?"

"That's why I bought the lotion and sun-block!" Marie admitted. "Need to get some tan before going back to pasty-old-Bean-Town."

Red chuckled at the remark. Then his ruddy brow wrinkled in mirthful concern.

"What time are you figuring on?" he asked.

"Ten-ish, maybe?" Marie offered. "Why?"

As Red headed the boat to drop off his passengers he explained.

"You might find this queer, but I think I need to be there to introduce these young folks to the not-so-official welcoming party that's sure to be there. Locals, you know; especially some busy-body girls I know who will want to know everything about Jan and, what's the other girl's name?"

"Celia," Marie offered.

"Right. I'm just saying," Red continued, "Dad and my brother will be off by dawn and my chores will be done so I could meet you. You drive, Miss," He looked at Marie. "I'll be along about that time by boat. Date?"

"Suits us fine!" Marie agreed. Once again, she didn't know why but figured why not let the locals break them into the scene.

Jonathon didn't seem to care either way as he stepped out of the boat but Jan decided this would be an important annotation in her journal. 'Tomorrow I meet the local girls'. That would earn a star by the entry.

4

The dark night was ending just as the sliver of moon passed back close into the unseen horizon. What light it had provided was shared by a contingency on the Maine coast. Jellyfish and squid had risen from the abyss to feed and be fed upon. Coastal waters had seen a timeless repeat of small fish trying to elude larger predators with predictable if varying success. All was as it should be; as it had been for time upon time.

Two figures lay side by side embracing on the rocky shore of a bay. The lush green, dark sea plants provided a cushion at mid-tide. The two bodies under the concealing black garments would have gone unnoticed by anyone or anything searching the bank.

Presently, the figures separated slightly and two sets of eyes gazed up into the star-filled heavens. The sound of the waves lapping the stone-strewn shore only accentuated the indescribable perfection of the long, profound moment.

Finally, one figure moved to rest upon an elbow and deeply kissed the one beside. Their dark capes and hoods intertwined once more. Tossing the hood back in a quick gesture, a face emerged in the scant light of the disappearing moon. It was masculine and strong with dark hair pushed back in wet waves. The sharp and freshly shaven features gazed down in intent and fervent desire and care.

"So you like me shorn?" he said, rubbing a slender hand across his jaw.

"I don't care how you come to me," a soft female voice answered dreamily.

"But you think I stay away too long?" the male voice queried.

"You decide that," the woman whispered. "I like the waves on the shore. Can I keep them in a box of tin to be opened when I please?"

"But I see in your eyes," he continued. "A longing? What can I do?"

The woman turned her back slightly. A silver white shoulder was exposed in the night.

"We both know what the times are," she whispered. "I fear for you,"

"Ha!" the male almost shouted. "You fear for me?!" He lowered his voice. "I don't care about what the Tribe thinks, I never have! I'll do what I want! But what are *you* doing? The ones from up north? What is that about?"

The woman nuzzled herself into the males' chest before continuing.

"You know who they are," she breathed.

"Do I ever!" the male hissed. "Who decided to bring them here? You do know that they are in danger? I can try to protect them! What if what they say is true and..."

"There's something else," the woman cut him off. "Something you don't know. I don't know how to tell you this. We have...other visitors. Twins. And their mother."

The male sat upright and pushed back the dark garment that covered him. A muscular torso gleamed in the night.

"Don't tell me," he asked incredulously, "That it's who I think it is? Don't tell me that!"

Her silence gave him the impossible answer.

"What are you living in, a House of Insanity?!" he raved quietly.

"What can possibly be the outcome of this? There's nothing, I mean, it's going to cause, I can't think!"

The woman pulled him down and embraced him strongly. Slowly the rage turned to passion. The questions were left unanswered like the darkness across the water near where they lay together.

A lone figure watched as a quiet splash passed beyond the dock. Rose colored fingers of light suggested early dawn. The figure clutched a carefully folded dark garment to its breast. One last languished look out into the blackness and the figure turned towards the dimly lit house. Pushing back the heavy hood, it brushed back a thick shock of dark hair.

Suddenly, the figure stopped and seemed to sense the early morning air. A cause of unknown urgency caused it to rush into the house without further fanfare.

This morning Jan had beaten both her mother and brother downstairs. Only Fin and his daughter sat at the table. Fin was drinking steaming coffee and Shere seemed as distracted as usual. In front of her was an untouched mug of tea and she abstractedly played with the string from the bag with her long fingers.

"What can I get you?" Fin offered.

"I'll manage fine," Jan returned with a small smile. Just as she was buttering some of the always present home-style bread, Celia and her brother came down the stairs.

Fin said his 'Good morning' as Hunter dove into the rather large oval plate of kippers that Jan thought to herself were always present as well.

Celia sat down next to Jan and smiled her close-lipped smile warmly.

"Sleep well?" she asked Jan.

"Ok," Jan almost sighed, "Until this morning at dawn. I thought I heard something out on the dock."

She watched carefully as Shere stopped playing with the tea bag but did not look up.

Fin said nothing as well and continued sipping his coffee.

"I can make some eggs if you like," he suggested.

"I'm fine," Jan returned. She hadn't figured on much of a response but she had to try. What she saw was more important than what she heard. But she let it go. She didn't feel there were going to be any revelations this morning.

Marie and Jonathon came down together. Everyone tucked-in and presently the subject of a beach excursion was mentioned.

As Marie told Fin that she was planning to take all four young people Shere looked up for the first time. Her eyes shot to Fin's and Jan thought they were rather wider than usual. This might be a good morning after all, she told herself.

Fin very calmly put his left weathered hand slowly on the right one of his daughter's.

"Sounds like an adventure to me!" he said. "Only, do me a favor and don't let any of you folks get a sunburn. Oh, and promise me you'll stay to where all the other people are. Those currents are wicked-strong and unpredictable. I wouldn't do more than wade in the shallows, and me knowing these waters all my life. Deal?"

"It's a deal," Marie agreed.

Celia seemed very excited about the prospect and asked Jan to the side if they would wear their swimming suits.

"Yep, why not," Jan said back, "But we'll put something over them just the same. You know, the sun dress thing you bought?"

This seemed to please the girl even further and Jan was again struck by how childlike some of her responses could be. She thought that actually her cousin looked much more advanced for her age but acted younger than she herself.

"Shucks," Jonathon jested, "And ah went-off and forgot ma clam-diggahs!"

Fin chuckled at the play on the local accent. Marie rolled her eyes.

Celia put a hand to her mouth and broke out in a full laugh that startled everyone except Hunter, who was inhaling more fish.

"You are so very funny! And smart, too!" she said, making Jonathon blush and avert his eyes from hers.

'Oh, brother,' Jan thought and rolled her own eyes. 'In the gothic novels didn't cousins get involved romantically?'

"Ok," Marie said finishing her coffee and toast. "Meet at the car in as soon as possible? Remember, we're meeting young Mr. Sanders as well. Jonathon, see that Hunter has what he needs? I know you girls will help each other."

Jan took that as a not-so-subtle sign of what she had to do; double-checking fittings and what should not show of her cousin's attributes. The razor would be ready for legs that had never seen one...

The drive to Popham took them past a large salt marsh and a few small campgrounds before the water came into view off to the right. They could tell by the GPS that this was just a sort of bay and a rocky island that their readings had told them was only reachable at low tide. Some tourists every year made the mistake of getting caught out there. The whole of the seascape was a protected park, but Fin had suggested they go on down to the old fort for parking as long as they got there early.

Marie indeed found parking at a premium but found a place just down from the restaurant and the general store that served the area. Unloading the normal beach trappings, they clambered up a small embankment and gazed out over the scene.

With the old brick fort on the left, stone boulders piled into the mouth of the river and to the right a beach stretched for as far as the eye could see. It curved around, as the maps showed, to form another area called Seawall Beach. Beyond that the jutting land was called Small Point. The old Lifesaving Station they had seen the day before stood out as a remembrance of times past.

There were already some tourists with blankets on the smaller beach in front of the newcomers and others were walking the shoreline. Scattered groups of fisherman were set up as well.

Marie guided the group down to the sand and they went about setting up for themselves. They had forgotten to buy long beach towels, but Fin had insisted they not waste money on such trappings so instead the four youths had towels borrowed from him. Marie had brought a low beach chair. She instructed the teenagers to apply the dreaded sunscreen, as she herself was doing. She removed her flowered beach dress and settled into her chair. She made sure to put the block on her bare shoulders as her light blue swimsuit was strapless.

Jonathon took off his khaki shirt, which looked like it belonged on safari. His shorts were equally baggy and of the same make. He had decided against the pith helmet and instead had the new camo ball cap. He turned his back and his sister started to apply the screen. She was telling Celia how to do this quietly and motioned that she could do the same to Hunter.

Celia put her hands on Jan's and stopped her.

"I'll do this," she suggested, "And *you* do Hunter?"

Jan was about to object when Celia looked directly into her eyes. "Please?"

Jan shrugged and stepped over to Hunter. She was a little shocked at what she saw.

Hunter had stripped off his skin-tight black shirt to reveal a very cut and muscular form. He seemed a bit confused as to what Jan was doing, but to her relief he didn't act like it was anything more than it was. Truth be told, it was Jan who realized it felt as if she was putting lotion on a warm marble statue. She had never put her hands on anything like it and it made her feel very strange indeed.

She finished as fast as she could and immediately regretted it. She felt herself blush and so returned quickly to Celia.

Jonathon appeared to have already caught sunburn as he was flushed and red. Celia was taking her time. Her smile was unabashed.

"Ok," Jan tried to hurry along the process. "Now how about you, Miss?"

Celia seemed to pout like a child who has had a toy taken away. But she smiled again and pulled her yellow sundress over her head. Her long dark hair fell back over her shoulders. Although Jan knew all too well what Celia's suit looked like, since she had uncomfortably been in the dressing room as she tried several on, she felt sure she heard her brother gulp audibly like a cartoon character.

Shaking her hair out of her eyes, she pushed it back and squared her shoulders. Jan had tried to keep the suit modest; it was a one piece with straps in a pink (at Celia's insistence) coral color. It didn't matter. Jan decided that not even sackcloth could hide Celia's form.

"How about *you* putting the stuff on?" she gazed at Jonathon.

Jan stepped in before her brother's knees gave out. "Oh, you don't need that much. And I'm taller."

"Ah, hey, Hunter?" Jonathon mumbled, his voice squeaking in his puberty, "Wanna throw the Frisbee?"

Hunter looked puzzled. He was scouring the beach with his sharp, dark eyes and Jan guessed that he was not looking for anything of his own gender.

"C'mon!" Jonathon pressed. He grabbed the Frisbee and off they went.

Celia watched them with interest but sat down gracefully on her towel. She reclined slightly but kept sight of the boys. Jan was just trying to figure out how she could look so lady-like in body and movement yet seem like a child in other ways.

Jonathon quickly realized that his cousin had no idea as to what to do with a flying disk. He demonstrated how to hold it and how to flick the wrist to make it sail. He backed up about twenty feet and threw it to Hunter.

The disk landed just to the right of the muscular youth. He made little attempt to catch it. Picking the object up, he studied it like it was an alien life form.

"Now, like I showed you!" Jonathon called. "Use your wrist! Throw it!"

Hunter cradled the disk in his bent right hand and arm. Jonathon could see from where he was the way Hunter's muscles rippled. First the forearms, then the biceps, and as he twisted at the waist more coiled sinew stretched and then sprang like bands of bent steel.

The Frisbee gratefully came nowhere near Jonathon. It might have decapitated him. Instead it sailed out over the water until it became a small dot and then slipped beneath the waves.

"Like that?" Hunter smiled.

Jonathon looked after the object. He could not be sure, but he guessed it had travelled well over a hundred yards out to sea towards the island with the lighthouse on it.

"Not bad," Jonathon tried in his best Vaudeville voice. "With a little 'woik' from me, who knows, kid? You might have a career."

"Can we try it again?" Hunter asked excitedly.

Jonathon walked back over and patted the rock-hard arm of his cousin.

"Not today, my boy," he said, adopting a W. C. Fields drawl, "Got to save that arm for the big Tiddlywinks Championship later."

He locked elbows with Hunter as they walked back towards the towels.

"Did you know I once attended the Tiddlywinks World Championship in Madagascar?" he continued in the Fields' voice. "Ah, yes, remember it like it was only yesterday…many people were killed."

Not long after Jonathon and Hunter rejoined their party, a

smiling Red sauntered up. He said his hellos to everyone. Jan noticed he looked a little out of place at the beach as he was dressed in cut-off jeans and a brown tee shirt without any logo at all on it. Then she realized it was the other tourists like her that were dressed oddly. Red was simply functional.

"Ma'am," he said to Marie, "If you wouldn't mind, I'd like to take these four up to the store to meet some of the other teenagers around here. If you don't mind?"

"No," Marie stated. "Just keep them out of trouble? And be back in about an hour? We can't take much more sun. I'll have a walk down the beach."

As Jan watched her mother stand up and put her sundress back on, she sidled over and caught her ear quietly.

"You want me to come with you?" Jan asked.

"Whatever for? No, you go with the others!" her mother suggested.

"Mom," Jan continued almost inaudibly, "Didn't you and Dad come here? You told me, remember?"

Marie looked not at her daughter but out to the rocky islands past the mouth of the river.

"You're a fantastic daughter and friend," she said equally quietly to Jan. "But I got this, Ok?"

Jan nodded and went along after the others.

The restaurant was busy with tourist-types clambering for beer and fried seafood. The greasy smell was intoxicating. The general store also looked crowded and small but Red did not lead them in there, only off to the side and down a small embankment to a rather more exclusive strand of beach. Here a group of youths sat on bright beach towels or stood in smaller groups.

Jan tried to not be nervous as Red was noticed with his group in tow and several people stopped what they were doing to check out the new arrivals. He headed straight for some girls seated in beach chairs that would have been the last group Jan would have wished to confront.

A semi-tall girl in a tiger-print strapless bikini with matching short skirt stood up and her court of two followed suit.

"Look what the cat's drug-in," the girl said, adjusting expensive sunglasses and placing a hand on a curvy hip.

"How are you?" Red started. "Gloria, here's some friends from away. I wanted to introduce them. They have family here."

Jan studied the girls as they studied back. The obvious leader, Gloria, with the tiger-print and designer glasses, had brightly highlighted blond hair pulled back with a tiger-print band that spoke volumes because Jan's mother would never let her do that to her hair. On the right side was a pink streak. She had to be Jan's age but bore a strikingly older manner.

"This is Jan," Red started, pointing as he went, "And her brother Jonathon, then their cousins Hunter and his sister Celia. This is Gloria Williams," he indicated the girl in the tiger-print.

She tipped her glasses in a much-practiced way and shifted her body to strike an attempt at a model's pose. Her eyes briefly flitted over the group but she turned her head down and stared intently at Hunter.

"Very nice to meet you," she said throatily, "Hunter was it?"

Jan disliked her immediately.

"And this is Denise Jones and Jenny Scotia," Red continued.

The Denise girl had black hair and also sported an advanced figure if a slight bit held-in by a one-piece black suit and long black skirt wrap. The other girl had deep, thick, shoulder length auburn hair and had a flirtatious look as well. She was wearing a green bikini with a see through green shawl around her arms.

"Hey!" Denise said, also to Hunter.

"What's up?" Jenny mouthed as she tossed her head and tresses back.

Gloria moved first and circled around the group. She extended a limp hand to Jan and shook hands if you could call it that. She eyed Celia up and down and smiled thinly, shaking her hand as well. She totally avoided Jonathon and instead stood at arms' length to Hunter.

"Girls?" she called to her friends, "Remember how I said this was going to be a boring summer? I've changed my mind!"

The other two locals twittered like birds.

Hunter stood with his skin-tight shorts and flexing muscles and smiled his closed-lipped snarl. He put one hand out. Gloria put hers in his and pretended to be hurt.

"Easy, Tarzan, I'm not Jane but you'll be glad of that!" she cooed, and her entourage giggled again.

Jan noticed other members of the beach had begun to crowd around slowly. Several groups now moved closer. They all bore pleasant smiles.

"I'm Jim," one blonde youth offered. "Any friend of Red's is OK in my book!"

"How are you?" a girl with wet dark hair smiled, "I'm Sarah. Good to meet you!"

Several more greetings were uttered from a rather congenial group of locals and Jan was beginning to feel warmth more than the almost blazing sun.

And then she noticed another group slowly circling the others.

Several wore the dark, even for the beach, black-clad gothic types that she thought were passé. In particular, she was concerned with four males who did not have a savory look about them. Enough time in Public School had taught her to bristle at the sign of trouble. Certain traits, certain eyes; a shark pack circling..."

The leader of the four came the closest behind the local girls. His shifty brown eyes made it look like he was treading on thin ice instead of sand around the Queen and Her Court. He had a shock of unruly dirty-blond hair and had on a pair of black surfer togs.

"You said they had family around here?" he sneered.

"Yep, Tommy," Red shot back, straitening to his full six feet of height. "Tommy Fields," Red continued to introduce.

Jan noticed Tommy flinch a bit when Red barked his name. He looked quickly to his sidekicks for support.

"Whatch'a know?" Red addressed the others. "This is Bill Glassman, James Henley, and Skip Donnelly. I think they're all joined at the hip!"

The remaining youth occupants on the beach found amusement in this statement and laughter rippled amongst them. This served to momentarily diffuse a situation that Jan did not like.

"So?" Tommy asked angrily.

"They're related to Fin on Parker Head," Red announced.

"Ha!" Fields cackled back, "That old relic and his spooky daughter?"

Red made a long step towards Tommy.

"You want to show some manners or you want me to teach you some?" he smiled.

Jonathon touched Red's strong shoulder and spoke up.

"Got a problem with my family?"

Jan was shocked but proud.

"What sort of AKC pedigree do you have?" Jonathon asked innocently.

Tommy started to speak but was confused by the new outburst of laughter from the other youths. Red smiled as well as Gloria and some of her friends got it but most missed the slur and reference to canine lineage instead of human.

Appearing wounded, Fields looked again to his crew. Glassman was big and blond but didn't appear to understand the situation. Henley had sharp blue eyes and an English-stock look. He seemed angry but stifled at the moment. Donnelly appeared to be of red-haired Irish decent and was content at the moment to study the curves of Celia.

Hunter now came to life and he finally let go of Gloria's hand and moved to stand next to Red.

The dark haired youth brought both fists together in front of his face and flexed his ample muscles.

An unfamiliar sound broke the tension. It was something spoken but short and bark-like from Celia. No one seemed to understand the utterance.

Except for Hunter.

He turned his head in anger and returned an equal growl of a response when Gloria diffused the scene.

"Boys, boys!" she scolded, "This is no way to welcome people! How about you guys drop the macho-thing and we all get back to getting to know each other?"

Tommy and his gang were already backing away, except for Donnelly. He was having problems committing Celia to memory and as such needed further scrutiny. The others knew Red and how sure a fighter he could be. The new guy looked like a nightmare.

"Anyway," Fields uttered loudly as a parting shot, "The whole lot of you, if you are related to Ole' Fin, you belong back on Malago!"

This drew some sharp hisses and oaths from everybody else on the beach.

"You idiot!" Gloria glared back at Tommy. "What a screwed-up thing to say! Nobody uses that anymore! Besides, all of our families here are probably tied there! You are *so* lame!"

Denise and Jenny showed equivalently fervent disdain at the comment.

"Hey, Jan is it?" Gloria continued, turning her back on Tommy in regal indifference. "Let's dig in the old cooler here for something for you guys to drink?"

"Thanks to Daddy's credit card!" Denise almost sang.

"Same thing!" Gloria flipped and locked elbows with a willing Hunter.

As the group moved towards The Queen's blanket pavilion, Gloria and her two ladies-in waiting falling all over Hunter, Jan caught Red's elbow.

"What did he mean?" she asked. "*Malago?*"

"Forget it," Red tried to brush-off, "He's an imbecile. Trust me."

Instead, Jan committed the term to memory.

As the group began to sit down Jan caught up with her brother.

"Are you crazy?" she asked him quietly, "Where did the confrontation thing come from?"

Sometimes she felt like his mother as well as his sister.

Jonathon continued to move with the small crowd but adopted a voice his sister was both used-to and almost hated.

"Sweetheart," he curled his lip in a Bogart way, "I'm gonna tell my grandkids about the time I stood-down the Maine Gang. But I won't tell them how I was sure of the play because of the muscle of the Lobsterman's son and the crazy cousin that makes Rocky look like a weakling. You follow?"

"You are nuts," she sighed.

"Riddle-me-this, Bat Girl," he continued privately. "Watch this…"

He dropped back and got Celia's attention away from the local boys who all wanted to be her friend. Within earshot of Jan he asked a simple question.

"Celia! What did you say to Hunter? I didn't get it?"

The girl brushed-off several would-be admirers and looked straight into Jonathon's face seriously. Then she turned her eyes downward in obvious embarrassment.

"I, I, I spoke in French," she offered, and then was swept away reluctantly by the new would-be friends.

Jonathon looked at his sister and switched voices to one of his favorite unsung actors from a Mel Brooks movie, Ron Carey.

"Yeah, yeah, it was probably French, yeah probably French!" he mimicked

Jan shrugged and moved on with the small crowd.

"That was no French!!!" Jonathon finished.

An hour passed there on the beach in a style not unlike any other activity that Jan could think of where adolescents were involved with or without supervision. This was the part she disliked.

Intellectually, she understood the pattern. There were the 'beautiful people' who were busy accepting Hunter and Celia into their fold as prizes to be won and then lauded over to their supposed friends. Handsome boys sat around Celia and vied for her attention. They tried to make her laugh or blush. All she did was look nervously as if she wanted someone to save her and continued the habit of covering her mouth when she smiled.

Her brother hid his smile as well. Jan wondered how he managed this since, unlike the apparent taboo of the boys touching Celia, every girl that could get close to Hunter had to feel his arms or brush their fingers through his hair.

He did not share his sister's apparent alarm at the attention.

It was all she could do for Jan not to shake her head and laugh at the whole situation. She felt like a scientist peering through a two-way mirror into an unsuspecting group of lesser primates.

Jonathon sat next to Jan talking quietly to Red. They slugged soft-drinks in a manly way and Red had this annoying way of sneaking glances towards Jan. Whenever she would catch his eyes, he would look away in haste.

This bothered Jan most of all. Were they not near-adults here? Were they schoolyard children? Gloria and her group were certainly acting out the roles of morally unfettered pubescent soon-to-be-regretting-bad-choices young people. Even if Jan was not remotely looking for a summer romance like the ones gaudily written about in some teen cheap novel, why didn't Red just walk up to her and say 'Hey, I like you'.

Not that the idea wasn't so far-fetched, she told herself. Guys at school had found her interesting. She suddenly hated that word. Usually it was the more studious ones who Jan told herself were only out to get what they thought they could.

But she had been kissed. And not in some faltering attempt, mind you. It was during a slow dance in the typically over-decorated rented ballroom, a year ago, with the 70's disco light going. The guy was unbelievably not in her sphere of existence. Everybody knew he had his own band. He had asked her to dance and talked so nicely, whatever he had said. So they danced.

And then he kissed her.

When the song was over he went back to his friends from the band, in the dark, where he probably had the booze she smelled on him hidden.

And they had laughed.

She got it. She wondered what he had won in the bet. But she laughed too to herself because whatever cruel joke had been played she had enjoyed it for a very short time.

Jan was jolted out of the memory by her brother's voice beside her.

"I can't watch this anymore," he said seriously.

"Watch what?" she asked, "The As-the-Teen-Turns Soap Opera?"

"She's not enjoying this," Jonathon stated.

Without a further word, he stood up and left his sister seated on the blanket. She looked puzzled and stared across the space he had vacated at Red. For once this afternoon, Red looked right back at her and shrugged.

Jonathon strode straight over to where Celia was seated encircled by the local wolves. He stopped right in front of her and all eyes were suddenly fixed on him.

The only ones he cared about were Celia's which were even larger now. These gazed back at him with what he had uncharacteristically counted on.

"Ready for that walk down the beach we talked about?" He was immensely relieved that his voice didn't squeak or crack.

Not waiting for an answer, he offered a hand to the startled young lady who put that hand in his and stood up.

Some watchers might have found it almost comical as she was a bit taller than he. She was certainly more athletic and of a different build. The local boys just stared in utter disbelief.

Celia smiled her closed-lipped smile larger than Jonathon had ever seen her do. They walked off together down the beach. The sand seemed to make the young man a bit faulty of step.

In his head, Jonathon was walking ten feet off the ground and the world was swimming. Yet, the one thing keeping him connected to Earth was the solid, firm grasp of Celia's hand.

"Finest kind!" Red almost whispered to Jan. "Wicked-cool, your brother!"

"I'm not sure that's my brother," she breathed back, watching the two figures leave the pack of would-be suitors gawking in their wake.

"My, my!" The Queen Gloria remarked loudly enough to be heard by all. "Kissing Cousins?"

Chuckles rippled through the court.

"Want to take a walk with me, Hunter?" she cooed very suggestively.

Hunter looked confused for a moment. Before he could speak Jan did so instead.

"I've got to check back in with my mom. Don't be gone too long, OK?"

Hunter nodded, but then strangely gazed over all the seated

heads out into the water. His smile faded and he took on a serious if not somber expression.

"I'll go with you," he stated, and broke away from the fawning girls and stood up quickly. "Let's go...now."

He started to stride purposefully down to the beach and didn't wait for Jan or Red. They got up and turned to follow him.

"I've got work to do back home," Red said to Jan. "Some folks got to work for a livin'."

"Nice to meet you," Jan said to the whole group.

"And you as well!" Gloria said, peering over the rim of her sunglasses again. "Hey, there's a youth function at the old church on Sunday. Why don't you and your entourage attend?"

"We'll see," Jan smiled. Right now all she was trying to do was to see why Hunter had left so abruptly.

"You do that, Dear. Red, you see to it, OK?" Gloria rather ordered.

Red was now by himself as Jan had rushed off.

"Right..." he smirked a little. Then he too was off.

Jan had to almost run to catch Hunter's long, strong strides. He made straight for where Marie was seated in her chair near the water's edge. She appeared to be napping. Her wide-brimmed hat was pulled down almost over her dark glasses.

Hunter strode straight past the dozing figure and entered the water up to his waist. There he stopped and stood stock still with his muscular arms tensed and his hands on his lean hips. His stance appeared defensive, defiant and serious.

Marie seemed to wake up with a start just in time to catch Jan wading into the water after Hunter. He shook his dark hair back and turned his head slightly over his shoulder yet not taking his icy stare away from something in the water. He raised his left arm and stuck it out towards Jan in a 'halt' fashion.

Not knowing why, Jan obeyed. She tried to look past him to see what he saw. All she could ascertain were two seals' heads about fifty feet offshore. The curious creatures were staring back like Jan had observed all day. They stayed their distance away but regarded the humans with interest. These two had larger eyes than she had noted in other specimens about the area. It was something about the steady scrutiny of them that made Jan think back to the incident on Fin's dock where the same scene had seemed to been enacted. Fin had rushed the group away quickly.

Hunter replaced his hand on his hip and resumed the lock of stares. Even with the swift tidal current, the animals were managing to stay perfectly in place. Only, they seemed to be trying to look past Hunter. With a shock Jan processed the impossible thought that perhaps they were interested in *her*. Or, maybe her mom, she couldn't tell.

"What's going on?" Marie asked Jan. "What are you guys staring at?"

Hunter gave another hard look over his shoulder that strangely Jan understood.

"Oh, nothing Mom, just looking at the cute seals out there." She suggested. This seemed to satisfy Hunter perfectly.

"Just don't get too far out in that water," Marie remarked. "That current is dangerous."

With her motherly duties dutifully enacted, she pulled her hat back down and her eyes seemed to be shaded from view.

Hunter looked quickly to his left and right. As there were no other people near enough for them to be seen he seemed more at ease. He looked straight back at Jan and caught her eyes with his. He placed his arms slowly to his side. Then he turned back to the two bobbing heads and made a curt but very deliberate bow from the waist.

Jan would have found the gesture romantic if arcane and suited to a by-gone gothic era had it not been enacted here and towards two sea mammals.

When he straightened back upright, he moved to the side so that he was not obstructing the view between the two heads and the girl.

Jan was not sure she could believe what had just happened. But she didn't have time to think about it because her eyes were glued to the ones watching her from the water. It was impossible to fathom, but the seals just stared and seemed to look straight into Jan's soul. She wasn't afraid. They almost communicated warmth and a greeting that Jan's logical side was trying to tell her fantasy side was merely misplaced cuteness in the same way people thought bears were cuddly and funny until they started to eat you.

Jan was startled back to the real world as Celia waded slowly out to join her brother. Her eyes were also riveted to the seals as well. She spoke softly to Hunter and he spoke back to her. Then he addressed Jan.

"Get your brother," he almost ordered.

Jan turned and motioned for Jonathon, who was standing on the shore with a very perplexed look on his face, to join her in the water.

He did so and when he was next to her he whispered "What...is...going on...?"

"I don't know," she answered back. "Just look at them. Now they're looking at you. This is not...normal."

"You can say that again," he agreed. "OK, if we're all in a dream, might as well play along."

With that he slowly raised his right arm and waved slowly to the bobbing heads. The animals appeared to wink both their eyes in unison.

"Oh, that didn't just happen!" Jonathon breathed. "They must be used to people and are expecting a handout or something."

The seals took their gaze away from Jonathon and now regarded Celia. She locked eyes with them and made a graceful curtsy.

"Hey sis," Jonathon asked quietly, "When did we enter The Twilight Zone? Or is it the X-Files?"

Jan just shook her head slowly in disbelief.

Suddenly the two heads slipped back under the water and were gone.

Hunter scanned the water beyond where the two had been and his eyes narrowed intensely. The others followed his gaze and saw three other seals approaching slowly.

Jan was sure she had seen them before. Even as animals of a same species may look alike, she was convinced these were the ones that had surfaced and chased the others away out from Fin's dock. They seemed to have done the same thing again here today.

With what little she knew about seals, Jan could tell that these were large males. The two smaller ones were still much larger than the two that they had chased away. The tell-tale features were the thicker, shorter and broader heads. Indeed, one of the two that had studied Jan and Jonathon before had such male traits but not like these interlopers.

The third one, who hung back from the others, was the largest of all.

Immediately, Jan felt a pang of fear that she couldn't put into words. A sense of foreboding or impending danger fell over the scene.

"Out of the water," Hunter almost barked. It was not said loudly but it carried the necessary authority.

Celia stepped in front of Jonathon, and Hunter's muscular back blocked Jan's further view. The two started backing such that Jan and Jonathon were almost pushed until they were completely out of the surf.

Hunter never took his dark eyes off the three seals as he spoke to Marie.

"Would you take us back now?" he asked, apparently startling her. "I think we've had enough sun."

"Oh, sure," Marie flustered. She began to collect things and asked

Jan and Jonathon if they had all their belongings. The two muttered as to the affirmative but they too could not break away from the three figures that now were circling and swimming back and forth in front of them. They were perhaps a mere twenty yards off shore.

Jan thought to herself that whereas the first two seals had appeared graceful and quiet and soothing, these three were positively menacing. Their lips were curled back to expose sharp teeth and these flashed snarls as they passed. She tried not to look into the eyes. She knew she would regret it.

As they moved back towards their car, Celia and Hunter kept passing quick looks to each other. They were obviously concerned and a bit rattled but Hunter played the role of male protector very convincingly.

Jonathon looked at Jan a lot as well. Their unspoken conversation seemed to say 'Do we have a lot to talk about later!'

For some reason Jan didn't even consider for an instant telling her mother what had happened. This was disturbingly uncharacteristic of her. It made her feel stranger still.

The ride back was punctuated by Marie's motherly questions about what locals had been met and what were they like and were they friendly and so forth. Jan was hoping her mother had not suspected that the four were not telling her something as every question was answered with the fewest syllables possible.

When they arrived finally at Fin's Hunter bolted out of the car and headed for the fish house where Fin was putting nets into his boat. The two disappeared around the corner as the youth was obviously intent on relating the afternoon's activities.

Jan put this down again in her mental notes as it seemed Fin knew more than he had so far imparted.

Marie collected things from the rear of the SUV and told her daughter that she was going upstairs to take a shower. This left Jan and Jonathon alone with Celia.

Before Jan could start the interrogation Celia turned to Jonathon.

"You are a gentleman!" she said softly. "You saved me from those...boys. I didn't like them. But I like you..."

Jonathon turned beet red and looked at the ground.

Celia suddenly hugged Jan very tightly.

"And I like you. You are the friend I always wanted."

She sniffed away some tears when she let Jan go.

"I want to tell you things. I want you to really know me, us." She said strongly. "Only, my family has rules. I can't break them. Fin is the Elder here. I must respect that. Hunter and Fin will talk. They will decide what I say and what I do. Please understand. This is how it is."

Then she hurried off into the house.

Jan turned to her brother.

"Hey, Romeo," she started.

"Cut that out!" he said, meaning it.

"OK, I'm just, you know, trying to process this? You're right; we're right in the middle of a fantasy-mystery-sinister novel here and I for one would not believe it if it hadn't just happened. So what do we do?"

"Leave Mom out of it for now," he suggested.

"I already thought that, and it makes me feel bad for not telling her! But I agree and I don't know why! She probably wouldn't believe us anyway but it seems right not telling her. Or, I mean, it seems right but it's wrong...I don't know!"

"What do you want to do?" Jonathon asked.

"I guess we wait but not for long. Fin is no dummy. He knows what Hunter is telling him and he knows we are not dummies and we know he's not told us everything and he knows he hasn't and did you really feel the way I did when those first two seals were looking at us?"

Jonathon nodded solemnly.

"I don't know about you," he decided, "But I've got some sleuthing to do, Sweetheart!"

"Ditto," she agreed. "I'm starting with the good ole internet and a remark said in spite."

"What's that?" her brother asked.

"*Malago*," she remembered.

5

The afternoon had given way to early evening. The events of the day seemed a lifetime away, if, indeed, they had really happened.

Jan had been quite busy on her tablet. Gratefully, the connection was working and as such she had a story to tell. What she had uncovered was hardly hidden. Rather, it seemed to jump out at anyone who wanted to inquire.

Hunter and Celia were not to be seen. Marie was relaxing in her room catching up on work related issues and Jonathon was out of his room and pretending to play detective. This left Jan to ponder the story she had discovered.

Malago was a local mispronunciation of a nearby island in Casco Bay known as 'Malaga'. The origins of the name were disputed. What was fact was that in 1794 a sailing Captain Darling gave his slave from the West Indies his freedom and enough money to buy a neighboring Horse Island. The free man took the name of Benjamin Darling. Most accounts have it that Benjamin saved his master and Captain's life during a ship wreck.

A man named Griffin settled on Malaga's east side in the early 1860's. Benjamin Darling's three granddaughters and their families settled there as well. All seemed to be of freed black or mixed races. As this was somewhat novel in Maine still the rest of the area seemed unconcerned for the moment.

The community continued to attract fishing types and by the 1880's about twenty-five families lived there. A man of Scotch-Irish descent was known as 'The King of Malaga' for his fishing prowess and became the spokesman for the island. The very idea of the place suggested somewhere where those who were not accepted elsewhere in the region could reside without consternation. Many groups were not year-round residents but came and went as they pleased.

Maine at the close of the 1800's was changing rapidly. A loss of ship building and depletion of fish stocks were substituted by a fast-growing tourist trade. Wealthy New Englanders could escape the city wiles by vacationing, hunting, and fishing in the green and clean state. Rocky coastal real estate sold expensively to folks wishing a get-away cottage or even affordable mansion with a view.

So it was surrounding poor Malaga. The Casco Bay Estates were today an affluent collection of homes. In the early 1900's, the new gentile ladies who took their weekend sailing excursions were shocked and dismayed at the sight of Malaga's mixed race womenfolk with their legs exposed in the shallow bay where they earned extra money doing washing. One could throw a stone from the tea-parties on the manicured lawns, if one were so gauche, and hit the island of such ill-repute.

That's where the stories started, Jan discovered.

Newspapers not just in New England but all across the investing-interested nation began to run totally false tales of inbreeding, debauchery, and squalor. The locals did nothing to stem the tide. Many were worried they might lose out on selling properties because of the 'blight' on the coast.

Jan stumbled upon a term that she had not heard of before. The very idea was so ludicrously taken for fact at this time in history as to be absolutely appalling.

The 'eugenics movement' had taken root in America like a creeping, choking weed after the Civil War. It sought to prove scientifically that certain 'unsavory' traits such as poverty, sloth, drunkenness, immorality, and even imbecility could be 'improved' through selective breeding.

Much made sense now to Jan as she remembered seeing printed cartoons of the Irish as monkey-like and deplorable as they tried to immigrate and get a chance in the New World. All the ethnic jokes for all but the firmly implanted WASP puritans were still being kept alive in schoolyards.

The same ideas would reemerge in the 1930's in Germany to hasten the destruction of so many innocent lives.

So what chance did a small mixed-race community of fisher-folk stand against a snooty high-browed political machine?

The answer was more diabolical than could be imagined.

Dispute over ownership of the island finally caused an edict in 1905 that placed the islanders as wards of the State and under the thumb of the 'Governor's Executive Council'.

That should have been heard as the death knell for the residents.

After a historic, at least as it was portrayed in the press, visit in 1911 the governor and a selected group toured the island and sang praises of the school the State had built there for the poor wretches who deserved a place to live.

Despite all this, a short while later the State published an eviction notice for all the island's inhabitants. They were to be gone by July 1st, 1912.

To help along some of those affected by the notice, a select group of eight people, many from the same family, were conducted to the newly built Home for the Feeble Minded nearby.

The State saw to the letter of the law in executing the evictions and then promptly burned anything left standing on the island to the ground. Except for the State afforded schoolhouse which was moved intact elsewhere. The island was purchased by the State for a pittance, to ensure no further settlement, and a few dollars were thrown to the displaced. As the ultimate insult, the buried dead on the island were dug up, their stones removed, and all were dumped into just eight mixed graves at the Home for the Feeble Minded.

Jan at least got a mixed sense of justice by reading that no one had managed to exploit the island for the supposed riches. It sat today as a stark reminder of wrongness. The State museum in Augusta had been running an archeological exhibit and learning experience on the place. It was deemed a source of embarrassment for the whole region.

And so back to the way in which it was still being used. The insult by the local bullies was meant to sting. It seemed to have backfired on them, but the malicious nature of the jab left some lingering questions.

There was just so much she needed to talk to her great uncle about.

Jonathon softly knocked on her partially closed bedroom door. He peeped in and then dramatically entered quietly.

"Have I got something to show you," Jan almost whispered.

"And me you," her brother sneakily smiled.

"Me first" she said, and began a presentation on what she had discovered.

With each new bit of information, Jonathon smiled wider.

"OK," he whispered when the article was through, "Now it's my turn."

He adopted the ridiculous Charlie Chan accent.

"Every-thing become most clear! You follow me, Missy! You see!"

Jan almost tiptoed after her brother as he led her down the hall and to the shadowed small staircase that Fin had said led to the attic and widow's walk.

"You didn't!" she whispered to her beaming brother.

"Ah-yuh!" he mimicked the local dialect, "Why not? It's not locked. It's almost as though somebody wanted me to go up there. Let's go!"

The two started up the stairs like burglars. Every creak made them stop and wait. Nervously, they finally reached the small open door at the top of the flight. Fading sunlight was streaming in from old, cloudy windows.

Jonathon led his sister past dusty antique furniture and old oil lamps that sat on crates and still smelled heavily of the fish, or maybe whale or seal, oil that used to fuel them. He stopped when he came to a very large and battered trunk.

Jan noticed at once that it was the type from the steamer era. Virtually everything a person needed could be stowed for travel. The thing was partially opened and revealed not clothes or shoes or such; instead there were numerous framed photos of very old subject matter.

"Here they are," Jonathon said quietly and reverently, "Here are all the pictures I said were missing from the house! Get ready for some shockers!"

Jan plowed into the treasure trove. There were old tin-types of nautical people; relatives she supposed. There was something about the sharp-set features and large eyes that just made her believe the traits were mirrored in Fin, Shere, and even herself and Jonathon. She felt as if she were staring at her family tree.

Each picture had for a background either a sailing ship, some salty people, a wharf full of some monumental catch of fish, or all three. The subjects were stoically serious as Jan remembered that people had to stand petrified for many seconds as the flash-pan went off and the slow shutter-speed made it imperative for stillness.

Jonathon abruptly looked over her shoulder.

"Recognize anybody here?" He indicated an aged photo of a sailing schooner apparently setting out on a voyage. There were some fifteen men in white sweaters and caps posed under the name painted on the prow.

Jan got a jolt of impossibility.

Jonathon's finger pointed to a face in the crowd.

"The year on the picture, as if you can't read it, is 1903."

"So it looks like him," she offered.

"Just like him. Not then, but now," he continued. "So what is our current host Fin doing in a photo from 1903? Impossible you say! But just look on…"

Jonathon had collected a small pile of specimens of particular interest.

"How about this?" he offered. "Is this taken on your island that you've been reading about? I think so."

He showed her a somewhat blurry photo of a bunch of people proudly displaying a large catch of fish. The subjects were indeed apparently of mixed-race. Small children played amid the bountiful harvest. All seemed to be clad in course white clothing that Jan recognized as being made out of necessity of flour sacks. The entire scene was wonderfully idyllic and simple and happy.

"You're right," she sadly told her brother. "It's on the island. I just know it. The guy there is the one I said was called 'The King'. Only, I guess you want me to look at the guy over his shoulder."

"Who is that?" Jonathon asked.

"OK, so it appears to be Fin." Jan conceded. "What do we do with this? Where does it lead? More scary crap? We're living under the roof of a guy that appears to have been around longer than he should be? I don't know."

"Just food for thought," Jonathon mused. "Let's get back."

The two retraced their steps and found that no one was looking for them. Their mother was still occupied in her room with either work-stuff or a nap. There was no noise from downstairs.

As Jan and Jonathon pushed open the door to Jan's room

Jonathon was about to go when Jan breathed in deeply and noticed something different in the room.

"What?" Jonathon asked.

"There," she offered.

On her bed, lying just on the pillow was a small book. Jan recognized it immediately as the one Celia had bought in Topsham.

Jan crossed the room and picked up the thing very carefully.

"What's this about?" Jonathon asked.

"Be quiet and we'll read this together. I think it's important."

Jan opened the cover and lay down to share with her brother. The first page was blank. Then, in stunning vibrancy, there was a colored pencil masterpiece. It portrayed a large eyed, small and impossibly cute seal nestled up to a mother seal on great grey rocks.

'Celia was a little seal' it read. 'She woke up by her mother.'

The next page showed the sun beaming down on a seal colony.

'Celia and her mother went into the sea. Celia liked to swim and play.'

The following page portrayed an undersea scene with urchins, wriggling pink squid, and green lobsters.

'Celia's mother taught her to catch fish to eat.'

Then there was a drawing of a desolate, wave-swept island.

'In the sunny afternoon, Celia and her mother went to a place where they could be alone.'

There was a picture of a sandy beach.

'Celia and her mother were special. They were not only seals. They were Selchies.'

Jan felt a cold shock course through her body. She didn't know if her brother felt the same.

The next page showed two pairs of human footprints on the sandy beach; one small and the other one larger.

'Celia and her mother took off their seal skins. They walked on the beach together.'

Following was a surreally drawn picture of a set of lithe, larger and graceful hands filled with flowers sharing with a smaller and delicate pair.

'They picked wildflowers in the meadow.'

The next picture was of the sun as seen as though lying on one's back, gazing up.

'The day was good. The sun was warm.'

The last picture was of a rose colored sunset over dark rocks.

'Celia and her mother put their seal skins on again. They went back. They were happy. Celia went to sleep snuggled up to her mother and dreamed of her good day.'

Jan closed the small book and her brother lying beside her whistled softly.

"As if things could get any weirder," he sighed. "So what do you make of this?"

"If I remember," she mused, "the term 'Selchie' comes from the Orkney Islands in Scotland. But we'll look that up. Anyway, I guess what you are asking is if I believe this or is it just a fantasy children's book written by our very strange relative."

"If I was four or five years old," Jonathon continued, "I wouldn't have any trouble taking this as fact. But I'm not."

Jan suddenly put the book down and stared seriously at her sibling.

"Exactly," she said, a bit animated. "But we both have seen things in the past week that grown-ups would say just aren't so. Now we see our great-uncle in pictures from a by-gone era that suggests he is who-knows-how old. You saw what happened with the seals today. You saw how Hunter and Celia acted."

"It sure would explain a lot about those two," he agreed comically. "I mean, they seem to have been brought up away from the things we call normal. But seal-people? C'mon, Sis!"

"And what about cousin Shere?" she continued. "What if she's one too? She sure doesn't behave like anybody I've met in a while."

Jonathon sat upright. He stared at his sister as if he had never seen her before.

"You're buying this!" he said incredulously. "Of all people! You are the very last person I would ever expect to believe something like this! Except for Mom, of course. Have you lost it or what?!"

"Just hang on and keep an open mind, will ya?" she asked. "Let's look into this a little bit."

Together they turned back to Jan's tablet and started researching anything on the subject of Selchies. Surprisingly, a lot existed.

They discovered that in fact the term was from the northern Scottish islands and simply meant 'seal' in Scots Gaelic. There were just as many stories and legends from Ireland, Iceland, The Faroe Islands (between Norway and Iceland) and even in American Native lore.

Of particular interest was the term 'Roan' used by the Irish for such beings. It also meant 'seal' in Irish Gaelic. It also happened to be the name used by their host and great-uncle.

The legends seemed to have a basic theme. Usually a fisherman would come upon a beautiful, dark woman shedding her seal skin. The man would steal her skin and then she would be forced to become his bride. Variations existed, and the Selchie women seemed to be perfect wives and mothers, until their hidden skins were recovered and they would return to the sea, leaving their husbands and children, forever.

Selchie males were portrayed as irresistible to human women and most stories had them seeking out the lonely and forlorn ladies along the rugged coasts.

Some of the stories had the Selchies luring humans out to sea to become as they. The humans would never be seen again, or if they were, it would be years from the time of their disappearances and the human would not have seemed to age at all.

"So," Jan posed the question, "Are we in the middle of a dream, a legend, or a Looney-farm?"

"I don't know," Jonathon muttered. "I'm going to have to see this to believe it."

"I'll bet you would," Jan smirked. "Didn't you see and read that when the Selchies shed their skin they don't have any other clothes on? You could sure see Celia in a different light..."

"Knock it off!" her blushing brother scoffed. "You know what I mean."

"I do," she considered, "But I'm not sure if I'm ready to truly believe this."

A knock on the door ended the conversation.

"Hey," their mother called without entering. "Dinner downstairs. Ok?"

"Ok," they chimed in unison.

After washing her hands, Jan almost ran straight into Celia who was heading to the stairs as well.

An awkward moment passed as Celia seemed to keep her large, soft eyes downcast. Abruptly, Jan simply threw her arms around the taller girl and hugged her tightly.

Celia sobbed a little as she returned the embrace.

"You are so very talented," Jan whispered. "Thank you. I loved the book. We'll talk later?"

Celia nodded quickly and went into the bathroom to dry her eyes.

Downstairs Jan found a new aroma permeating the air in the kitchen. On the table were four large boxes of the pizza variety bearing the name of a local eatery.

"You're in for a treat!" her mother remarked. "Your father took me to the place they make these! It's in Bath right across the street from the ship yard. Thanks, Fin!"

The older man smiled slightly. He was drinking coffee and leaning against the counter away from the table where Marie, Jonathon, and an ever-hungry Hunter were seated. Jan left a spot for Celia, who was just coming down the stairs. The smell was intriguing. There was the usual sausage and pepperoni pungency but something else. Jan couldn't quite figure it out.

"I got one like you might find anywhere," Fin drawled, "But I hope you're adventurous and will like the white ones. It's a specialty."

Marie opened one box and showed her children. The pie had white Alfredo sauce instead of tomato and was topped with a generous amount of small pink shrimp.

"Gulf of Maine shrimp," Marie smiled, "Small but so sweet. What do you say?"

Hunter didn't need any convincing. He opened another similar box and dove in.

"I'll bite," Jonathon shrugged. "Celia?"

"Yes, please," she nodded and accepted a slice from Jonathon with a beaming, if still closed lip, smile.

Jan opened a box in front of her and tried the same. The lack of words for the next few minutes spoke volumes.

There was some small talk from Marie to Hunter, who had problems taking his attention away from the food, and Jan agreed with everybody else that the fare was top notch. Only when the white pizza was gone did anyone reluctantly turn to the 'regular' one, which was equally good in its' own right.

"Fin?" Jan finally asked, "Is Shere going to join us?"

"Ah, no," he said slowly. "She's off to contact a friend of ours. I hope they get back soon. Weather's turning nasty."

As if on cue, the small radio that was the only seemingly modern device on the kitchen counter crackled to life. It was always left on and now Fin strained an ear as a marine advisory came on.

"Sounds like it might blow-over," Fin concluded. "Shere should be back in the morning with our friend. We need some, ah, help around the place."

"Anything we can do?" Marie offered.

"Ah, no, Missy... Thanks just the same," he said.

"She didn't take the boat, did she?" Jan asked flatly. "And you just got back in the truck."

Fin simply smiled a bit and looked at the girl.

Jan was expecting a glare or a verbal rebuke from her mother at being rather rude. Instead, there was a surprising silence from that end of the table.

Fin turned slowly and walked over to the sink. He reached in the cabinet above and took out a dark bottle there and poured a fair amount into his empty coffee cup. He replaced the bottle and sipped with his back to his guests for a few moments. Then he walked back and sat down across from Marie.

"Well, no use beating around the bush," he stated. "Marie, I need to talk to you."

"Sure," Marie said strongly. "Fin, you go ahead. There's an elephant in this kitchen and we might as well discuss it."

Celia swiveled her head all around the room with wide eyes even wider.

Jonathon patted her right hand on the table with his left.

"Figure of speech," he whispered. "I'll explain later?"

The white haired man just smiled his slow smile back at Marie.

"Look," she stated, "I know this concerns both my children and me. I don't like keeping things from them. It's time. I don't like to admit it, but they're almost adults. When I decided to come up here I expected something like this."

Jonathon looked at his sister and both shared a collective shock and expectation of something important about to happen.

"Marie," Fin said softly, "I'm only thinking about what I promised your husband."

"You've done everything just as Manny wished," Marie continued. "You've stayed out of our lives. I love you for that. It was Manny's idea to try and protect them. But you and I know that sooner or later...well, it's time."

"Hello?" Jan blurted. "We're right here, you know!"

Marie smiled a sad smile.

"Hunter, Celia, can we trade places?" she asked.

With a shuffling, they rearranged seats until Marie was sitting between her twins. She clasped hands with them before continuing.

"So," she started with a determined air, "First off, Fin, I'll bet you were about to say that we should leave. That there are things happening here that worry you. Do you think we are in danger?"

Jonathon and Jan both sat alert and waited for an answer.

"No," Fin said flatly. "If I did, I would ask you to leave; I'd make sure of it."

"Spoken like the gentleman you are," Marie noted. "That being said, then who were the three stooges that threatened my kids today at the beach?"

Before Jan or Jonathon could recover from the shock of the question, their mother addressed them.

"Thought I was asleep under my hat? You don't give me credit for the mom I am. I saw everything."

Jonathon physically put the hand not in his mother's grasp up to his jaw to check if his mouth was open in disbelief. Jan just let out a short chuckle.

"Hunter?" Marie caught the seemingly uninterested youth's attention. "I want to thank you for first showing what good manners and bearings you obviously learned from very fine parents. Secondly, you and your sister moved to protect my children. You do your Tribe great honor."

"Tribe?" Jan started, but a squeeze from her mother's hand cut her short.

"Celia?" Marie waited for the shy eyes to lift from the table. "Your beauty and grace tells me instantly that you are truly of royal blood, as your brother. Am I right?"

The strong but demure girl lowered her large brown eyes again in a slow nod. Her brother seated beside her stiffened as to attention in his seat. Pride and a fiery masculinity filled his wild dark countenance.

Jan and Jonathon sat dumbfounded.

Marie kept looking at Celia and Hunter but spoke aside to her children.

"Unless I miss my guess, guys, your distant cousins here are from a very old Tribe in what we now call Canada. The coasts of Nova Scotia and Newfoundland, the Gulf of St. Lawrence, Hudson Bay, the Labrador Sea, the Davis Strait and even to the Arctic Circle and Greenland; that is where they roam."

Hunter nodded sharply and spoke strongly.

"You do us great honor as well. I have heard all my life the stories of how our blood ancestors left the Old Country of Eire and came here together. I am proud to meet cousins who have the blood of our fathers in them."

Hunter looked quickly at Fin. The white haired man smiled and nodded.

"Fin is the elder here," Hunter continued. "I have kept quiet as he wishes out of respect well earned. But I have wanted to greet you as my family would want me to. So…"

With that Hunter shot straight up out of his chair, knocking it over, and faced Marie, Jonathon and Jan. Celia stood up slowly and gracefully. She let her eyes wander up briefly but then returned them to a downcast posture.

Hunter bowed curtly at the waist as he had done for the seals that afternoon.

"Hail cousins of the most revered blood-line of MacLir!"

Celia curtsied as well before passing a rather dreamy, almost secret smile and flirt of the eyes to Jonathon.

"He means you two," Marie offered to her astonished offspring. "It would be proper to respond with equal respect?"

Numbly, Jonathon stood and rather clumsily bowed to Hunter and Celia. Jan stood but could not manage a curtsy like Celia so settled on a serious head nod.

As everyone sat back down Jan said out loud what she was thinking.

"Mom? Want to tell us just what is going on here?"

"You mean to tell me," her mother said softly, patting her hand, "That my intelligent children have not figured out yet that Hunter and Celia are Selchies?"

"Oh, brother," Jonathon sighed. "Captain's log entry... just left wormhole into new dimension!"

"Ok," Jan conceded slowly, "So if I have this right they turn into seals and go merrily on their way around the coasts until they decide to turn back into...well, like us, and then shed their seal skins and walk around on dry land."

"Something like that," Marie agreed jovially. "We can go into particulars later. Anyway, stop me if I'm wrong, Fin, but I also think that Hunter and Celia here are the, well, for lack of better words, the 'Prince' and 'Princess' of their Tribe? I suppose their esteemed parents sent them here to get a different view of life? They are to learn some new things about not only their relatives, but about the land ways as well?"

Fin continued to smile and nodded.

"Wait a minute!" Jonathon reasoned. "They just, I mean, Mom, you said they were royal, and then they did something and said we had royal, ah, blood or something, and..."

"Calm down, sweetheart, I'm getting to that," his mother soothed. "Fin? A little help here?"

"Suit yourself," he shrugged in a warm way.

"I'm a simple man," he started, and took a swig from his cup. "I say things in simple ways. You two youngsters, Jan and Jonathon, you can use your new-fangled machines to fill in the gaps later. There's just what I know, and if you want, I'll tell it."

He waited until Jan and Jonathon nodded for him to continue and Marie smiled her consent.

"Fair enough," he huffed and leaned back in his chair. Everyone else at the table leaned forward.

"I was born in the year 1804. Believe that or not, it doesn't matter to me. That's what I was told. I was there, but I don't recollect the exact date. I just know later that it seems to fit."

Fin let that sink in before continuing.

"Anyway, my mother was a part of the local Seal-People Tribe. That's what we call it, in English. There are other names, to be sure, but it never was a subject of debate. Her father was a shipwright and fisherman. Her mother, also of the Seal-People, chose him, so she said, because he was handsome and honest and worked hard and never told a lie and never said nothing to nobody outside of the family that his wife was, well, what she was. I know there are a lot of fancy stories out there about the Seal People. Well, most of them are just that; stories. Of course, here I am saying 'stories' when my own mother spent most of her life as a seal!"

Jan found herself smiling and caught-up in the tapestry Fin was spinning.

"See, here's the thing," Fin continued. "Like Hunter said, years and years and years ago some of our family left the west coast of Ireland, because there were too many people moving in, and made the grand and dangerous crossing to the New World. Our origins? I'm talking about a time when the people who now call themselves Irish came to that island. As I've been told, our blood-line goes back to that magical race that was there first. Great shape-shifters, they were! Too many stories for now! But anyway they chose to go away. Our mixed-race folk were left. I don't pretend to know how it works, it just does. The skins, you see. I'll get to more of this later, but the skins are magic! They mold to the person who accepts them! And not all who try are accepted, oh no! The skins must *want* the wearer! There was made only a certain amount of them! If one is lost, it's gone forever! Anyway, more on that later..."

Another sip from his cup and Fin pressed on.

"So," he resigned, "To the particulars. The original Tribe was up north as your mother has stated. The native people were more than gracious. Many of their people became as we. Their blood is as equally revered as any of the old stock. But the Tribe had troubles. Several splinter groups moved into vacant areas but always fights broke out. I think it's a fault, it is, and that we can't get along just as the people on land can't. Somebody wants more power, wants more position, wants to dominate the breeding, sorry, that's just the way it is. That's why Tribes were formed along the Maine coast, before it was Maine. Anyway, the groups were consolidated before I was born. A few tried going south, but the fishing could not sustain them and land people grew too numerous."

"Where do we come in?" Jonathon interjected.

"Smart as paint!" Fin remarked. "Here we go."

"You two," he indicated the twins, "Your father was born of my brother and his wife. They chose to remain at sea. Here's where things get a bit complicated. See, there is always a choice. It seems to be there from the beginning. A child is born, on land, and when a skin accepts them, that child must choose, in time, whether to be a part of the Tribe at sea or spend most time on land. Some choose the land for good. I chose a life straddling the two, at first, until I found the life here on shore more rewarding. I also found myself a use to the Tribe, but again I'll get to that later. I found a wonderful woman who made my choice to stay on land easy. She gave me my daughter, who you might have guessed also has chosen to be a sometime part of the Tribe. So, back to your father; I was asked to raise him when he decided to choose the land-dweller path. I did what I could. There was never a smarter, nicer, more respectful soul. He too found a way to help out the Tribe in ways you can't know. But of all the things he did, the greatest was finding your mother."

Fin stopped here and seemed to choke up a bit. Marie pressed her children's hands tighter.

"Anyway," the man continued, "I don't know how long I'll live. I've seen things and done things and so many of my friends are gone. I have to change my name from time to time to not let-on. I'm just glad to finally get to see you two understand your heritage. It makes me happy."

A moment of silence settled on the room.

"Again," Marie broke the trance, "Who were the three today?"

Fin finished his cup. He looked hard at Marie before continuing.

"First off," he said, "The two who wanted to see Jan and Jonathon; I believe it was my brother and his wife. Your grandparents..."

"And then," he continued with a wave of his weathered hand, "That had to be the embarrassment of our current Tribe who wants to be called 'King'."

"Like on Malaga?" Jan asked.

"You are a wicked-quick-witted young lady!" Fin noted. "Yes, like on the island. Only this 'King' has his two goons. Did you guys find the pictures in the attic? I hoped you would. Yes, where else would my family find a place? It was so nice there. Not to be bothered by prying eyes and wagging fingers. For a brief while, anyway. I still believe that someone who will be left unnamed in the State House wanted to use his connection to the Seal People for dirty profit. That so-and-so wanted to cash in on the land grab and also get rid of our kind on the island. I miss it greatly."

Marie took up the story.

"See," she said to her children, "Your father never kept anything from me. He brought me here and imagine my surprise when he told me about his family. His grandfather, Fin's father, was a great chieftain of the Tribe. He led for many, many years with his wife at his side. They say she was a beauty who had come from local native stock."

"So they say," Fin continued, "When she passed, he brought her to an island close by. Me and my brother helped him. He shed his seal skin, gave up hers, and he bound them both, embraced, in rich imported bands of silk. There were rocks wrapped at their feet. We rowed them out past the island now called Sequin. He nodded goodbye, and without a word he hauled himself over the side to be with his love forever in the cold depths."

The silence in the kitchen was broken after a time by the static of the old radio repeating the forecast.

"So," Fin started again. "That left the Tribe without a chieftain. It could have fallen to my brother or me because of our blood ties to The Old Ones. He tried. It wasn't for him. He was and is a very placid, peaceful soul. I had my place here. I had a new bride. And so, an ugly creature enters the picture. Pardon me..."

Fin went to refill his cup with the black stuff. When he returned, he frowned a bit.

"I don't like talking bad about anybody," he stated, "But hang-it, there's just some that has nothing good a body can talk about! This 'King' as he wants to be called, I call him 'Julie' because his mother named him 'Caesar' and he hates it when I say that, has a very, very bad background. His mother was a conniving, skulking, witch of a seal-woman. She took-up with a land man who owned some boats, I won't call him 'captain', who's name still we don't say. He made a fortune in the seal hunting trade."

"You've got to be kidding me!" Jan breathed.

"Now look, Missy," Fin waved a hand, "Don't get me wrong here!

We, that is, the Seal-People, don't pass judgment on hunters. We hunt. We kill. But this monster used his seal-witch wife and others like her to drive thousands to their deaths. All for money! Riches! Big houses near here and 'proper' friends from away! Some of our northern brethren were even driven from their fishing grounds in order to avoid the slaughter. The thing was, just like so many other times with the land people, greed and quick money blinded common logic. Like the beaver, and the whale; you can't exceed what nature can put back. Even farming today! We, the Seal-People, know not to overfish an area. And we grieved for our brothers the murdered seals! But you also have to understand that our relationship with them is, well, strange. They don't seem to know who we are. They accept us. They are not social creatures, despite what you see with them collecting together on rocks to sun. They have a sense for safety in numbers, which led to the carnage they endured. But, trust me, if one seal can beat another to a fish there is no sharing; they look out for themselves! They leave their young so quickly. They only return to a place to breed where the fishing is good. And bullies much like our 'King' dominate harems of females."

Fin paused to sip the cup.

"Every year," Fin said almost wistfully, looking up to the ceiling, "The Tribe has a meeting, a Gathering. It is held at a prescribed time after the birthing season at a time-honored place. At this time, problems or grievances can be brought up. It is from The Old Ways, The Old Laws; it must be done. Here also a chieftain can be elected or deposed, depending on his or her leadership the past year in finding fishing stock, seclusion, and any other matter of peace and harmony."

Jan must have given Fin a quizzical look.

"Oh, yes, Missy!" he continued, "Females can be chieftains too! Check your Irish lore; we don't hold that only a male can lead!"

"Anyway," he pressed onward, "This 'King' has bullied and pressed most of the members of this Tribe for so many years and it seems only a handful will stand up to him. His goons do his dirty work. Like any bully, or rather any unsuccessful leader, he is paranoid and sees everything as a threat to his continued dictatorship."

"What happened to his father and mother?" Jonathon asked.

"Ha!" Fin laughed. "His father died at sea amid the stench of the hides he collected. His crew tossed him over the side to rot with the carcasses of those he had created. His mother, well, let us just says that not all our Tribe was pleased with her activities. She...met with a bad end. Her son has ever after tried to find out who had something to do with it."

"Ok," Jan summed up, "Then what happened with our dad? Wouldn't he be in line here?"

Marie again pressed her daughter's hand.

"Absolutely," she admitted, "But your father wanted nothing to do with the turmoil that had started to grip his Tribe. He had, well, other ideas. He set his mind and energy to helping his Tribe increase both their monetary gains here on land, thereby ensuring a safe place for them away from prying eyes, and in making contact with the old side of the family."

"In Ireland," Jonathon suggested. "That's why he and you, Mom, started the business. You insure mostly companies coming and going from Ireland, don't you?"

Marie nodded and smiled at her smart young man.

"Something else," Fin added. "He restarted the passengers of our kind travelling securely by fishing or trade ships. You have to see, in this modern world, hopping on a plane with a seal skin under your arm won't fly, to coin a phrase. Too many questions and activists rights groups. Might take longer by boat, but everybody used to travel that way and enjoy the ride."

"Fascinating," Jan breathed. "Well, nothing like having your world turned upside-down after dinner!"

"Say," Jonathon asked slowly, "If Dad was involved in all this, in Ireland as you've told us, Mom, then doesn't this have something to do with his disappearance?"

Silence again filled the room.

"We don't know, son." Fin said equally slowly. "*I don't know. I've tried for ten years to find out anything I can. Your poor mother drove herself sick trying to do the same. Truth is, no matter what we suspect, we just don't know nothing.*"

"I think this 'King' thing had something to do with it!" Jan seethed.

"Easy, Missy!" Fin warned. "Thoughts like that, without proof, will mess up your thinking; drive you batty."

"He's right," Marie agreed. "Of course I thought the same thing. But the Tribe has strict rules. Even if one was cruel enough to break them there are consequences."

"Back to here and now," she announced. "Who is it Shere is going to fetch?"

"He's sort of a rogue," Fin smiled oddly. "He's not really a part of the Tribe. He goes his own way. And, he has no respect or fear of 'King' and his thugs."

Jan asked what to her was the obvious, "And he's Shere's...boyfriend?"

Fin let out a short, sharp laugh. "That's between them! But I guess you could say that!"

Marie joined back in. "He's coming here as protection? What's his name, or rather, what does he go by?"

"Dearg," Fin replied, "And I won't call it protection. He's just a friend that I think should be around right now."

"Ok," Marie conceded, "If you think so then its fine with me. Now, I have to ask a few favors here..."

She looked around the table and made sure everyone was attentive, even the shy Celia.

"Now that...things...are out in the open, I'll bet some other things are going to be wondered about and thought about. First, Jan and Jonathon, do you want to stay?"

They both nodded quickly and each started to say something. Their mother's well-known hand raised stopped them short.

"Fine," she continued, "I figured that. I also figure you are going to want to 'explore' your new-found heritage even more. Let's start, tonight, with a room all three of us have been avoiding."

"Dad's room?" Jonathon asked quietly.

"Yep," his mother nodded. "Fin says there's a TV still in there. Jonathon, it will come as no surprise to you that your father loved the old comedies. I remember a VCR player and a small collection of classics. Celia, Hunter; please join us. It will do me, at least, some good to laugh. Ok?"

All four youths nodded in agreement.

"One more thing," she said, holding a pointed forefinger aloft, "I'll need to go back to Boston for a few days. I simply must see to some stuff at the office. I want to check on the house, catch up with the mail, and get a few of my things that I didn't pack. So if Fin agrees?"

"Sure," he said, "Tomorrow both Shere and Dearg will be here."

"There's the get-together at the church day after tomorrow," Jan suggested. "Red can take us!"!"

"I'm Ok with that," Marie stated, "Everybody else?"

Hunter sat up and nodded his approval.

"I...don't think I'll go," Jonathon said slowly. "I think I'll stay here, if that's alright?"

Marie was about to question her son when Jan squeezed her hand, got her attention, and silently indicated Celia. The girl had drooped her strong shoulders when Jan had suggested the outing. Now she actually looked up and smiled at Jonathon.

"I don't want to go either!" she said, relieved. "Can I stay here?"

"Ah, sure," Marie said very slowly, "As long as the adults are going to be here?"

Fin barked a short laugh. Celia and Jonathon both turned boiled-lobster red.

Jan rescued her brother. "I'll bet Celia would love to watch some of those old movies and have a knowledgeable commentator? Hunter and Red and I'll go. Do you have his phone number, Fin?"

"I think I can dig it up," Fin scratched his head.

"Wait," Marie took control again, "Before we all go off on a tangent. One more crucial, important thing here..."

She waited for complete attention again.

"I mean this...I want a promise from all of you here..."

Another pause for dramatic effect...

"Under no circumstances are Miss Jan and Mister Jonathon here to go into the water. That means without...*or with*...seals' skins."

A shock ran through both teens that had been addressed collectively. Jan's mind raced. She had not for an instant considered the impossibility that she might be asked or taught to be like her newly-found legacy might suggest.

"Until I get back!" her mother said sternly.

Jan thought she might faint. Had she heard correctly?

Marie pointed at Hunter but smiled as she did so.

"On your Honor?" she asked, "I'm leaving you in charge of this!"

Hunter smiled a crooked, closed-lipped, proud smile and stood up again. He placed his clenched right fist over his heart. Bowing slowly, he stared into Marie's eyes when he straightened.

"You have my word!" he said seriously.

"Good," Marie smiled wider, "All that's settled. I'll leave tomorrow, after the 'Dearg' character gets here and I can talk with him. Now, let's go watch some movies! You guys go along first and I'll follow in just a bit."

Jan shuffled off behind the others. She had a thought running through her numbed brain, like a scene from the old TV show 'Leave It to Beaver'. Mrs. Cleaver had her pillbox hat on and her white purse was tucked under her arm. 'Now boys!' she scolded, 'I'm going to the PTA meeting and I don't want you two turning into werewolves and terrorizing the neighbors or howling at the moon! Not until your father gets home!'

After the youths were gone, Fin scratched his head again and looked at Marie.

"Didn't you just leave something out, there, Missy?" he smiled knowingly.

"I think they have enough to digest right now, don't you?" she inquired.

"Suit yourself!" he said, crossing his plaid sleeved arms and leaning back.

Marie stood in front of the partially closed bedroom door for a protracted moment. She could hear the sounds of her children and the two others in muffled conversation. This was not going to be easy. She knew that everything behind that door would remind her of the love-of-her-life. Everything would hurt.

But, she told herself, she wouldn't let on.

She knew she had to be strong for her kids. This was going to be hard for them too. They simply did not know their father for very long; they had not had enough time with him. Instead of this being a mausoleum, she decided, this was going to be filled with happy things. Here were things that every child or person chooses to surround themselves with in the place where they go to sleep. That was how she was going to play it.

With a smile and a forced-set jaw she opened the door.

"Mom! Check this out!" Jonathon greeted her excitedly. He was standing with Jan beside him looking at what was lying on a somewhat dusty small desk. Celia was looking curiously over his shoulder and Hunter was surveying pictures on the walls.

Marie grinned as she recognized the old cigar box filled with numerous and varied old coins.

"There's got to be a small fortune in here!" Jonathon marveled as he ran his fingers through the gold and silver pieces.

"Do you know what any of them are?" she asked.

"Uh, this one looks like Spanish writing," he mused.

"Close," she corrected, "Portuguese, actually. But this one is..."

She picked up a larger one and handed it to her son. As he was turning it over in wonder she dug and found a similar one.

"Pieces of Eight'", she announced, "Like in the pirate stories. It was the Spanish dollar called *real de a ocho* because it was worth eight *reales*. The English coined the phrase 'pieces of eight' because it was also known as the *peso de ocho*."

"Nice pun, Mom!" Jan laughed.

"It was at that!" Marie agreed. "And there's English silver, Dutch gold, French as well..."

"Hey!" Jonathon observed, "So how do you know so much about old loot, Mom?"

"You forget, me hearty," Marie said in a fake pirate voice, "My mother's side of the family was sponge-divers in Florida? All the summers I spent with them I learned a thing or two about treasure, Arrrr!"

Jan and her brother chuckled together. What a day for discoveries, or rediscoveries.

"So then how did Dad come by all these?" Jonathon pressed.

"Want to share an answer?" Marie asked to Hunter. He was still intent on studying the pictures on the walls.

"I know," Celia said softly, "He found them. We all find them sometimes, but not so many now as I have heard stories from long ago."

"Found them where?" Jonathon asked with visions of treasure chests buried on lonely beaches in his head.

"In the wrecks," Hunter said without looking away from the pictures. "In the shipwrecks on the bottom; where land people can't go."

"Right...!" Jonathon whispered. "So, how much is still out there?"

"Who knows," Marie shrugged. "Most of the hulks have been found, either by land people, as you put it Hunter, or by...Sea People."

"You mean *Seal People*," Jan corrected.

"Sure," Marie added rather quickly, "Even in the south waters where my family dove most treasures have been lifted. But there are some still that have yet to be found..."

"Cool," Jonathon muttered.

"The Tribes made a lot of money," Hunter said distractedly, "Trading that metal stuff to land people who probably cheated them on the worth. That is until we found out what it was worth. Then those land people got...punished."

He turned his gaze away from the pictures and smiled a not-so-nice grin.

"Wow," Jan changed the subject, "Look at this other stuff!"

The desk had all sorts of memorabilia strewn about. There were report cards from the local high school, seashells, a small partially encrusted ship's bell, a tattered baseball and glove, and an old, cloudy jar of hundreds of different kinds of buttons from clothing.

"I know what that is!" Jan almost whispered. "You can still find them today, I read, on Malaga, in the shallows where the women did the washing!"

Marie nodded. "What sort of pictures have you found, Hunter?"

The rest of the group started around the walls. The pictures began with a young brown-haired boy trying to pull nets into Fin's boat. The smile, the eyes; unmistakably those that Marie remembered and the twins dreamed about.

"Dad," Jan almost sobbed.

A lump started in Marie's throat. She bit her lip hard to stop it.

"Wow," Jonathon mouthed. "He looks like me. I mean, I look like him!"

Marie kissed the back of her son's head. "Yes, yes you do," she whispered.

The other pictures painted a time line of Manny's life. There was a Little League team photo. More great hauls of fish with a Fin who looked as he did now. Only, a dark haired, lithe beauty was is several of the pictures.

"That's Shere!" Jan noted, "Except she has her hair done and she's not wearing men's clothes! She's a knock-out!"

"Jan," Marie said seriously, "Don't make a big deal out of this! It's a touchy subject around here! Promise me?"

"Sure, Mom," Jan promised without understanding.

"So where's Fin's wife?" Jonathon wondered out loud. "I don't remember even hearing her name?"

"More sad stories," his mother sighed. "Your father told me that she died in the late 50's during a terrible winter's influenza outbreak. He also said she looked just like Shere, which partially explains why she dresses now the way she does, but that's not all to the story, and it's not my place to say or yours to pry, Ok?"

The twins nodded respectfully.

The pictures stopped with a handsome and proud young man showing a battered leather suitcase with a Boston College sticker prominently displayed. He was off to another world.

"Shall we see to a movie?" Marie suggested. She had had enough of Memory Lane and needed to hear her children laugh.

"You won't believe this!" Jonathon spouted, "Dad had some movies here that they haven't transferred to DVD yet!"

"Has," his mother corrected. She refused to speak of Manny in the past tense.

"Has," Jonathon agreed, "So what'll it be? Marx Brothers, Charlie Chaplin, W. C., Abbott and Costello..."

"Well," Marie suggested, "Have you told your cousins that you are related through my father to the Costello family?"

"His real last name was *Christillo*, Mom, but that's all right!" Jonathon remembered. "I'll find one!"

With the lights dimmed and the flicker of the small-by-modern-standards television, Marie breathed a deep, pleasant release of the tensions that had plagued her since arriving in Maine. She was propped up reclining on some pillows on the small double bed with her soon-to be-too-old-for-this daughter snuggled by her side. She could not decide if it was her straining imagination or did she actually *smell* Manny's scent?

Hunter was sitting next to the bed reversed in the desk chair. His strong arms draped over the back of the chair and he laughed with his hand sometimes covering his mouth, in the way he and his sister always did. He found the ridiculous slapstick hilarious.

Jonathon sat on the floor at the foot of bed and closest to the TV. He guffawed out loud as well and Marie had to admonish him countless times for saying things like 'Watch this!'

Seated next to him was a silent Celia. Marie had noticed that the straight-backed young girl was amazed and fascinated at the black and white figures on the screen. Any dancing or singing number, which drew disinterest from the boys and even Jan, had Celia entranced. Marie could see what an impressionable, tender soul resided in that strong feminine body.

When the movie was over, Jonathon turned on the dim overhead light to hit the rewind button and find another selection. He actually wiped tears of laughter out of his eyes. He began to repeat some of the jokes in the film and then stopped cold and looked at Celia.

"What's the matter?" he asked genuinely.

Marie noted with her mother's eye that Celia's eyes were brimming with different tears as she looked at Jonathon.

"It's beautiful," she started, "But why do you laugh when the mean man hits the little fat one? He didn't do anything wrong! He wants to be nice to people but he gets hit all the time!"

Jonathon faltered for a moment.

"Celia?" Marie offered, "Come here, sweetheart!"

Celia got up and sheepishly lay down next to Marie. Jan shifted over to make room.

"Honey," Marie soothed, stroking the girls long brown hair, "It's make-believe! The little man didn't get hurt! People laugh at stuff like this! Like a clown!"

"They don't have to hit him!" Celia said sullenly. "It's not funny!"

"Oh, Lady!" Marie cooed, kissing the top of Celia's tense head. The girl relaxed a bit at the touch.

"I guess The Three Stooges are out?" Jonathon tried in his Woody Allen voice.

The stern look from his mother changed his tune.

"Hey, I got an idea. Marx Brothers...song, dance, silliness...absolute pandemonium. Please?"

He extended a hand to Celia and she accepted. As she held his hand and returned to her seat she looked intently at the young man.

"You don't think its right?" she demurely demanded. "You wouldn't hit the little man?"

"No way," Jonathon smiled back, "I'd pop that Abbott guy smack in the kisser!"

Celia still looked confused.

"I wouldn't let him do it," Jonathon explained.

Celia tried to smile broadly but put her hand up to her mouth in the way now expected. Her eyes, however, made Jonathon blush and Marie smile a worried, if proud, smile.

The night ended after a riotous romp on board an ocean liner and into the world of opera with Groucho, Chico, Harpo and Zeppo. Everybody laughed out loud. Jonathon explained a few finer points of humor to a very attentive Celia. She found the comedy amusing and the song and dance fantastic.

As Jonathon explained things to Celia during the course of the film their heads got closer and closer together until Jan had to nudge her mother and ask a question.

"Just how close a cousin is she?"

Marie pushed her daughter in silent jest.

"Guess I might have to find out," she said.

6

With the early morning light just streaming into the room, Jan awoke to the quick knock on her door followed almost immediately by her brother's head appearing in the opened crack.

"He's here!" Jonathon loudly whispered like a child announcing Santa on Christmas morning.

"Who?" Jan asked blearily.

"The guy!" her brother answered back. "You know, Dig, or whatever his name is!"

"It's Dearg," Jan yawned. "Irish for 'red' or 'reddish'..."

"Come on! Downstairs!" Jonathon urged and slammed the door.

Surprisingly, Jan discovered, she was not the last one downstairs. Her mother was seated across from the new comer, Hunter was next to her, and Jonathon sat next to Fin who was sitting by the figure of the moment. Celia and Shere were nowhere in sight.

At a glance, Jan was mildly frightened that the creature of so much interest this morning might possibly be the most darkly handsome 'man' she had ever seen.

He glanced up from listening to Marie and nodded as Jan came down the stairs. She felt as though she flushed immediately and hoped her feet didn't trip her on the way down. He smiled slightly and she almost put her hand to her hair to check if it was brushed properly. Now she regretted hurrying in the bathroom and that bothered her even more.

Somehow she made it down the stairs and sat down next to Hunter. From somewhere far away she thought she heard her mother introducing her. This time, when the slim angular face with a slight black stubble of beard looked at her, he smiled wider and she was shocked to see behind his thin lips very white but very sharp-looking teeth.

Even this did not deter her from studying him, as he went back to listening to her mother, since she could not stop looking at him anyway.

His hair was jet black, long, and somewhat curly. It framed his long face and shook carelessly down his strong but not so wide shoulders. The eyes were so black that Jan thought she saw a glint of red, instead of blue, in them. He was wearing a grey, tight tee shirt under a black leather jacket. Like Hunter, his build was lithe and very muscular. Long fingers of strong hands were clasped in front of him on the table.

The face and eyes were looking at her again. She heard her name. It was her mother calling.

In a rush she forced herself back to the reality of the moment.

"Glad to know you," Dearg was saying, his sharp teeth bared in not an evil but still a disarmingly, if hauntingly pleasant, way.

Jan nodded, which was the best she could muster.

Fin was speaking now and Jonathon hung on every word and stared mesmerized at the subject of conversation.

"Did you meet any…welcoming parties this time?"

Dearg looked at the white haired man and grinned a now menacing sneer.

"They leave me alone," he said in the thick Irish brogue. "Those two lackeys have scars from times they got into my business."

Hunter barked a sort of short liking at this news.

"As for the silly 'King-ie'," Dearg continued, "If he were to meet me without his lap dogs I'd bring you his skin for the vault and let the hagfish pick his bones."

He looked quickly to Marie.

"Sorry, Lady, I just get carried away."

"Understood," Marie nodded.

Jonathon picked up on a thread. "What vault?"

"We'll talk about that later," Fin said without looking at the youth. "Marie, I told you that Dearg was not part of our Tribe. He moves, respectfully when warranted, from place to place. He and I have a sort of...business relationship."

Dearg sat back in his chair and the warm smile returned to his hard features. He regarded Marie again.

"I'm from The Old Country," he offered. "I only came to this coast just before Manny was born. I guess I had a few too many unfriendly dealings. Anyway, I looked-up old Fin here, as a friend of my family, and together we've managed a tidy income in the salvage trade."

"I knew it!" Jonathon blurted then looked embarrassed.

Dearg just put his head back and laughed loudly.

"Just like your father!" he said to the youth. "Manny was a part of our little enterprise, too! And after college he..."

His sentence trailed off and he regarded Marie again.

"Later?" he tried.

Marie nodded again, stifling for the moment her children's peaked interest in more of the story.

Jonathon pressed ahead anyway.

"Salvage?" he asked, trying not to sound too excited. "Like, sunken ships and gold and all?"

Now Fin chuckled sharply. "Not so much the stuff of movies and books! Although, once in a while, well, but see times have changed. The real treasure nowadays is not in old locked chests. It's the wrecks themselves."

"Let me guess," Marie mused, "You find a wreck and you alert the insurance company that had an interest. If the ship was really old, the policies were paid out long ago and anything you salvage is yours; as long as it can't be claimed by a government."

"Ah-yuh," Fin agreed, "But mostly the cargoes have been lost, in one way or another, but that's a different tale. What pays now is the antiques; the fittings and bells and wheels and instruments. If ya can prove which ship it is, mores' the better!"

"How do you find them?" Jonathon asked.

"Well," Fin smiled, "That's my secret, but in all my days I've made some friends in some of the museums hereabouts. Old log books and proposed sailing charts can tell a tale, if you know how to read them."

"You could say," Dearg added, "That I'm a perfect scout. All of the Seal People are. We don't need diving gear; that comes later after we know what we've found."

"Nice!" Jonathon smiled. "Was Dad a scout too?"

Dearg looked at Marie before continuing.

"Sometimes," he said, "But mostly he did the detective work with Fin. That's more important. Finding where a ship may have gone down beats combing a very big ocean bottom."

Jonathon sat up in his chair with the proud realization of where some of his interests came from.

Marie spoke up.

"I'll bet I can name the companies you two use to do the heavy stuff," she said knowingly. "Want to bet?"

Fin and Dearg looked at each other like school kids caught cheating.

"Never mind," Marie sighed. "At least now I'll know when I sign the policies exactly who is behind the operation!"

The two men smiled sheepishly.

"Anyway," Dearg changed the subject, "Hunter, where is that sister of yours?"

"Upstairs," he answered nonchalantly. "I don't know why she acts so shy, especially around males of our people."

"She's uncomfortable," Jonathon started then stopped the train of thought.

"Never mind," Dearg said shooting Jonathon a sly look. "She'll find out I don't bite. Well, not friends, anyway!"

Hunter and Fin smiled at the jest, but it was a bit disturbing for the MacLeers.

"So," Jan ventured bravely, "So where's Shere?"

There was a tense silence all of a sudden.

"She's shy too," Fin stated.

Dearg changed the subject again.

"Marie, Fin says you have to get back to Boston for a few days."

"Yes," she replied, "I want to leave today but I'll be back by Monday. Jan and Hunter are going to a church social day tomorrow. I need to know, Dearg, if you are willing to look after my children."

"Of course," the dark man assured. "And when you get back, well, let's just say I would think it an honor to help…train…a few young pups? I'm very good at it. And you wouldn't have to worry about the local bullies."

Jonathon and Jan were on the edge of their seats.

"We'll see about that," Marie said solemnly. "We'll see about that. In the mean time, Fin, I'll bet you'll find some things for two teenagers to do around here?"

"I might," Fin scratched his head, "I just might at that."

Upstairs again, Jan and Jonathon helped their mother get her things together. They protested as usual at the constant barrage of repeated instructions and do's and don'ts. In the end, Marie just looked at her twins in a way that made them both feel very grownup.

As they walked to the SUV, all Marie had to say in parting was short and heartfelt.

"I'll be back Monday afternoon," she promised. "You two have had a rollercoaster of emotions lately. I didn't know if I was doing the right thing by letting you in on all this. I trust I'm right. But responsibility comes with discovery. I know you'll honor my wishes. That doesn't mean you can't have a good time. Within reason?"

They both nodded in promise then embraced their mother and she was off.

Jan and Jonathon looked at each other after the vehicle was out of sight.

"What next?" Jan voiced their collective question.

"I've got to check on Celia, and don't you make fun of me," Jonathon warned.

"Gotcha," his sister agreed, "And I'm going to play your role of sleuth and see if I can break some ice with Shere."

"It's a plan," he said seriously.

The soft knock on the door caught the inhabitant of the room off guard. From the outside of the door, Jonathon's voice broke the silence again.

"Hey," he said quietly. "It's me."

Celia stood up from her seat on the bed where she had been looking out the small window at the trees with the bay hidden beyond. She could never have guessed how gracefully and lithely she moved. Crossing to the door, she put her cheek against the old wood and closed her eyes.

"Are you alone?" she breathed.

"Of course," Jonathon answered back. He somehow guessed where her voice was coming from and put his own face to the door. He had to stand on tiptoes to match.

After a long moment, Celia whispered again.

"What do you want?"

She was dreaming that his cheek was close to hers with just the panel separating them.

"I want to see you," he answered back strongly.

She smiled. That was exactly what she wanted to hear, word for word.

Opening the door, she looked straight into Jonathon's eyes. His knees went weak but not as weak as before. He was getting used to this.

"Come with me?" he asked, reaching for her hand and lightly taking it. "Let's go exploring. Ok?"

He meant the widow's walk with its supposed great view, but his mind thought of another meaning.

"Ok," she said, without smiling and never unlocking their eyes.

He led her up the old stairs and showed her the pictures he had discovered. She showed a slight interest but not as much as she seemed to want to hold hands, stand very close to him, and look into his eyes.

Breaking the tension, he found two dusty wooden folding chairs and with these in one hand he let her take his other and they walked to the even smaller staircase against one bare beamed wall. He went first and was grateful that the latch worked and the creaky door opened upward. Celia kept her hand on the small of his back and followed.

The morning sunlight was subdued by the canopy of trees hanging over the roof. These would not have been there in the original days of the walk, he guessed. Twigs and old leaves and even bird droppings littered the once fine cross-planked path that spanned the length of the roof. An ornate waist high railing and wall was now faded by years of sun and snow but spoke of an earlier gilded elegant time. They came to the center and out from under the trees.

The view was spectacular.

Celia was finally transfixed on something besides Jonathon and she gazed out at the vista of bay and rocks and the many colors of the picturesque quintessentially Maine village across the river.

Jonathon set the two chairs up and guided her to sit down. She did so, only after scooting her chair as close to Jonathon's as could possibly be.

Many moments passed as the two sat and clasped both hands, rather awkwardly, looking first at each other and then at the scenery.

In a move he would have never even a week ago have dreamed himself possible of; Jonathon suddenly let his left hand slip from Celia's and placed his entire arm around her shoulder. Their right hands remained together.

Celia seemed almost as surprised as he, but within seconds she smiled and nestled her head into his neck.

After what Jonathon thought was a blissful eternity Celia began to speak very softly and in a way that he surely believed was that of a Siren in legend.

"I have never felt so close to anybody except my mother before," she cooed. "I like this better. I am not afraid. Well, maybe a little, but in a way I don't know how to say. It's good. How do you feel?"

Jonathon wanted to sum it up by giving a cowboy 'Whoop-eeee!' but thought better of it.

"I've never felt like this," he admitted. "I'm always so nervous around other girls. I don't even like them but I'm nervous. Why am I not nervous with you?"

"The same reason I feel so safe with you," she whispered into his ear, sending him into a frenzy. "The others, the land boys and the Seal People ones...they look at me but don't see me. They see...things...that are not nice. They act like the males in the seal colonies. My mother told me. They want something and then they go away. You see me, I think."

"I want to," Jonathon confided. "I want to get to know all about you. I want to show you who I am. I want you to know my world. And I want to know yours."

Celia snuggled closer. Jonathon continued.

"I'm just figuring out who I am," he said. "I thought I was this person, now I find out I'm not. It explains things but it makes more questions! You know who you are."

Celia shook her head slightly.

"It's not nice," she almost sobbed. "It's hard and mean. My brother is like my father and so many others. They have rules and seem so proud. But they know only 'fight' and 'take'. I think my mother wanted me to see your Tribe. Your grandfather and grandmother, Fin and his wife, your father and mother....they stay together. They..."

"Love each other," Jonathon said, not believing he said it.

Celia was very quiet for a time.

"It's beautiful up here," she finally said. "I have never been so high. To see the water, I am drawn to it. But I don't think sometimes it is my home."

"Why did you bring me here?" she asked suddenly, moving her head to stare into his eyes again.

"Because," he said with his face very close to hers and their eyes still locked, "I thought one beauty deserved another."

Celia looked a bit confused for a moment. His words didn't seem to get through.

Without thinking about it, Jonathon moved towards her to kiss her.

Celia's eyes softened into something he could not describe. But just as suddenly, she turned her head away and put a hand to her mouth.

"I'm sorry," Jonathon started. "I just..."

"You don't know things about me," she said, her head still turned away. "You won't like me..."

"Wait a minute," Jonathon realized. "Hey, I saw Dearg earlier. His teeth...hey!"

He gently touched her chin and moved her face back close to his.

"Are you worried because you have...teeth like his?"

"They can change!" she said, her eyes filling with tears. "Those of us that spend most of the time in the sea, they are like this! But if we stay on the land a long time, they start to look like...you!"

He could not help himself. With his mouth moved to her ear, he whispered "You just don't know, do you? You just don't know how beautiful you are and that makes you even more beautiful!"

He brought her surprised eyes back to lock with his.

"Everything about you, to me anyway, is perfect. I can't wait to get to know every little thing about you, and whoever told you that something like teeth different than others would make you unattractive just doesn't know anything about anything!"

She gazed into his eyes in a very happy but hesitant way.

"I'm not going to ask you to do something you don't want to," he said. "When you want to, smile for me. I promise it will be, in my eyes, the most beautiful smile in the world!"

Lost in her deep eyes, Jonathon's distant memory center of his busy brain decided this was a moment to sear forever into whatever creases of his grey matter retained cherished moments for life.

Then, everything in his head and body got suddenly short-circuited or overloaded.

Celia kissed him ever so lightly but meaningfully on his lips.

She returned to nestling her head into his neck and snuggled tighter into his one-armed embrace.

Shock and electricity seemed a pitiful way to describe what coursed through Jonathon's very core, but he decided for the moment the terms would do.

He wondered how she could not feel the tense war that raged inside his frame. Newfound male hormones tried to shiver and shake his frame. Uncanny strength of reserve restrained the awkward show.

Detached, a part of him hovered over the scene and calmed him in the indescribable peace of Celia snuggling him so near and looking out at the thing that so far defined her.

He simply let go and inhaled the moment.

Jan had found Fin and Dearg talking out on the dock. She waved and walked out to them.

"Your mother left?" Dearg asked. His height of well over 6 feet and then some was now apparent and the thin, muscular build in the black jeans leaned casually on one of the dock piles.

Jan nodded. "What did you have in mind, Fin, for us to help you with?"

Fin smiled and pushed his plaid hat back on his head.

"Well, now, let's see...it's like this, Missy. I know your mom wants you to stay busy, but I still think you are my guest and on vacation. So what I need is for you and your brother to tell me how you can keep from being bored in an old man's house!"

Jan smiled back at her benefactor.

"Are you any good at sewing?" Dearg asked with a smile of his own.

"You know," Jan said, lifting a finger, "That in today's world a man asking a woman that is considered chauvinistic and in bad taste?"

Dearg laughed out loud.

"Right-so," he admitted, "So I'm archaic and an eedgit. I didn't mean anything by it, just had an idea, is all." Jan could discern the Irish accent even more in this exchange.

He looked sideways at Fin for some kind of approval.

"Oh well," the older man sighed. "Your mother's not gone 15 minutes and here we are setting you into untested waters."

Jan must have looked puzzled. Dearg spoke again.

"If you wish, go inside into the kitchen. Look for the small door in the far left corner. Knock like this…"

He rapped on the metal covering the top of the piling.

"Slowly… one, two….wait a bit…then faster… three, four, and five."

"What am I going to find there?" Jan asked.

"What's the fun in no surprises?" Dearg queried as he leaned towards Jan and winked an eye. The red sparkle twinkled in the black pool.

Jan slowly turned and strode robotically back towards the house and whatever new secret awaited there.

Passing through the 'mud room' and into the kitchen, the old marine radio crackled a static-laced report of fair weather for the rest of the day. She found the door where Dearg said it would be. She raised her hand to give the knock Dearg had suggested but stalled as a sound came from behind the door.

It took a few moments, with her hand raised there, for her to imagine what was causing the whirring noise inside. It rhythmically purred in staccato fashion for a few seconds then stopped. It would start again in a few moments.

Jan decided it had to be a sewing machine or something similar.

She threw caution to the wind and gave the 'secret' signal.

The sound ceased. There was a rustling noise and then the sound of a latch or lock being turned. Then the old worn brass doorknob turned and the door creaked open slightly.

As much as Jan was surprised to see the eyes and face of Shere peering at her so were those eyes widened in confused recognition.

Without knowing what else to say, Jan simply said "Hi…"

There was silence from the face with the somewhat unkempt dark hair. The eyes continued to register a mixture of fear and concern.

"Ah," Jan tried, "Dearg and Fin asked me to give you a hand."

Nothing seemed to get through.

"I'd like to help," Jan offered. "Can I come in?"

Slowly Shere opened the door wider and lowered her dark eyes.

"I don't need help," she said neither meanly nor cheerfully.

"I don't imagine you do," Jan tried to sooth. "It's just, I mean, they said I could do something."

She had a thought and pressed ahead.

"I thought I might learn something. You know, to be helpful? I'll bet you are a good teacher."

She wasn't sure, but Jan might have caught a glimmer of something softening in Shere's demeanor.

The woman stepped away from the doorway and with her back to Jan she descended a short stone stairway without a railing. Jan supposed it was the best invitation she would get.

The room below smelled musty and was obviously the beginning of the basement. As Jan passed carefully down the steps she saw the only lights were a series of hanging naked light bulbs that glowed yellowish and only partially pushed back the inky darkness.

Following Shere, the teenager caught sight of shadows of basement things; old garden tools, an ancient wooden snow sled, and cast-away nautical stuff hanging on rough hewn beams. The same smell that had permeated the attic was as pungent here and ever so much more intense. It was a fishy, oily, and somehow leathery aroma.

Shere moved past some long shapes that hung down on pegs on either side of the close corridor. Jan realized with a shock that the dark garments were the hooded clothing that she had observed in recent occasions. There were many of them. She guessed as many as twenty or more. The old fear she had of a coven of witches or a bunch of druids or devil worshipers came flooding back. Then she reminded herself that it was only shape-shifting Selchies after all.

The dark haired woman had stopped and seated herself on what must have been a low stool. She bent to handle something that covered a heavy and homemade table.

Jan, convinced she would not be invited to do so, found another stool close to Shere and sat down as well.

The contents of the table were panels of the black material that obviously made up the strange garments. Jan forced herself to touch the stuff and found it was indeed oily and leathery but slick and not rough.

To Shere's left was a brighter lamp with a broad green glass shade like Jan had seen in antique stores and might have come from old-timey banks. Under it was an equally ancient industrial-looking sewing machine.

"You really want to learn?"

Jan jumped at the sudden, if softly, voiced question from her 'cousin'.

"Yes," Jan answered, hoping she was not telling a lie. "Did you make all these?"

Shere cocked her head in a funny way, like a raven Jan thought, and looked at the girl for the first time since opening the door.

"Not most of them," she said wistfully. "But I made some and I repair all of them."

She suddenly reached and took one of the robes down from a peg. Turning it so the inside could be seen she indicated sheepishly for Jan to feel the thick, rich, black satin-feeling lining.

"Wow," Jan breathed. "It's like a soft pillow."

"I did that," Shere said, and smiled a very quick and proud smile.

"Amazing," Jan said genuinely. She imagined that without the lining the wearer would be rather uncomfortable and the odd word 'chafed' came to mind.

"They tell me you know," Shere asked and turned her head away again.

"Oh!" Jan understood. "Yeah, I know. I just found out about my Dad. Mom didn't tell us until now. Guess she had her reasons.

Anyway, I didn't know when I first got here and I'm very sorry if I was rude to you in trying to figure things out."

Shere waved a slender hand. She looked up into the blackness of the basement ceiling before continuing.

"I was maybe six years old when I found out everybody wasn't like my family."

Jan suddenly felt a completely new set of emotions towards the woman.

"I was happy," she started again. "My parents gave me such happiness and warmth. One day some other children came with their father to get the fish. While Fin was getting the fish I tried to play and be nice to the children. They said I wasn't like them. You guess the rest."

Jan stayed quiet.

"Anyway," Shere broke the moment, "My mother took care of the robes. She taught me to repair and even make new ones. Most of them are very, very old. Do you know what they are for?"

"I can guess," Jan tried. "I saw you with Celia and Hunter and you all had them on. Then I'm thinking I saw you after you had met Dearg somewhere, right? You wear them when you change back to land people because..."

The connection suddenly fell into place for her.

"Because," she mused slyly, "When you change you don't have any clothes on! I can see how the material keeps you dry but the linings keep you warm and comfy!"

Shere actually smiled again.

"But not everyone likes it," she said sternly. "Some think it's sissy. But not many..."

She shot another almost playful look to Jan.

Now Jan offered up a question.

"Why so many, Shere?"

"Did Fin tell you about the Gathering each year?"

"Oh, yeah!" Jan remembered.

"I have enough for the whole Tribe. I like helping."

"So," Jan looked down at the panels on the table, "What are we doing here?"

Shere turned her attention very seriously to the heavy material.

"I have to rebuild this one. Some of the skin has gotten too old..."

"Skin?!" Jan jumped.

"Oh, not what you think," Shere assured, "We gather seals' skins when one of them dies. We don't kill them. We just honor them. Some of these robes are made from seals I remember fondly."

"Ok," Jan admitted, "I'm just gonna say that *that* is creepy. No offense, right?"

"Guess it could be," Shere almost but not quite chuckled. "So you want to help?"

"Sure," Jan told herself as much as Shere, "But I'll never look at a seal the same way again!"

"Would you hold the panel for me?" Shere asked. "The machine is old but strong and it can really hurt you if the skin gets bunched. The cord is waxed and stiff. But I know what I'm doing."

"Let's go!" Jan sighed.

Shere used her foot to start a large treadle and the sewing apparatus whirred to life. With a gentle, guiding hand she taught Jan to feed the material to her. It seemed to be a great help and soon the two were communicating silently as the panels moved this way and that, up and back and slowly became one of the long black robes.

Straightening from the machine, Shere used a short, sharp knife to cut the cord. She stood up stiffly and rubbed the back of her neck. Then she hung the robe on a peg.

With her back turned, she addressed Jan.

"Maybe, if you want to, in the next day or so we'll do the lining. I'm tired now."

Just as Jan was standing to brush back her hair and stretch as well, Shere suddenly turned and put her right hand lightly on Jan's shoulder.

"I haven't had help since...since my mother..."

"Thanks for letting me be here," Jan finished.

Shere nodded and pushed her own wild hair back away from her eyes. Even in the dim light, Jan again caught a glimpse of a very pretty if well hidden face. Not the kind of manufactured pretty found in fashion magazines, Jan decided; more the strong classic features that Renaissance sculptors strived to capture for all time.

Shere looked towards the door from whence they had come.

"I need to go," she said as if to no one but herself. "He'll be wanting lunch and..."

She stopped and realized Jan was listening and starting to smile.

"Don't tell me he can't make his own lunch?" Jan chided playfully.

Shere almost laughed but caught herself.

"Big strong hunter," she joked back. Her eyes were half closed and could have twinkled.

"A woman's work is never done!" Jan found herself saying, but her own mirth was apparently lost. "Let's go, Cousin."

As Jan and Shere exited the basement, Jonathon and Celia were coming down the stairs. Their somewhat embarrassed look was gratefully passed over. Together the group went out to join the two men still talking on the dock.

"Look at this crowd!" Fin jested. "Don't know if the dock will support the weight!"

Jan looked inquisitively to see the interaction between Dearg and Shere. Almost as shy and unsure as Jonathon and Celia, Shere just sort of stood there looking down until Dearg sauntered over and wrapped a strong arm around her. She smiled nervously at the show of affection.

"Been talking," Fin started. "Got something you young ones might want to help with."

"Anything!" Jan offered.

"Well," Fin continued, pushing his hat back in his way, "Hunter has already been at it. If you follow down that path, just there, that leads away from the dock and towards the other point on the bay that's hidden by the trees; you'll find an old boat house. It was never really meant for a boat. It's hidden, as I said, from all prying eyes. It's got a place for private, well, changing, so to speak. A body can change clothes, you know what I mean, and then easily slip into the water. Nobody can see. I suppose it could be boys at one time and girls the next. We don't hold much problem in that sort of thing but I know some folks, especially new comers, might."

Jan and Jonathon exchanged glances.

"Anyway," Fin started again, "It hasn't been used in some time. Young Hunter is down there sweeping out spiders' webs and dust. He could use a hand."

Ok," Jonathon agreed. 'We'll go, right Celia?"

The girl nodded cheerfully.

Jan noted that not but just a week before if asked a similar question her brother would have answered after consulting his sister and then returning an answer including her.

"Fine," Fin smiled. "Tools are down there. Just be mindful. Lunch in..."

"Forty-five minutes," Shere offered, "That good?"

"I might have starved by then," Dearg pretended, rubbing his flat stomach.

Shere swatted a playful hand at his cheek and they went off together towards the house.

Jan and Jonathon and Celia started down the small path towards the water. The trees overhead made a perfect canopy. The midday sun only barely mottled the way with splotchy color. The boat house came into view and was a plain looking planked shack affair that was indeed hidden from view from the water.

Opening the weathered door, Hunter could be seen stabbing purposely into the low rafters at old webs and egg cases with an old broom. He was attacking the job as Jan supposed he attacked about everything he did.

"Hang on," Jan ordered. She took the broom from an astonished Hunter and started sweeping the rafters instead of jabbing. The effect proved much more productive and she gave the broom back to Hunter who mimicked her lead. Then she found another worn broom and began to sweep the dusty floor.

"We'll check to see if anything's broken," Jonathon announced. Jan just gave him a 'whatever' look and continued on her task.

This gave Jonathon, with Celia very close in tow, a chance to check out the place further. There were grimy windows facing the water and on the two sides adjacent. On the water side, the trees created a tunnel sort of passage out into the bay. The other sides were so clouded that nothing except the shadows of supposed thick branches were visible.

In the center of the shack was an apparatus that needed further study.

There was a raised box-like area of about six feet square where a thick, smooth-sanded wide plank sat half off and half on like a sort of diving board. The end of the plank on the box rested in the dead center and seemed to have a latch device attached.

Jonathon approached and did his best to figure out the function. He turned the latch, and with a slight creak the plank started to teeter down and then came to a stop just a foot or so into the space below.

"Check this out!" he called to everyone. Jan and Hunter stopped their broom-ing and came to see. Celia only needed to look over Jonathon's shoulder.

The now up-swung part of the plank acted as a counter weight and the lower end just touched the water below. It became apparent that a body could open the latch, let the plank sink down, and scoot into the chilly bay waters.

"This is nice," Celia spoke up. "After you put your skin on or come out of the water with it on, it's hard sometimes to roll off of or climb up onto a dock. And the rocks don't hurt with your seal skin on, but they cut land-skin."

"This brings up a whole lot of questions," Jan summed up. "Mind answering a few?"

Hunter and Celia didn't say no, so Jan sat down on the edge of the box thing and motioned for the others to do the same.

Celia waited for Jonathon to sit and then managed to get as close to him as she could.

"First of all," Jan began, and wondered if she could get through the question without her logical side stopping her, "What does it feel like when you put your skins on?"

Celia looked at her brother and neither seemed to know what to say. Finally, Hunter offered an attempt.

"I remember when I was very little. Not the first time. But I remember being on land for a long time once. I don't know why so long. When it was time to go back, it felt...strange. You start with the skin around your feet. Then you pull it up. It...it becomes you. It grabs you. I don't know how to say. It takes over. You pull it up but it helps you. It wants to be you."

Celia looked very serious and added her own thoughts.

"When you put it over your head, you have to be ready. You can't be standing up. Well, some of the males do but I think just for show."

She shot a nervous glance at her brother but continued.

"After you pull it over your head, you can't stand anymore. You are like a seal. Land is not easy. The sea is where you are free."

Jan and her brother took all this in with quiet awe. Neither had heard Hunter say so many words in a row. It was just faintly apparent that he had an accent. Much more distinct than Celia had. Jan couldn't quite place it; possibly a Scottish or Newfoundland lilt?

"Ah," Jonathon posed, "What sort of seal do you become? I mean, I've seen a lot of species on TV and in books and the internet. I've always loved studying those types of things. I don't know how many times I've been to the Boston Aquarium and seen seals..."

He stopped short there.

"Hey, I didn't mean anything about the seals in the Aquarium. I mean, I don't agree with it or anything..."

Hunter shrugged. "I have heard about such places. It doesn't bother me. It sounds like the land people give a seal a good life with a lot of easy fish. Maybe they don't like the place, I don't know. I think the males would not like not having mates..."

"I think they think of that," Jonathon tried to recover.

Hunter just shrugged again.

"I don't want to be in a cage," Celia stated. "But we are not seals. They don't think like us."

"So back to the question," Jonathon reminded. "What sort of seal do you look like?"

"I hope," Celia said aloud but meant for only Jonathon, "That you will see for yourself!"

Jan diffused the moment with one of her trusty devices. She had pulled up pictures of several species of Pinnipeds. She motioned for Hunter and Celia to look at the images and placed the I-phone where they could see.

Immediately, both Hunter and his sister giggled at the first photo.

"That's a Harbor seal," Jan noted. Hunter spoke up in obvious mirth.

"That's the funny ones! They are small and not so smart. They don't talk to us much. They just look and stare. They don't understand but they are still funny!"

Jan was a bit taken aback but switched pictures.

"The Gray or Common seal," she pronounced.

"Ah!" Hunter nodded, and Celia followed suit.

"That's mostly who we know," he said. "They are smarter and let us sun with them. They sport with us, too. They can be fun, but mostly they just want to find food and mate and stay away from the Seal Killer Fish."

"Seal Killer Fish?" Jonathon perked up. "Are you talking about...a shark?"

"Oh, what do they call them?" Hunter looked to Celia for an answer. She lowered her head and seemed not willing to speak but did anyway.

"White?" she almost whispered.

"A Great White?" Jonathon wanted to know.

"That's it," Hunter said, pointing a finger at Jonathon. "We just call them Seal Killer Fish. We can tell when they are hunting. We can see them below. The seals don't see them as well. So they can get eaten. The young ones, mostly; and the old and sick."

"Really?" Jan voiced. "It doesn't sound like an easy life you guys have!"

Celia and Hunter just looked at her as if they had been Indian youths growing up on the fringe of the jungle where tigers still carted off children in the night and it was all just a part of everyday life.

Jan tried another picture. This drew a sharp smile from Hunter.

"The Northern Hunters!" he proudly proclaimed, and for the first time his sharp teeth were seen without a hand to cover them.

"The Leopard Seal," Jan stated. "They are one of the largest and most predatory species. They are in the cold north waters..."

"What hunters!" Hunter added in admiration. "My father took me two seasons ago up to learn by watching them. They move fast, like us, even out of the water. They hunt with great skill and don't need a large colony around them. They kill the Ice Birds with speed and great surprise!"

"Ice Birds?" Jonathon asked again for clarification.

"Penguins," Jan suggested, "That's their favorite target. And these?"

She brought up yet another image.

"Oh," Celia recognized, "That's the Pretty Ones!"

"Fur Seals," Jan again categorized.

"Very far north," Hunter noted. "They are the ones the land people wanted to kill most. Their skins were wanted for…"

"Yeah," Jan stopped him, "We know. It's horrible."

Celia spoke again. "We don't see them much. They stay where it is so cold. But they are nice. And sad…"

"I can imagine," Jonathon said, and found Celia's hand to hold.

"So," Jan continued her brother's original question, "Which ones do you look like?"

Hunter seemed very intent to search for an answer but Celia spoke first.

"Not like any of them," she said. "And like all of them. We are not…fat or slow. We can blend in with many colonies. We are not as big as the Northern Hunters but we move like them better out of the water than most. We can see each other but the seals and even the land people don't see us as different. If…one of us dies like a seal…no one will ever know. It's the magic."

Jonathon posed the next question.

"So you eat fish like the seals do?"

"Depends," Hunter shrugged, "On where we are hunting. This bay here; we look for the brown fish that turns blue when they move to deeper waters…you call them…ah,"

"Pollock," Celia remembered. "I like the small shrimp like what was on the…pizza? Only they are wriggly when we catch them. Oh, and squid…"

"Oh, yes," her brother agreed. "They come up from down deep at night. They are fun to catch because they are so fast and good at getting away."

"We eat smaller fish," Celia said rather excitedly, "When they get together and the other hunters move them into a...pack?"

"A school," Jan corrected without sounding condescending.

"What other hunters?" Jonathon asked.

"The small whales with teeth," Hunter suggested. "The ones the land people think are so smart."

"Dolphins?" Jan wanted to know. "Porpoises?"

"Yes," Celia confirmed. "That's what you call them. They are good hunters. They work together, not like the seals who only come in after the work is done. But they are not like the land people think they are."

"What do you mean?" Jonathon asked.

Hunter smiled his sly look again.

"The mothers are good to their babies, but the males will sometimes use a group of them to get a female."

"Not nice," Celia shook her head and her brown hair swished across her face.

Jan sighed.

"Looks like we got a lot to learn," she said to her brother.

She looked at Hunter.

"Do you think we will be able to try, I mean, to be like you?"

"Why not?" he shrugged. "Fin is the Keeper of the Skins."

"What?!" Jonathon blurted.

"Oh," Hunter remembered, "Let Fin tell you about that."

With that, he picked his broom back up and returned to attacking spiders.

Jan shrugged as well and stood up.

Jonathon came up with an idea.

"Celia and I will try to wipe these windows," he suggested. He kept holding her hand and led her over to a pile of old rags and they started smearing the cloudy glass together.

Jan just shook her head after them.

Lunch was another chowder with everything it seemed that came out of the bay with small potatoes thrown in. The scallops, especially, were large and so fresh and savory and unlike anything one could buy in a store. There was enough butter to almost color the stuff yellow. The thick, course bread was in abundance as usual. Still, it was far better Jan decided than anything she had ever had in a restaurant or fish house.

Shere served the affair and kept having to dodge the playful antics of Dearg. Jonathon though it was nice to see Shere in another light and Jan was equally glad to see their cousin seem to lighten up a bit.

Fin just smiled and acted as though he was very happy to have such company around his table.

The afternoon was lazy with Dearg and Shere disappearing somewhere and Fin out working in the ripe fish house. Hunter joined the older man there to learn and help.

Jonathon wanted to watch some more old movies and Jan went along to their dad's old room as a self-appointed chaperone. Looking through the small collection Jonathon suddenly came upon a find.

"Wow!" he said quietly. "Look at this box set!"

He showed Jan a six-video cassette edition of The Undersea World of Jacques Cousteau.

Explaining to Celia who Cousteau was he excitedly put in the first tape.

As they sat on the floor at the foot of the bed again her brother was enthralled and explained things to Celia, who at first seemed more interested in snuggling up to him than anything else. Jan reclined in their father's old bed and caught up on a few non-important e-mails from not friends but school acquaintances then took a call from their mother saying she was safe back in Boston.

Slowly, as the tapes progressed, Celia became fascinated as well. It seemed she had never seen anything of the oceans outside of her own northern clime. The vivid, if old by modern standards, captured footage of especially the reefs mesmerized her.

Jonathon told her how he and Jan had been down to Florida many times to visit their mother's family and had snorkeled on similar structures. Celia looked like a wild bird let out of a cage for the first time and seeing the wide world around.

"The colors!" she marveled. "The little bright fish...I don't think I could eat something that pretty!"

"Oh, but you saw the sharks as well!" Jonathon warned. "Although, unless you are doing something to agitate them, Mom and my family down there say they will not bother you."

Suddenly Celia put both of her slender hands on both sides of Jonathon's face and looked him square in the eyes seriously.

"Will you take me there?" she almost pleaded. "Say you will take me there!"

Jonathon was once again flustered but again he was getting used to it.

"I'd like to," he said earnestly. "I'd really like to!"

"Promise?" she implored.

"Ok," he conceded. "I promise."

Even with Jan just a few feet away on the bed Celia kissed Jonathon again, this time longer, and then went back to nuzzling into his neck.

He looked innocently to his sister, who was staring at him as if she didn't know him.

He smiled, shrugged, and went back to watching the series.

Jan shook her head and went back to her tablet.

She must have dozed off at some point and woke suddenly not

sure of her surroundings. Jonathon and Celia were gone and the TV was off. The light suggested late afternoon. She remembered some strange dreams where her father's smiling face came in and out of focus in scenes replayed from her long-ago past.

Then there was another half-remembered dream.

She was streaking through the water at an unbelievable speed. When she turned her head, her long and slender dark body followed instantly. She could feel the water flow over her flippers which were where her arms used to be. Raising one on the left side and lowering the other made her double back in a move no human spine could have withstood.

Her eyes could see everything under the water. There were dark rocks down deep where wavy strands of water plants swayed like living dancers. Fish darted by in small schools; alarmed at her presence. She dove deeply and then shot to the mirrored surface and out of the water into the cold air above. There was a giddy feeling as she arched and took in the surrounding shoreline. Then she knifed back into the water and glided for a moment.

The remembered dream was over. She was back, lying in her father's old bed, wondering whether to take the dream as a fantasy or a gift-preview of things to come. It was a long moment as she savored the scene and then reluctantly got up to see what was going on in the strange house she was now a part of.

The evening was spent with first dinner and a bit of a surprise. It seems Shere had actually gone into Bath and bought provisions for a meal that she thought was more suited to a 'land lubber's' repast. This consisted of the famous New England 'boiled supper'. Spuds, carrots, an onion and a pot roast were bubbling on the stove when all assembled.

Hunter was not impressed but stoically picked at his plate. Jan supposed it was because it did not contain something from the briny deep.

Celia as well daintily moved things around with a fork until she heard Jonathon thank Shere and remark that this was one of his favorites. Then she smiled closed-lipped and tucked-in as if she relished it.

Dearg acted as though he was comfortable with land as well as sea fare. Jan could not help watching his handsome features and easy style of trying to constantly woo Shere. As Shere seemed embarrassed and kept him at bay, Jan recalled a line from literature and thought 'Methinks the lady doth protest too much'.

With the dishes cleared away and Dearg insisting to help Shere wash-up, which meant he got to stand ever-so-close to her at the sink, Fin asked what the 'youngsters' had in mind for the evening.

Jan reminded him of the social tomorrow and he dug into some drawers until he came up with Red's phone number.

"Would you mind calling?" he asked Jan.

"No, not at all," she somewhat fibbed.

It was a bit awkward for her to use the telephone right there with Hunter and Celia and Jonathon and Shere and Dearg and Fin not so much talking but just being there.

Her worst fears were realized when she made the classic blunder as a male voice answered.

"Red?" she inquired.

"Ah, no, but Ah'll get him for ya, Miss. Can Ah ask who's call-in'?"

Jan froze for a moment. The thick Maine accented voice must be Red's brother or father; either way it was a faux pas.

"It's Jan MacLeer...family staying with Fin Roin?"

"Ah-yuh, hold on, Dear," the voice replied, and she could not be sure if she imagined the chuckle or not. Now she felt the voice was older and so that of Red's father.

There were sounds of feet crossing a floor. A door creaked open and the voice recently talking to Jan shouted "Jo-ey! Hey, phone for ya!"

More sounds of feet shuffling were heard. Then an older woman's voice away from the phone said "Who's on the line?"

"A girl callin' Jo-ey…the one stayin' with ol' Fin." The male voice reported.

"Oh?" the woman cooed, "What's she look like?"

"Now how would I know that?" the man rebuked. "She's on the phone, not at the front door!"

Jan wondered how anybody could not realize they could be heard on the open line. Or did they care?

The sound of the door opening brought her back from the embarrassment. Red's voice could be heard now.

"Got the last trap fixed," he said, and the sound of tools clanked on a cabinet or table.

"Good work, now there's a girl on the line for ya," his father said, and Jan imagined the wink or nudges that followed.

"What's she look like?" Jan guessed his mother repeated.

Red gave a hushing 'Shhhh!' noise and picked up the receiver, which Jan guessed, was just as old as the one she was holding. There was a poised moment before Red spoke up.

"Hullo?"

"Hey, Red, it's Jan."

"Oh, yeah, hey Jan…"

"I'm calling because I was hoping to get you to take us to the social tomorrow?"

"Oh, yeah, almost forgot. Hey, I'd love to take you."

Jan noted the singularity of his statement but put it down to male bravado with his parents listening.

"It's just me and Hunter, you remember him?" she asked.

"Oh, sure. No problems. Hey I can pick you up for church at 10:30?"

"What time's the actual social?" she tried.

"'Bout 12:30" he figured.

"Let's say noon? Unless you are going to church yourself..."

"Nope, just wanted to give you an option."

"Great...are we going by boat?"

"Nah, I'll be there in the truck...plenty of room."

"See you then..."

"Yep, see ya Jan..."

As she hung up Jan had a nagging feeling she had just made a date. That would surely be the way Red's parents saw it; the forward city-girl calling to set up a rendezvous. Would it appear in the local paper or just be transmitted by the gossip line?

"Ok," she announced, "That's settled. Red's picking up Hunter and me at noon."

Fin nodded. "Shere and Dearg will be around if Jonathon and Celia get bored."

Both Jonathon and Jan thought they caught a little jest but then Fin just continued and there was nothing to it.

"I've got work to do on the boat motor. Even though it's Sunday tomorrow I might have to go into Bath to get some parts from a guy I know. Runs his shop outta his house so his hours are not limited."

"Hey," Jonathon mused, "Maybe we'll catch a ride with you. I could stand to see some more of Bath. How about you, Celia?"

She nodded as if to say 'If you are going'.

"Suits me," Fin agreed.

With the table cleared and the dishes done, Jan was about to wonder what the rest of the evening might hold. Then her brother spoke up.

"Fin?" he asked, "Would you mind telling us about some of the things you have seen?"

"You mean stories from an old man?" he chuckled.

"No, I mean..." Jonathon started.

"Just joshing with you, son," Fin smiled. "If you don't think I'll bore ya?"

"No way!" Jonathon replied.

"Well, let's go into the parlor. Don't get much use out of it these days."

As the light outside faded Fin sat in his chair and faced his audience. Jan sat on the brocaded couch with Jonathon and Celia seated in front of her on the floor. As was now apparently the custom, Celia sat as close to Jonathon as was possible without sitting on his lap. Hunter sat in the other arm chair and appeared attentive but not enthralled. Dearg and Shere were off together on other business.

The tapestry Fin wove with his words was indeed a salty and magical piece. As his mother was teaching him in the ways of the seal-people, Fin was totally taken with the many ship wrecks they encountered. As he learned to work and live among the land people, he was equally fascinated in how sailors risked everything to go to sea. Many of them at that time did not swim a stroke. Yet, they still braved the waves and tempests and rocks and shoals to earn a very meager wage. Such were they willing to gamble to feed their families.

As a youth fishing in the community of Malaga, Fin saw firsthand how people can be good to each other and how prejudices and misinformation can lead to travesty. His family could have lived anywhere, given their sly 'finds' of money and other goods. Also, their natural sense for finding fish, when no other land-person could, set them apart. But they chose to be among the folk who cared not for things like color or race or social position.

A curious, adventure-seeking young man named Fin decided to see things for himself.

The white haired man described at length how he signed aboard ship after ship that was built, launched, and set sail from Bath. He watched, he worked, and he listened to the men who made up the crews. What he learned would fill enough storybooks for a lifetime of reading.

Unlike most of the Hollywood depictions of sailing life, boredom and constant back-breaking tasks filled most days. The ships from Bath sailed down the coast with seasonal cargos. Some were timber ships; their hulls able to open in the bow to allow loading and unloading of tall trunks. Coal was the most common store. A vessel would carry various goods from the north to places like Boston, New York and Philadelphia, then pick-up coal from Pennsylvania and reverse the stops in the same cities with enough left to fuel the home fires.

One of the most odd journeys that Fin was part of several times was a very nasty but profitable run down to South America where the ship would take on tons and tons of 'guano', or bat-droppings. This was mined from caves and the stinking mess was used in munitions factories for the United States government for making explosives.

Surprisingly, Fin told his young listeners, a schooner crafted in Bath or any other period shipyard, was only expected to last for about ten years. Even after the advent of steam power, it was much cheaper to sail the ships that had 'fore-and-aft' rigged sails so perfect for Atlantic coast travel down and back again. Indeed, some of the largest sailing ships ever built were constructed right here. Six-masted giants, no, behemoths, would lumber down the Kennebec into service hauling more coal than had ever been imagined.

Fin learned a few other things during his cruises.

The real money to be made in shipping was from investors. A ship, built in Bath, paid for by a group of as many as thirty-or-so individuals or companies, for a percentage of profits for each voyage was insured by firms also in Bath or other maritime cities against loss.

This led to some obvious attempts to cheat the system.

Ships had for the history of sailing been subject to bad weather, wrecks caused by so many variables and snares, and even piracy.

Danger was ever present and communication was impossible at sea. Even with the invention of telegraph in Fin's day news was long in coming.

Some ships' captains were also investors. Some even smarter captains used far-flung family members as investors or had companies under other names. Some just were in cahoots with other ill-meaning parties.

A ship might happen to run aground on a terrible reef that was really not so terrible because it was accessible by 'wreckers'. These were specialized people who could strip a ship of anything useful that could be sold right down to the very timbers and planks that it was built of. When a ship was nearing its' end, an enterprising captain could pay-off the crew to keep quiet, or simply not tell them, wreck the ship, and get a kick-back from the sale of the hulk. This way he would profit more than the whole group of investors back home when it was dismantled there. A captain's salary was not as much as one might think. Then if he were an investor, he would stand to be paid the insurance as well.

Insurance companies tried to discover any false claims but with the many underhanded deals it was difficult. Sometimes, even years after a pay-out was made, loose lips in sailor's drinking establishments might prove the only clue to the truth.

Then, of course, there were the real disasters.

Whether it was inept captains or navigators, decisions to forgo prudence after warnings of gales or storms in lieu of profits, or simply drunken or slovenly dereliction of duties, many fine and equally shoddy ships went down often taking their crews to a watery grave.

These and more Fin discovered in his travels both above and below the waves. So it was he resolved to make use of the knowledge.

Jonathon sat riveted to Fin's every word. It appeared that he shared his father's keen interest in the subject.

Hunter seemed distant and distracted.

Celia fell asleep dreamily curled up to her chosen beau.

Jan watched it all with a chronicler's eye. It was important to her legacy but equally important was the way in which every person in the room reacted to the telling.

Fin seemed to be in his element and enjoying the opportunity to share more than a normal life's experience.

The evening ended with a strange twist. Jonathon asked Fin a question.

"Fin, what is 'The Keeper of the Skins'?"

The old man smiled a wily smile and only replied "That I'll have to show you. Maybe when you mother gets back? We'll see!"

With that, Jonathon carefully awoke Celia and helped her upstairs. Hunter confirmed with Jan that they would be going to the social on the morrow. Then he went aloft as well.

Jan sat looking into the face of her great uncle.

"I'm proud to get to know you," she finally said.

"And," Fin said back, "Your father would be very proud of you, Missy."

7

Waiting for their ride outside of the house, Jan nodded approvingly of Hunter's second attempt at public attire. He was wearing a black polo shirt that still showed his powerful build and a pair of khaki pants. His first choice of the tight black and shiny shirt and bathing suit had met with consternation on Jan's part. Reiteration of the term 'church event' had forced the change of apparel.

Jan was wearing soft pink jeans that came down to mid calf and a matching flowered sleeveless button-up blouse. She had her light brown hair pulled tastefully back into a loose ponytail. She had debated how much makeup to apply but when she had looked in the mirror before coming downstairs she was proud of the outcome.

A candy-apple red 1950's style pickup truck came into view in the driveway. Jan thought the color fitting as 'Red' was behind the wheel, beaming.

Fin came out of the house and smiled his approval as well.

"Wicked-nice job on the old girl!" he appraised.

Red stepped out and admired the ride as though for the first time.

"Dad and Andy and I spent a lot of time on her!"

Jonathon and Celia appeared.

"Wow!" he breathed, "Very cool!"

As Red told Fin when he would have the two back Jan realized the sudden seating arrangement. Hunter opened the passenger door and sat down without a word. This left a still smiling Red with his door open and with a sweeping gesture he indicated that Jan should slide in.

She did so with some trepidation. Red sat down behind the wheel and closed the door and now she was uncomfortably sandwiched between the two young men. Hunter seemed oblivious and as the truck started Red was all too chipper over the situation.

At least, Jan noted, the machine had the gear shift on the column.

Rumbling along, Jan exchanged sentences with the driver but never eased. Even that made her self-conscience as her back was ramrod straight and she wondered if it appeared that she was pushing her chest out. Gratefully, the ride was not a long one.

The old churchyard had been set-up with long tables for the youths that milled about. There was a grill manned by adults and the smell of cooking meat filled the air that clinked with the sound of horseshoes being pitched. Younger members chased each other and tossed balls while the high schoolers clumped in predictable quiet cliques.

Red introduced Jan and Hunter to a woman who gave the appearance of a leader. Her pleasant manner and style was in keeping with what one would expect from a church youth leader. Jan did her best to answer the standard questions. Yes, they were visiting 'from away', no, they didn't need a church home; yes they felt welcomed, thanks for the invitation...

Jan wanted to explain to the lady that her cousin was a deaf-mute but thought better of it. Hunter was much too interested in looking at the girls who were interested in looking at him.

The three new arrivals moved over to the food table and Red gallantly got Jan some lemonade. Hunter dove into a hamburger after first sniffing at it. Jan decided to wait a while. Then, they were spied by the Queen and her court.

Gloria, Denise and Jenny sidled up in typical style. Gloria tipped her sunglasses to regard Hunter as she spoke to Jan.

"Why, hello, dear, certainly glad you could make it!"

Denise added "Red, people are going to talk! You riding around with a pretty girl in that pretty truck!"

Red tried to play off the remark and some small talk ensued about the weather, who else was here today, and the like. Finally the girls moved off and took Hunter with them to introduce him around.

Jan and Red moved about awkwardly and took in the sights and sounds. Their conversation was light and Jan made sure to leave a proper distance between them so as not to draw more attention. They exchanged stories of their schools and their likes and dislikes. Jan realized that Red was actually quite the gentleman and easy to talk to. Her mood and demeanor lightened by the minute until she actually caught herself laughing with him.

The youth leaders tried to involve the groups with various activities but only the middle school ages complied fully. Obviously the adults knew better than to push the limits on the older ones. Their games continued in their own way with different smaller groups jockeying positions and intermingling intermittently.

Red noticed a small crowd gathering at a distant part of the yard and Jan followed him to check it out.

Some of the older boys were ringing a small table where two of them were seated across from each other. An intense arm wrestling match was under way.

Jan unfortunately recognized the larger of the two as Skip Donnelly; one of Tommy Fields' gang. He was apparently the master of the game as opponents were lined-up to try their strength.

As Jan and Red watched, Skip put down two contenders with a familiar Irish grin. Girls had begun to watch the spectacle, much to the delight of Donnelly.

Then things got quiet. A shock of regret ran through Jan as she saw Hunter sit down to face the champ.

Before she could do or say anything the two were wrist-locked and someone called 'go!'

Behind Hunter closely stood Denise and Jenny. They were obviously the reason for his show of bravado. Jenny whispered something into Hunter's left ear and he smiled the close-lipped snarl.

The group began shouting encouragement to their champion. Skip smiled as well but as the seconds passed he started to strain and his face got even redder. He could not budge Hunter's arm.

After a full minute the crescendo of voices became stilled.

"Ready?" he said over his shoulder to the two fawning girls.

In a split second he whipped Skip's arm to defeat.

Surprisingly, in the stunned silence, Donnelly wrung his wrist and then offered his hand to shake with Hunter. They did so and stood up to the face the amazed crowd. It appeared everyone wanted to congratulate the new winner.

Jan was a bit proud when she overheard Hunter remark to everyone that it wasn't fair since Donnelly had faced many arms that day.

Hunter was reveling in his victory when Jan heard a voice in her ear.

"Darling," Gloria cooed, "Could I bend your ear a little?"

She locked elbows with Jan and walked her away from the throng. Red followed as well and Jan was glad of it.

"Just wanted to get to know you a little better," Gloria said and Jan somehow felt uneasy.

"It must be…interesting…spending time at old Fin's place? Spending time with his…daughter?"

Jan immediately felt a rising tension even though Gloria's words were as soft as silk. She muttered something about not really knowing her great uncle that well when Gloria stopped walking and faced her. The sunglasses came down again.

"But really, darling, surely you've heard things. Red must have told you, at least?"

Red spoke up.

"What are you driving at, Gloria?"

She looked over her glasses at him now.

"You haven't told her about the mystery of the Gaither brothers?"

Red slumped his shoulders and appeared to be getting angry.

"Why in the world," he said with exasperation, "Would you bring that up? If it's not Tommy Fields doing his best to insult these folks it's you dragging up some tongue-wagging gossip!"

Gloria struck a pose as if taken aback by the remark. She gazed at Red with a not too pleasant look.

"Ok," he said with a flourish of his hand, "Why don't you just come out and say whatever it is you have to say. How about that?"

Jan must have looked confused, as she really was, but she waited for some kind of explanation.

Gloria looked back to her.

"Never mind his rather rude tone," she started. "I just thought that you were aware of how some people around these parts regard Fin and his daughter after an incident that still has yet to be explained."

Red was shaking his head in disbelief as she continued.

"Years ago, what was it Red, in the early seventies? Two brothers named Gaither...disappeared...after saying they were going to pay a visit to Fin's daughter."

"What she's not saying," Red interrupted, "And pardon me for saying so, but these coots got liquored-up one night and told some drinking buddies that they were going to see, ah, Sharon, isn't it? Everyone knows the story. They did not have good intentions I'm sure and they sure didn't have any sense as my father always says."

Jan looked at Gloria who did not give away a trace of emotion.

"Anyway," Red continued, "These idiots got into a skiff and I guess planned to sneak up on Fin's place. The night was dark and the waves were up and nobody ever saw them again."

"Not a trace, I might add," Gloria remarked.

"Of course not!" Red admonished. "Gloria, you know that just last summer two guys capsized right under the Bath Bridge, with boats all around, and one was picked up alive immediately and the other one was never recovered. The currents and bottom have a way of keeping secrets. Everybody who works around the river knows those Gaither boys foundered their boat in a drunken state and the water got 'em. That's all."

"I'm just saying..." Gloria started. "Word is that Fin's daughter was a 'dark, wild beauty'. These days, when she's seen at all, she sure doesn't cut that figure anymore..."

"Right," Red said and took Jan by the arm and pulled her away from the Queen. They left her looking after them with a strange smile playing around her face.

After several silent moments and when they were out of anybody's earshot, Red turned to Jan.

"I don't know why, but I find myself apologizing for people around here. I'm very, very sorry."

"Don't be," Jan tried to assure, and before she could catch herself she touched his arm and gently squeezed his working man's tight bicep. "I guess she just wanted to see what kind of rise she could get out of me. I've met her kind before, trust me. Boston is full of girls like her. Only, unless I miss my guess, the Blue Bloods there have a much more cultured and dignified class snobbery. She's an amateur."

Red laughed and before she could redraw her hand he took it into his own somewhat rough, toughened ones.

A long silence ensued.

Jan broke slowly away and continued to walk towards nowhere. Red followed not too closely at her side.

"Don't lump me into that group," he suggested. "I'm not like either of those types that want to be mean or, what's the word, condescending? My parents taught me manners better than that and..."

"I get that," she cut him off. "I have to say you are the most well mannered guy I've met in a long time. I like that. I like *you*."

The sudden tension between them intensified as Jan realized she had opened a whole new door. Honesty had gotten the better or her usual discretion.

They walked on and Red moved just a bit closer and let his right hand brush against her left, but she was not ready for such show; not just yet.

"Hey," he finally asked, "Is Jan short for Janet?"

"Yep," she returned.

"Could I call you that?" he wanted to know.

"My mom calls me that when I'm in trouble."

He laughed again.

"Yeah, if I hear 'Joseph Michael Sanders' I know either my mother or the priest has a bone to pick with me!"

"Why do you ask?" Jan shot back, realizing they had more in common as he was surely Catholic as she.

"It's just," Red almost stammered, "*Jan* is like something out of 'The Brady Bunch' on reruns on TV. Now, 'Janet,' that's a classy name and more in fitting with your personality, as far as I see it."

Another awkward silence ensued.

'This guy's good', Jan thought. 'Is he for real?'

"You can call me Janet," she mused, "As long as I can call you Sir Red-gin-al? You sure know how to save a damsel in distress."

He looked around uncomfortably.

"Ah, I'd be, ah..."

"Forget it," she teased, and touched his flushing cheek. "Red will do, and you call me Janet but you can explain it to my mom if she asks."

He nodded and they continued their walk with a renewed purpose.

Deciding to try the local fare offered and after a few hot dogs done in the true New England style which were red skinned with a 'snap' to the bite and presented on the split New England type roll, she and Red found Hunter.

He was still enjoying the attention of numerous females but Jan managed to tell him it was time to leave. The girls all tried to get him to promise to call them, text them, e-mail them, and Jan found it amusing that with his silent, unspoken inability to do any of these he only increased his mystique and surely soon-to-be-talked-about popularity.

The ride back to Fin's found Jan a bit more apt to rub shoulders with Red as they rounded a curve. Their legs touched several times without Jan pulling away in haste.

Pulling into the dirt driveway, Jan saw a familiar and welcomed SUV in the yard.

Red got out of the truck and offered a hand to Jan; which she accepted. Hunter moved off without another word. That left Jan and Red looking at each other.

They both tried to speak at the same time and laughed together at the comedy.

Jan decided to throw caution to the wind.

"I had a great time," she confessed. "And, I can't figure you out, Joe Sanders."

She waited for the blush and downturned eyes but instead received a steady eye-to-eye smiling gaze.

"Do you treat every girl this way?" she continued, in what she hoped was a brazen city-tempered way. "Or are you just trying to impress me for the season?"

Red did in fact blush a bit at this but gathered her right hand in his two and, smiling wider, kissed it gallantly.

Jan's mother suddenly burst out of the house and the scene was quickly over.

"Hey!" Marie beamed, "Thanks for driving these guys to the affair! Back a day early!"

Jan hugged her mother but with a slight difference that only two females could pick up on.

"Good to see you, Mrs. MacLeer," Red said. "My pleasure, believe me!"

Marie looked quickly to her daughter's eyes, but not too obviously, and then back to the young man.

"Hope to see you again soon," she remarked.

"Me too," Jan blurted without realizing how fast her response seemed.

Red waved as he pulled out of the driveway and headed home. Marie had her arm around her daughter's shoulder and started to talk about the trip back down. Something was left unsaid for another time, they both felt.

Jonathon and Celia had clambered into Fin's truck and rambled into Bath. Celia sat between the two males and craned her neck to look at everything they passed. She seemed always fascinated with trees, or at least being so close to them. Jonathon put this down to her usual coastal habitat.

Fin dropped the two youngsters off at a small but pleasant park in front of the town library. He told them he was not worried about anything concerning them out of the water. He would only be about a half hour and he would be back to find them. Jonathon had an idea and told Fin to look for them in the library, which he had seen was luckily open on this Sunday on a few small signs.

After walking the sidewalks, hand in hand, Celia stopped them under an ancient tree and simply gazed up into the spreading branches. Jonathon felt a little uneasy as he had never walked in public holding anybody's hand except his mother's. He felt alive in a new way.

He turned Celia's attention to the grand old building with a copper-sheathed roof parapet and led her up the steps and inside.

The first thing to gain her attention was the change in climate. She let go of his hand and wrapped her graceful arms around her shoulders.

"It's cold!" she exclaimed. "But it feels good!"

The air conditioning was obviously novel to her but so too was the place. Jonathon didn't mind stretching up to whisper in her ear that people talked in low tones where other people were reading.

Celia simply smiled closed-lipped and grabbed his hand again. She put a slender finger to her lips and giggled a 'shhhh!'

Passing the desk, he read the signs over the rooms and led her into the heart of the impressively extensive yet small collection. He explained in whispers how the marking worked and how one could find a book. She was just wide-eyed with total fascination.

Jonathon quickly found the section he was looking for. He didn't admit to Celia how back in Boston he was at home in a place like this or how it might be viewed by some young people as 'nerdy'. He felt that was a word she had gratefully not been privy to up to this point and he certainly was not about to give a definition, especially when some people he knew would use him as a Poster Child.

The reference section was not exactly where folks their age flocked to. But, Jonathon found a very large book that he was satisfied with and he took Celia over to a heavy, tasteful table.

Thumbing thorough, he used the almost over-sized atlas to first show his attentive partner Boston and in ever going detail just where he lived. He had thought about doing this on Jan's tablet but he also had a flair for the showman and felt this was much more grandiose. Of particular genius, he congratulated himself, was the way he showed Celia where he figured she was from and then in increasing detail related the distances of their separate worlds.

After establishing this, he moved even further through the maps to bring her attention down the long coastline of the Atlantic. His final point on the map was where he had spent time with his mother's family in Florida on The Gulf.

Replacing the atlas, he retrieved another large book on reefs and allowed Celia to devour the vivid pictures of coral seas life. These were much more extensive and brilliant than the old television show and it made him feel very good to see Celia's reactions.

All too soon, Jonathon heard a librarian at the front desk greet Fin in a voice louder than expected. The woman remarked how good it was to see him again and so on and so forth. Jonathon's great uncle said very little but was as polite and genial as ever.

After leaving the library, Fin suggested that the three make a stop at the local grocery store. He hoped that Jonathon could come up with some ideas for meals that were more in keeping with what the twins were used to. Jonathon agreed and silently was more grateful than he let on since all of the food at Fin's, while great, was of the seafood variety.

The white haired man pulled the truck into a parking lot and the three went inside and got a shopping cart. Celia was glad to push and seemed delighted in the endeavor in her almost childlike way.

Jonathon tried to remember to be frugal since he figured Fin was to foot the bill. He was admittedly a good shopper as he regularly helped his mother in the chore. He chose some different rice dishes and fresh vegetables for one of his and Jan's favorite stir-fries. Fin was pleased to help pick out potatoes and some parsnips.

Planning for several days, Jonathon found some chicken and some hamburger and the fixings for a grill-out. Fruit juices and milk rounded out the nearly full cart.

Several times during the excursion some other shoppers would stop and try and engage Fin in conversation. It seemed as if everybody knew him but admitted to not seeing much of him. Always pleasant but tactfully aloof, he smiled and said as few words as he could while still being genial. He introduced Celia and Jonathon as 'family members from away'.

Just as they were almost to the checkout lanes another woman's voice addressed the group.

"Why, Fin! What a surprise to see you here!"

Jonathon turned to regard the person. She was behind an overstuffed cart that was piled high with what seemed a little bit of everything in the store. It took a moment for Jonathon to fully take-in her somewhat garish appearance.

The woman had a rather wild mane of streaked-blonde hair that framed a long face heavy with makeup. Green eye shadow and long false eyelashes didn't exactly match the black-outlined ruby lipstick. Her age was not given away but Jonathon guessed somewhere in the trying-to-hide-but-failing group. The smile was wide but something insincere was there as well.

A gold and sparkly knit top was cut very low and her full figure, now a bit sagged with age, was quite provocatively displayed. Multiple strands of pearls and silver and gold chains surrounded the too-late-to-hide-it wrinkled neck. Gratefully, the too tight and made for a younger person designer jeans were mostly hidden by the over-filled cart. However, plainly and painfully in view were the gold spike-heeled shoes.

Jonathon was shocked but he put on a game face since he had been brought up to be polite and there was obviously, he hoped, some reason for this person's choice of attire.

"And Fin," the woman continued in a smoky, raspy voice, raising a hand that was gaudily bejeweled and jangled with countless bracelets, "Who *are* these adorable young persons?"

Jonathon suddenly caught the sense that something was wrong.

Fin seemed to change his ever-genial character. His smile disappeared as quickly as the crest of a wave on the bay he knew so well. His aged face went stony and Jonathon had never witnessed such a rapid transformation. The usually twinkling eyes changed to the steely blue-grey of a storm sky.

"That," he said lowly but steadily, "Would be none of your business."

The woman just continued to smile her painted mask grin and Fin urged a confused Celia around the woman and down to a further checkout lane.

Jonathon was more shocked at his great uncle's uncharacteristic cold and rather rude behavior. He had to continue to watch the woman tell the cashier to get someone to unload her cart. In a haughty manner, she then ordered that someone should be available to take the mountain of groceries to her name-dropping luxury car.

Just as suddenly as Fin had gone seriously unfriendly, he switched back to a warm tone with the young man who was their cashier. Jonathon heard the familiar small talk between them but he couldn't help sneaking curious glances to the strange woman who seemed to be used to ordering people around. The employees attending to her were tight lipped and didn't appear to be enjoying the encounter, although it seemed they knew the drill all too well.

Outside, as they loaded the bags into the bed of the truck, Jonathon expected an explanation from Fin but again strangely did not get even a hint. His great uncle was just all smiles and kindness. It was as if the odd meeting had never taken place. Or, as if Fin did not care to speak of it in the slightest.

As they were pulling out of the parking lot, Jonathon caught one last look at the strange woman who was now directing two young store workers to stuff the trunk of an expensive automobile. Two other women had gotten out of the vehicle and were watching with caddy mock interest and waved cigarettes. They, too, were dressed in a way Jonathon had not up until this point thought possible in this idyllic conservative New England community.

He decided the three of them would have fit into one of the old movies as 'painted ladies'.

8

Back at Fin's place, a jovial reunion took place. Marie filled-in Jonathon on all the news from Bean Town and how everything was going just fine without any of them. The mood was light around the kitchen table as Fin had produced some delectable cold lobster and crab salad. As was now the usual, Celia ate without taking her eyes off Jonathon, Hunter was intent only on his food, and Marie and Jan carried most of the conversation.

Shere and Dearg, Fin had announced, were off fishing to fill the curing shack.

When the talk turned to Jan and Hunter's experience at the social, as Jan was telling of the arm-wrestling match, Hunter shocked the assembled with a casual remark between mouthfuls of bread and seafood.

"That guy Red, he likes you," he said, pointing a fork at Jan.

The silence that ensued made Jan want to cringe, but she tried to diffuse what she felt was coming, especially from her surely smugly happy mother, with a shot of her own.

"All the girls like *you*," she almost scolded.

Hunter smiled and was about to go back to gorging when Jan pressed further.

"Hunter, Celia," she tried, "You haven't said too much about where you're from. You've got to feel comfortable with us, right? Why not tell us. Do they have get-togethers like this one? What's it like?"

Celia looked to her brother and didn't speak. Finally, he cleared his throat and put his fork and bread down and looked uncharacteristically intent.

"North," he started. "Islands near Newfoundland...fishing places. Not many people. Small. Some seasons we stay, on land, on islands near Nova Scotia. Same thing...places where people maybe know who we are but don't ask questions."

"Like Malaga," Jan pondered out loud. Her imagination and what she had seen on TV also clicked as to figuring out the accent he had.

"Just like it," Fin agreed, and ran his old fingers through his white hair. "Places where a body can just be what they are."

"Television? Computers?" Jonathon wanted to know.

Hunter shrugged. "I guess, but I'm not really interested in all that. Some of our tribe is. Not me."

Jan remembered something.

"Hunter, Jonathon and I heard you and Celia say a few things in a language I didn't catch. Do you speak anything other than English?"

"Huh!" Hunter barked with a wicked smile. "We speak a lot of different ways."

Jonathon looked at Celia and held her hand before he cared who saw it.

"Like what?" he asked.

"Well," she said with head down, "What you heard was the language of our Tribe. I don't know what you would call it."

Fin spoke up. "A very old form of something that influenced Irish Gaelic. Probably from the 'People Who Came Before', as the Irish say. That 'magical' race I know you kids have read about"

Jan nodded. She would have to investigate this at another time.

"And?" she further queried.

"French," Hunter remarked casually. "But they say it's old French. The people that came and settled along the big river, Saint Lawrence, you call it? Oh, and some of the older members of the Tribe speak the native talk. Like from the people who were there before the French and English. I haven't learned that; just a few words that don't have any other way to say it. It's a good tongue, I think. Father told me, when we were leaving to come here that in the Old Speak the name of this river is 'Kennebec'. One word. In that speak it means 'long river that has no rapids'. Why say so much?"

Marie and her children and Fin chuckled at this logical and simple truth.

"And then," Hunter continued, "There is the Seal Speak."

"That's different from your Tribe's language?" Jan wondered.

"Sure!" Hunter nearly scoffed. "You can't speak any other way when you're in the skin, in the water!"

Jonathon was as confused and marveled as his sister and mother. The new concepts were flying around his head so fast it was hard to grasp them.

"You mean," he tried to sum-up, "That when you are seals you communicate another way?"

Now Celia laughed softly.

"Of course!" she said as if talking to a child. "We use barks and eye and body movement and...oh, how do I say?"

"Well," Fin broke in, "You can't explain, dear. But just maybe by tomorrow at this time they'll understand. It happens naturally when you make the change. That leads us to the question of the moment."

He paused for effect and looked at Marie with a serious but playful eye.

"Are we ready to go ahead?"

Marie looked in turn to both her children. The gravity of the occasion was perfectly clear if not somewhat precarious.

"Do you two want to find out? What it's like, I mean? It's your heritage and I would no more deny you of it any more than I regret keeping it from you for so long. I just wanted you to be ready. And I just want you to be sure."

"Yes!" Jan blurted before she even knew she had.

Jonathon completed the reversal of roles with his sister as he hesitated before answering.

"I feel like I have to," he admitted.

"No, you don't," Fin warned. "Your father would just as much respect you, as I would, if you choose not to. Up to you."

Celia had been sitting on the edge of her chair. She squeezed his hand a bit and spoke lowly to him.

"I want to show you my world," she soothed. "I want to share it with you."

"Of course," he seemed to snap back. "Of course I want to see what it's all about. I'm still not sure I believe it, but let's go!"

Fin smiled broadly.

"You asked me," he said knowingly, "About the Keeper of the Skins. Well, now's the time. As you say, let's go".

Fin stood up and motioned for Marie and Jan and Jonathon to follow. Jonathon paused long enough to grab his gray fedora for the adventure. Fin led them to the small door Jan had entered to help Shere. They in turn filed in and followed the spritely step of the older man. He called over his shoulder as they passed the rows of hanging robes and casually explained what Jan already knew about the use of them at the Gathering of the Tribe. They followed him past a few more walls covered in shelves with ancient fishing apparatus that smelled that way and finally to a small more open area where they all could just crowd together.

In front of them was the apparent rock that made up the

foundation of the house. It was dark and smelled earthy and even had some trickles of water slowly cascading down in tiny beaded rivulets. Fin had produced a flashlight and his slight grin could just be made out in the gloom.

"The fellas who made this, before the house," he said proudly, "Were all trusted friends of the family. They're long dead now, rest in peace, but the secret is now only known to a select few. If you didn't think yourselves family before, then you better start now. I can't tell you how important this is. I think you'll figure it out for yourselves. Anyway, the job was left to me and I take it very serious."

Jonathon and Jan and their mother all sensed the change in Fin's normally jovial and easy manner. Just as Jonathon had witness not long before on this very day, the old man's face almost lit with something from within and his face became as hard as the rock in front of them.

"No going back now," he said mostly to himself.

He thrust the flashlight to Jonathon, who took it with a fumbling motion. Before the young man could turn the light back towards the rock wall Fin's arms and weathered hands moved so quickly as to defy logic. A series of presses with the surprisingly nimble fingers that had been so abused by years uncounted of torturous abuse from nets and lines and ropes, and a low rumble was felt and heard.

Fin pushed slightly and the entire wall slide inwards and swung to the right to allow passage.

"That," Jonathon whispered loudly, "Is the coolest thing I have ever seen."

Retrieving the light from the open-mouthed Jonathon, Fin stepped into the passage without fanfare or a word. Marie followed and urged her children as well. The darkness was closing in at their backs.

The most remarkable thing about the place they entered, at first, was the sound. Or rather, the lack of any. It must have been carved out of the black rock that the large river ran through and yet there was no reverberation as in a large stone room or cathedral or church. And yet, it had an indescribable similarity to just that sort of place in the reverence that it seemed to command.

Jan summed it up with a whisper that did not carry far.

"Silent as a tomb."

Marie and Jonathon expected Fin to shush the utterance but he said nothing for a moment. He let the place cast its spell.

The light had been cast on the smooth black floor. Now Fin turned it towards the far end of the oblong space.

"Our family," he said lowly but proudly. Even these words were somewhat muffled as if they all were enveloped in invisible velvet.

The flashlight shone dimly on a set of heavy wooden doors. Great black aged rings and tastefully wrought hinges and straps completed the décor. From floor to ceiling, they were together about ten feet tall and equally wide.

"Pardon the show," the old man said, "But a flashlight don't belong down here."

He took out an old Zippo lighter and touched it to something on the right wall, then did the same to the left.

Slowly, two rather large torches made up of big round pots with thick wicks set into the walls with more black iron fittings sputtered to dim life. It was apparent immediately that these were powered by oil from something that came from the sea.

Fin switched off the flashlight. He smiled faintly at the other three for a fleeting moment then turned serious again.

Stepping forward, he placed his weathered hands on the heavy rings, paused for another silent moment, and then swung the doors slowly open. He stepped back and to the right so as not to obstruct the dim view.

Jonathon wanted to give another 'wow' or the like but decorum gratefully choked it in his throat. Jan had the feeling she should genuflect, like in church. Marie just slipped her arms around the shoulders of her twins.

Similar to a mausoleum, the interior space behind the doors was an extensive shelving system. Each cubicle was about two feet high and wide but the darkness did not permit the depth to be ascertained. Jan and Jonathon collectively thought that with a squeeze each could contain a body or what once was a body. There appeared to be about twenty-five spaces.

"Come on, then," Fin said softly. "Come closer."

Moving as one, the mother and children advanced until they were within arm's reach of the recesses. The realization of what lay in most of them came as not a shock but a revelation.

Neatly folded in the niches were furry seals' skins. As the amazed newcomers looked further and drew even closer, the flickering torch light revealed neatly carved small plaques with inscribed names. Some of the skins were lighter, some darker, some larger, some smaller.

Marie finally spoke.

"How many, Fin?"

"Right now," he returned, "Seventeen. The other spaces, well, let's leave it as saying it's the last resting place for some of the Tribe's, ah, remains."

He waited before continuing.

"Some of the skins are here permanent, awaiting such a time as might be, and, some, well, I'm just holding...for now."

Marie looked quickly towards him with an almost frightened, unasked question.

The old man smiled and moved to gently step between the three and the cubicles. Slowly, reverently, he reached two rows up and almost center and slid a bundle out of its place. It was about three feet in length, doubled and folded. He gingerly but strongly held it in his cradled arms and tuned to the waiting faces.

All three noticed together that there were tears welling up in his eyes.

Marie realized first and tried to stifle a sob.

Her children looked to her in surprise and then slowly something became clear. An idea that was impossible, but nevertheless they felt the sadness and the shock of realization.

"I'm holding and keeping this," Fin said, the tears now spilling over since he couldn't brush them away, "For when he gets back."

Marie now started to cry in controlled strength as her twins were there, as she always did, but this time without keeping anything back. She guided her children with her down on one knee. Then she took her hand from around Jan's shoulder and reached a slightly trembling right hand towards the dark shape.

"Go ahead," Fin urged. "Go on, Missy. You know wherever he is he will feel it somehow…"

Jan and Jonathon stood stock still.

She stroked the fur tenderly.

Sniffing back a tear, she composed herself a bit and continued to touch the bundle.

"Your father's," she managed to say to her children without breaking down.

They looked first at her, but it was startling to see her in such strain. They looked back at the thing in Fin's arms.

Jan reached out without further thought.

The first sensation was as touching any real fur; a brush of coarseness against the grain, but a sleek and soft sensation the other way. Then something else hinted at her mind.

Slowly at first, then gradually stronger, she felt her father's presence. She logically told herself it was because of the power of suggestion, but either way it was all the same pleasant. She remembered strong hands picking her up and hugging her. A voice, a face, and words that were not clear but male and happy and loving. It was then she realized what her mother must be going through.

"Mom!" she whispered, "Mom...can you feel it? He's...not gone, is he?"

Jonathon managed to overcome all his fears and incredulousness and touched the fur as well. It was apparent his feelings were just as shocking and soothing as well.

"You're right," he finally said. "Or at least, I just want it to be true. But I feel like if he was really, you know...dead..." He never used that word in talking about his father. He knew it shocked the other two as well.

"If he was, I don't know why but I feel like I would know it."

His mother sniffed again and hugged his shoulder with her arm that was still around it.

"You're right," she said lowly. "You're right, son."

Fin spoke up again.

"I feel it too. I come down here sometimes just to talk to him and let him know I'm still waiting. We'll have to talk about this later, you three, now that it's out in the open."

He gently moved to break their touch with his bundle. Reluctantly, they all longingly kept their fingertips on the fur until it was out of their reach and back in its place.

"So," Fin started, and he seemed to be back in control of tears, "Now for the Choosing. We have to figure out which skins want to meet you. Even then we won't be sure it's a match, but we have to start."

Marie, as well, had tried to compose herself. She stood up with her offspring and after wiping her eyes replaced her arms on their shoulders.

"How do we do that?" Jonathon asked.

"Well," Fin said, scratching his head, "Let's let ladies go first. Do you trust me, Jan?"

She nodded and tried to tell herself that she believed it.

"Best thing is to make a little experiment. See, I think I have a notion, maybe a small one, of what you are like, dear. Or I should say, I think I know what you don't like. Bear with me..."

He stepped to the right into a darkened corner and carried back an old wooden hand-made ladder. It was the type like from over in the Old Countries that was wider at the base than the tapering top. He placed it on the left side of the shelves and motioned for Jan.

"Third shelf," he indicated, "Third one over. If you would, Jan, climb up there and read the name for me? But don't touch until I tell you to. Read the name like in church and then say your name and your father's name."

Jan did as requested. She figured this was a formal introduction.

"Your father's full name, dear," Fin amended as she climbed.

In the torch light, she could see a very old black plaque with what looked like yellowed ivory letters embedded in it. She drew up her shoulders and read the words.

"Sheila Macha O'Ferguson..."

She had tried to sound as loudly and firmly as she could. The air seemed to deaden the sound less than before. Was it the words?

"I am," she continued with real pride, "Janet Marie Costello MacLeer, daughter of Mannanan MacLeer."

She could hear, or thought she heard, her mother breathe-in with her own pride as Jan had included her grandfather's name as well.

"Well done!" Fin said lowly. "Now, ever so slowly, reach in and put your hand flatly on the skin. No petting; this is like a handshake on meeting for the first time.

Jan did as directed. At first there was just the feel of fur. Then, slowly again, some images started to waiver in her head. Wild, wind-swept rocks...dark nights...lightning and thunder in the not-so-distant ink-black sky.

Then a jolt caused her to stiffen on the ladder. She could just make out, behind her eyes it seemed, some disturbing things. A room, a smell of wood fire and strong tobacco and…beer. Then clanking metal tankards, rough-sounding male voices, and above all a haunting, throaty, hoarse female's laughter.

Jan withdrew her hand as quickly as seemed politely. She rocked a bit on her perch.

"Easy, now," Fin warned. He stood just below her ready to steady her. "Come on down, now."

She looked at the older man with wide eyes and a puzzled face.

"I'm sorry," he admitted with a slight sly smile. "I figured that wasn't a match, but I wanted you know how it works."

"What did you feel?" her brother wanted to know.

She looked a bit embarrassed but tried to convey the message.

"Stormy coast, black rocks, kinda scary, and then a…a tavern, I think?"

"Sorry, again," Fin chuckled softly. "I guess she was just showing off."

"Who was she?" Jan asked, and in so doing realized she knew the woman was deceased.

"She was a story to tell, she was," Fin shook his head with a smile. "I only heard of her. Not directly related to us. Her father came from the old country way back. She lived here in the Tribe oh, around the early 1800's. Her mother was local, as fiery as she turned out to be. She lived both in the sea and on the land with a reckless abandon and a love for danger. That's why I figured it would not be a match, Jan. Gratefully so. She would be the only crazy one of the Tribe to actually seek out storms and play in them. That killed her, finally. It took days of searching to find her cracked-up on the rocks north of here. They just saved her skin, I heard, before she passed."

"One of the things," he continued, "Is that *her* skin there, well, it was from a woman from way up north. Like where Hunter and Celia live, I think. Her father introduced her through someone like me to the skin but that seal-woman was not as reckless; only maybe wanted to be. And before her it belonged to a woman from The Faroe Islands and before that I don't know. Anyway, the last personality seems to leave the biggest impression. Only, I can say for me, I learned to pick up on the past lives of my skin. Maybe because I wanted to..."

"OK," Jonathon summed up, "So what next?"

Fin scratched his head again. He looked at Jan with a furrowed brow in scrutiny.

"Let me ask you," he pressed. "Since coming here, have you had any dreams? Dreams about being a seal? Dreams that were..."

"So real!" she finished. "Yes, yes, I have!"

"Tell an old man more." He leaned back and crossed his plaid-sleeved arms.

Jan tried to collect her thoughts and tell the tale without any giddy fluff. It was after all, only a dream?

"I was racing through the water," she started, looking off and up and to the left where everybody does when trying to remember. "I was sleek and fast and free. I could turn so quickly. And I was happy. I was so happy that I shot up out of the water and..."

"What was that?" Fin interrupted with a raised finger. "Say that again, missy?"

Jan looked at him as if she had said something wrong.

"I jumped out of the water," she stated. "It was wonderful. I looked all around and it felt like a rollercoaster and then I dove back like a knife...why?"

A large smile had crossed the old man's face. His eyes seemed to twinkle in the flickering light. But Jan sensed there was some sadness in the smile.

"You jumped out of the water...up into the air," he almost sighed.

"Yes," Jan said quizzically.

Fin looked at Marie and Jonathon.

"Seals don't do that," he continued to smile. "I mean, you might see something like that in a show where one has been taught to do it for a fish, or if being chased by a shark or an Orca, maybe. But that is not something a seal does for fun. They arch out of the water when moving quickly to gauge a shoreline. But not for sport."

His smile seemed to widen with wisdom.

"But *we* do! Sometimes, if the mood strikes you, but not normally."

He laid a finger alongside his nose for effect.

"However, there was one of us..."

He moved the ladder over to the right side and then motioned for Jan. She started to climb but Fin put a gentle hand on her shoulder and whispered something for her ears only. She nodded in agreement and started back up.

"Fourth row up," he said aloud, holding the ladder. "First on the right."

Jan paused before the darkened recess. She let her eyes get accustomed to the light and then read the name, first to herself. She noted the spelling of the family name with keen interest. Then she read out loud.

"Margret Shannon MacLir," she said as proudly as she could. Then she paused and did as Fin had requested.

"Maggie-Shannon," she said in a slightly lower and less formal voice. "Janet Marie Costello MacLeer, daughter of Mannanan Mac-Leer. Hi. I'm Jan."

With a little less hesitation as before, she placed her right hand on the tawny, light brown fur. It was almost her own hair's color and even in the dim light there appeared to be some blond and red tints present.

Her thoughts were immediately greeted. Again, as if behind her eyes, it seemed there was a pretty cottage door that was just barely opened. As if Jan had knocked, a presence was looking at her through the slight opening. Nothing was clear, just a sense of shy eyes and a genuine, girlish interest. Jan looked back and tried to convey a smile. It was returned. Still no face was visible in her mind, but the door was opened and a sunny, salty-sea-smelling yellowish light beamed out. Jan moved into the room in her mind. Her real body could feel herself press against the ladder as if she were really moving.

Inside everything was wispy pink curtains that blew about in the sea breeze from many open windows. The warm sunlight flowed in like touchable waves. Jan sensed a form in the shape of a shimmering light hovering in an area of a soft sofa adorned with fabric of colorful flowers. Without fear, in her mind she sat down. There was a small low table and on it were dainty tea cups and saucers. The pot was covered in a hand-made cozy of orange yarn.

"Hi," Jan said again, out loud or in her mind or both. "Everything is so pretty."

She heard a voice then. Or, something like one. It tinkled like a wind chime in a summer breeze. Behind it were the gently lapping waves on the rocks outside. No words were spoken but the meaning was clear.

"Thank you," Jan blushed. "I never think of myself as pretty. I'm really new to all this."

The presence reassured her it was alright.

"I just found out about all this, my family, I mean, just a little while ago. I was scared," she admitted, not knowing why she felt comfortable to do so.

"But now I'm not."

The shimmering form started to change into something that looked more like a person. It was about Jan's size and very feminine. But it wasn't totally clear.

Abruptly, she heard from somewhere far, far away a voice she knew. It was Fin telling her it was time to go. She didn't want to. But she knew she had to.

"OK," she said to the form that was starting to fade again into light. "I'll see you again? Please?"

And with that she took her hand off the fur and seemed to zoom back out of the room, the door shut quietly, and with a start she was back in the dim light on the ladder.

"So," Fin smiled warmly, "You met Maggie-Shannon. Just one more thing to do. Pick up the skin, Jan. It won't feel heavy. If she wants you to, you'll know. Bring it down with you."

Doing as told, Jan had to hug the skin tightly as she descended. It felt like an old, familiar blanket or quilt. She used her left hand for gripping the weathered wood of the ladder. Gratefully, she accepted Fin's strong assistance.

On the ground again, she placed both arms around the skin like a child would a favorite stuffed toy. She looked at Fin in the same childlike way for explanation.

He knelt to face her eye to eye. His were again a bit misty.

"I'm going to tell you some things," he said soothingly. "Some are pleasant, some are not. That's how things are, ah-yuh?"

Jan nodded. The feel of the skin and the faint sea-smell was almost intoxicating.

"Maggie-Shannon," he said with a gleam. "Everybody loved her. She was the brightest spirit I think we ever had around this place. Oh, yes, I was lucky enough to know her."

"She was born around the 1900's," he continued. "She was the only daughter of your great aunt Maureen, my only sister. Her father was never disclosed. It never mattered. From the start she was as bright as a summer day. Always bubbly and cheery. As innocent as the days are long. She marveled in everything, no matter how large or small. And, she was always known for her playful jumping. Everybody warned her about drawing attention but she didn't care. She just loved life. As far as I know, and I would swear to it, she never said or did anything bad or malicious to anybody or anything. That's why I never figured out..."

Fin trailed off his narration with a sad eye.

"What happened?" Jan spoke up. "I feel some sadness..."

"So very strange," Fin said wistfully. He looked straight at Jan and the skin she was holding.

"I was so happy to be around her, whenever I could. She had this cozy little place just up the shoreline from here. It was done-up like a doll house. Up on the rocks, she could watch the waves and the ships and it was all a story book."

His face changed again into what Jan knew was coming.

"I got home from a trip salvaging down in the islands where a lot of ships had been recently sunk by German torpedoes. Fand, my wife, met me at the door wringing her hands. Maggie-Shannon was upstairs. I went into to her. She gave me her skin and told me she was tired."

The old man paused and sighed.

"It's something I didn't want to talk about just yet. That's what happens. We don't know how long we live if we stay mostly as seals. It's on the land that we age more. So, sometimes, many times, really, some of us just decide that it's time to go. Usually, we are old and we find a safe, comfortable place and just...fade away."

"But she was young," Jan stated.

"That she was," Fin nodded. "In land-people years she looked no more than twenty. I tried to ask her, but she just used that bewitching smile and said she was tired of being in this world. Maybe, I have thought over the years, she started seeing how bad this world can be. It's ugly. This was the 1940's and the Second Great War was on. So much fear; we were worried about U-Boat attacks in the Kennebec. Maggie-Shannon was just too good to stay here. She would be happier elsewhere."

"She died in this house," Jan added.

Fin nodded with a puzzled look of his own.

"In the room where I'm staying," she added flatly.

"I hadn't noticed before," he admitted. "But you're right. I have to say that a lot of people have left this world here on these grounds. It's one reason I built the place. More about that later, OK? Right now I think you have found a friend and you need to bond with her. You'll keep her with you for the rest of the day and sleep touching her tonight. You'll know in the morning if it's a fit."

"Now," he turned to Jonathon, "About you, my young man."

Jonathon had been watching with keen interest. He shrugged as he spoke.

"So who do you know up there that was a nerdy library-bound dreamer?"

"Jonathon!" his mother admonished.

Fin held up a hand.

"You sell yourself short, son. I can see through a lot of things. Comes with the job. You have the smarts and a heart as strong as any of our family. And a sense of style and a good funny-bone. Let's see…"

The old man rubbed his chin and looked up into the niches.

"Ha!" he chuckled out loud. "Could it be? Why not…"

He moved the ladder again to the left and pointed.

"All the way to the top, son. First one on the left."

Jonathon stepped to the foot of the ladder and started to take his antique fedora off.

"Leave it on," the old man grinned. "Oh, but son, don't get startled by some of the contents of the spaces up higher. OK?"

With that warning, Jonathon climbed but of course could not help peering into the spaces he passed. The bottom three rows had skins in them. On the next row and above he could just make out eerily white and yellow bones. Gratefully, he did not see any skulls but he guessed they were in there as well, as were the skins.

Reaching the last niche, he read the plaque expecting a noble name from long ago. What he read aloud was quite puzzling in the simplicity.

"Loki Larson," he spoke slowly. "I'm Jonathon Sean MacLeer, son of Mannanan MacLeer."

With that he said lowly to himself "Here goes nothing, kid..."

As his hand settled on the dark fur, darker than his father's, he heard a haunting strain of music. It grew louder, in his head he guessed, and he recognized it somehow as a tinny orchestra playing a song he found vaguely familiar. The tune was a jaunty but somewhat sad number that epitomized The Roaring Twenties.

A room came into his mind. He moved through the open door and immediately smelled the acrid cigar that lay smoking in an ashtray on a small table against the far wall. There was a smeared and dingy mirror with several dim light bulbs around it. Stepping closer (he found he didn't feel his feet) he could see a corked bottle on the table that bore some small letters on the label and 'GIN' in larger ones. The half-full squat glass beside it needed washing. A well - worn black leather case was open and pancake makeup and grease paint and cold cream were strewn inside. A streaked dirty casement window let in street noises and an alley breeze with a pungent refuge odor rustled the Variety paper on the un-swept floor.

Looking around further, Jonathon saw a battered steamer trunk against another wall. Too many stickers from too many trains and boats covered it. A hat rack by the table had a faded black jacket and a straw hat as well as a crunched fedora much like the one he had on.

He suddenly realized the music was coming from an old Victrola somewhere behind him. The song was now clear to him as a voice crooned *"When you and I were seventeen and life and love were new..."*

Jonathon joined in.

"The world was all a field of green and skies were smiling blue..."

From somewhere a gentle but hearty laughter could be heard. It too chimed in, in perfect tenor harmony, and made a trio.

"That golden spring when I was king and you my wonderful queen...Do you recall when love was all..."

The ethereal voice rose for a 'Show Biz' finale. Jonathon followed suite and took the lower part.

"And we...were...sev-ven-teeeen!"

More jovial laughter followed. It faded out with a slight coughing as the room did. Then Jonathon was alone on the ladder.

"Does he want you to bring it down?" Fin asked.

"I think so," Jonathon answered back. He bundled the fur under his right arm and descended past the cairns.

After he was back standing next to his mother and sister and great uncle, he whistled to himself, pushed his hat back with his free hand, and shook his head in amazement.

"Don't tell me," he said to Fin. "This guy was an entertainer. Vaudeville, right?"

"Ah-yuh," he agreed. "Need to hear more?"

"You darn-tooting" the youth expressed.

"First off," Fin explained, "That skin is so high up because it has a place of honor. The older the skin, the higher up. Just out of respect and reverence. None of us know how old it is. It's like this..."

He scratched his chin and thought a moment.

"One summer day sometime around 1890 this thin man in a worn suit shows up at my door. He says his name is Loki 'Lucky' Larson. He gives the right credentials by way of introduction from really old members of the family in the old world. It seems he came from Iceland. See, when our people left Ireland and Scotland and the like they naturally ventured first to Iceland and The Faroe Islands. They were the closest and had very small land-people population, if any.

What people there was, they knew magic when they saw it and gave us a wide berth. They were also a sea-going lot."

Fin paused to collect his thoughts.

"So this Loki..."

Jonathon interrupted him.

"Loki the trickster...from Scandinavian mythology."

"Right," fin smiled back. "Anyway, his family must have been very, very, very old. Maybe back to Norway and before our people's time. None of us had ever seen but a few skins near as old as his. Mind you, ours go back to a time well before written history, but this was something even older. And he was not so interested in the whole Selchie life. Maybe it was because he or his skin was so old and had seen so many years as one, I don't know. But he had other plans."

"The Stage," Jonathon said with a slight flourish of his left arm crossing in front of his face like curtains.

"Right again," the old man continued. "He needed a place for the summer. He relaxed here and rejuvenated each summer for many years to come."

"I know why," Jonathon mused.

"No air conditioning," the young man explained. "The shows all had to close for most summers. Too hot in the theaters. Only work was out west in carnivals or in Circuit Chautauqua tents."

"Seems like you know a lot about this," the older man said. "Guess I was right in the matching."

He smiled and took up the story.

"So Loki was a stage man. He went under many names. He was Lucky Larson if he was playing the comic fool Germanic or Swede clown. It was Lucky Lannagan for the Irish. In some places, he even spoke Yiddish and was billed as Lucky Leftowitz. Always the clown. Always with the slapstick and funny accents and pratfalls. He used to show me play bills and newspaper clippings. He never made it big, but he said he didn't want to, that it ruined a comic when he got a big head. I never understood how he could make such fun of people who came to this country not speaking much English."

"It's a dying art," Jonathon sighed. "People are too serious now and too PC. Back then, everybody enjoyed making fun of themselves, right?"

"I suppose," Fin conceded. "I never got it. I went to see him perform once only, when my ship was docked in Boston. He paid for my ticket and took me out to dinner afterwards. I just didn't get it. But the crowd roared when he got hit or fell down or said something like a dim-wit. He didn't seem to make much money, anyhow. But he didn't care. He loved the stage."

Here Fin winked at all three with him in the vault.

"I'll tell you true," he almost whispered. "When he arrived that first summer a big wagon with a four horse team delivered his trunk. It was so heavy it took four strong busters to get it down. Know what it was full of?"

No one answered.

"Gold," he winked again. "All melted ingots. A king's ransom. He said he brought it from his home. We banked it for him but he rarely drew from it. I never asked where he got it."

"So what happened," Jonathon pondered, "When the 'Vaude' started to lose out to movies and reviews like Ziegfeld's?"

"One summer, I think it was in 1931, Loki just stopped coming. He had always left his skin with us for safekeeping. He just never showed up again. We knew, as time went by, that he was gone. But nobody knew how or where or when. No trace. I contacted some of the numerous partners he worked with but nobody knew nothing."

"I think," Jonathon thought out loud, "That he had one last really good show. You have to go out on top. When he knew it...that was enough."

Silence had returned to the place.

"Well, let's get back into the air," Fin started. He moved to usher the three out so he could close the massive doors.

"Wait!" Jan blurted. "What about mom?"

Fin looked at Marie who looked in turn to her children.

"This is your legacy, not mine," she smiled. "Someday, you'll understand. OK?"

With that they stepped back and Fin shut the doors and told Jonathon to switch on his light and wait for him outside. They did so, and in a few minutes he joined them, pressed some more unseen buttons, and the wall slid back as if it had never moved.

In the kitchen again, Hunter and Celia were waiting. Jonathon and Jan extolled on what had happened. For once, both of the northerners were attentive and downright reverent. Celia seemed especially pleased in that soon she could show Jonathon 'her world'.

A voice from outside called Fin's name. It was Dearg. He called for help with the unloading of fish from a full boat.

"Help me, Hunter?" Fin asked. The youth moved off behind him with stoic resolve.

"I feel like some herbal tea," Marie stated, and busied herself opening cabinets and starting a pot of water.

Jan and Jonathon sat down at the table with their bundles in tow. They looked at each other for a moment.

"Would you have believed?" Jonathon started.

"Never," Jan finished.

"Do you feel anything now?" he asked.

"Not like before," she frowned. "I mean, we're holding them, but I don't get the same images. Anyway, what did you see?"

He painted the picture, with a few glances towards his mother when he got to the cigar and gin bottle.

Another uneasy silence descended.

Celia was all about sitting close to Jonathon and smiled at him constantly.

Marie found the cups and the kettle boiled and whistled and she served all three youths even when Jonathon protested. She sat down with her own steaming cup.

"Forgive me yet?" she asked her twins.

"For what?" Jan immediately asked.

"I don't know," her mother said in a recent not-so-surprisingly uncharacteristically childlike tone. She sipped the lemon grass tea.

"For not telling you sooner?"

"Oh, mom!" Jonathon said for himself and his sister. "What were you supposed to say? And when? 'Hey, kids, have fun at kindergarten but remember all your new little friends are not seals like your family!' Gimme a break!"

Marie had to laugh at his mirth.

"Really, mom," Jan added. "Don't you know how much we respect and love you for trying to raise us by yourself? Now we get the bigger picture. I'm more amazed."

Marie fought back more tears.

"You are a good mother," Celia suddenly said, looking with her large brown eyes to Marie.

The remark took everyone at the table by surprise.

"If I can say," the girl continued, "I would be proud to be your daughter. My mother, she tried to be close to me. We did some wonderful things together. She taught me so much, but now, she is gone to me. She has other things to do. It's hard to say. I wish she was still in my life. But I am supposed to treat her like any other female in the Tribe. I am supposed to be big now, but I don't feel big."

Jan reacted first and with her right arm still cradling the fur at her side she reached out with her left and touched the girl's strong shoulder. Jonathon was quick to take her right hand. Marie smiled and stretched her left hand out across the table to touch Celia's left hand.

"Hey," Marie said. "I'm far from perfect, sweetheart. But I

promise, if you want, to be a friend to you. I will watch out for you, protect you, as I can. Maybe we will find more in common than you think. If you want to...?"

Celia nodded quickly.

The interlude was cut short by the boisterous entrance of Dearg and a quieter Fin. Hunter and Shere followed behind with their usual silence.

The men smelled liked the catch they had unloaded. Fin and Dearg were pleasantly arguing over fishing sites and Hunter started rummaging around the kitchen for food. Eventually Dearg turned to the twins.

"Aaragh! I heard you did some skin-matching! That's grand, right-so! Then the morrow is the big day, is it?"

A slight awkward pause followed. Fin broke it.

"We were to discuss it, yes," he said with a bit of deflated surprise. "Any objections?"

Marie smiled an answer and Jonathon and Jan both felt that twinge of excitement they had first experienced when coming to Maine. Only now it was impossibly magnified with a supernatural twist.

"We have to talk about some rules and stuff like what to expect," Fin stated. "You have to listen to me, right?"

The twins shook their heads in promise.

"This will take all of us," Fin announced. "Let's have a seat..."

The old kitchen table was again filled with figures.

Fin started by laying down the law in that under no circumstances were any of them to leave the small bay just beyond the dock. There would be no venturing out into the wide part of the river; just yet. He further instructed that Dearg would be first in the water, followed by Hunter, to wait for Jonathon who would be instructed by Dearg. After the 'men', then Celia would follow, then Jan as helped by Shere. Fin would be watching from the dock.

Jan interrupted with a question.

"You won't be changing?" she asked and realized how easily she now accepted the improbability.

"No," he answered. "I'll be watching."

Jan caught an idea but let it go for now.

"What about mom?" she further inquired.

Marie smiled a long moment before offering an answer.

"Your dear mother," she said slyly, "Has decided to try out these frigid waters for herself. When I was back in Boston, I took the chance to bring some of my old diving gear from the Florida days. I doubt I can stay in for too long, but I'll try to snorkel-around and see my children in their new adventure."

This both pleased and excited the twins.

Next, Fin led a discussion on just how the transformation would feel.

Dearg and Celia offered some minor personal information but it was agreed that it was different for every person and every skin.

Again, Fin instructed that the twins were to keep their skins touching them for the entire rest of the night. Shere had made a quick trip into the cellar and produced two black satchel-like bags with a shoulder strap for each of them. They could put the skins there so they were still in contact with the fur through the open top.

Shere also quietly stated that she would provide everyone with a robe in the morning so no one would have to strip in the boathouse.

That part left Jan and Jonathon a bit nervous. Both of them had been wondering about that part of the equation.

The round-table discussion ended with Fin suggesting that he and Shere would make use of some of the salted cod they on hand for a dinner later. Marie said she was going up to her room to read a while. Jan decided to do the same. Hunter looked somewhat dejected in that dinner was so far off. He wandered into the parlor and picked up a book on the local shipbuilding history.

Celia and Jonathon strolled hand in hand out on the dock.

Around the dinner table, the conversation was light or non-existent. Jan wasn't too thrilled with the baked fish, which had been reconstituted from the hard, salted state in much less time than she had read about. It had a distinct, almost fermented quality to it as well as the potent salinity. Red potatoes and parsnips in a butter sauce helped.

Afterwards, the eldest member present declared that everyone should get a good night's rest. Jonathon doubted that was going to be possible. His sister felt the same way.

Everyone helped clear the table but Shere insisted on doing the dishes. Dearg grabbed a drying towel and snapped to attention like a sailor. His goofy salute brought some mirth to the room.

When the only ones left in the kitchen were Fin, Dearg and Shere, the old man gathered up his boat coat and reached for his cap. As he was heading out the door Shere put a soapy hand on his shoulder.

"Not to worry," he assured his daughter. "Just got to be done, that's all."

"Do you..." Dearg started.

"Ha!" Fin cackled. "No, thank you kindly. But I don't need no help with the likes of these."

With that, he was off into the growing darkness towards his moored boat.

Upstairs, Jonathon had said goodnight to a pleasantly clinging Celia. She was just bubbly with anticipation of the coming day. She had given him a quick kiss on the cheek in parting.

Dressed in his tee shirt and gym shorts for bed, he did as Fin had instructed and took the fur out of the satchel and laid it next to him as he tried to settle in for sleep.

Surprisingly, in less than fifteen minutes of anxious thought, he drifted off.

He heard laughter. Faint at first and then more pronounced. It was a crowd. He couldn't see them clearly for the flickering glow of gas footlights in front of him on the un-swept stage. If he strained, he could just make out a garishly shadowed couple of rows of guffawing faces. But the laughter came from many other places. From balconies, from seats beyond, from boxes above both sides of the stage...and all of it directed at him.

He realized this was not the kind of derisive making-fun-of kind of laughter he had unfortunately been the brunt of numerous times in his young life. Like when he failed to hit a baseball or run fast enough or tripped over his own feet in a school hallway. This was ever so much more of the kind of laughter he had figured out could overcome his weaknesses. This was the coveted response when he cracked a funny joke or made a comical parody of a teacher or well-known leader. This was what got the girls to notice him at all, even if for a brief moment.

He looked down at his hands. They wore dirty white gloves with the fingers cut off and were tucked into the belt of baggy, ragged trousers. The stuffed big belly over them jiggled in pretend yuk-yuk-ing.

He felt a whap upside his shaggy wigged head.

He looked, as the crowd roared, at the fellow beside him onstage. The character was supposed to an 'upstanding' personage. A false, pointy, up-turned nose with small glassless glasses pinched on the bridge and a battered once-fine top hat completed the look of putting-on-airs. The fellow had a stuffed carpet bag that obviously had dealt the blow.

Jonathon heard a trilling, high-pitched sound that he realized was coming from him.

"OOOOOOOH! By Yimminy! You zay you don't vant no fish today!!"

The crowd went wild. The fellow with the bag hit him again, even harder.

"OOOWWW!" Jonathon heard himself, or rather 'Lucky', he realized, say. "Vould you taken-out-en ze brix before on mine noggin-you hitten!!!" he said, grabbing his head and imploring the audience.

The crowd lost their minds.

Slowly now the laughter drifted away and he was seated before another small lighted mirror like the one he had seen before. The gloves came off and were tossed in a chair nearby where the coat and shabby vest and false stomach lay as well.

The hands, not controlled by Jonathon but feeling like his own, struck a match and lit the crumpled stub of a half-used filter-less cigarette.

The face in the mirror was long and lean. The grease paint and burnt-cork beard stubble didn't give much of a hint as to the man beyond, but with a shock Jonathon thought he perceived his own likeness merged with 'Lucky's'.

Someone passed at the open door behind.

"You killed 'em tonight, Lucky. We're goin' for a drink. Comin'?"

A silent, waved hand sent the man off.

Jonathon sensed an overall sadness in the room. A sort of melancholy as if the only solace could be found in the stage lights.

The scene changed abruptly and Jonathon was streaking through the water at incredible speed. His body effortlessly twisted and made corrections to catch the school of fish he was chasing. Behind him, other seals had fallen way back in the hunt. It was as if he was the fastest, most nimble, most experienced hunter.

Even this brought with it a slight sadness. It seemed...old.

Several more snippets of places and people flashed by in his dream. Small fishing villages with colorful puffins wheeling overhead, grand parties with clinking champagne glasses and dancing couples; and yet always, it seemed distant.

With a start, Jonathon awoke to the sound of his smart phone on the bedside table.

It was playing a song he had downloaded earlier that evening.

But he had not set it to start playing now.

"When you and I were seventeen and life and love were new..."

He looked at the skin under his hand.

"I think I get it, Lucky," he said slowly.

"You got tired. Nothing was new, was it? So...you want me to make it that way again, don't you?"

He sighed.

"Well, it's going to be new for me, that's for sure, pal. It will all be new. I'll try to breathe some new life into things, I promise. Partners?"

Without waiting for an answer, he added, "Only, let-en me get-en zome sleep-en und I promise to taken-out-en ze bricks before over your head I'm hittin'."

He thought he heard a ghostly, coughing laughter.

Jan was staring at the ceiling over her bed the way she had started at it many times since coming here. She had memorized the cracks in the plaster and the way the light made different shadows depending on the time.

Right now, she was having a different kind of thought train.

She moved the fur skin from beside her and placed it over her chest like a child with a favorite toy. She inhaled the musky, salty aroma.

"Was it different then?" she said to it. "The ceiling, I mean. You must have looked at it too. A lot, I think. I'm sorry you died here. Maybe that's not what you call it. You moved on, huh? I want to see things like you did. Mom says, and she's right, that I'm cynical sometimes. Actually, a lot of the time, if the truth be told. I always think about changing myself or becoming somebody else but that is not what this is about, is it? I'm not changing into a seal as much as I'm becoming myself, right? Just, maybe, a different side of me."

She cuddled the skin tighter.

"Is this really happening?" she asked. "I've spent my time finding out about things in the real world that people used to call magic. Now look at me. I'm hoping, praying that tomorrow I really will turn into...something."

She had another thought.

"It was you, wasn't it?" she asked, looking at the fur in the dark. "You woke me up when I needed to see something. You sent the dream to me. You know, I can count my friends on one hand? We are going to be closer than friends, aren't we?"

With the warmth that suddenly came over her, she sailed gently into a calm sea of sleep.

The old boat cut its motor some distance from the expensive but unlit dock. Drifting perfectly and now silently, the craft was masterfully guided alongside the boards by its lone occupant. An older man stepped strongly out of it, lashed it, and strode purposely towards the large chain-link fence and gate that separated the pier from the looming, dark and massive lone modern house on the small island.

Without pausing at the gate where a security box waited for begged admittance, the figure reached under a plaid jacket and brought a heavy, short hammer up and then down on the strong electronic entrance system barring the way.

The lock shattered with the superhuman blow.

Striding up the path to a large front door, the figure stopped and rapped with the hammer on the expensive wood. It left deep scars in the polished teak.

After several ever increasingly louder and more destructive knocks the door was partially opened with a heavy chain hoping to preclude further advancement.

In front of the soft light that shone out was a frightened, painted older woman's face.

"Coward!" the old man with the hammer addressed the inside of the mansion. The voice cut above the sounds of the waves all around like a thunderclap.

"I'm talking to YOU, *Julie*! I know you're in there!"

The frightened woman behind the chained door looked nervously over her shoulder. Her wild, platinum mane appeared dingy in the backlight. The bangles on her tanned and liver-spotted arms jangled.

"Hide behind your pathetic consort, will ya?!" the white-haired man in plaid almost laughed. "You make me sick! All right! Have it your own skulking way, then!"

He gathered himself up to full height, thrust out his barrel of a chest, and roared.

"I'm giving you fair warning, you lout! I have guests in my house! You may already have guessed, but hear me now, you son of a witch! Some are royalty from The Northern Tribe! Others are of my kith and kin; from a bloodline you are required to pay homage to!"

After letting the words sink in, and with the woman at the door cringing at the weight of the words, he continued.

He pointed the hammer at the cracked door menacingly. The woman behind it flinched and disappeared from view.

"If you do not extend the Sacred Rights of Hospitality to any and all of these, then you will find me, Finley Roin Magnus Og Brian MacLir, to answer to!"

He waited for any response.

"That goes for your embarrassment of a goon-crew as well! Are you going to send them out tonight so I can end their filthy lives and take their skins back with me? Not that I would have them mixed in a place of honor, but maybe I could use them for doormats!!"

"No? And you won't show your ugly face?"

The man smashed the hammer into the door with such force as to lodge it there buried past the head.

"Puppy!" he snarled as he spun and scornfully strode back to his craft.

9

The breakfast seemed in keeping with a theme; a preparation of sorts. Cold herring and cold cod from the night before was the only fare.

After the plates were cleared, Shere and Dearg passed out the dark robes to all concerned.

As if that was the signal, without further fanfare everyone except Fin went quietly upstairs.

Jan sheepishly took off her clothes, everything, and quickly put on the robe. It was surprisingly not as heavy as she had expected, and indeed it was more than comfortable to the touch; almost too comfortable. The whole experience was exciting and somewhat taboo and this was only the beginning. She cinched the belt tight and looked down to see if anything was 'showing'. This was a moot point, she told herself, at the thought of things to come. She had always been extremely self conscience about undressing in front of girls at school in gym class or sleep-over's or anything else. She had shunned the rite of passage of other friends who had marveled and wondered about their changing bodies and wanted to compare.

The robe had an inside large pocket fixed just at thigh level for the skin that was to accompany her. It was most discreet and personal and intimate.

The hood she did not need and so with it thrown back and with only the robe on and a pair of flip-flops for prudent foot protection she gathered her resolve and stepped into the hallway.

Her brother was there, and a quick glance told her he was not in the least comfortable with this either. It probably didn't help, she thought, that Celia was already latched onto him and she looked positively stunning. Her robe was casually worn low on her shoulders and open enough to show ample cleavage and skin down to her waist. Her brown hair cascaded back in a wild fashion. Her eyes were aglow.

Gratefully, Marie stepped out of her room to diffuse the moment. She wore a wet suit vest and a set of tight running shorts that came to mid thigh. In a bag at her side she had fins and a mask and snorkel. Over her shoulder was another rather large gym bag of sorts that Jan figured held towels or something like it.

"OK," she smiled. "Ready? Let's go!"

Jan thought her mother sounded as if they were headed to the water park for slides and wading pools instead of off to transform into...something.

Downstairs, Jan thought indeed it was a scene from her early fears of the place. All assembled except for Fin and her mother had the black robes on and it looked to the world like a coven of evil-doers.

Except, it seemed, it was light and mostly happy.

Hunter seemed as ready to go back to the sea as a hound in a cage ready to be set loose on the fox. Dearg was all smiles and the red in his dark eyes was even more pronounced. Shere was her usual quiet self but she was intently listening to her father who gave her some last minute low instructions.

"Gentlemen," Fin finally announced, and simply pointed to the door.

"Stay in the bay!" he repeated sternly as Hunter, a stumbling Jonathon, and Dearg exited.

Waiting in the kitchen seemed like a lifetime. Jan nervously tried in vain to look out windows but nothing could be seen except for Fin and her mother on the far end of the dock. Fin had a very serious eye out towards the open water and her mother was sitting with her legs dangling over the edge and was putting on fins and spitting into her mask and rinsing it and preparing for her own plunge.

All of a sudden, Shere motioned. From her position casually gazing out of the doorway it seemed her father had waved a signal.

Jan filed in between Shere and Celia like a prisoner headed for the guillotine. She was lost in the moment and was only vaguely aware of her surroundings. She saw the door of the boat house opened and she stepped through as if in a daze.

Inside, she remotely registered the piles of robes that suggested her brother had already undergone the transformation. With that thought as something to steel her resolve, she continued.

Shere was saying something to her but the voice seemed to come from somewhere far away. The opening to the water was clear and with a slight smile to both the women left in the room, Celia dropped her robe and stood for a brief moment proudly naked to the world.

Jan tried not to stare but it was impossible not to do so.

With a more serious but still dreamy look she sat down on the plank over the water and placed her feet daintily into the open end of her seal skin. Slowly, almost lovingly, she continued to pull it up over her legs, then waist, and then raised her arms and closed her eyes as the magic took over. The skin kept moving up and over her until her arms became flippers and her pretty face was engulfed in a seal's whiskered muzzle.

The transition completed, with a short bark she tumbled into the water and was gone.

"Right," Jan said rather loudly. "Ok...I just saw that...I think..."

Up until this very moment all she had heard about was just stories and legends and fantasy. Now, she had to believe or think herself in a dream she couldn't escape from.

Shere prodded her gently.

Jan stood up and took out the skin from its place inside her robe. She rather awkwardly undid the cinch of her robe and fumbled clumsily to let the vestment fall.

Shere was there to help her.

"When you enter the water, look for the others," she offered. "Don't worry, sweet. This is who you are."

With that, Jan forgot her embarrassment and sat down with her skin. She could not remember the last time, if any, she had been stark nude in front of anybody, and that included her mother.

She tried just a slow wriggling of her feet into it. It felt like a warm, welcoming blanket. Without realizing she was doing so, she let the fur climb up her body in a way she thought might be too pleasing. It engulfed her, it caressed her; it felt so good. She had never experienced anything to match it. Her senses were alive and yearning for more.

Following Celia's lead, she raised her arms and surrendered as her whole world changed forever.

With a jolt, she felt her legs become useless for standing. Instead, she wanted to move her now powerful front flippers. Her eyes had undergone a profound change. Again, with Shere's help, she floundered into the water with a splash and entered her new world.

The first thing she became aware of was no need to worry about breathing. Her nostrils had automatically closed when she hit the water. Unlike when, as a human, she had swum before, she sensed a long-lasting sense of air that she instinctively knew would sustain her.

Next was the sight. As in her dream, the underwater world

was more vivid and sharp than anything she had experienced using diving gear. Everything was crystal clear and vibrant. The bubbles under the boat house were diamonds. The waving sea foliage was green and brown and beautiful. The rocks held mussels and moving crabs and small fish. As if a magic mirrored ceiling, the surface above shone brightly different.

She became aware of the others.

Gathered just a few yards off in a sort of waiting were two seal forms. She darted to them with a freedom she could have never dreamed of.

Unbelievably, she recognized both of them. Bobbing to the surface for a deep breath of air, she regarded them further.

Dearg was easy to identify. His wide eyes, now set as a seal, burned with the red twinge she had grown to know. He was sleek and powerfully built and very, very masculine. He was the first to greet her.

"Welcome, little one! You are beautiful!"

Jan realized what she heard was a short series of barks and grunts, but she had understood. Hunter was also easy to see as he held his male posture strongly and stoically.

Next, she looked for and found her brother. She had expected to find him floating silently by himself and not too sure of what was happening. She was wrong.

Two seal-forms were undulating and playing together in unabashed excitement. Their wake caused waves to ripple on the tide. One was brown and slender and feminine and wrapped herself in twisting, touching, sensuous arches around a darker, beguiling male specimen. The two stopped long enough and surfaced for the dark one to raise his head and communicate.

"What's up, Sis!" Jonathon managed to get out before Celia nipped at his whiskered snout. "I.....like....it!"

With that they were off racing around the bay at great speed.

Jonathon was playing at learning that he could out-swim the obviously ecstatic Celia.

Jan nodded to Hunter and could not help feeling that just as he made a macho land-person he was even more of a hot item as a young seal. He snorted back a greeting and then went back to chasing a school of brown-backed fish. Shere came up from behind to complete the assembled.

"Oh, Mom!" she barked to Dearg and Shere, who had just swam up to complete the party. Together, they ducked under the waves and headed for the dock.

Jan was absolutely astounded at the ease with which she adapted to her new form. It felt so natural and even if she was a novice she craved further exploration. Her senses were so in tune with everything under the water. With a glorious recognition she saw the form ahead of her.

Her mother was diving in a slow arc that just a few moments before Jan would have considered very graceful, only now it seemed clumsy and...human.

Racing up to meet her, Jan hoped that her seal face could smile. Her mother certainly did, around the snorkel and through the mask. She reached out and stroked Jan's sleek head lovingly. In turn, Jan moved her body around her mother in a sort of embrace.

Shere and Dearg greeted Marie as well but stayed aloof a bit. Jonathon came speeding up with Celia just behind and created a bubble net by circling round and round. Then the two were off again.

Marie motioned for Jan to go about without worrying about her. Reluctantly, Jan did so.

Following Dearg and Shere, Jan allowed herself to be schooled in various aspects of her new life. In the shallow bay, sharp rocks and deep crevices were to be avoided. Things which were supposed to be tasty, to Dearg and Shere at least, like small lobsters and urchins with prickly spines and squid that hid in the seaweed was not to her liking. As yet, she told herself.

Always there was the boundary.

Before, as Jan had looked out over the bay in front of Fin's house, it had seemed vast. Now, the opening into the river basin beyond was like a choking invisible fence.

As she flitted around the area, merrily enjoying her impossible freedom and new-found sensations and all, Jan found Dearg and Shere were there to close off the entrance to the big water that beckoned beyond. There was no logical explanation for it, but Fin's warning words came back to her thoughts. Surely, the elder had reason for his limits. But, the open river and then the expanse that lay unexplored beyond were as tasty as the salt water that strayed into the bay and then as exotic as…

She caught and bit and swallowed the soft cephalopod that she found venturing too far from its favored rock hiding place.

The sensation caught her by surprise but she savored the wriggling salty flavor and realized she had found her first 'kill'.

Dearg swam up alongside her and flashed an approval.

The affair left her thoughtful. But with odd indifference she pressed on.

A thought ran through her mind and giving into it she gauged the bay in a way she did not know how previously possible and then began a fast circling of the expanse. After several circumnavigations of increasing speed she ignored the concerned glances of Dearg and Shere and even Hunter and her brother and Celia and, at a dizzyingly top speed, she shot out of the water and arched, as in her dream, out of the water and into the air.

The sensation was everything and more than she had expected.

Something deep inside her exalted in the moment and she felt the connection not only from Maggie-Shannon but from something older still. Dark, dormant images seemed to awake and take pleasure in the youthful playing.

She let the moment continue as when she entered the water again and Celia was there to celebrate and revel in her actions. The two shared a new moment as Celia circled and brushed against her and pressed her seal body against Jan's to produce a not-so-unpleasant sensation.

Jan decided it was like a sisterly hug, albeit she had never allowed any of her friends to get that close.

Following Celia, she joined in a playful game of chase but Celia was too fast and nimble. However, Jan was learning and getting more accustomed with every passing minute.

Her brother shot by at an alarming speed. She figured it must be his skin, as Fin had described how old and powerful it was, and she was so very proud that her brother was appearing to have a great time in his new-found prowess.

She thought about jumping again but Shere and Dearg made it clear they did not think it was prudent. Understanding their concern for drawing attention, she settled for exploring every rock and shell and creature in the small bay. She even snapped at some fish that swam too close and ate a few. It was more than a novel experience to have something squirm down your throat. She didn't even taste them, so much; just a sensation of salt and a coppery scent that she supposed was blood.

Anyway, it seemed as if it was what she had to do. Just as natural as it was that she always shot to the surface instinctively to get air. But what a dive-time she had! She didn't try her limits yet, but she was able to stay down well over five minutes on a single short breath.

The morning passed blissfully and so much was learned. Even more was longed for. The boundary of the bay kept coming back as an incredible hindrance. It was after several hours or more when Jan realized there were no other seals in the area. This was a puzzle, but she felt Fin could answer later.

The old man could be seen each time Jan surface and looked to the pier. He smiled but was also keenly alert and watching beyond the protected cove.

Her mother could also be seen waving warmly when one or both of her children looked for her. She seemed proud and happy, if a bit bitter-sweet as when the twins had took their first steps, started school, been in plays...

Every so often Jan would have to remind herself at the shear impossibility of what was happening. This was magic, or something that defied modern thinking at least. Sure, stories had existed since man could pass down thoughts about such transformations. But who believed it nowadays? And, she further wondered, since this was obviously happening to her, what else might there be that had hitherto been brushed off and explained away as legend or fairy tale?

After about three hours Dearg and Shere rounded-up the two novices and made signs that it was time to return to the land.

This was a crushing realization.

Jan could not put into words how much she wanted to stay and continue to marvel in this existence. But, she also realized, there was no use in acting like a child on this first time out. Perhaps Fin was testing them, as he had with the rules of not venturing beyond the bay. She bowed to experience and venerability.

Shere swam under the boathouse first, in a reverse order of their entrance. After a few minutes, Jan followed.

It was not as easy to shuffle her body up the plank as it had been to simply flop off of it. It took some rather strenuous wriggling and Jan told herself this was something to practice for later for getting up on rocks.

There to help, Shere had obviously just changed back and had not had time to put her robe on. Her black, wild hair did not even appear wet, Jan noted. Also, as the woman helped scoot Jan out of the water, it was apparent that she was still a beautiful specimen.

Now nearly helpless, Jan heard Shere tell her to *think* about changing back...to ask the skin to allow her to.

Closing her large seal eyes, Jan did so and in just a few moments she felt her muzzle retreating around her head and then down her neck. Slowly, the skin melted like warm honey until she could move her feet and legs out of it.

Then she was the second nude figure in the room.

She and Shere both retrieved their robes and in an unexpected moment the woman turned and hugged Jan quickly.

"How do you feel?" she asked softly.

Jan knew the tears of joy were about to spill out of her eyes. She couldn't speak.

"I know," Shere nodded, sharing the secret. "I know."

Celia glided up the ramp like a seal in an aquarium show. Ever so gracefully, she shed her skin with loving, tender movements as if in a dance. She also rushed to Jan and grabbed her arms to begin a flood of questions and congratulations.

"Ah, wait, I, uh, robe please?" Jan stammered. She was just not yet at home with all this nakedness.

Shere ushered them out as the 'boys' started to return.

The rest of the morning was a blur of smiles and questions and half-answers and hugs and pointers on all things seal. They got changed back into 'land people' clothes and congregated in the kitchen.

Jonathon was lauded for his ability to take on the seemingly overpowering ancient skin. The ease with which he showed in meeting the responsibility was indeed remarkable.

Jan got some good-natured chiding about her flourish with the jumping but all in good spirit as it was collectively understood about the background circumstances.

All in all, it was a celebration that rocked the house and posed more questions than were answered. It seemed that indeed a 'new' life had been infused into the family. Strong, proud feelings ran rampant. Hunter and Celia were amazed at how well the newcomers had adapted.

Only, Jan noted a strange thing to be pondered on.

Her mother, while all smiles and perfect excited praises, seemed somehow slightly distant and not as interested to ask all about details of the underwater life. Jonathon did not seem to notice, but Jan did. She remembered back to when the three of them had first gone to visit relatives in Florida and her mother had introduced them to the waters there. A sort of underlying familiarity had made the experience rather simple.

Now, Jan pushed the thought out of her mind that her mother might feel left out. She was absolutely confident that her mother had not a jealous bone in her body and in fact had always strived for her children to push the limits and go further in everything.

So why not now, was the question?

Wasn't it her mother who had set all this up? Wasn't it all her doing in bringing them here to find out all about this incredible adventure?

So why would she now seem a bit distant and almost secretive?

Jan let it go for the moment and let herself be swept away in the joyous celebration.

Her mother did remind her children of her favored phrase of 'bread-winner' as she went back down to the dock and returned with a washtub full of squirming lobsters.

"Hope I'm not breaking any laws," she looked towards Fin. "Just couldn't help myself."

"I won't say anything!" he replied with a grin. "I know you didn't get 'em outta anybody's pots, so all's well!"

Again, as the group began preparing for yet another meal, Jan was strangely interested in how her mother could have harvested such a haul.

"Mom," she tried, "I didn't see much of you in the water. How did you...?"

"Hey!" her mother returned lightly. "I spent my summers down in Florida, remember? These things just have claws to watch out for; otherwise they are just as dumb as our spiny ones down south!"

Jan just let the thing go for the moment and got caught up in the excitement and mirth.

The afternoon was a lazy postlude to the morning's impossible happenings. Dearg and Shere disappeared somewhere, Fin said he had to see to his boat, and Marie had made a strong suggestion that Celia and Jonathon get some rest most definitely *apart* for a while. Hunter had gone to help Fin. This finally left mother and daughter alone in the hall.

Marie smiled and invited Jan to come into her room. Words just seemed to get in the way and before long Jan was asleep in her mother's arms on the bed as if she were three again.

Jan loved her mother for not asking questions. She just rocked her and was there.

Without realizing it, Jan had dozed off with her skin pressed between her and her mother.

The dream wasn't anything unwanted or annoying; instead it was just as natural as her being cradled by her mother. The wind-chime voice tinkled sweetly.

'I'm glad you like my mother,' Jan said to Maggie-Shannon. 'I know she would like you too.'

'Why are you giggling? Jan asked. 'You know something I don't, don't you?'

'Well, if you're not going to tell me,' she said, in her dream, almost cross...

The twinkling voice soothed and presented a gentle sound and feeling of the waves that Jan now had such a different appreciation of. She drifted back to blissful slumber.

Down by the dock, Dearg caught up with Fin as he was throwing the lobster-feast remains back into the water. He spoke lowly but with great seriousness.

"There was something...odd...out there today," he started.

Fin cast an interested eye towards the dark man.

"Something...was watching us. A sound. Like a dolphin or whale, but it wasn't any of those I've ever heard before. It was just quick and came from everywhere but nowhere. Just a click or a blip ever so often..."

Fin slowly smiled.

"Nothing to worry about," he assured.

"I don't know," Dearg confessed.

"Trust me," the older man stated. "I'll explain when it's time."

"As long as you're sure, right so," and his eyes flashed the red tint.

"I am," Fin nodded.

The evening turned out to be anything but what had previously become the norm.

Jonathon had been seemingly empowered, perhaps by the skin he had fit into that day, to rather take charge of the usual order of things.

Since he had had a great hand in grocery shopping with Fin and Celia he began to suggest, maybe give orders, as to the various roles associated with his planned meal.

Dearg and Fin had been relegated to fire up the old charcoal grill. This produced some sparks not related to the fire as the older man and the younger one argued friendly about the ratio of hardwood to commercial briquettes. At any rate, soon the smell of the outdoor fire permeated the open windows where Shere and Marie and a confused Celia, with Jan coaching, were slicing up tomatoes and onions and peeling lettuce and readying condiments.

Jan found she could not help but feel a pride in how her brother had risen to new heights and commanded a quiet but forceful effect on the family.

He chose a rather reluctant Hunter to help him in mixing, by hand, the ground hamburger with spices and steak sauce as directed. At first, Hunter turned up his nose at the mixture but slowly the concoction seemed to draw him into an unaccustomed interest.

Jonathon demonstrated to his cousin how to pat-out the burgers in relatively equal patties.

As if following a school of fish, Hunter keenly brought up the rear as Jonathon presented the meat-discs for introduction to the grill.

Keeping a sharp eye out and making sure to see to proper cooking technique, the young man in the gray fedora 'allowed' the two older men to save face and do their manly duties in the searing of the flesh. Several flare-ups were masterfully attended to by Jonathon's timely dousing with a dark ale Dearg had been downing. The crowning achievement was the cheese slices at just the right moment to melt perfectly.

The results, when presented at table, were at least to Jan, a welcomed respite from the land-lubbers nightmare that had been previously presented; despite the flavorful fare.

Fin had anticipated the affair and had set a separate ring burner afire with a cauldron of grease or oil in which sliced potatoes had been fried. But, in a northern twist, Shere had made brown gravy that was to be pored over the spuds with melted cheese curds in a manner in keeping with an eastern Canadian favorite.

The moment was forever captured when, after a lengthy silence around the table of enjoying the messy feast, Hunter looked up with a genuine greasy smile.

"This," he managed to say, "Is better than the stuff you get at the road-side places!"

Jonathon beamed in the spotlight.

After dinner, Jan managed to get her brother away from Celia long enough to walk out onto the dock. The two had not had a moment to talk and they soon gushed with words to describe their magical encounter.

They took off shoes and socks and sat with their legs dangling in the now seemingly cold water. They talked like they were used to; sharing things that only twins could know about.

Jan teased about Celia, Jonathon about Red. They giggled at private jokes until there was a moment of pleasant silence.

Then Jan spoke of her feelings about their mom maybe being left out. Jonathon dismissed this at once. With that thought over, she tried another.

She related what had been said at the church social about the two men who had disappeared en route to their present location.

Jonathon confirmed her fears by suggesting the two might have reached the residence. He asked if she had told their mother, and Jan shook her head to the negative. His suggestion, which sounded much more mature than Jan had ever heard him, was that it was to be disclosed.

"I just think," Jan mused, "That it might explain a lot as to why Shere doesn't want to look... pretty. I mean, she sure could, right?"

"You can say that again, sister," Jonathon reverted to his Film Noir character.

After another short silence, Jonathon realized he had not told his sister about the strange women they had seen at the grocery store. This produced a quizzical line of conjecture from both of them.

"Well," Jonathon finally summed up, "Guess we are going to have to do some asking. All we can get is either the truth or the run-around, right?"

"Right," Jan agreed. "Oh and how do we play this? Do we act like we can't wait to get back into the water or play it cool?"

"I can't wait!" her brother admitted.

"I want to swim to Ireland!" Jan whispered excitedly.

Jonathon switched to his W. C. Fields voice and mannerisms. "Philadelphia will do!" he sneered.

10

The Maine Maritime Museum in Bath was situated on the grounds of a once vibrant shipyard on the Kennebec. The small but extensive exhibits and buildings told the tale of shipbuilding life from the time of the wooden schooners up through the colossal steel hulled six-masted behemoths of the Wyoming class right up to the WW II era.

A tidy and shiny launch boat with open seats for over twenty with a canvas sun top ran several times a day down the river towards Fort Popham. The tourists were treated to lighthouses, picturesque islands, the fort, and of course the ever present seals bobbing their heads looking back at the humans and basking on the rocks.

On this summer's morning excursion, a small group was busy clicking away photos of about fifteen animals that were hauled out on one rather small outcropping. One woman nudged her husband to look off to the right away from the rocks.

"Look, Harvey!" she almost screeched. "There's a whole bunch of them coming to join their friends!"

The balding man looked casually at the group of racing black backs headed towards the rock.

"Must be a convention," he muttered to himself.

The group stopped as the boat passed. Six heads regarded the passersby.

"Oh, they're looking at us!" the woman squealed.

"Yeah, yeah, Cathy, so they're lookin' at us...probably want a hand-out!" Harvey said, annoyed yet again.

"They look like they're talking to each other!" Cathy cackled, disclosing her Bronx accent.

"Oh, for cryin' out loud!" Harvey moaned. "They're just confused by the boat! Look at the fort, will ya?"

"They're harmless," Dearg pointed out as the boat slipped past. He addressed the younger seals who were staring with wide, brown eyes.

"Can you imagine?" Jan barked lowly, "They're taking pictures of us and when they get back home they will show friends and nobody could ever in a million years believe who we are!"

The group bobbed on the waves a while longer as Dearg repeated for the tenth time the 'rules' for venturing out of the bay today.

It seemed maddening for Jan and Jonathon as well as they waited through it again. The current was so fast and strong. It was high tide and as such the river was running towards Bath, not the open sea beyond. Everything was just ripe for exploring. The depths were well near ninety feet and the rocks below were tumbled by the ancient river's power and promised nooks and crevasses and who knew what?

"Now," Dearg growled, and they understood, "We move very slowly towards the rock. The seals will at first look at us like strangers who are here to steal fish or worse steal mates. You know what to do. Also, you'll 'know' if anybody else shows up. I think they will. Word is out."

With that, he ducked back under the waves and the entourage followed suit.

Approaching slowly as directed, when they got close to the rock that was covered in seal forms, they waited with their heads just showing. Almost immediately, some commotion started on the outcropping. Barks and brays and growls alerted the colony to possible theat.

One large male reared his now sun-dried brown head and bared sharp teeth. Jan was almost alarmed before she realized she had the same type in her mouth, only not as large.

Gradually, the newness wore off and since Hunter or Dearg or Jonathon didn't try to make any aggressive moves, and indeed postured around Shere and Celia and Jan as to tell the colony 'these are under our protection, they are not available' the group on the rock settled back down and went back to snoozing.

Jan could not help wonder at the five or six pups that peeked out sheepishly from under their mother's flippers. Natural curiosity was made cuter by downy coats and huge eyes.

Satisfied that no show of force was intended, Dearg moved the group off and up river.

It was another thrilling, exhilarating romp as the younger ones explored everything and anything. Celia chased Jonathon, who allowed himself to be caught when he wanted to. Jan spun and twisted and cavorted and played like a mad thing.

Even Hunter seemed to enjoy the openness and appeared to be having a good time.

With a shock, Jan found the first wreck.

She had been briefed about how many boats and hulks of boats, big and small, were littered on the rough bottom of the river.

This one was an old small wooden fishing or lobster boat that was resting on the rocks and covered in barnacles, mussels, and thick, soft moss-like green and brown seaweed.

Her brother soon found the thing as well and he and Celia and Jan poked their snouts into the old wheel house and looked at the remnants of rotted lines and such.

Dearg was quick to swim up and with motions reminded the youths that such lines and traps and cabins were the real danger here. A seal could get caught up and drowned.

But even the warning, while heeded respectfully, did little to diminish the joyous nature of the outing.

Shere, uncharacteristically, started to swim closer to Dearg and spun around him as they moved. It gave Jan a good feeling and made her think again as to the mystery as to why she always seemed so dour and sad.

They moved with the current past places they had learned by studying Fin's nautical charts and which Red had pointed out. There was Lee Island, very large and with a shallow landward passage to be explored maybe later. Goat Island was small and flat. Local lore had it that it got its name from sailors returning to Bath leaving livestock there so as not to have to go through a lengthy quarantine or more likely having a tax levied on them. Goats and small sheep were good items for voyages since they ate little and were a source of meat that didn't need preserving.

Several more ships shared the waterway with the Selchies. Most were pleasure craft with sport fishermen trying for the trophy sized Striped Bass that were deep in the channels. They were elusive to the fishermen, but Jonathon and Hunter chased the giants for their own sport.

Of all the underwater oddities present in the great river the one that caught most attention was a submarine of a fish that silently glided along the bottom. Copper-colored wavy backs and long, thin snouts with barbells that looked like whiskers; the primitive sturgeon prowled as it had for eons unchanged. Jan remember that they were protected now as they had been fished to almost extinction.

The most unwelcomed inhabitant, or so Jan felt, was the abundant black and slithering eels that made the cracks in the rocks home. These, too, Jan had read, had been a staple for humans in days gone by. Now, they were mostly caught for Striper bait.

Crab traps were another constant danger to be avoided. The lines were shaggy with aged seaweed and waved hauntingly in the tide.

With Dearg in the lead, they raced hurriedly past the industrial Bath Iron Works. There was no reason, as explained beforehand, to hang around the area. Patrol boats kept all human traffic away as well.

Passing under the tall bridge that connected Bath with Woolwich, they lingered just long enough to get a good seal's eye view of the pretty town. Gone were the docks and warehouses of yesteryear, but just as it was on dry land, the town gave off a pleasant and timeless quality.

Jonathon had been noting all along the trip the birds overhead. Not only Ospreys but Bald Eagles had their great aeries, or nests, in the tall trees lining the ledge-like shore.

They came to a swirling meeting of waters where the Androscoggin River met the Kennebec. Numerous small islands, many with little camps or cabins perched on them, dotted the area.

Moving just beyond, they came into a calmer wide area known as Merrymeeting Bay; possibly named from the early fur traders' Rendezvous or to give the area an appeal to Puritan English settlers.

Here, Dearg selected a low, uninhabited rock and the group slowly hauled themselves out for a sunning and a rest.

The warmth of the sun was lazy and produced a sleepy quality associated with all seals, it seemed.

Jan noted that Shere lay close to Dearg. Of course Celia was nestled into Jonathon. Gladly, Hunter seemed oblivious to his loner status and stretched out and yawned. His white teeth were long and showed promise as to his future alpha-male status.

That left Jan to dreamily allow thoughts of not only Maggie-

Shannon but other, more distant hints of personalities to share in the simple pleasure of the solar radiation.

She felt, just at the dim twilight of her mind, a feeling of utter peace as a motherly presence suckled a roly-poly pup. Also, a strong and alert slender female searching an unfamiliar coastline that smacked of a cold, salty wind.

Then there were snippets of hearth fires...smoky, peaty heat with the sounds of the ocean just outside the small cottage. Another presence was holding her close...a welcomed and comforting male presence.

That new sensation caused her to open her eyes. Or was it something else?

As she looked out into the calm bay waters two sets of seal eyes were watching her.

She recognized them straight away.

Without alarm, she made a short bark to the others.

"I think the family's here," she said.

Dearg shot his head up in sudden interest, but he softened as soon as he perceived the heads floating not ten yards away from the rock.

"Jonathon," he rumbled quietly, "Why don't you and your sister go say hello to your grandparents."

He looked down at Shere.

"Introductions might be in order?"

Shere gracefully slid into the water and motioned for the twins to do the same.

As they approached the male and female waiting for them, Shere surface and breathed the greeting.

"Uncle Augus, Aunt Margret," she said lovingly, "So very good to see you."

The two nodded back politely. The female was the first to speak.

"You are as pretty as ever, my dear. We don't see enough of you, but maybe someday things will change."

The male, his muzzle somewhat gray with apparent dignified age, took up the conversation.

"Indeed," he voiced in a deep and silky way. "Perhaps, my beautiful niece, these youngsters here might have a say in a new order of things?"

Jan was touched by the voice. She had thought for so many years about not having a grandfather and now here he was; only he was a Selchie, a seal for now.

Margret moved first.

"You are Jonathon," she indicated the young man. "I see your father's eyes in you. And what a brave young thing! If I'm not wrong, that's Loki's skin?"

Jonathon nodded, trying to look proud.

"That speaks volumes," Augus stated. "You have been given a great honor in this, and it brings even more honor to all of us in the family."

"Oh!" Margret gazed at Jan. "Janet! My sweet, wonderful girl! I sense you have such a soul! And it's my beloved Maggie-Shannon that has chosen you!"

Jan thought that if a seal's eyes could cry, both her and her grandmother surely would be.

Margret moved to nuzzle Jan and a flood of emotions opened up.

"We're so very, very, very sorry!" Margret almost pleaded. "We wanted to know you, to see you grow, but..."

"We'll have time to explain later," Augus said deeply. "A great injustice has been done to us, but I feel the reckoning is coming."

"There's so much to tell, so much to catch up on!" Margret gushed.

Jonathon interrupted rather coldly.

"You could say we've been wondering,"

Jan was shocked, as this was not like her brother at all, but he was of late quite different and more forward.

"Lots of birthdays, Christmases, grandparents day...you know."

"You have a right to be jaded," Augus conceded. "Only, there are reasons."

"Sure," Jonathon said rather too quickly.

Jan shot a glance at him but it was no use. He was locked with his grandfather's eyes.

Margret backed away from Jan slowly.

"In time," she started.

"Hold on," her husband said, still looking at Jonathon a bit differently. "I like what I see. He has his father's pride and strength and the warrior spirit he doesn't know about from The Old Ones."

"I wouldn't know much about my father except what I've been told," Jonathon said back. "And it seems that what I *haven't* been told grows exponentially every passing day."

If she had feet, Jan would have kicked him.

Augus stared at the youth with steely pride.

"Niece?" he asked sideways to Shere. "May I have an invite to my brother's house?"

"Of course," Shere remarked demurely. "Always welcomed, and you will honor us."

"Then," he said to Jonathon, "Can we travel together?"

Jonathon just turned and started to swim away.

"Hold it!" Dearg barked, jumping into the water as he could see there was no time to waste in following the hot-headed young man. Celia and a reluctant Hunter followed.

As they swam, Augus and Margret greeted Celia and Hunter with much fanfare and courtly manners. The group retraced the trip, only now with the outgoing tide.

Jan finally managed to catch up to Jonathon.

"Will you slow down!?" she gasped. "What has gotten into you, anyway?"

He finally slowed his pace, which was a relief to the whole group.

"Nothing!" he snarled.

"Come on, Jonathon!" Jan pleaded. "We finally get to meet our grandparents and you all but slap them in the face with a flipper!"

He turned his head and bared his teeth in a manner very different from the brother she thought she knew.

"I'm just not going to get all mushy when they haven't bothered to make any sort of contact with us up till now! And, I might add, I'm just a little 'miffed' at our own mother for not telling us they exist! How's that for starters!" He ducked back under the waves and Jan followed.

They both winced suddenly at a piercing, audible high-pitched noise.

"And what the heck is *that*!" he surfaced and further ranted to his sister who had surfaced as well. "I've been hearing it all day and it's driving me nuts!"

"Please calm down," Jan implored, "Let's just give them a chance? OK?"

Jonathon seemed to tone down his ire. Celia slid up next to him acting like she had done something wrong. He slowed further; as it was obvious he was making her struggle, and nuzzled her muzzle to reassure her.

Jan moved back to the others.

"What is that noise?" she asked Dearg as they breached to breathe.

"I don't know," he answered back strangely. "But I don't like it. Augus?"

"I'm not sure," the venerable Selchie admitted. "We'll talk to Fin. I have not heard it before today, at least, not around here, I think? It sounds like a porpoise, maybe, but no..."

"It goes right through you," Shere noted. "Could it be the humans, the Navy people?"

"I've never heard it around here before," Augus repeated. "Only, maybe…"

He let his thoughts trail off and the group focused on keeping close to Jonathon.

As they passed the Maritime Museum the tour boat was just returning from the trip out near Sequin Light. As Jonathon was still in the lead, much to the annoyance of Dearg, they had to slow as the boat turned to position and dock.

"Oh, look, Harvey!" the woman at the side stood up and shouted. "It's the same ones again! They came back to say goodbye to us!"

"For Pete's sake," Harvey winced, "Give it a rest, already?! You seen one seal, you seen them all, they all look alike, don't go on like…"

The boat was struck by a small but forceful wake from another passing boat. It jarred the occupants slightly but not too badly.

However, Cathy had to hold on to her camera with one hand and grab for the seat back with the other. This left no hand for the floppy pink flowered hat on her head. It tumbled into the river.

"Ow! My hat!" she howled as the thing floated out of reach.

"Fah-get-a-bout-it!" Harvey railed. "I hated that thing anyway. I'll get ya a better one, ah-right?"

Like a shot out of a cannon, Jonathon burst with a speed not available to either seals or most Selchies. He swam under the floating hat and shot up with it poised on his seal forehead. Racing back towards the boat, with Dearg bubbling an underwater 'No!' Jonathon looked up at the woman and her gawking husband and with a flip of his head he sailed the wet thing straight into her face.

She fell back onto her seat with a flopping motion.

Harvey stared at the brown seal eyes looking up at him.

"Really?" he asked.

Jonathon snorted loudly and ducked back underneath the waves.

Pleased with himself, alone in the thought, he spun and cavorted all the way back to near the opening to the bay that lay in front of Fin's abode.

That's where he felt the unsettling presence.

Something made him slow up and go on the tense defense without knowing why he did so.

The others schooled up around him and it was obvious they felt something too.

Augus and Dearg moved to the front and motioned for the rest of the group to get behind them with their backs to the bay.

Jonathon swam up and nudged Hunter and the two youths joined the other males.

Slowly, leisurely and casually, but nonetheless menacingly, three large forms glided into view.

Just as Jan had recognized their grandparents, Jonathon had no problems figuring out who the interlopers were.

It was the three males they had seen before. The two that circled around the third were darker and just a bit smaller despite the hulking thickness of all three. After a few more terse minutes of silent posturing they broke the surface with their large, knotty heads.

The brown one in the middle was the only one to speak.

"Well, well, well..."

Jonathon immediately decided the oily voice was as insincere and annoying as any he had ever heard in person or in film. It might have been conjured-up by George Sanders, who played many sleazy roles as well as debonair ones including the voice for the tiger in Disney's 'The Jungle Book', or maybe by Edward G. Robinson as a patronizing, dirty gangster.

"So what do we have here?" 'King' slithered the words, "A jolly little party that I wasn't invited to? Pity..."

"My, my...what an interesting group," he continued in nauseating fashion. "I demand you introduce me, Augus."

The 'demand' made the fur on Jonathon's neck bristle.

"You know full well who these are," Augus said shortly. "And you know what homage you must pay."

'King' frowned a pathetically false face.

"Oh, very well," he huffed.

"I suppose you," he pointed his snout at Hunter, "And the girl, there, are from The Northern Tribe. Very well…"

He made a phony nod of his big head.

"I extend to you the Rights of Hospitality. Whatever."

Hunter now made a move forward in anger at the obvious slight but was held in check by Dearg and Augus.

"As to you two," 'King' flipped towards Jonathon and Jan, "Here we are. This is my Tribe. You would do well to remember that."

"Enough!" snorted Augus. "That's yet but another insult to my family and your betters!"

The two darker forms on either side of the brown one started to move forward.

Hunter and Dearg and Jonathon and Augus bared teeth in unchecked aggression.

The brown one stopped the other two with raised flippers.

"Oh, don't waste time here!" he oozed. "The Gathering is coming. We all know where we stand here, don't we, Augus?"

There was a tense silence.

Jonathon looked to his grandfather but was confused to see something conciliatory in his manner.

"Anyway," 'King' continued, "It's good to see you bringing new breeding stock in."

His eye roved sickly over Jan and just as Jonathon was about to forget everything and charge the monster an overwhelming underwater sonic wave stopped all of the forms in the bay.

Like a wall of sound that burst through the water and rattled teeth and inner ears and even skin and blubber and bones, it stunned everything to shocked silence. The overall effect was one of mindless, primeval fear and made flight seem the only option.

'King' and his goons shot off without further fanfare like frightened rabbits after the hunter's gun.

Augus and Dearg shook their heads but after a moment of collection they quickly led the group into the safety of the bay.

It was again decided for the women to 'change' first.

Shere came out first and ran to gather another robe for her aunt to use. She returned just as Margret was in need of the garment.

When she had shed her skin, Jan was a bit stunned that her grandmother did not look like the white haired, stout, wrinkled and smiling little old lady she had imagined. Far from it, she was as tall and lithe as Shere with long black straight hair. Her eyes were hauntingly blue-green and large and almond shaped. She did not appear to be much older than her niece.

Remembering what Fin had taught about Selchies that spend most of their time in the sea not aging as quickly, she was still struck by a smile that she half-remembered in her early memories. It must have been like her father's.

The graceful lady helped Jan on with her robe and then she turned her around and played a long, slender and delicate hand along Jan's cheek.

"May I, my Dear?" she almost whispered.

As Jan could do nothing but get caught up in the spell, the woman bent tenderly and lightly kissed the younger girls flushed cheek.

Celia glided up the ramp and shakily but still lovingly took of her skin and robed as well.

Shere began to hurry them out of the place before the men arrived.

Celia and Jan went upstairs to change. Their ears were still ringing from the whatever-it-was strange sound. Their knees were a bit wobbly on the stairs as well.

Shere and Margret sought out Fin. He had been watching for them out on the dock and could just barely make out the confrontation with 'King'.

Margret embraced Fin warmly and then Shere started in with wild, dark eyes imploring an explanation of the eerie blast that had rocked all of them so. Her father did his best to calm her down and said everything was alright and he would talk to the men and she and Margret should get upstairs and change before any passing boat spied two women in black hooded capes with more men dressed the same way soon to follow.

Shere did as told reluctantly but she was also very rattled. Margret shook her thin head in puzzlement but had a sense of grace and tact about her as the two moved towards the house.

Fin did not wait on the dock and went to meet the men in the boathouse.

Hunter came out of the water first and didn't even seem to notice Fin very much. He just shed his skin, packed it neatly in the pocket of the robe, and donned the garment.

"What's for dinner?" was his only question.

Fin waved him away with a smile.

Expecting Jonathon, surprisingly Augus was next and after the very personal shedding of the skin, the younger white-haired brother handed the robe to the older reddish-blonde haired one who looked taller and quite younger than his sibling.

The two hugged and slapped each other on the back in a fast but meaningful exchange.

"Quite a day," Augus started.

"Good to see you, brother. Let's wait and talk later?"

Augus nodded to prudence.

Jonathon finally appeared and, this being only his second time, he launched himself up the ramp as if it were child's play. He rather sullenly shed his skin and didn't seem as embarrassed as before. He picked up a robe and slammed his arms through it and stalked out before the two brothers could get a word in.

"That's different," Fin remarked.

"He's very angry. At me, at everything, I think," Augus sighed.

"Good," Fin shot back, "He needs some growing up. He's got worse ahead, ah-yuh."

Dearg splashed out of the water with one red eye peering over his back. When he had robed, he started in with the rant.

"I let it go before!" he almost yelled, "Now I want to know what you know! I think me teeth are loose after that blast! I don't know what it was, was following us all day, but I admit I liked seeing 'King' and his lackeys turn tail and fly like pigeons when the cat's among them!"

"Slow down!" Fin said with hands raised. "Tell me everything!"

Dearg described the day with the sound following them around from nowhere and everywhere and then the massive shock wave that affected them all.

Augus was stroking his red-bearded chin in thought and waited a moment before offering a statement.

"I've been around for a few years and more. I thought I had heard everything in the sea, as well as on the land, and yet I'm struggling to put a finger on this. It's certainly no whale or the likes. It's so much stronger than even the Belugas' song way up north. But it's not whale or dolphin; and it's not the man-made sonar that we know they have around here to protect the shipyard. I feel it's made by something...alive. My poor old memory wants to believe I've heard it once before...on a trip...but where?"

Fin smiled wider.

"Right-so!" Dearg railed. His eyes were blazing red coals. "You spill the beans, Fin, or I swear I'm going hunting tonight and I might run into some beastie that might do-me-in but I have to know!"

"Simmer down," the white-haired man chuckled. "Don't get your beans in a boil! What I'm going to tell you has to be kept a secret. For a while, anyway…"

Jan had just entered the hallway, dressed now in shorts and a tee shirt, when she saw her brother slam the door behind him into his room. Celia came out as well and looked perplexed. She started towards Jonathon's door but Jan stopped her with a look and a gentle hand.

Marie appeared out of nowhere and was toweling off her hair.

"Hey!" she voiced, "What are you girls up to?"

"Mom," Jan started, "Something happened today; something weird. It's gotten us all shook up, I think."

"Really?" her mother asked, furrowing her brow. "What was it?"

For some reason, Jan got a strange feeling and didn't feel like going into details.

"Let's wait and talk to the others, OK?"

"OK," Marie smiled. "I'll check on your brother."

"I wouldn't do that," Jan warned. "He's not in a very good mood. There's something else. Our grandparents are here. We met them today. I think they are downstairs."

"Oh," her mother said matter-of-factly, "Yep, I saw them on the way up. I've only seen them once myself. As land-people, I mean. You should get acquainted."

With that, she smiled again and went down the hall to her room, towel in hand, without further adieu.

Jan looked at Celia as if to get some reassurance of the odd behavior but only got the blank stare back.

Shaking her head, she motioned for Celia to follow and started downstairs.

The parlor was cozy with bodies. Fin motioned, when he saw Jan and Celia, for the two to come in. Jan heeded a smile and a long, graceful, beckoning hand from the beautiful, black haired lady seated on the old sofa.

She was wearing an old style white dress with an embroidered front panel that had to be many, many decades old. Still, it became her and brought out her dark features that were in contrast to her husband who sat beside her. He wore a yellowed once-white cable knit fisherman's sweater that Jan realized must have come from Fin's old closet as well. The tan pants were a bit more contemporary but not by much. His wild, red-blonde hair and beard made him seem timeless.

Both of them were casually barefoot.

Jan perched herself on the sofa arm next to her grandmother who beamed at her and stroked her bare arm. Celia gracefully folded herself on the floor in a cat-like reclining pose.

Dearg and Shere and Hunter were not present.

The conversation was between brothers. Both had mugs of what Jan figured was the black rum. Her grandmother had a small, dainty cup and saucer of steaming tea on her small lap.

Fin was answering light, polite questions about land-people that Augus had known. Some had passed, most really, and with each name the red bearded brother closed his kind eyes and nodded in reverence.

Then it was Fin's turn to ask after apparent members of the Tribe. Surprisingly, Jan noted that her grandfather did not appear to know a lot about anything going on around him aside from reports of numbers of fish and changing channel patterns.

Finally, a quiet silence fell over the old room. The ticking of a clock on the wall and faint static from the weather radio in the kitchen were the only disturbances.

"So," Jan's grandfather said softly, only it sounded like a gunshot in the thick void of sound, "I imagine you have some questions of your own, Janet?"

"I prefer Jan," she said automatically. It was not comfortable to be the center the attention suddenly.

"Of course," her grandmother soothed.

Jan had often heard it said, but for the first time in her life, here was a voice that could have read the phone book or a dictionary with eye-closing, rapturous results. The velvety tones were like a gentle wave washing up a smooth sand beach and then soothingly fading back down again.

As it was apparent it was her time to speak, Jan waited longer than she wanted to.

"I, that is, my brother and I, just need some time. We've had a lot to process, lately. I don't know what to ask, what to say, or even what to believe anymore."

Fin, his brother, and his brother's wife smiled in a way that should have felt comforting, but it didn't feel that way to Jan.

The next words spoken completely took Jan by surprise.

"Do you have a comb, my sweet?" her grandmother asked.

Startled, Jan blinked and then found some words of her own.

"I, I've got some brushes," she admitted.

"Then," the dark haired lady smiled back, "Would you two pretty young ladies help me untangle a year's worth of knots?"

Not seeing anything wrong with the long, black tresses, Jan shrugged and she and Celia stood up. Margret did the same in a slow, somewhat unsteady way and placed her tea cup on a side table.

"I don't have my land-legs, yet!" she purred.

Celia offered a strong arm and Jan did likewise. The three left the room and started back upstairs.

After they had gone, the conversation in the parlor did not resume. Only the occasional sound of sipping could have been heard.

Jan ushered her grandmother, who did not look anything like a grandmother, and Celia into the room Jan had been occupying.

Pausing at the door, Margret peered in with a slight smile but hesitation.

"I know," Jan said. "Maggie Shannon died here. But she's OK with it, and so am I."

"Of course she would be!" her grandmother agreed. She allowed herself, stronger now, to be led to the small bed. Seated, she obviously saw no mirror.

"I'll have to trust to you ladies," she beamed.

Jan produced her own brown brush and a silver-handled one that she had found earlier in the bedside table drawer.

Celia took the silver one and the two began to slowly move the instruments through the luxurious, raven strands that fell well below the older woman's thin waist. With each passing stoke, the hair seemed to shine brighter with a blue-black hue.

Presently, Margret spoke through what was obviously pleasing to her.

"Celia, I have met your father. Once; at the Old Sow. He is...regal."

Celia blushed and curtsied slightly.

"I'm talking about," Margret now said to Jan, "A very special place right on the border of the two Tribes; between Maine and Canada. It's an area that flows around many small islands and the mainland and creates whirlpools in the changing tides. They call it the Old Sow perhaps from the sound of the water. It is a sacred place."

Margret continued.

"Jan, your mother is very special. More than you know. I sense some things about her that I don't understand. I only know that she made my son very, very happy."

"I'd prefer," Jan said flatly, "That you don't speak of him in the past tense."

"Of course," Margret said after a small silence. "My Dear, you have to understand that we didn't see much of him after he decided to stay with Fin."

Jan stopped brushing.

"And why would that be?" she asked, sounding now like her disgruntled brother.

"Sweet," her grandmother continued, "We stay at sea. We don't have a land house like some of the Tribe. We prefer..."

"Excuse me," Jan tested, but not too bluntly, "But you prefer to not see your son? Or his children? I'm beginning to see why Jonathon is so upset."

"I didn't mean..." Margret started.

"Again," Jan tried to control her rising blood in the way her mother said was Irish, "Excuse me, I mean no disrespect, but I'm not ready to get all sentimental and teary, despite the fact I want to like you and all, but what if I do? You'll soon go back and what then?"

Celia had paused her hand as well.

A tense moment filled the room. Jan felt something deep inside her longing for a connection she had been denied for so long. But her anger took over.

"I'm sorry," she said, placing the brush on the bed and stalking out.

She ran blindly into her mother's arms in the hallway and simply broke down crying.

Marie moved the two of them into her room to the bed and they sat and just rocked together until Jan's tears subsided. Then a flood of words started that could not be stopped.

Jan told her mother about what had happened with her grandmother, what had happened with 'King' and his thugs and the wall of sound. Then she spilled what she had learned about the young men who had disappeared and what she now thought about Shere's not wanting to appear alluring because of that incident and maybe because she looked so much like her mother.

Marie let her talk until she seemed to want another side to the questions.

"I think you and your brother deserve to feel slighted about not having your grandparents in your life. I did, for many years, and the same with Fin. Only, I didn't make much of a point to do anything about it either."

She let that sink in before continuing.

"As for them, I don't know them. There is a lot more to discover here, I'm sure. Your father said some vague things about them having a place on land once, but that was long before he arrived. I just don't know. I do think that they want to know you but I'll bet they are just as nervous and not sure of what to say or do as you two are."

Jan realized, no matter how she wanted to look at it and be mad or feel sorry for herself, that it was probably true. And she had just driven a wedge that probably hurt deeply.

Marie pressed on.

"As for the thing with Shere, I could ask Fin but I didn't hear the story. You will have to do that. I think he has been fair in telling just about everything he can without going too far. Right?"

Jan sniffed and nodded.

"That leaves just one other point and I'm going to ask you to trust me again. About what happened with 'King'...let me say that you are being watched-out for. I haven't told you everything all your life because I have my reasons and, right or wrong, that's my call to make."

She put her forehead against her daughter's and stared into her eyes.

"We tell each other the truth. Later, when I ask you how a date went or what happened in certain situations I expect you to tell me what you need to tell me. But I don't expect everything. Do we understand each other?"

Jan was shocked but in a mature way and she hugged her mother in an answer.

"Now," Marie said, straightening her back, "I have an idea. See what you think."

Jan was suddenly attentive and serious.

"I asked Fin a few days ago if he knew anybody in the area who did women's hair. I need a trim. So do you. I certainly think Celia would jump at a chance to girl-up. Think we could talk your grandmother into it and maybe with some careful and skillful lady-charms get Shere to agree?"

Jan smiled.

"I had a few moments with her over the past week or so. She might agree if we play it right. We have to get Dearg involved. What did Fin say?"

"Well," her mother smiled back, "he suggested a friend of the family from years back who has her shop in her home nearby. Can't get much better than that. Apparently, this elder lady knows just who the family is and everything."

"Let's get to work!" Jan agreed.

Margret and Celia had just gotten to the foot of stairs when Jonathon caught up with them. Without a word but with a now warm smile he placed himself between the two and, arms in arms, he walked the stunned but smiling ladies back into the parlor.

Fin and his brother were sitting just as they had been.

Before Margret could speak, Jonathon did so instead.

"Grandfather, Grandmother, I apologize for my rude behavior. It is an honor to meet you and I hope to get to know you better very soon."

Margret smiled her beguiling smile and took a seat next to her husband.

"Thank you, son," Augus said slowly and softly. "I realized now what a fool I may have been in staying away so long. I had my reasons, but that may change soon. We shall talk of that presently, yes we will."

Jonathon nodded in a very grown-up way. He was amazed at what he was doing. He put it down to his recently discovered 'partner' Lucky who seemed to bring out the things he had been wanting to bring out in himself for a long time. He felt strength and courage and was not ashamed to admit he was quick and childish in his earlier manner. He knew he didn't know everything. But he was learning. And he was a keen student.

And he knew how to wear a fedora.

11

The phone in the small office of the Sequin Island Light Observatory jangled for almost a minute before it was answered by Kim the intern scientist. Instead of putting the call on hold she simply put the black hand piece on top of some jumbled papers on the desk and yelled. That was all the 'on hold' function the grant money would buy.

"Dave!" she called. "Dave! It's for you!"

The older man shuffled in with his wind-tousled wispy hair and picked up the call. After some time answering the questions he hung up and found Kim outside jotting down bird numbers in the log book. He had to speak-up to be heard over the din of squawking sea birds.

"That's a new one," he said. The girl let one thin eyebrow rise in interest.

"That was the Navy up at the shipyard. They wanted to know if we had seen anything unusual in the way of marine mammals yesterday."

"Where?" Kim asked.

"Didn't say," Dave continued. "The commander just said that their hydrophones had picked-up a...a bloop."

"Really?" the girl asked with an excited smile. "Like *THE* bloop?"

"I think that's what he meant. It's got them worried. I could hear it in what he said and didn't say. Words like 'anomaly' and 'undetermined acoustic signal origin'."

"Wow!" Kim almost laughed. "They have it recorded?"

Dave nodded.

"I'd sure love to hear that!" she admitted. "We've all heard the declassified one but I've heard there are others. Nobody can figure out what it is. Just a massive blast of underwater sound. What do you think?"

"Not my line of study," Dave shrugged. "But you know how touchy everybody is since the courts ruled against the Navy here in Maine and blamed some whale deaths on them. They have spent oodles of our tax dollars flying over the Gulf and marking numbers and migration patterns in the settlement. We could have used some of that money!"

"I don't think the Navy had much to do with any whale killings!" Kim conjectured. "More likely, the very volume of commercial maritime shipping traffic has messed-up the animals' acoustic habitat. Just like I don't think this new mandatory sinking lobster pot line has anything much to do with saving whales. The big whales are too far out to get caught in lobster lines. All it's done is cost the poor fisherman more money that they don't have."

"That's not the thoughts of most of the marine biology community," Dave warned.

"Sure," Kim waved off, "They have the ear of Washington right now. We can't even get new cameras when we need them."

"Especially ones that keep getting smashed," Dave sighed. "Whoever was doing that in Seal Cove has their way now. We can't afford to keep changing them."

"So back to 'The Bloop' and all," Kim stared again. "Any thoughts on the matter?"

Dave scratched his balding pate before speaking again.

"I would bet a few beers that it's something of theirs that not everybody is in the need to know enough to know about. One hand not knowing what the other is doing. Those Aegis Class destroyers they are cranking-out up river are some sophisticated, scary war machines. And I'm glad of it. And the new one? Even more secret and scary. But that's what makes the Navy nervous when somebody else might be snooping around for secrets."

"Right," Kim agreed. "Oh well, back to the birds."

Marie and Jan strolled together in the bight morning sun down onto the dock and out to where Fin was loading fish into several waiting skiffs. The skiffs would in turn take the ripe beauties to lobster boats ready to start their day on the out-going tide.

It was too late to turn back when Jan spotted the second boat in line's helmsman.

Red waved to her and Jan waved back hoping she had not turned a bright crimson color.

Just as Fin finished with the first boat and Red motored up, Marie shaded her eyes with a hand to gaze off into the river. It seemed rather busy today.

One rather large boat bore the unmistakable orange and white and blue stripes of The Coast Guard. It seemed to be prowling first one steep rocky bank and then crossing to go over the deep portion of the river near the mouth of Atkin's bay.

Fin only looked up casually at the women and greeted Red.

Red greeted Fin but kept shooting glances to Jan.

"How are you, Red?"

"Good, you?"

"Load 'er up today?"

"Yep, Dad's waitin'...I'm taking ma brother's place today as Sternman!"

The news was spoken with great pride.

"Finest kind!" Fin congratulated. "Just for that, here's some I've been keeping for a special occasion like this!"

He pulled the lid off of a dingy plastic container and held it for the young man to whiff.

Jan and Marie tried not to wince even from their distance.

"Much obliged!" Red savored as if sniffing fine brandy.

Fin replaced the lid and handed it to Red. Then he started to transfer the wooden tray of the other bait. It was apparent that Red wanted to say something and Jan selfishly thought it was to her when all their attention was diverted to an approaching vessel.

It was a Zodiac inflatable boat with an unmistakable three man Navy crew aboard. All wore the heavy, protective float coats and Kevlar helmets and dark goggles. The man at the wheel slowed the craft long enough for the Petty Officer in charge beside him to stand and wave a greeting. The man in the stern was armed with a tactical assault rifle. All three had side arms.

"Ahoy, Sir! U. S. Navy...Permission to come alongside?"

Fin waved him on.

"They've been swarming all day," Red said quietly. "Don't know why. There's no launch scheduled up to the yard until next month."

"Reckon we'll find out soon enough," Fin said lowly.

The boat didn't throw a line; instead the man at the wheel masterfully kept the craft in place with forward and backward slight bumps of the motor.

"Good day to you folks!" The spokesman called dutifully. "Gentleman, we are inquiring of all persons utilizing this stretch of waterway, especially professionals like yourselves, if there have been any sightings of marine mammals other than seals in the vicinity."

Red looked at Fin, who only smiled like an old native senior.

"Like, dolphins and such?" Red inquired.

"More to the point, Sir, something larger. Pilot whales or the like? Perhaps even larger."

Red shook his head in a negative fashion.

Fin still grinned a buffoonish confused smile.

"We have reason to believe," the serviceman continued stiffly, "That such an animal may be stranded close by and in danger. We wish to see to its' safety."

"Whale?" Fin cackled in a voice Marie and Jan didn't recognize. It sounded simple.

"Ain't no whales up in he-ah, sonny. Ain't no dolphins, neither. Tell ya what, though. Go over to Boothbay and they got boats what'll take ya out to see 'em!"

After a moment of silence punctuated only by the Zodiac's motor, the man standing next to the wheelman snapped a finger to his brow in a sort of salute.

"You folks have a fine, safe day!"

The craft backed away and swung towards the open river when it suddenly slowed again. The man in the aft section placed his automatic weapon against a gunwale and produced a net on an extendable pole. He scooped something from the water in the small cove. Then the Zodiac sped off.

"See that?" Red pointed when they had gone. "They're all over the bay. But just in the bay."

Jan craned to see what Red was talking about. There were floating, dead fish scattered sporadically on the surface of the water.

"I've seen 'em," Fin said, back to his natural voice. He didn't look at the younger man as he cast off the line and so signaled the transaction and conversation was over.

"Navy or Coast Guard must have churned 'em up with all this commotion."

"Maybe," Red said without believing it. "Thanks, Fin. My father will thank you too. I'll pay you when we haul the catch in, tomorrow or next day."

"I know you will," Fin smiled and waved. "Good hunting, young fella!"

"See ya, Janet!" Red called, and was off.

Jan blushed and waited for the kidding to begin from her mother. Oddly, there was none.

Instead, Marie was looking at the floating fish.

Fin finally caught her eye and they looked at each other for a moment.

"Not a good day to venture out into the water," he finally said flatly.

Marie nodded. Then she seemed to snap back and spoke to him.

"Fin, Jan and I have had an idea but she wants to ask you something first, OK?"

"Sure," he shrugged, back to his warm self.

Marie pressed her daughter's shoulder and then turned and stiffly walked away apparently lost in thought.

Jan started lightly by telling Fin about their plan to give all the girls a make-over. She avoided using Shere's name but she figured by Fin's silence he knew she was to be included. Jan tried to paint a picture of a girl's day out and a pampering. Fin smiled but didn't agree just yet. He finally looked at Jan in the way she had come to know meant 'and what else?'

He wiped his hands on his overalls after splashing them in the water and motioned for them to start back down the dock. Jan figured it was now or never.

"Fin," she started, "The other day at the church social, I heard something. Something about something that happened with two brothers."

"Always wagging tongues in Phippsburg," he sighed. "What do you want to know, dear?"

Jan gathered her nerve and just said it.

"Do you know what happened to those boys?"

Fin's smile seemed to diminish slightly. They had come to the end of the dock and he sat down on an upside down blue plastic bucket. He motioned for Jan to use the white one there in a similar fashion. She did so and started to stare at the ground, beginning to regret she had started the whole thing.

Gently, Fin placed his rough, weathered index finger under Jan's chin and lifted slowly until their eyes locked.

"You are family," he said in a serious voice. "Like my father, I will not tell a lie. But first you have to get a picture in your mind. These Gaither 'boys' were not innocent little lambs. They were black hearted ne'er-do-wells that had done things to a string of young girls that I won't talk about. Get it?"

Jan didn't have to say or do anything. Her eyes did her talking.

"You are almost grown," Fin continued. "You have probably seen a lot more than I care to think about in the city. You certainly have already run into things here that can and will be dangerous. Life is ugly with some people. Maggie-Shannon knew that."

He let the thoughts sink in.

"Those criminals came here that night, to my house, to the house of my family, with evil thoughts and planned evil deeds. Now, let me ask you. If I were a farmer, and two foxes came one night to kill my chickens, would I catch them and turn them over to people who would rant and rave and say they weren't to blame for their wicked ways and that they could be rehabilitated and we should find out why they wanted to kill my chickens and then say it was somebody else's fault they went bad and then let them go again...?"

"Or would I make sure they would never hurt anybody ever, ever anymore?"

Jan could not hold her gaze with his any longer. She stared at the ground again.

"I'm not asking you to agree with what I did or to judge me for it. I'm from old times and old ways. I used what I know and what

I am and what I've learned to make sure what I protect is safe. You have the same powers watching over you, you just don't know it fully yet."

After a time, Fin spoke again.

"I know Shere took it hard and you don't know how close she came. I think, since she has been changed by young Dearg, that she is ready to change some more. She likes you. I can tell. Talk to her."

Jan smiled and put a hand on Fin's strong shoulder as she rose.

When she was almost to the mudroom door, she heard Fin say something quietly.

"If two foxes came to harm a chicken, don't the chicken have a right to harm them first?"

The shock made Jan freeze at the door.

She shook her head out of the fog and went in.

Jan talked to Dearg. He was very interested in the plans. Then she approached her grandmother, who was more than happy with the thought. Marie and Jan both explained to Celia about the process and she was hesitant until Jonathon suggested slyly that he would like to see the outcome. Then Celia was all about it.

Finally, that afternoon, Jan had a rare chance to catch Shere cleaning some clams at the kitchen sink in preparation for dinner. She joined in the task.

Elbows touching from time to time, Jan finally got up the nerve to speak.

"Shere," she started, "My mom and my grandmother and Celia are trying to plan a trip to see a local hairdresser your father told us about."

"I heard," the dark woman said with little emotion.

"I want you to go with us," Jan said matter-of-factly.

There was a silence for a moment with only the sound of the water from the kitchen faucet running before Shere spoke.

"Why?" she asked, without looking up from her task.

That took Jan aback for an instant. She opted for the naked truth.

"Because," she said softly, "I think it's time for you to pay some attention to yourself. I've seen some of the old photographs and you were and still are a beautiful woman. Why not pamper yourself and let things go. I'd like that. I really would."

Jan braced for the coldness and the excuses or the total lack of any and a simple closing up like the clams they were washing off.

"OK," Shere said abruptly.

Jan was stunned.

"Really?" she asked incredulously.

Shere nodded and her wild, black hair shook.

"Great!" Jan smiled. "Great!"

The rest of the clams were cleaned without further conversation.

The following morning a sensible silver SUV pulled up to a quiet house off the main drag and down a short side road in Phippsburg. It was loaded with people.

Marie and Jan got out of the front seats and opened doors for Margret, Celia, and Shere in the back. Lastly, Marie opened the rear hatch and Jonathon and Hunter tumbled out of the cramped rear.

The house was situated close enough to the church yard where Jan and Hunter had spent time with the youth group. The young men had insisted on going as 'protection' and whereas Fin and Dearg had silently feared nothing, they treated the gesture with respect and bravado.

Marie knocked at a side door and it opened to a flood of female voices.

The matriarch was a round faced and round bodied cherub of sweetness. Her curly, short black hair with streaks of gray framed the beaming smile and small mouth.

"Come in!" she bubbled, "I'm so glad to see you! Margret, get in here! It's been ages! You look so wicked-good!"

The two women hugged like family.

"This," Margret introduced, "is Mother Annie. She won't let you call her anything else!"

Jan saw immediately that the features of the warm woman were a bit different than any she had seen locally so far. Her complexion was a bit darker and her little black eyes shone with a timeless sparkle. Still, she could not place the thing exactly.

Mother Annie introduced two other women in the room, which was equipped with three salon chairs and a sink with a chair for shampooing. Another table suggested a small manicuring station.

"This is my daughter Edna," Mother Annie indicated a middle aged lady that indeed looked very much like her. "And this is my Daughter-in-Law Peggy!"

Peggy was thinner and had straight blondish hair but also smiled as warmly as one could.

"I'm so glad you are here!" Mother Annie gushed again. "It's been so long since I've seen your family! Welcome back!"

Margret introduced Marie and Jan and Celia. Shere sheepishly hugged Mother Annie as they quietly appeared to remember each other.

Then the women of the salon commenced to fuss over Jonathon and Hunter. Quickly, the two made a hasty retreat for outdoors.

Outside, Jonathon had brought a soccer ball and in the grass of the church yard he began to instruct Hunter in the usage of it. He paid particular attention in letting his cousin know not to kick it too hard. It was the only one they had. Little by little, Hunter began to catch on and admitted he had played a bit when he was younger. Jonathon didn't bother asking where or under what conditions. It just felt good to pass it around.

They got to the point where they could run together and dribble back and forth. Jonathon realized all they needed was a goal and perhaps another chapter could be started in their getting to know each other.

Just as Hunter passed the ball a little ahead of a sprinting Jonathon, a rushing figure came out of the woods on the side of the yard and clumsily kicked it away. It sputtered over to the far side of yard some twenty feet across from the players.

Standing where the ball had been recklessly kicked was a black clothed, rather dingy Tommy Fields. Behind him soon appeared his crew of Glassman, Henley, and Donnelly.

Hunter jogged up as Jonathon faced the sneering, zit-marked face of the interloper.

"I'm guessing soccer isn't your forte," Jonathon said with a smile.

Fields just turned his sneer into a frown.

"Sissy sport!" he spat back.

"Funny," Jonathon mused, rubbing his jaw, "Where I come from wearing dirty out-of-style Goth rags and hanging around with only members of the same gender constitutes a questioning of masculinity."

Henley's sharp blue eyes widened and he coughed a bit of a laugh.

"That's funny!" he remarked lowly, and there was no animosity to the comment.

Glassman just stared numbly but Donnelly was looking at Hunter and not seeming to enjoy the intended confrontation.

"Hey, man!" he said to Hunter. "What's up?"

Hunter nodded back.

Fields tried to take back the moment.

"What are you two doing here? You don't belong here!"

Jonathon looked around in mock surprise.

"I didn't see any signs," He said icily, "restricting anybody with an IQ over, what, a sea slug? If so, Hunter and Donnelly and Henley and I will leave. I haven't heard Glassman speak, so the jury's still out."

Donnelly and Henley both chuckled at the remark and that

infuriated Fields even more. He got red in the face but before he could think up another comeback Jonathon pressed ahead.

"Look, guys," he said, "So we're from away. So what? What have we done to you? You want to act big and bad, so do it. Whatever floats your boat. Only, two things here; one, I only see two of you guys here who are big and bad. Henley seems decently intelligent. So where do you fit in? Why do they back your plays?"

As Fields got even redder, Jonathon continued.

"Two, we'll leave and you can make up any story you want as to how you kicked our butts or whatever. That will avoid the skull-busting my cousin Hunter wants so badly to unleash on you."

Hunter flexed his arm muscles into epic bulging shape. Then, for the first time Jonathon could remember, Hunter smiled widely and let his sharp teeth flash.

"What-the..." Glassman spoke for the first time, and backed up in fright. Henley and Donnelly also took a step back.

Fields almost jumped out of his pimply skin.

"We'll leave," Jonathon stately calmly, "Only Mr. Fields, you go and get our ball back for us. That's the deal."

"Whoa!" Donnelly breathed.

"Cool!" Henley agreed.

Fields looked around at his companions.

"Better do what he says," Glassman said.

"I will not!" Tommy shrieked, some hot tears welling up in his frightened eyes. "Are you guys gonna stand for this?!"

"You're on your own," Donnelly said flatly. "I got no beef with these guys."

"I'm tired of being your back-up," Henley shook his head. "But I'll stick around to see what happens to you, Tommy."

Staring at Glassman as his last hope, the big blond kid shook his head and took another step back.

"That leaves you," Jonathon said, not believing he was doing this.

Just a few weeks before he would have found some way to get out of a situation like this by cow towing or comedy or simply walking away. Now he heard himself saying further...

"If you have to be so physical about it," He shrugged, "Then I guess I'll have to make you be a good sport and go get the ball for us. How about that?"

The look on Tommy's face went from rage to stark fear. He looked at the flexing Hunter, who at least had covered his teeth with his tight, serious lips.

"Oh, you would think that!" Jonathon said, shaking his head. "Hunter, do me a favor, OK? If anybody tries to get between Tommy-Boy and me, just break them in half, right?"

"Gladly!" Hunter barked.

"So how's that?" Jonathon faced Tommy. "You're bigger than me, you have insulted my family, and you have tried to bully me...so?"

The other three boys backed away. Fields was left panting and white with fear. He looked around for some answer and instead in a rush with a shout he put his head down and came at Jonathon.

The smaller youth simply stepped to one side and as Fields blindly fumbled by used a foot to trip him.

Tommy fell in a heap on the grass. The laughs from his ex-gang hurt more than the fall.

"Step right up!" Jonathon called in a barker's voice. "Today only! See the amazing tumbling boy!"

Fields got up, now with real tears streaming down his face, and rushed Jonathon again.

This time Jonathon feigned left then moved right and without touching Fields the youth fell flat on his face again.

"He defies gravity!" Jonathon said with one hand cupping his mouth like a megaphone. "First he's up, then he's down! You won't find another show like it on the Midway!"

Donnelly and Glassman and Henley were really laughing now.

For a third time Fields screamed and, arms flailing, ran at his mocking opponent. Jonathon didn't even look as he raised a knee into Tommy's stomach and crumbled him to the ground.

"How does he do it, Folks? An absolute wonder of nature! No refunds..."

Fields lay sprawled for a time and Jonathon was about to go over and begin the reconciliation. But suddenly Tommy put his hand in his black jeans' pocket and fumbled for something. He rolled onto his back and flashed a large opened pocket knife in his dirty hand.

"Hey, wait a minute!" Donnelly called out.

"Not cool!" Henley shouted.

Hunter started to move towards Fields but Jonathon stopped him.

"This really what you want to do?" he said to Fields.

The boy was wild eyed and crying and his face was blotched white with fear and mottled red with anger and hurt.

"OK," Jonathon said, not knowing why he was so calm.

"*Get up*," he said in a voice that didn't sound like his own.

It had a strange effect on the other youths as well. The voice was as cold as a Nordic coastline in winter or an Irish warrior's invitation to one-on-one mortal combat.

Jonathon felt a wave of strength come over him. It could have been the hot blood in his ears but he heard a slow, steady drum sound. It was low and had the tones of an animal skin stretched tight over a wooden frame. The drumming brought something out in him he could not describe then or later.

Fields scrambled to his feet and tried to wipe away the tears with his grass covered forearm. He brandished the weapon hesitantly.

Jonathon calmly walked towards him and began to crouch into a stance. He raised his left arm as if there was a round shield there. His right arm cocked itself back like it held a sword aloft.

Then, with all eyes on him, Jonathon casually let his arms drop to his sides and leisurely stuck his hands into his pockets. He smiled rather comically and shuffled to where his back was to everyone but Fields. Shrugging his shoulders, he stepped closer to his antagonist and opened his eyes as wide as he could. They changed into first black seal's orbs then flashed to glowing red.

Tommy started to back up. After a few steps, he trembled in all his limbs.

Winking, Jonathon cocked his head and drew in a sighing breath. "BOO!"

The sound made everybody present jump, even Hunter.

Fields dropped the knife and turned and ran as if the devil were after him. He screamed as he fled.

Jonathon slowly returned to his easy-going posture and his eyes lost the fire. He looked at Fields' remaining friends and shrugged.

"Guess I was right," he sighed. "Not a soccer man. Cross country seems to be his event."

The din of conversation within the home salon was nearly frightening. It indeed produced an effect that had Celia wide-eyed and looking for an exit.

Jan touched the bewildered girl on the shoulder and led her over a seat where they went over pictures in many magazines of styles and glamour shots. It all seemed too strange for Celia to comprehend, but she started to giggle and point at photos she thought interesting.

Mother Annie had chosen Margret to be first and as such placed her in a chair and carefully combed out her long black hair. The rotund woman fussed over the exquisite length and quality of the locks. She began a careful trimming of the edges and in so doing reminded the matriarch of much overdue split-end repair.

Mother Annie's daughter sat Marie down and settled on a sensible trim. Her daughter-in law motioned for Jan.

Jan followed and got the dowsing and shampooing necessary.

With Celia at her elbow, Jan allowed the skilled woman to cut and style her hair in a sassy but not too new-style close cut.

The conversation in the room was all too interesting.

Mother Annie spoke to Margret about old times.

"I remember," She said fondly, "How my mother talked about taking the boat out to your place to cut and style the Tribe's ladies' hair there!"

Jan picked-up on the reference.

"Yes," Margret agreed, "It was a good time. Before..."

And here she trailed off. Jan could not help but dig.

"What house?" she asked innocently.

Silence was her answer.

Jan felt compelled to seek further answers.

"Mother Annie?" she tried. "Were your family on the island? On Malaga?"

The woman shook with laughter as she snipped the long dark hair of Jan's grandmother.

"Of course!" she stated. "But that's not the house I'm talking about! Look at me, child! I have a lot of mixed blood running through these old veins! I'm proud of it! Most of my people were of the Abenaki stock, but I'm told there was black and Creole in the family as well!"

Jan filed all this away.

"My people," Mother Annie continued, "Lived next to your people and we all got along."

Here she looked slyly sideways towards her daughter and her daughter-in-in-law.

"We know who you are. We respect you."

There was a wink to follow the statement.

Peggy finished with Jan and the youth looked in the mirror and nodded approval at the results. As Jan stepped out of the chair Peggy beckoned for Celia.

"There!" Mother Annie pronounced, spinning Margret to view herself in the wall mirror. "How's that?"

The thin, dark lady smiled and placed a long hand on the chubby one of her stylist.

"Fine!" she breathed.

"Beautiful, I'd say!" Mother Annie said back.

"Now, Miss Shere," she started, "I think you are next!"

Jan looked over as Celia had been smothered by Peggy and was enjoying a tense but rewarding shampoo.

Shere had been trying to conceal herself along the wall. With slow movements, she allowed herself to be seated and placed herself at the mercy of the Queen of the Salon. The wild, black hair seemed in danger of being tamed.

Jan kept an eye on the woman who was flashing away with silver scissors at Celia's brown mane. The girl was wide-eyed and seemingly frozen with delight and mixed terror.

Then there was the long moment of Shere getting a long overdue shampoo and conditioning. Mother Annie sat her down and closed one small black eye as she envisioned the end result. Her daughter Edna had started the manicure on Marie.

In a statement of pleased finality, Jan heard Peggy say she was through with Celia.

Walking over to stare behind and join the girl's eager gaze at herself in the mirror, Jan had to draw breath.

The woman had cut Celia's hair into a modern, irregular, shaggy-length masterpiece. The spiky tips framed Celia's oval and long face like a model in a fashion shoot. The effect was stunning.

"Wow," the stylist said, "Better than I thought. You are one hot number, girl."

Celia stared at her reflection as if she did not recognize the face.

"May I," the woman suggested, "Do a little make-up and eyelash work and brow trimming?"

Jan nodded for the stunned subject.

Then she turned her attention to Mother Annie's chair. Another stranger sat there.

The expert shears of Mother Annie were transforming Shere into the real woman she was. Not just one who helped with the fishing nets and sewed robes and did housework, but a true timeless beauty.

The wild hair was now feathered back at the sides and allowed the fine-chiseled classic lines of her face to be fully appreciated. Without asking, Mother Annie trimmed and plucked the dark eyebrows into thin arches that highlighted the dark orbs below.

Shere sat without looking up. Even when the work was done, she was reluctant to look into the mirror.

Jan walked over and placed a gentle arm on Shere's hand that clenched the armrest.

"Hi," Jan said to the beauty in the mirror, "You are so very pretty."

Shere cast a quick glance at her reflection, then sneaked another, and then locked eyes with herself. A very small smile crept along her full lips.

She looked at Jan, and they smiled at each other for a short while.

As the door to the salon opened to the small parking lot, much debate was being bantered about over why Margret got to pay for everything. Marie argued, Jan joined her, and in the end tips and money were forced into hands and laughs echoed all about.

Marie looked up and saw Jonathon and Hunter just a little way off in the church yard surrounded by three other boys. At first she was concerned, but her worries were laid to rest by the light chuckling and posturing of young men having a good time. She couldn't see what they were doing, and that suited the youths just fine. They curtailed their game rather quickly when they realized they had been spotted.

Donnelly and Goodman and Henley were teaching their new-found acquaintances a time-honored game called 'Mumbly-Peg'. A knife-point was balanced on a pinky finger and then spun in order to get the blade to stick point down in the ground. Each round the number of spins increased with players falling out of the game if they didn't make the prescribed turns.

Hunter and Jonathon looked towards the women and it was obvious their time was up. They both looked at the other three youths and all nodded and said some form of 'later, man' or 'see ya' or the like.

Henley bent down and covertly picked up the open lock-blade knife in the turf and slyly closed it and palmed it as he went to shake Jonathon's hand.

"What's this?" Jonathon asked quietly.

"Yours, man!" Henley said back, "Spoils of war!"

Goodman and Donnelly nodded their solemn agreement.

Jonathon slipped the thing into his pants pocket without his mother seeing. He didn't think it would matter, but it seemed the correct course of action under the circumstances.

As Hunter and his cousin drew near to the ladies milling around the SUV, each had different reactions.

Hunter stared at all the women as if pleasantly confused and at his sister for several long seconds before recognizing her. Celia had her large eyes downcast again and Jan was about to motion to Jonathon to say something but she didn't need to.

Jonathon walked straight up to her and, not caring who was watching (everybody was) he took her right hand in his left and with his right he touched her chin and raised her face. He tried but could not control his smile and wide eyes.

"Wow!" he whispered for her alone. "I told you so! You are beautiful!"

Celia locked eyes with him and stared to tear up but he 'shhh-ed' her instead. So she just went on smiling with him.

He took enough time to look around and compliment all the women on their looks and he did it in his own way.

"Saints preserve me!" he lilted in a Hollywood Irish brogue. "I'm sur-rounded by Nymphs!"

Back at Fin's, the older man and his brother made many compliments of their own as to the coven of beauties who had returned. He was misty-eyed when he looked at his daughter.

Dearg sauntered in and his red-black eyes nearly shot out of his head.

He didn't care as well about who was watching (everybody was) and he embraced Shere lovingly and kissed her. She did not protest but did finally motion she had to come up for air. This produced laughter all around and Shere joined in the mirth with a wider smile than Jan had witnessed before.

"Things they are a-changing," Jan said to herself.

As the group broke up to their own ways, Jonathon asked his mother if he and Celia could walk out on the dock. She agreed but gave a stern, if smiling, look of warning to her son. He rolled his eyes but got the message.

Fin went into the parlor and sat down with a newspaper. Jan followed and sat down just an arm's length away on the brocaded sofa.

Presently, Fin folded the top of the paper down and stared at the girl with a whimsical eye.

"I know, I know," she said. "You're going to think I'm such a pest. But I have to know…"

"What?" the elder man asked with some comedy in his voice.

"I couldn't help but overhear," she started, "Mother Annie was talking to Grandmother about a house they had; where all the Tribe got together?"

Fin sighed. He put the paper on the sofa and crossed his arms.

"Yep," he said wistfully, "Used to be like that. I helped to find the workers and drew up plans and even did some of the work myself."

"Where is it?" Jan wanted to know.

Fin shook his head.

"I swear, Little Lady, as they said in the old days, you could worry the horns off a Billy-goat!"

Jan missed the old meaning.

He sighed again.

"It's around the point, on a small island; right-near Seal Cove where the Tribe has been meeting for The Gathering since I don't know when. The land was deeded to our family but it's been hidden by a group of trustees so nobody nowadays knows who owns it. The taxes get paid from a fund and so the state doesn't care. A house was built there to be used by all the Tribe. We built it in the early 50's to be modern and not such a relic. You can't get there by road. Only by boat, or, the way you now know about. It has a room bigger and better than the boathouse for changing and enough room for as many folks as here, only better hid from prying eyes. But, neither the Tribe nor your grandparents, who used to live there, use it now."

"Why?" Jan almost demanded.

"And why didn't I know you were going to say that?" Fin huffed.

"This gets complicated and ugly," he said, closing his eyes and rubbing them with his thick fingers.

"Fine," he resolved, looking at her again and drawing closer.

"It started with my mother. She was such a busy, smart thing and just as my grandfather and grandmother passed like I told you, my mother was…afflicted."

Jan shook her head not understanding.

"She just up and one day became…confused. She just stared out into nothing. We had to force her to eat; she couldn't take care of herself and didn't know any of us. All the Tribe tried to figure it out because none of us get that way, the way old folks do and now-a-days you call it something else. But we couldn't figure it out."

"Then," Fin said sadly, "Julius' witch mother proclaimed that it was a curse befell the family. One fall day my poor father had gone down to the boathouse to get some oil for the lamps and my mother just wandered out into the bay and was drowned. He didn't last another full season after she was gone. I still think he died of a broken heart."

"Augus was then in line for the Chieftainship. We decided he needed a place for all of us because so many ships were passing and people were watching. So we built the house. He was Chieftain for about three seasons. Julius' mother said we had made a mistake with the island. Of course we didn't believe her, but then just a short time later my sister Maureen, Maggie-Shannon's mother; fell into the same sort of state and died within four months, wasted away. Julius' mother, I will not say her name, said she had divined it was because we had built the house on the island over a spot where old spirits didn't want us to. Again, I didn't go for any of that hogwash no matter what magic we all seem to hold to."

"But my brother, he's a different lot," Fin said sadly. "He listened to the witch and moved out before his beloved Margret came down with the same. Julius became Chieftain because most of the Tribe thought this family was cursed and took over the house and there was little I could do about it. Only, he stopped having The Gatherings there because of the curse, he said, which hasn't seemed to hurt him, and now it's his playhouse. I told you his mother met with a ghastly end, and I'm glad of it, even if I had nothing to do with it. She was found as a land person chained to the rocks and gagged where the tide would submerge all but her head. The crabs and lobsters and the like slowly ate her until she died. "

Jan shuddered but continued to think out loud.

"But how can he control the house if he doesn't own it?"

"Really, I don't care," Fin admitted. "But he had some sort of hold over the accounts and money of the Tribe; I don't understand it all.

Now in this new age it has something to do with computers and passwords or something, or so Dearg says."

Jan nodded, understanding a bit more.

"Anyway" the elder continued, "He lives there now with his crew and he has a ...a woman who has been with him for a long time now. She's a horrible old biddy. She brings other women for the other males."

"Is that the woman Jonathon saw at the grocery store?"

"Ah-yuh, that would be her."

"Jonathon told mom and I about her,"

"I went out there just a few days ago, to warn him to stay away from my family, but it didn't seem to do any good."

His face hardened suddenly.

"I guess I'll have to get another message through,"

A voice familiar to Jan suddenly interrupted.

"I think we'll take care of that very soon ourselves," Marie said coldly.

Fin and Jan looked as the woman was casually leaning at the wall leading into the parlor.

"Sorry, I wasn't eavesdropping," she smiled strangely. "But I'm not about to sit by and let this monster threaten my children or my husband's family. It's time he got taken down a peg or two."

Jan didn't understand what her mother was meaning but Fin just smiled a broad, slow grin.

"Wait a day or so for things to calm down," he said with a wink. "Then we'll fix his little red wagon."

Perhaps it was the new hair style or the dangerous looking hands in slacks, but leaning so slinky and smiling so foxily Marie reminded her daughter of a *femme fatale* from one of Jonathon's old movies. She could have been Marlene Dietrich or Lauren Bacall.

Somehow Jan had an odd feeling deep in her stomach that Marie

Costello MacLeer was more a force to be reckoned with than any of the pretend serious dames.

12

The morning's excursion promised to be the best ever. And yet, Jan had that butterflies in the stomach feeling that was associated with the impossibility that was about to transpire.

Despite the fact, yes fact, that she was about to magically transform into a seal and go cavorting about the underwater world, Jan was thinking of something else. She sensed that something was coming that was at least if not more world-shattering than what had already happened. She just went along with everything because she felt she was as caught-up as she soon would be on the outgoing tide.

The boundaries of the bay had been broken with the last outing and now the whole of the big, mysterious open water was the subject *du jour*.

Dearg was ranting away like a captain of the cavalry in making sure Jonathon and Jan were sufficiently warned about the many and dangerous and lethal 'things' that could go wrong 'out there'.

The plan was to leave the bay, after everyone of the party had formed up, and proceed past the fort, between the sand beach and rocky islands, into the lesser area of The Gulf of Maine. Sequin Light was the outer boundary. Under no circumstances was any of the group to venture beyond it.

Then, a slight turn to the right would bring them to explore areas

Jan so wanted to see. The Holy Grail of Malaga was not immediately promised on the trip due to some tricky obstacles.

Jan believed this was the real reason for the trip, despite what Fin and a very nervous Dearg had been obviously sworn to secrecy about.

The proposed introduction to Seal Island and the venerable place of The Gathering also brought them in close proximity with her grandparents' former abode and as such into the lair of 'King' and his squad.

The night before, Marie had gathered her twins together and gave them a very strange pep-talk prior to the next day's activities. Sitting in the kitchen, making sure they were alone, the mother had held her children's hands as she spoke.

"I'm so very proud of you," she beamed. "I know tomorrow is going to be wonderful. Each new experience will be. But..."

Her face hardened here. She was even prettier when serious, Jan decided.

"I don't want you to be afraid. I want you to remember who you are and who your father is. I want you to know that you are being protected and this is something that has to be done. You'll understand later. We have to show the world that we fear none. Understood?"

Jan laughed a bit inside as she thought that 'we' didn't exactly cover what might befall her and her brother. But, this was their mom and she had always been there for them before.

The morning broke perfectly and the time allotted was upon them. Dearg and Hunter and an almost swaggering Jonathon went to the boathouse to change. When it was their turn, Jan followed Celia with not as much trepidation as before.

Celia faltered for a moment until Jan assured her that the new hairdo would survive and the makeup could be reapplied afterwards. She then entered the water as gracefully as ever.

Jan didn't wait for coaching this time and easily slipped into the warm, embracing skin with a 'hi' said to Maggie-Shannon.

In the water, she joined the team as Shere slid up to complete the group.

Passing out past the rocks that formed the base of the old fort, they encountered other seals that were busy being other seals. The fine weather had many people out as well and Dearg once again needlessly pointed out fishing lines that might ensnare an unwary Selchie. Jan found this touching as he was obviously doing his supposed duty. But her eyesight underwater was so keen as to pick out even the thinnest of monofilament lines. The humans wading in the cold water, despite the sunny skies, looked on and snapped pictures the way Jan had done not so very long ago.

Jonathon was having a grand old time shooting along the sand bottom with Celia just nipping at his back flippers. As the entire group gained the vast sandbar they fanned out and worked together for a while to corral fish onto a frenzied bait ball with bubble nets and quick maneuvers. The ensuing feast was satiable, to say the least.

Always there was the open expanse luring both Jan and Jonathon. Hunter seemed as aware of it and he kept glancing out into the void from time to time. Jan caught Shere drifting away from the shore as well. Only Celia, who was still only concerned with Jonathon, and a concentrated if not bothered Dearg seemed to avoid the temptation.

It was just so…free, Jan thought.

While she knew the open expanse held untold dangers and no landfall and how would she navigate, it nonetheless also held the unbridled opposite of what she had known in her life so far.

Sidewalks said go here; roads did the same. You can't go there. You must go here, don't do that, you'll get in trouble, sit here, eat this, don't eat that…don't DO that.

But out there, she thought, none of those rules applied. Surely, if you made a mistake, you paid dearly. Life was in the delicate balance between good judgment and blind luck.

But there was no one there to tell you what to do.

The thought was intoxicating.

Dearg broke the spell by barking that they should all be in reverence of the ragged group of islands they had come upon.

Jan realized this was what was known as Seal Island. It had a small low area of rocks that could be used to haul ones' self out upon. Beyond was an area that only had some small green plants or algae growing there. It did not seem to Jan that it was conducive to any extended meetings of any kind.

Bristling for a slight moment, Dearg relaxed as another group of seals swam in close-by. These addressed the newcomers warmly.

They introduced themselves but Jonathon and Jan had trouble remembering all the names. They were members of the Tribe and they were keenly interested in Celia and Hunter. They bowed in turn when Dearg gave the lineage of the honored guests.

Then it was Jonathon and Jan that got nearly a hero's welcome as one after the other of the some twelve Selchies present marveled at the offspring of 'Manny'. Everyone seemed to love and be concerned after any news as to what had happened to him. They were formal enough not to overstep prudence since Jan and Jonathon did not seem to hold any answers.

Three rather proper and dainty females swam up to coyly and respectfully inspected Jan and Celia. They spoke to Shere as intermediate.

"Oh, and aren't they the pretty things!" one would say.

"Have you seen such eyes? And they are so well behaved! Royalty, I say!"

"Yes, yes, we know that!" another smiled. "But so humble! And do you recognize this sweet one's skin? Manny's dear daughter? Could it be?"

"Och, I'd know it anywhere!" a gray-snouted matriarch proclaimed. "It's Maggie-Shannon as I live and dive!"

The others fussed over Jan until it was almost too much.

Dearg held court with the males that had circled.

"Fin sends his greetings," he said. "He says to look sharp. Things are moving. You can't be content with how things are."

"As well I'm not!" one male sounded off. "I've been tasked with a-breaking the human's cameras on the Island! I dunna know how I haven't been caught so far! At least they have seemed to lay-off, for now."

"You are being watched?" Jonathon asked.

The entire group of Selchies, male and female, turned to look at him.

"I would imagine you are also being watched via satellite from space. Did you think about that?" Jonathon continued.

"Aye, so we have been told," the breaker of the cameras answered back. "Do I know you, Sir?"

"Look deep," Dearg suggested. "It's Manny's son, to be sure, but who do you suppose chose him?"

"Faith!" one male swore. "Loki?!"

"Is it?" another asked.

"It is," Dearg confirmed.

A hushed silence came over the colony.

"That is epic," another older male noted. "There are indeed changes in the tide. I have grievances. As do we all. But can we count on...?"

"More on that later," Dearg growled. "For now, you feel it; clear off. You know what's coming. But stand close by. A thing is about to change all. Don't be alarmed. But be ready."

The heavy-set man cinched the silk belt of the black and gold silk kimono under his big belly and continued to search through the cabinet he had his large head stuck into. He cursed under his breath, which puffed-out the long mustache that covered his thick lips.

Cursing louder, he started to toss empty plastic 1.75 liter bottles that used to contain coffee brandy over his shoulders to bounce on the once cared-for expensive hardwood floor.

"We better not be out!" he shouted for the only other person in the room to hear.

He withdrew his head and wheeled rather unsteadily around.

"We're out!" he bellowed, and the brown and gray mustache under the rather red and bulbous nose flew again.

The person he was facing cringed at the onslaught of ire. She was a woman of considerable age who was trying not to look that way. Her dingy platinum hair was in need of attention. She put her browned and spotted arms up in defense. The gaudy baubles and bracelets jangled cheaply.

"I just bought a case at the first of the week!" she protested.

"Don't interrupt me!" the man yelled with blood-shot eyes bulging. "All I ask is for you to keep my house and what do I get? Incompetence! I'll bet there's not even food!"

The woman grimaced again and lit upon an idea that might stop the inevitable blows from starting again.

"I can go right now!" she pleaded. "All I need is my purse and I'll be back before you know it!"

"You better!" the bully roared.

"All I need is money..." she started.

"WHAT?!" the man screeched. "I gave you money last time!"

"It's gone!" she said, nearly in tears she knew mattered not. "Everything is so much more expensive nowadays!"

"Ahhhh!" the man shouted in fury and raised a heavy hand that made the woman flinch but gratefully it was not directed this time at her.

He turned and kicked the empty bottles with his heavy and bare feet as he padded across the expansive, tastefully furnished kitchen. The wide and long marble counters had ample seating for many, but the barstools had dust on the seats from nonuse.

He did not even look at the panorama of breathtaking scenery the large picture windows presented of the open sea beyond the island where the house was perched.

Snatching open some fine French doors that now were in sore need of cleaning the dirt and smudges and grime from the etched glass, he stalked down a thickly carpeted hallway that had numerous doors on either side. These had not been opened in a very long time and as such could not show off the spacious and comfortable rooms for guests behind them.

The cursing man stopped in front of a door at the end of the hallway and punched some numbers on a cipher lock above the handle with his pudgy, sausage-like fingers with yellow nails. Once inside the leather and chrome office, he opened an old but still very secure heavy safe and grabbed a stack of currency from many like it.

Slamming the massive door and resetting the lock, he retraced his steps with more vile, ugly curses.

Nearing the bleached-haired woman who stood shaking, he tore some bills from the stack and pushed them forcefully into her open satchel of a purse. The gesture almost made her drop the bag.

"You better be quick!" the man warned with malice in his narrowed eyes. "And I want receipts from now on! I think you're stealing from me!"

The hurt on the woman's face was almost more than when she suffered the physical abuse.

"Surely you can't think! Why, I've been with you so long and I would never..."

"Right!" he sneered back, interrupting her. "You've been with me soooo long!"

The mocking tone and mean look was the one she feared most of all.

She turned and was about to head towards the front door that had a repair where a heavy hammer had caused a hole not very long ago. Just as she put the ridiculously large white sunglasses down over her frightened eyes, another voice made her stop.

"King," the bass male voice started.

The man in the gold and black robe wheeled as if very annoyed.

"WHAT!" he ranted. "What do you want now that's important enough to bother me? This better be good!"

The man he was facing was dressed in a white, cheap terry robe. It appeared he had hurried from the room built for changing from one form to another. His once muscular frame now sagged a bit in opulent inattention. He was still a big and formidable person with a shock of black hair and a low brow that did not do much for suggesting intelligence. This brow was furrowed in apparent worry and his oddly oblong head was bowed.

Another figure similarly attired filed in behind the first. This one was big as well and had close-cropped red hair with a close-cropped red beard. His head was bowed as well.

"Well?!" 'King' berated, "Are you just going to stand there and drip all over my floor!!??"

"King," the black haired one started again. "Most of the Tribe is out there just off the Meeting Rock. They are talking with some others."

"What others, you nitwits?" 'King' implored, but with a slightly less incoherent rage.

The red one spoke now.

"You know, King; the four young ones, the old man's daughter, and that disrespectful Irish red-eyed troublemaker!"

"Ahhh!" 'King' seemed to ponder with a black-hearted sneer. He ran his thick fingers through his brown hair with gray flecks that looked unkempt as it always was.

"I don't know what ideas they might be putting into the Tribes' heads," the black haired one said quickly, looking to his master.

"And," the red one added, "It being so close to The Gathering and all. I'll bet old Fin is behind this."

'King' stroked his brown and gray mustache thoughtfully. When he spoke again, he had reverted to the practiced, oily, suggestively foul voice he considered 'posh'.

"So, gentlemen," he oozed, "I do believe it's time we went out and saw to the well being of our 'Children'. They may have forgotten, since we have been so generous and non-violent these many years, as to just who is in control here. What?"

The other two curled sinister smiles.

"I think it is high time," 'King' continued, liking the sound of his sleazy voice, "That we furthermore put an end to this meddlesome Irish vagrant. He does not... amuse me?"

The two henchmen chuckled with the idea.

"Come then, my stout right and left hand fellows!" 'King' motioned with a theatrical flair. "Let us sally-forth and crack some heads! I rather took a fancy to one of those nubile females. And to think I thought today was going to be just like any other!"

With a slapping of fists into palms, the two in white turned to go before their leader.

'King' suddenly had an afterthought and spun around dramatically. He looked somewhat aloofly at the older woman who stood stock still and wanted to be forgotten.

"Are you still here?" 'King' asked in his fake British accent.

The woman said and did nothing.

"GET OUT!" 'King' bellowed again, even louder than before. "GET OUT OF HERE!"

The woman almost fell to the floor but collected her things and started weak-kneed for the front door.

"You better be back quick!" 'King' ranted after her.

He turned again to his waiting men.

"I'm going to want to celebrate tonight," he said more to himself than anyone else.

Jan had an indescribable feeling and foreboding that something important was about to happen.

The Tribe members had reacted to Dearg's words and had slowly moved away from the group of relative newcomers. Several males had lingered and asked if they could be of assistance but Dearg was insistent that things were under control. With that, and a sidelong look to the females, they had moved away as well to a distance not discernible.

"Remember now," Dearg called out as the six of them bobbed on the surface. "Leave a bit of space between you, but don't let the enemy get between any of us."

Jan didn't like the sound of the words and in her mind she replayed the many reassurances from Fin and Dearg and her grandfather, who wasn't here, as to the overall safety of the presumed impending encounter.

Something in her gut did not want to see the figures she knew were about to be there.

In an attempt to change the subject, she craned to see an island not far off that had a prominent house on it. The structure filled the small island and she marveled at the way the glass windows sparkled in the sunlight. It looked inviting.

"Is that," she asked, "The house of my grandparents?"

Jonathon looked as well as all the others. Dearg confirmed the sighting.

"T'is," he stated. "But you know all too well who lives there now."

"Look!" Celia noted. A small white motor boat had just left the house on the island. A woman with windswept, wild bleached hair could be seen steering the outboard as it putt-putted away from the dock.

"That's the lady," Jonathon remarked, "That we saw at the grocery store!"

"That's no lady," Dearg snorted, "But you're right."

Jan had told her brother all about what Fin had made known to her and they had traded thoughts on the nefarious goings-on at their grandparents' former place.

"Get ready for it," Dearg warned. Indeed a superhuman sense had filled the surrounding water with something almost palpable in the way of danger.

Jan reminded herself that she did not want to see the figures she knew would soon appear. She was concerned and anxious. She peered out towards the island with the house on it and ducked under water in apprehension of spotting...

Them.

The two large males rolled up in the lazy, supposedly easy fashion she had come to expect. They kept their eyes ever searching as the circle of intended interest was observed.

Keeping to the game plan, Dearg was out in front and Hunter was positioned to protect Jan and Celia. Jonathon was strangely postured to swim beside Shere. They made small adjustments in unspoken twitches and whisker messages.

After a tense few moments the two males moved off to the sides of the gathered group and signaled the approach of their leader.

He lumbered up looking more like a small tusk-less walrus than a seal. His bulk was not at all suggestive of power or strength and Jan wondered if the skin had stretched over the years. He rolled his bloodshot, yellow eyes as he surfaced.

"Inciting my subjects, are you?" he said sickly to Dearg.

"Subjects!?" Dearg shot back. "Is that what you really believe?

What an insult to the Tribe! You are *elected*, why I don't know, but you have no *subjects*!"

"Call them what you will," 'King' huffed through his drooping whiskers, "You ignorant Irish nobody, but they're my subjects just the same, as are all who enter my territory. You have ignored my position long enough. It's time you showed me the respect I'm due."

Hunter interrupted with a growl and a flashing of sharp, young teeth,

"How dare you!" he seethed. "My family bows to no one, especially a blubber-ridden fool such as you! The insults you do will be heard in the north! You may well have MY people to answer to!"

'King' blinked and seemed to realize he had overstepped himself. A small shadow of fear crossed over his yellowed eyes.

"Oh, I didn't mean you," he tried to smooth, only it came out as oily and sleazy as ever. "You are welcomed to leave anytime. The sooner the better. And you should not believe anything this Irish instigator has to say or anything as well from that old fool Fin."

Hunter was about to attack when Dearg stopped him with a raised flipper.

"You are nothing but a wind bag!" he almost laughed. "You and your gang here may at one time have been passable fighters. But look at you now! Your already dim brain is soaked in cheap booze and the years have not been kind to you! I know how you operate! Your boys here will drive at the females, you cowards, and try to make us make a mistake by trying to protect them. Then you think you will have an opportunity to strike like the cur you are!"

'King' started to snarl and reddened under the insults, mostly because they were true.

"You know," Dearg continued, his eyes flashing menacingly red, "That by myself I could rip any of you three apart, even if ganged-up on, or you would have tried it already! Hunter here could best any of us. And has it escaped your blurred attention that Loki's skin has returned? AND it's being worn by a MacLir? You make me laugh!"

The other two males had started looking nervously at what Dearg had been alluding to.

'King' looked stunned for a moment and moved slowly to have a closer look at Jonathon. There was a furrowing of his thick brow as he locked eyes with the youth.

"BOO!" Jonathon barked suddenly and made the hulk of 'King' jerk his head back in alarm.

"But don't worry," Dearg took up again. "We don't have to fight you. And here I'm giving you fair warning, you pathetic excuse for a Selchie. Leave us now, and slink back to your stolen lair, or face the consequences. You have no idea what you are about to get yourself into."

He addressed the two goons who were now visibly alert and looking around for something they felt but couldn't see.

"Why do you do his dirty work?" Dearg asked them. "For what? The filthy vices that have made you soft and hated among your Tribe?"

When they didn't answer, he turned back to 'King' who was also troubled-looked but still mad and redder in the muzzle.

"I ask you one...last...time! Do you mean to do us harm? This is your last chance to save yourself."

'King' looked blankly at Dearg.

"That and more!" he bellowed and made a sideways attempt to lunge and bite at Shere.

Jonathon moved with lightning speed and nudged her out of the way. As the huge body passed, Jonathon opened his mouth and let his sharp teeth rake 'King''s large left flipper. Blood ran red in the water.

Barking in pain, 'King' returned to the surface with a thrashing of his head.

"You will pay for that!" he sputtered to Jonathon.

"Wrong," Dearg said hollowly. "You will."

Jan had been all but petrified at the ordeal. She had drifted on the surface to be just behind Shere when the strike came.

Now something shot by her under water. It was so fast that she did not get a good look at it. It appeared to flash silver as it moved like a torpedo past Shere and Jonathon to smash into the bulk of King. All the air was knocked out of the great blubbery body and he doubled up in a sick groan of pain. As his head fell under the waves, he could not help but gasp and in so doing inhaled a short breath of salt water. He floundered on the surface choking and wheezing.

Jan caught sight of the thing again as it reappeared from the open water side. It was again so fast; faster than any seal and that included Jonathon. It seemed to have a dark or black front and a shining back section. Sleek and streamlined, it flashed in the sunlight and headed for 'King''s henchmen. They tried to move, but the closing speed was overwhelming. As the thing passed them, it appeared to use a strong tail or fluke to thump first one of the would-be-attackers and then the next. The cracking ribs were audible above and below the water.

The creature, for Jan now felt it was something living, spun miraculously and returned to further punish the two large seals with more heavy tail blows. Certain internal damage had to be done. The silver tail flashed a light show of differing shades of red.

Jan remembered seeing something similar on TV as marlin attacked fish. But this was no marlin, although it was longer by far than any of the seals present.

The two goons had surely had enough and tried desperately to escape. Their broken ribs and bruised internal organs made it impossible for them to do anything but weakly try to swim off. Jan felt sure that if it chose to, the creature could have killed them both with one more salvo of lethal blows.

But Jan's attention was momentarily diverted to the gurgling hulk of 'King' who was now very near to her. In the confusion of the attack by the silver-tailed creature, Jan had drifted much too close to 'King' without realizing it.

But 'King' noticed.

Even through his pain and half-drowning, he turned his sickly yellow eye on her and bared his teeth in a drive to bite her.

This time the thing rocketing through the water actually brushed Jan aside as it passed. 'King''s eyes widened as it zeroed in and wheeled to slap his head with the wide tail. The blow knocked several yellowed teeth out of his jaws and sent him reeling backwards.

'King' sank under the surface and started to limp away like his gang. Jan saw something coming back and so she ducked under as well.

What she saw surprised her more than anything she had up to this point experienced.

The 'creature' was returning but now at a speed, although still fast, that allowed a closer look at it.

As it approached the stricken 'King', who was bleeding now from not only his flipper but also his smashed mouth, it slowed to stop his retreat.

The thing had arms. The upper body was human-looking and the torso was black. But the arms and face and neck were almost the color of Jan's skin when she wasn't a seal. It appeared to have dark hair pulled back in a woman's way and securely braided. The lower part was shimmering silver and still pulsed with the red luminescence of anger or attack mode. The tail was fan-like and wide and graceful but obviously immensely powerful.

In the hands of the thing that confronted 'King' was a strange, murderously deadly looking object. It was like a stick about three feet long that had been covered in varied and

differently shaped sharks' teeth. Both ends were tapered to a point where two very large and slender teeth made spear points. The middle was wrapped in some sort of skin, gray and suggestively shark as well, that allowed the weapon to be held.

The spear point of one of these ends was now leveled at 'King's' muzzle just inches from his bleeding snout.

Jan could not help but look at the face of the creature. There were large, round eyes that looked indeed like a tuna or billfish. Small but definite gill plates moved slowly just below the human-looking ears.

That's when Jan first thought the unthinkable.

The black part of the upper torso was a wet suit vest she knew. The nose and ears she knew as well. Even the hair was done up in a way she could not mistake.

The large eyes flashed quickly to Jan and momentarily away from King.

Marie smiled quickly to her daughter and then returned a cold stare back to her prey.

'King' was struggling to remain conscience. Fear showed in his eyes through the pain.

The sharks' teeth weapon was shifted to the other graceful hand but never moved from right in front of King's shaking muzzle. The now free hand was raised to 'King's eye level. A slender index finger that ended in a sharp and curved claw and was attached to other digits that were connected by webbing wagged back and forth firmly in an unmistakable warning to the injured hulk.

In a lightening flash, the sharp weapon sliced along 'King's jaw. He blew bloody air into the water and turned his head expecting the death blow.

Instead, in a shimmering flash of silver the creature was gone.

King moved as quickly as he could towards his abode. The gash on his jaw showed bone underneath and trailed a faint ribbon of crimson as he left.

Jonathon was saying something to his sister. He repeated it for the third time before she realized he was speaking to her.

"Was that what I think it was?" he demanded.

"You mean who?" Jan finally managed.

"Guess it was," he tried to shrug but found the gesture impossible as a seal.

Jan looked at him as if for the first time in her life.

"Is that all you have to say!?" she barked, and as a seal the noise was louder than she expected.

Celia had moved to get as close to Jonathon as she could. She still looked bewildered and a bit frightened.

"Well," Jonathon mused, "So our mother is a mermaid, or something; I suppose she'll tell us the right term now. And, our father and his family are seal-people. We are Selchies. Is it so strange to be talking about it all in seal barks and yips and growls?"

Jan just shook her seal head.

Dearg swam up rather coyly with diverted eyes. Shere joined him and they kept as close as Celia and Jonathon.

"You knew," Jan accused.

"Ah, right-so, I did yeah," he faltered. "And I was told to keep quiet about it. That's your mum and Fin. Sure and it was a grand thing now! Did you see the way she settled their hash? Faith!"

"Come on, Sis," Jonathon started. "I'm getting used to this. I'm just waiting for what's next. Do we have a side of the family that has wings? I know, maybe centaurs. Didn't you always want a pony?"

"Ah," Dearg said, looking around nervously, "We're supposed to meet yer mum away from prying eyes. I just have to explain a few things to the Tribe over there. Oh and I'll bet they've never seen the likes of this."

"And you have?" Jan asked as incredibly as everything else going on.

"Well, maybe, just once," he admitted. "Years ago when I first left Eire I came here, then spent a while a-roving down the coast and just wound-up down south in the islands. I caught a glimpse of them down there. They didn't want anything to do with me."

"That's it," Jonathon stated. "Don't you get it, Sis? Mom's people...where they came from...remember how strange some of them were when we visited? All closed and secret-like."

"I guess so," Jan admitted, thinking back to her past.

Dearg swam off to speak to the Tribe. Hunter appeared and kept looking around as he took on the role of protector.

"You were really brave," Jan said to him. He blinked at her and she could tell he was still nervous from the encounter.

"I don't like that 'King'", he snarled. "If my father hears about him and how he treated us he'll..."

He stopped and looked strangely at Jan.

"Well, your mother took care of that."

Jan just let it go in all the improbability.

"For now," Jonathon noted. "It ain't over, Ladies and Gentlemen. It ain't over..."

After what seemed an eternity, Dearg swam back and motioned for the rest to follow. They passed stealthily around the part of Seal Island that was open to the gulf and fought some strong currents between it and the peninsular. When they were secluded behind the island, they all surfaced and waited again.

As if materializing from under the water, the creature who looked like Jan and Jonathon's mother appeared and broke the surface as well.

Marie smiled but it was a different smile than her children were used to. Her eyes were non-blinking and much larger. She held the weapon in one hand and put up the other to stop any questions.

"You can't speak to me like you are," she started in a somewhat familiar voice. "I don't speak seal but you understand human. I can't stay above water like you very long because I breath water."

She ducked under as if to prove this point.

"I know you have a lot of questions," she said when she surfaced again. "We'll talk when we get back to Fin's. I have to be careful. Lots of people see seals and that's fine but nobody sees my kind and doesn't freak-out. I also have to be extra careful going back because I can't use my sonar-location as much. It's caused a lot of trouble lately that I didn't think of. But I was just worried and protecting you."

Jonathon barked anyway and nodded his seal head vigorously as if to say 'You go, Mom!'

Marie got the gesture and laughed sharply.

"I'll see you back at the house," she said, and was simply gone.

With the changing all completed and the confusing questions and short conversations Jan was the first to rush out of the boathouse and look around.

Fin was the only one to be seen and he might as well have asked his questions to thin air as Jan rushed past him and, in her dark robe, searched up and down the dock and the back of the house for her mother.

The masculine group was quicker this time in arriving and Jonathon was soon at his sister's side in like robe and like determination.

Dearg started to relate the details to Fin but Jan and Jonathon left everybody else to dash towards the house. No words were needed.

As the twins crashed through the screen door they were met by the figure of their mother toweling off her hair which had been loosed from the tight braids. She bore a sheepishly uncharacteristic smile and had changed into a Red Sox gray T-shirt and green gym shorts.

"Wait," she ordered lightly with the same raised finger that her children has so recently observed warning 'King' before the carving was done.

"Give me a minute?"

Jan and Jonathon stood mute but both wore an expression of utter disbelief and shock and confusion.

"Do you mind," their mother asked calmly, "If I explain this all at once to avoid redundancy?"

Neither Jan nor her brother could muster a response.

Suddenly the kitchen was full of black robed figures. Shere and Celia and Hunter were quiet and stared at Marie with wonder and confusion. Dearg and Fin were in heated discussion about the day's events and the possible outcome it had on The Tribe.

They soon fell silent and all eyes were fixed on Marie.

"Hi," she said flatly. "Guess I have some explaining to do."

That being said, she turned sharply and walked gracefully in bare feet into the parlor.

Everyone followed.

"I wish," Marie started, facing the oddly dressed throng, "That I could have told my kids about this before...well, before I had to, but I hoped I wouldn't have had to get so involved."

She sought out her twins' eyes now.

"I was only watching. I was just protecting you. Then things got out of hand and I lost control and blasted those...those bad guys and then it killed all the fish and...I'm sorry!"

Fin broke the awkwardness.

"Who could blame you?" He tried to reason. "It's just your way."

Jonathon shook his head to clear the cobwebs.

"That was you we heard 'pinging' and following us?" he surmised.

Marie nodded like a child caught with a hand in a cookie jar.

"How does it work?" Jan wondered out loud. "I mean, we get it. I remember now the way our family in Florida was so weird and I get the whole sponge fishing thing and how better to get ahead in the business than to have...what do you call it... 'mermaids' in the mix?"

"We don't use that term," Marie said, looking up to the ceiling.

"Mermen and mermaids...too trite. We just call ourselves 'Sea-people'...there's too many other names in too many languages."

"So how does it work?" Jan pressed.

"Oh!" Marie understood. She sat down on the floor in a graceful crossed-legged posture and beckoned for everybody else to get comfortable.

Jan remained standing but Jonathon sat down on the floor as well and was followed closely by Celia. Shere sat on the sofa as well as Hunter. Dearg and Fin hovered behind.

Marie held up a large gym bag that her children remembered seeing in a closet in their condo forever.

"It's not unlike you Selchies," she continued. "I suppose, but don't know for sure, that we are related somehow. Back in pre-history, I mean. See, the tail...we slip into it like you do your skins. Only, it doesn't cover us completely, but the transformation takes place. My skin changes and my eyes change and my teeth, well, they get sharp to catch fish like you. And I get gills. I told you about that."

"What's with the wet suit vest?" Jonathon asked simply.

"Oh," his mother blushed and put her hand to her mouth, "First off, it's bloody cold up here! I'm used to tropical waters! Our people came first from the Greek and Sicilian and Mediterranean islands; then we got pushed out by people and found the Caribbean and later Florida hunting grounds. But, there's another reason."

Dearg laughed a short male chortle.

"See," Marie continued to her son, "I said the tail only extends to the waist. I didn't want to shock you guys with not only the fact that I'm who I am but also with a bare-breasted mother."

"Thanks for that," Jonathon remarked through his own flush.

"I think it's a silly thing," Marie mused more to herself, "And something to do with people who come from cold climates. The men there don't see women without heavy clothes on and when they do they get insane over...well...you know. In the islands in Greece or Italy or Sicily girls go topless all the time and everybody's used to it."

"Sorry," Marie noted as her rant had varying effects on her listeners.

"Anyway," she continued, speaking mainly to her offspring, "Imagine the comedy when your father brought me up here and explained about his family. He was so impressed when I didn't go nuts and accepted everything. Then I take him down to Florida and show him my side. We laughed....!"

Marie noticed her mirth was not felt by the assembled.

"We wanted to tell you," she said again to her children. "We decided we would know when the moment was right. But that never happened."

"Hey," Jonathon suddenly thought out loud, "So, could we be...?"

"It's not the same," Marie caught the thread. "Fin has been so good to find the right skins for you. But, my people are not so kind and...nice. We fight. We are brutal. We cling to our secrets and don't let many in. I'm breaking every rule by saying what I'm saying now to 'outsiders'. I don't feel that way about you all, but it's our way."

Dearg and Fin nodded in understanding if the idea escaped the rest in the room.

"I got my tail when my aunt was killed by a rival pod. I was expected to avenge her death. My grandfather was murdered likewise."

"What did you do?" Jan asked softly.

"I don't want to talk about that," Marie answered. "OK?"

"So we thought," she changed the subject, "That one day you two would learn the quiet, peaceful life of the Selchie. But, here we go again. I've managed to bring violence here..."

"Wait a minute!" Dearg started. "You've done naught but put things in place! We've needed help for forever and today you started something a long time in coming!"

"Still," Marie looked down to the floor.

"Mom?" Jonathon asked rather strongly. "I want to know more about this and I understand how hard this is for you, but I really, really want to see that shark-tooth stick!"

That broke the tension in the room and with a proud smile Marie reached from behind a chair and retrieved and brandished the weapon in question.

All the males in the room moved to inspect it.

"It's terribly old," Marie stated. "It was started before anyone knows and passed down. There's Mako, Tiger, Hammer Head, Bull...even some Great White teeth. They each have their own function. Some are serrated, some jagged, some slice; there are even some porpoise and dolphin teeth. Those are razor-sharp. I have replaced ones that have fallen out with use..."

Here she batted her eyes and seemed to recall past memories better left alone.

"We use cement gathered from oysters and mussels. They have the best bond..."

Jan felt again detached from the moment as the wicked tool was gawked at and marveled-over. The facts that were trying to sink into her head were just as fantastic as her slipping into a seal skin and transforming but somehow the thought of her mother in her new role was not as alarming as sad. She could not figure out why.

A quick look transpired between mother and daughter as the group in the room surrounded them. It was a poignant reminder of how things had changed so quickly.

13

The older woman with the bleached platinum hair could barely manage to bring the short glass filled with clinking ice and strong spirits to her lipstick smeared mouth. The jangling of the bracelets on her liver-spotted arms sounded like finger cymbals in a cheap belly dance.

She jolted yet again as the howls from the other room reached a pitched crescendo.

Peeking around the doorjamb, she saw 'King' sprawled on a sofa with the doctor she had brought by boat from the mainland hovering over his great mass. This doctor was aged as well and had been sworn to secrecy with vile threats and copious payments. Still, he was having trouble tonight as never before.

"You have to be still!" the old man pleaded to his patient. "I have to give you a shot to numb your jaw so I can suture it!"

"Aaaaagh!" 'King' bellowed. "You saw-bones! Do something to help me!"

"I'm trying!" the doctor tried. "But this is too much! I need to get you three to a hospital now!"

"Forget that!" 'King' ranted, pushing the old man away for the umpteenth time. He tried to raise a plastic bottle to his lips.

"Don't do that!" the doctor ordered yet again. "It will run straight out of the cut on your jaw! Can't you understand that?!"

Groaning from two other hulks sprawled on chairs in the room started again.

"I'm telling you," the old doctor tried to sound impressive, "I need to see what damage has been done here! It looks like you three were beat with major league baseball bats! I can't imagine what has been damaged internally! I know there's broken and probably splintered ribs...you, King, have teeth knocked out and a surely broken nose and this cut was fouled with salt water...what do you want me to do?!"

"Do what I pay you for!!!" 'King' shouted almost incoherently. "Fix us!"

"You don't get it!" the doctor said sadly. "I don't know how bad you're hurt!"

"OK," the Doc sighed, resolutely, "Here goes..."

He stabbed a short needle into 'King's gaping jaw wound.

The result was more oaths and foul language and howls of pain.

The doctor continued in his unpleasant task of pushing the anesthetic into the length of the wound.

"There!" he finally almost shouted and grabbed the bottle 'King' had been so attached to.

"Give that a few minutes and I'll sew you up." He gulped a long draw from the bottle. "But I have to do some interior and some exterior! This is almost surgical! What did this?!"

"Never you mind," 'King' mused foully. His demeanor blackened a few more shades of deadly intent. "I know how to deal to this!"

His henchman said nothing in their pain. He suddenly bellowed out for the woman in the other room who had prayed beyond hope that she would not hear her name.

Failing to set her glass down without spilling it, she shakily peeped around the door frame.

"Get in here!" 'King' shouted with palpable malice.

When she had presented herself before him, his crazed gaze was enough to turn her knees weak.

"You know what we are going to do?" he slurred. The drink and the drugs to numb his face were catching up. "We are going to bring back the curse on that old coot's family..."

The older woman seemed to cringe further with the thought.

"I'm going to send you..." 'King' blurrily pointed to his consort. "Oh, yes, I'm going to send you. I'll say more later... And you know what will happen if you fail me?"

Her shaking satisfied his sadistic humor for the moment.

"All right," the old doctor resigned; a semi-circular suture needle and thread in hand. "This is going to hurt. A lot. It can't be helped. Ready?"

The bleached platinum blond moved out of the room as the screams started again.

The first day after the incident with 'King' and his men was like a prison sentence to Jan. Everyone had to remain inside and away from windows. Fin and Dearg kept watch outside and for the first time Jan saw her great uncle visibly worried. He carried a long double-barreled shotgun cradled in the crook of his arm.

Celia stayed close to Jonathon and they watched his tablet for entertainment.

Hunter searched for food in the kitchen all day.

Strangely, Shere spent most of the day close to Marie. Jan could not discern the majority of the conversations but caught snippets here and there. Marie answered questions not so much about her underwater adventures as to what she did for a living, how she spent her days, and what it was like running a company.

At one point Jan must have looked particularly forlorn and her mother included her in the newfound interest. Her mother wanted her to show Shere a program on her computer that was giving Marie a hard time.

Jan easily found the problem and fixed it. Then she had to endure the praises of her mother over her cyber prowess and the keen, fixed look of Shere who seemed to suddenly be wishing to enter the present era.

Indeed, Jan had noted, Shere had taken to grooming herself in a most feminine way ever since the make-over. She was back to looking like a lady and now she seemed to be a lady with a renewed purpose; whatever purpose that might be.

The early afternoon brought so many protests and protracted questions that Fin finally raised his arms, minus the shotgun, in surrender and decreed that Dearg and Hunter should go investigate the situation in The Tribe.

Jonathon wanted to go but he was outnumbered and after a suitably short period of indignation he was secretly happy enough to remain with Celia beaming at him from very close quarters cooing about his courage.

He decided it was Lucky who whispered 'stay on the stage, kid, while they want ya!'

Everyone waited tensely for what felt like forever until the two males had returned just before sunset with news.

It seemed The Tribe was in fact in an uproar but one of a positive note. There was great optimism in the besting of 'King', even though almost everyone agreed it was not over. He had not shown himself and for that matter neither had his henchmen. There were wonderings if all survived. At any rate, a boat had been observed bringing a doctor and then returning him to the mainland. That had most convinced the Chieftain and his men were severely injured but not dead.

Moreover, much had been asked about Marie and her further intentions. More political water-testing was in now real thought that there was a chance in a few weeks to oust the bully at The Gathering.

The most important thing, in Jan's mind, was the continued hounding questions she had about how safe it was now to resume 'training' in the water. She wanted to be free to explore.

Maggie-Shannon was calling to her.

After several such barrages Fin reluctantly agreed that there had never been a safer time.

Celia hugged Jonathon even closer at the news. She had her own playful agenda in mind.

Marie was the last one to admit that it was, for now, a plausible idea. Only, she was opting not to follow along if Dearg and Shere were there to look after her children. She mused that she had had enough chances of being spotted for the moment.

Dearg of course vowed to play the continued role of protector.

Again, strangely, Shere voiced an opinion that Hunter was very suited to being a guard as well, and Jonathon was his own force to be reckoned with.

Dearg looked at her briefly with a questioning glance but was not returned any answer except silence.

"I'd like to spend some time with Marie," Shere then stated.

Jan noted that her cousin did not look downward or away with the type of whisper she was associated with. Instead, the statement was direct and strong.

"Right-so," Dearg said rather slowly. "We'll go tomorrow if anybody has a mind to."

"Good!" Hunter chimed in. "I'm hungry!"

If the previous day had been a prison, this one served as pure joy to Jan.

Back in what she was beginning to feel was her natural element, the unbridled freedom and the very magical impossibility of her seal life was almost overwhelming.

Dearg had chosen to take them exploring the area surrounding Booth Bay. Avoiding the somewhat busy little town, as it was tourist season and whale watching and other excursion boats were plentiful, the seals had plenty of small islands and rocky coast to keep their attention.

It was enough for Jan to just be experiencing the underwater views with more and more familiarity. She had never felt so alive and vibrant and...free.

The word kept coming back to her. The way she felt was impossible to describe, she thought, but wonderfully open and boundless. The sheer vastness of the ocean, the smallness of her, and the way she seemed to fit in seemed in harmony. She reveled in Maggie-Shannon's constant presence and tuned-in to further get to know all the hushed voices that wanted to get to know her as well.

The group paused around noon to bask in the sun again on a small uninhabited outcrop of rock. The gentle crashing of the waves was like a lullaby.

Normally, Jan dreamily pondered, she was always quick to ask those around her about shared experiences, especially her brother. Now, as she gazed sleepily at him with Celia as always so close, she didn't need words or felt it was necessary to jot down images on a device to be looked over later.

The thought suddenly struck her that she was at peace.

This was a novel thing to her. She had always filled her time with what she deemed 'important' things. Ever since she could remember it had been that way. But now she was just content; content to just accept the whole ridiculously impossible scenario and just...be.

On the way back, the group was treated to a rather special meeting.

Seeming to just come out of nowhere, a small pod of harbor porpoises appeared.

Clicking and whistling (much like her mother, Jan thought

strangely) the small cetaceans were not particularly interested in the seals but at the same time seemed mildly curious.

If she could have, Jan would have smiled at the appearance of the mammals. Whereas she had seen pictures and videos of them, she could not help but find them funny looking compared to the bottle nosed dolphins she had seen in Florida. These cousins were much smaller and their snouts were more whale-like.

Jonathon was the first to engage the newcomers in a sort of game. He raced alongside them and matched their moves. This seemed to signal a playful mood and several of the small group of maybe six took up the chase.

Dearg seemed his ever-present watchful self and did not approve of the sport but Jan could not help getting into the moment. She picked out one of the younger looking ones and playfully rolled and dove and matched its moves. Then she took the lead and, with the animal following closely, she did her jumping routine.

As they were in mid air, their eyes met and Jan felt that she would remember the moment as one of priceless beauty and deep meaning.

Of course she knew she would get a chiding look from Dearg, but she also thought that he looked a bit impressed.

Just as quickly as they had arrived, the porpoises were gone again.

Their clicks died away and they were off to find food again or do whatever porpoises do, Jan decided.

Upon reentering the waters near the Kennebec, a few of The Tribe greeted them and they stopped to bob on the surface and chit-chat as no mere seals could do. To any other peering eyes, it would have looked like just that; seals bobbing on the surface. In fact, introductions were traded and as expected talk soon turned carefully to the delicate subject of Jan and Jonathon's mother and of the coming Gathering. No cards were tipped, but it was apparent that change was in the wind.

As Jan was brushing her hair in her room there was a knock on the door and her mother's voice.

The two spent a tender time sitting on the bed and having Jan enthusiastically telling of her day. Her mother beamed at her daughter's exuberance.

Then it was Jan's turn to ask about what Marie and Shere had done all day.

Marie frowned a bit as she explained how Shere had continued to be interested in things like spread sheets and on-line banking and a slew of other 'modern' subjects.

"I don't know what to make of it," Marie shrugged. "She's so different. I don't mind showing her all I can, it's just a little strange given what we have come to expect out of her."

"Yeah," Jan agreed. "Still, it's good to see her coming out of her shell."

"Agreed," her mother nodded. "I think she opened her eyes after the run-in with you-know-who. I think she has decided she has to play a front seat role in her own life."

"After what we know," Jan mused, "About what happened with those two guys we know she can take care of herself. That's for sure."

Marie nodded again.

"Guess we'll either find out what's up or we won't," she admitted.

The mother and daughter hugged and they were back to being what they both cherished so much.

Marie had just stepped into her room and shut the door when her cell phone on the night table rang.

A cold wave rushed over her as if her blood had turned to ice.

It was not the unexpected reception of service that she had come to accept in the area but more a sense of foreboding dread of something she had been waiting for.

On the third ring she knew that she had to pick up despite her distaste to do so. She recognized the number.

"Marie," she said in what she realized was too business like and unnecessary.

"My dear cousin," the female voice on the other end blurted. "Are you alright?"

"Yes, I am," Marie responded flatly.

"We have all been so worried!" the voice continued. "We knew, given the location of the situation, that it had to be you up there, what, visiting your husband's people?"

"My children were in danger," Marie stated. "I had no choice."

"How can we help?" the voice asked in a way Marie felt too trite.

"I have everything under control," she said.

"Of course you do but there is the matter of containing the ever-prying eyes."

Marie tried not to show her ire at the obvious reference to her underwater blast and the consequences. At least, she thought, nothing was mentioned so far as to her altercation of late.

"Not to worry," the voice tried to soothe. "The Matron has seen to the particulars and silenced any unwanted inquiries."

"Please thank her for that," Marie said genuinely. "And what does she want in return?"

"Now, please!" the female continued. "Don't be like that."

"All the same, how may I return the assistance?"

The conversation continued and Marie resigned herself to the inevitable.

All through dinner that night Jan had the feeling that Fin was up to something. He was more reserved than usual but not in a worried way. He kept shooting silent glances at Dearg.

Finally, Shere spoke up after the dishes had been cleared.

"Well," she said uncharacteristically to her father, "Are you going to tip-toe around all night or will you just ask?"

Dearg laughed silently.

Fin looked at Marie for a bit before beginning.

"I don't like to ask personal questions," he started, "But, Marie, how are you fixed...financially."

Marie must have looked a bit shocked.

"I mean," Fin floundered, "I know you make a good living and I know you have provided everything for the kids, but..."

"What are you getting at?" Marie asked calmly.

"Well..." the old man paused.

Dearg jumped in to save him.

"He wants to know if you care to do some business with us."

"And what kind of business?" Marie asked. Her son and daughter had perked up their ears and were keenly becoming interested.

"It's like this," Fin started again. "I need to tell you a story first."

"Go ahead," Marie said, sitting back in her chair.

"You see, you know that I do salvage work. Your Manny was involved, I've told you. I'm just getting so old that in the past few years my heart's just not in it anymore. Until, that is, I was approached today with a whopper of a tale."

Jonathon sat forward and his eyes grew wide.

"A contact that we have used before called to broker a deal. It seems that an article was being shipped. Now, I don't want to get into anybody's business, but I guess they have to be careful in the way they shipped whatever it was. They have to be secretive, I suppose. Anyway, this thing and the courier left Canada aboard a fishing vessel bound for Boston. They figured it was the safest way, they said. And I bet you know the next part."

He waited for effect.

"Storm comes up and down goes the boat. All hands and the guy with the shipment lost."

Marie sat forward.

"I'm sorry for the loss of life," she said slowly.

"Everything is legal and above-board," Fin continued. "Boat's in international waters and there won't be any questions or filling out forms and whatnot if we act fast and quiet-like."

"And?" Marie asked with a raised eyebrow.

Fin looked like a schoolboy trying to come up with a good story.

"Well," he stammered, "See, we, that is Dearg and me, we know where the boat is, our broker sent the last known coordinates and we figured out the rest. Just, see, nobody's willing to pay to investigate a fishing boat in 300 feet of cold water for insurance purposes. Unless, of course, there's a treasure in that boat, but the owners don't know about the article in question. Other salvagers would want a huge percentage to determine what happened to collect the insurance. Only..."

Marie waited, as did her children.

Dearg jumped in again.

"Only it's too dangerous for a diver. It's too dangerous for...one of us. You know how wrecks can be. You can get caught-up in something...it's just too dangerous. Trying to find an unknown article in the hulk of a ship? It's just too dangerous. Except for..."

Silence filled the kitchen. The old weather radio crackled with momentary static.

"Except for..." Marie finished, "Someone who isn't restricted by breathing air, right?"

Fin smiled. Dearg sat back in his chair now.

"Can you guess," Fin almost whispered, "How much it's worth to these guys to get their thing back? Can you guess?"

Marie was silent but her children thought they could just see a slight smile cross her set features.

"I don't need the money," Fin admitted. "But I like to think I can still do for my family. Marie, you would never, ever want for anything ever again. And the kids..."

"I take care of them just fine," she roused.

"I know that!" Fin waved. "But...just think of it?"

"Mom," Jan stated seriously. "I don't want you doing anything so dangerous. You could get hurt..."

"Yeah," Jonathon agreed. But then a small voice in his head added something.

"Anyway, it sounds too hard to do. Even for you..."

He thought he heard a smoky chuckle.

Marie looked at her son with her best piercing gaze.

"Too hard?" she laughed, "Too hard?! You don't know the things I've done and the dangers I've faced. This is nothing compared to..."

She trailed off her thoughts.

"Clever, son, clever..." she smiled.

Jonathon smiled as well.

"Anyway," Marie said matter-of-factly, "The answer is already yes and I can tell you all about this article and about what we are getting into if you wish."

Now all eyes were attentive to her.

"First, I also received a call today from my kin in the islands," she started. "It seems that my little demonstration in sonic blasting of course reached their attention. The military and scientists and other parties that have searched for us for eons are eager to pursue this but all has been silenced by my people's long reach. But there is a price for me to pay. A favor for mutual friends. That is why you got the call, as my people know where I am and who you are. Shall I go on?"

The silence served as an answer.

"We are to retrieve a metal box about the size of a guitar case, although I am quite sure there is something else in it that I am not to know about. The person who we will return it to is something of a character that operates in the islands of my people. A pirate, for a better name, or a privateer of sorts that I know only by stories and more secrets. Goes by only 'Dovarchu', *Doe-var-koo*, whatever that means."

"You didn't say what I just heard you say!" Dearg blurted.

Now Marie looked puzzled.

"Go on," she said slowly.

"The name you spoke of," Dearg said lowly, "It means 'sea otter' in Irish but is used to describe anything out in the water that can't be explained. Like a monster. Lake monster even. Terror. The legends in the Old Country tell of a character who plundered and murdered along the coasts in the New World and beyond to support the Irish cause. Back in the 1600's it started and the title was passed down to subsequent generations."

"Makes sense," Marie continued. "If that seems at all plausible. They have acted in the past with the blessings of my people in some sort of mutually beneficial capacity. The current one, so I have heard in my youth, prays on other smugglers, mostly drug-runners, to keep the peace in my family's waters. Also involves other countries in secret to thwart the traffic. Real piece of work. Not the one to be involved with, but I have no choice. Definably not one to cross. So we better not mess this up. Let's do this."

"Finest kind!" Fin stated.

"Here we go!" Jan sighed.

"This just gets better by the minute!" her brother smiled.

14

Jonathon knew he was dreaming but it was so real he couldn't resist giving in to it. The smell of stale sweat and cigarettes and booze wafted through the dark air of the back stage side wing. Scenery drapes and ropes and discarded props were everywhere.

A single light source came from a small window in a shabby box with 'Stage Manager' painted above it. Seated inside was a fat man with a worn derby hat and stained shirt with shabby suspenders. His stubble-covered round face looked nervously towards the door that must have led out into the ubiquitous alley. The stump of a cigar glowed as he heavily breathed.

He almost jumped when the thin dapper figure appeared out of the shadows. He knew this was always the last of the performers to leave. He was counting on that.

The thin man wore an overcoat of once-fine material. He stopped long enough to extend a gentile gloved hand into the widow.

"Dah, OK, Lucky," the fat man stammered. "Here youse go. Cash as always."

The cigar stump never left the puffy-lipped mouth as the manager forked over some greasy folded bills.

The thin figure counted the money and pocketed it into the over coat.

With a nod he flicked the brim of his fedora in a sort of parting gesture. He then produced a card and spun it deftly onto the small counter.

"Sure, sure," the fat man acknowledged, "Dah, we'll send youse's stuff to dis address, don't you worry none, Lucky!"

The dapper man turned and in an instant was out the stage door.

Craning the thick neck to listen, the man with the cigar stump smiled a bit as he heard the scuffle in the alley. There were sounds of crates being smashed and garbage cans being tossed about. He grinned an evil grin as he thought of his cut of the money the two robbers outside would be bringing him.

There was a protracted silence from the alley.

The stage door exploded open and in a move no human could follow a thin figure in an overcoat was standing before the manager's box. A lithe arm shot out and the fist attached connected in a lightning blow to the fat man's Adam's apple.

Before the fat man could even grimace at the choking pain, the same thin arm reached into the box and grabbed the oily hair on the back of the thick head. With a tremendous force, that head was smashed down onto the plywood counter in front of it. The nose was mangled and the forehead split open but the most horrible pain came from the lit cigar that was now burning into one of the porky cheeks. The acrid smell was appalling and the cries from the would-be villain were horrific but the head remained pinned down.

The thin man looked away from the awful scene as if peering into an audience out in the darkness.

"I don't like showing you this," Lucky said to Jonathon. "Only, it's what happens. Always somebody wants to take advantage of you. I'm telling you this because things are going to happen and I want you to be ready. Follow?"

Jonathon nodded in his sleep.

The scene faded into wispy smoke but the meaning was crystal clear.

The sensible silver SUV was more than a bit cramped on the journey down to Portland. Jan was squished in between Dearg and Hunter in the back seat. Fin rode up front with Marie driving and Jonathon and Celia did not seem to mind being delegated to sitting rather prone in the otherwise cramped very back.

Jan recounted in her mind how the day before had been filled with nautical charts spread out on the kitchen table and depths and currents and water temperatures being pored over. She had tried to not get in the way, as had her brother, but she found the whole ordeal exciting and yet potentially dangerous.

The most intriguing part had come when blueprints of the type vessel now lying on the sea floor had been studied. Although every boat was slightly different, Fin had taught, these prints were from the small shipyard in Canada where the fishing vessel was built. Of particular interest was the layout of the few small cabins below the operational decks. Here, Fin was convinced, would be where a 'passenger' would have been berthed and also where said passenger would have most likely been when the ship went down.

As to what led to the disaster, only knowledgeable speculation could be called upon.

Fin figured that the boat headed out in rough weather to avoid scrutiny from most others. No real fishing was planned, as the idea was to get the man with the shipment to Boston as soon as possible. Unfortunately, the waters in which they sailed were known to be frequented by 'rogue waves' that formed in bad weather and would strike a ship amid-beam or sideways where a captain or wheelman did not expect and as such drive a boat down to either capsize or roll into a dive where water rushed in and sank the poor lot.

Where Dearg and Fin had been briefed as to the underwater location of the boat was further evidence of the scenario. Sonar readings from rescue vessels had it resting on the seabed on its side with a list of some 40 degrees. The wheelhouse was smashed in and the port side outriggers were bent-in as if a huge force had crumpled them.

Now, the group minus Shere was headed to Portland to set Dearg and Fin on board their salvage ship that would then be motored to the Kennebec. There, it had been decided that Marie and her two children would join them for the expedition. Hunter, and likewise Celia (who seemed mortified to be left without Jonathon) would stay at home to be watched over, as well as the house, by Shere.

Fin and Dearg were dropped off on a commercial wharf near what was called 'The Old Port'. The older man had left instruction on some sightseeing and so Marie found some paid-parking and they embarked on a visit to the historical area.

Cobblestone streets and old warehouses were now home to interesting shopping and restaurants and pubs and tourist traps with cheesy souvenirs.

The architecture struck Jan more than anything else. Jonathon was amazed at the sights he realized had been viewed by the great stars of Vaudeville, as this had been the end of the line for the East Coast Run. The likes of Burns and Allen, Sophie Tucker, the Marx Brothers and countless more had played here before making the jump by rail to Canada. One of his favorites, W. C. Fields, had memorized the American Native names of places hereabouts and included them in his most famous, classic, boastful routines. 'Once in Passsamaquoddy...'

Leaving the old, Marie guided them to the new. New, at least, as far as Maine goes.

The Maine Mall was so named because at the time it was constructed it was indeed the only such structure in the state. Others had now sprung up in Bangor and the like but this was still the original.

Strolling through the place, Jan was struck by how few people seemed to be about. Conversely, her mother reminded her that this was 'teeming' as far as state populace was concerned.

Jonathon thought he would lose blood flow in his arm as Celia clutched it in wonder and frightened delight. She whispered to him that she had never been around so many people and he shook his head in thinking of Boston. He secretly and selfishly studied her gaze as he wondered if she found any of the many other males present interesting.

His fears were unfounded as she only clung to him more tightly with each passing moment.

Hunter was in a dilemma as to whether to stare at the girls or search out the food smells. He struck a happy medium in both.

After some frivolous shopping of no real need Marie spent a short time at Shere's request purchasing a laptop computer and associated gear with money she had sent. Then she managed to pull Hunter away from the food court with a promise of something new.

The entire group was then herded by car again to a nearby Mexican restaurant that Marie had spied.

As everything was new to Celia and Hunter, the twins and their mother had a field day introducing them to things they had never before encountered. Jan and Jonathon were glad to have some fare not of the sea, even if they had been spoiled so far.

The entire experience would have been a complete success had it not been for the ride back to Fin's.

Tactfully, for the sake of all those in the SUV, some thirty minutes into the return trip Marie had to breach the subject of when it was appropriate and not appropriate to give into the gastrointestinal results of spicy food to the newcomers.

Giggles and downed windows resulted.

Back 'home' at Fin's Shere recounted no troubles and so everyone waited for the salvage ship's arrival. The trip up Casco Bay was not long but paperwork and fuel had to be negotiated and it was not until almost dark that Shere called them all to the dock to witness an impressive fifty-plus feet long vessel moving silently past the Lighthouse into their bay. Shere launched the small boat and another hour passed as the large ship was tethered and put to bed. Finally, the two men came back with Shere.

Immediately, Fin uncharacteristically asked to borrow Jan's cell phone. Not Marie's, but Jan's. He passed it off by saying he did not want to draw attention. He needed to contact the broker to iron out particulars. The old man disappeared into the boat house for privacy as the rest of the house went in to forage dinner.

Some hour later, he returned and motioned to speak to Marie.

Moving to a far corner of the kitchen for relative privacy, he fished in a drawer for a scrap of paper and a well-worn stub of a pencil.

"We're all set," he said matter-of-factly. "As soon as you want, tomorrow, I hope, we'll leave. I want Dearg to help me keep the ship over the target. That's not easy. I have a specialized tent-thing over the stern for, ah, changing. I want your two to act as go betweens. They can take turns keeping track of where you are and what's going on. I don't want them anywhere near the wreck. They just watch..."

"Agreed," Marie nodded.

"Now," Fin added, "Afterwards, we go direct to a spot set-up already down off the New Hampshire coast. They meet us; we give them the goods..."

"You're supposing I'll find them," Marie interjected. "And you don't fear a double-cross?"

"I know you will find it," Fin smiled thinly. "And I also know it won't be pleasant. But these people have their own code of conduct. They will act in good faith. Anyway, afterwards they send the money e-lect-tronic-like to an account down in the Islands, by way of Switzerland. That way the taxes and any prying eyes..."

"I've been thinking about the taxes," Marie mused. "I don't know how I'm going to explain the windfall."

"Unless you don't want to," Fin suggested. "Don't you pay enough tax?"

"Well, yes," she thought out loud. "I guess it would depend on how much I would have to pay. I mean, it would bother me to think I didn't…"

Fin passed her the scrap of paper where he had scrawled a figure.

"I could get over it," Marie said after a moment.

Jan flitted about the house for the remainder of the evening and well into the early night with a shared sense of nervous anticipation.

Fin and Dearg and Jonathon pored over the charts and boat blueprints. Her mother was bent on teaching Shere how to use the new computer and they made some phone calls to discern what Internet availabilities there were in the area. Celia vied for Jonathon's attention and Hunter just wandered about sniffing out snacks.

Finally Fin announced that an early start was in order and as such rest was ordered.

A shuffling followed with each associated member of the household doing whatever was necessary to ensure compliance.

Marie showed Shere how to 'log out' and save data. Hunter took a bag of tortilla chips aloft with him. Dearg rolled up the documents and made a sheepish attempt to not look like he was going to Shere's room. Celia pouted until Jonathon walked her up the stairs under the watchful eye of his mother.

After a brief moment of quiet, Jan realized she was alone in the kitchen with her great uncle.

"Didn't figure on all this, did ya Missy?" he asked with a warm gleam in his old eyes.

"No," she admitted, "If I had written a book I could not have ever dreamed this."

"But you are meant for it," the old man winked playfully.

"Ah-yuh," she mimicked, "Suppose I am..."

The dawn had not thought of breaking when the rap at her door startled Jan awake. She didn't know who had done it, but it didn't matter.

She forewent the usual shower (which was laborious anyway in the antique claw-footed bathtub with a retro-fitted hose and nozzle) figuring she would be on a boat and eventually in the salt water before long. Gathering her skin, and cell phone for no reason, along with her black robe and a backpack with several changes of underwear, she started downstairs.

The kitchen was somewhat silently filled when she got there. A make-shift breakfast had been packed by Shere into a wicker picnic basket that looked like a cast-off prop from The Wizard of Oz. Marie was rechecking her own bundle of gear and speaking to Jonathon who was trying to listen while also doing his best to stem the flow of tears gushing from Celia.

Fin announced it was time to go and further stated that two trips were to be made in the skiff. He and Dearg and Jonathon would go first, piloted of course by Shere. He gave final stern orders to an attentive Hunter as to looking after everything.

While the men and Shere were gone, Marie did her best to console Celia and reassure her that they would back in a few days. Her natural motherly way did seem to calm the girl who was acting, as far as Jan was concerned, much too childish.

Then it was their turn and in the blackness of the early pre-dawn Shere motored them masterfully out across the bay with no words spoken to come alongside the humming hulk of the big ship. Dearg assisted in their transfer and with an unabashed long kiss he left Shere to go back.

On board, it was apparent for the moment than Jan and Jonathon and their mother were not to get in the way. A very quick run-down of the ship's layout, with particular attention being stressed as to areas where they were not to venture, was shouted by Dearg over the constant din of motors and the like. He directed them to stow gear in two small cabins below, one for Marie and the other to be shared by the twins, and then suggested a small but well stocked galley as a place to be.

Even as Jan and her brother were looking at the little bunk beds and sparse accommodations of their cabin, the ship lurched with a powerful commotion and the trip was underway.

The siblings found their mother in the cramped passageway and they exchanged a collective look of 'we ain't staying down here!'

Cautiously treading up the steel stairway they found their way onto the main deck and a choice presented itself. One stairwell led up to the wheelhouse where no doubt Fin or Dearg or both were seriously bent on navigating the vessel and as such would be no fun.

The other way led out onto a wide dark deck and looked like way better sport.

Like three children, not mother and offspring, they crept quietly out into the growing sunrise to survey their surroundings.

They were not disappointed.

The few and far between lights of dwellings along the rocky shore were beautiful. The beam from the now mechanized Sequin Light was picturesque. As the horizon started to glow with an impending dawn, the dark shapes of small islands came into clearer focus. Birds wheeled overhead and a few smaller lobster boats were now visible.

Jan thought of what a lonely, tiring, hard job that trade was. Jonathon was thinking how free and exciting it was to match wits with the sea and its treasures.

After an hour or so the land was no longer seen and even though the waves were mild, the novelty had worn off. The three went back inside to find the 'head', or bathroom, and then the galley.

Marie found some cold breakfast things in the basket and after they had tried and failed at civil conversation over the constant hum of motors, they just sat and waited.

Presently Dearg popped in and took each of them in turns up to the wheelhouse to see the goings on there. It was interesting, more so for Jonathon than any of the other two, but it was a break from what turned out to be a long, very boring morning.

The afternoon proved no more exciting.

Trips up on deck, more waves and water, back to the galley...the early evening dragged by.

It was unspoken but neither Marie nor her children would entertain the thought of asking Fin 'are we there yet?'

Jan had laid her head down on the small galley table for the umpteenth time and was almost asleep when the engines slowed.

Mother and twins perked up and looked at each other hopefully but with a shot of fear of the unknown at the same time.

After what seemed an eternity Fin stuck his white head into the room.

"It'll be dark soon. Radar shows nobody around for a hundred nautical miles, and that suits me just fine. Get yer gear and we'll assemble on deck when the sun drops." Then he was gone again.

"We're going *at night*?!" Jan blurted.

"Sweetheart," her mother smiled, "Have you forgotten that none of us need light?"

Jan pondered on this.

"Guess I should have mentioned it," Marie mused. "Anyway, it will be more discreet and our eyes can see just as well in the dark as in the light. I know you two have not had that experience yet, but no time like the present."

Jonathon smiled at the thought of the adventure.

"Anyway," their mother continued, "You guys are not to come anywhere near that wreck, you hear me? I want you to work in shifts just watching out between the boat here and the wreck on the bottom. Take turns surfacing at the front of the boat, I say the front of the boat, and avoid the props at the rear. They will have to be spinning back and forth to keep us on top of the hulk. Just let Fin and Dearg know everything's alright."

She touched both of their cheeks for added emphasis.

"You will hear me 'sounding'...clicking and locating as before. If anything should go wrong, I'll make a noise you won't have trouble understanding. Ok?"

The two nodded solemnly.

"Ah, one more thing," Marie remembered. "These waters, according to Fin, will have a lot of sea life around the wreck; especially at night. Blue sharks are the scariest. But they won't bother you and they are beautiful. I promise. The other reason Fin chose a night dive is that any Great Whites in the area usually only feed at dawn and dusk. If I detect any of those about, the whole thing's called off. And I will know if they are about. Trust me."

The darkness all about the vessel was complete. A slight breeze made sounds as it whistled through the wire riggings. Lapping waves were also heard against the constantly moving sides.

Dearg was aloft in the wheelhouse moving the power levers back and forth to keep position. His red-black, keen eyes were switching from a GPS screen to the controls.

Lights above the deck illuminated the assembled.

Jan had been the last to come topside. She wore her black robe and immediately saw that it was overkill.

Her brother wore only a pair of plaid boxer shorts, despite the surprising chill of open waters in the Gulf of Maine in the summer. His skin was folded over his elbow.

Marie's attire as well shocked her daughter. She was wearing a large towel wrapped around her and tucked in under her strong arms and apparently nothing else. Her hair was braided tightly and bound so as not to be cumbersome in the twisted passages of the wreck.

Fin did not seem to approve or disapprove of Jan's choice but only seemed a bit preoccupied with getting on with the job.

He led them aft across the deck, which was pitching and lurching with the efforts of Dearg above. The older man had no problems navigating the deck with the seasoned sea legs that no mere human could have amassed over the years of experience.

It was a bit different for Marie, Jan and Jonathon, but they followed as fast and as surely as they could. Jan bumped into and then held on to her mother for support.

On the fantail, or very rear portion of the ship, Fin had indeed erected a tubular frame now surrounded by dark tarps that made up a tent-like array of about ten feet square. The thing extended out over a flat transom that would allow them to slip into the water unseen. This hardly seemed necessary, Jan thought, given the fact that there was no one anywhere near them, but then she realized the genius of her now-modern-thinking great uncle in that satellites were always watching nowadays.

"Not so many frilly-stuff out he-ah," Fin stated, "You all know your jobs, we know ours. I need you three to change as fast as you can. Marie, you first, then Jonathon help your sister then you. I can only kill the props for a few minutes and even then it'll take some doing to get us back on top. Ready?"

Jan did not like the idea that had just been laid out but there was no time to argue.

The three passed through an opening in the tarp that closed again with Velcro patches. Before Jan could say a thing, her mother kissed each of her children and said a last minute set of orders.

"I love you, I'm counting on you, and I'm doing this for us for the rest of our lives. Don't go near the props or the wreck. Get it?"

"Got it," the twins said in automatic unison.

"Good!" their mother said.

Then, in a whirl that did not leave the twins much time to feel embarrassed, she whipped off the towel and called out to Fin. He whistled loudly and the engines stopped dead.

"Sorry," Marie said to her children, "No need for the wet suit vest. It's too cold down there to worry about."

Trying to avoid their mother's obvious lack of clothes, realizing it had been many years since either of them had seen each other this way, it was still impossible not to watch as she unfurled a shimmering lower body and tail and simply, gracefully, impossibly slipped her legs into it and sat down on the transom.

Her features changed rather suddenly and profoundly. The eyes became larger and definitely not human. The gills appeared behind her ears. She kept her mouth shut but her offspring knew the sharp teeth were now there.

Communication now a problem and with the obvious need for her to breathe water not air, she tried to look lovingly on her children but it was lost in the hardened features of her kind. Grabbing the belt that she had prepared, which had the sheathed shark-toothed weapon on one side and a crow bar and several more tools on the other, she flopped into the dark water and was gone for the moment.

"You're up, Sis," Jonathon reminded.

"I don't think so!" she blushed.

"Come on!" her brother shot back, "No time! I'm not watching, right?"

He indeed turned his head and she trusted him. She tried to picture all the early years when the two of them took baths together and changed clothes in the same room and…

The robe fell away and she could hear Maggie-Shannon singing and then she was flopping around on the hard transom. She looked up as her brother gave her a gentle shove and she was into the inky blackness.

Or so she had thought.

Nothing could have further from the truth.

Yes, at first, there had been darkness. But then everything came into focus and she realized with a thrill that what her mother had suggested was in fact true.

She could see into the abyss.

There were no words her human mind could conjure up to express the feeling.

Whereas before, in the daylight, the underwater world was all about moving, waving seaweeds and darting fish, this was monumentally different.

Her wonder was briefly interrupted by the splashing of her brother entering the same wonderful realm. He swam to her and motioned that they should swim clear, just as the props roared back to life.

Then, their mother was there. She again tried to convey tender emotion but it was apparent that this was difficult. Her tail swished powerfully to keep her in place and her arms were crossed to cover her unclothed chest. She did make motions with her large eyes to tell them she was not at all happy with the cold temperature of the waters. They found this amusing, but both realized again that she was more accustomed to tropical locals.

She raised a webbed hand to remind them to remember her instructions and then she flipped her wide tail and was off in a dive.

Jan realized her brother was going through the same epiphany she was in their surroundings.

There was the surface above. It was noisy with the boat sounds and the waves and she knew she had to return there to breathe.

Below was nothing. At least, nothing she had explored yet. Unlike in the river and bay, all about her was freedom. There were no boundaries. She swam and dived and turned and spun and it all took place in a medium that seemed to have no end. She equated the new sensation with flying in space.

The concept of 'space' and the vested interest of such exploration suddenly seemed silly and downright stupid to her.

She remembered reading that 'mankind' knew more about the surface of the sterile moon than the bottom of the sea. Why?

Adjusting her eyes to the wonders around her she now saw life everywhere.

Timid, probing squid moved up from the depths to forage. Jan had also read that at a time in Earth's history this creature had been the most intelligent life form on the planet. Its' mysteries still had not been explored.

The very substance of the water was a soup of plankton and small krill and untold animal life. Below she knew would fall the snow of the ocean; a steady mix of organic substance that fed untold legions of bottom dwellers that far outnumbered even the insect population of the land. Here was the Earth. The waters had been here innumerable years before the rising of the upstart dry places. Here too was the tumult and violence that created the places above the waves.

For the first time in her short life, Jan believed she touched the vastness of what it meant to be alive.

Jonathon swam up to her and through his eyes she knew he was having the same revelation. But he did remind her they had a job to do.

Rising together, they bobbed on the surface in front of the ship until someone; they could not be sure who, waved back at them. Then Jonathon looked at his sister and communicated in their seal language.

"I know what Mom said," he barked, "But do you think I'm not going to see what's down there?"

Before Jan could yip a rebuke, he was off. She had to follow.

Diving down into the depths, she realized how pressure changed but her seal body adapted. They passed through a couple of different water zones; different temperatures and salinity that was a source of amazement.

When she spied the thing for the first time she had an overall sense of dread.

It lay just as Fin had pictured it. Sort of. The outline was unmistakably that of a fishing vessel. Heaved over on the starboard or right side, it looked both abandoned and forlorn and suggested a violent end.

Jan looked for her mother, who would have certainly disapproved of the disobeyed instructions, but instead saw Jonathon cavorting along the fouled deck of the wreck. He was chasing a smaller school of Pollock that belonged to a larger school of the same that mingled with a slow moving mass of Cod that looked to feed on countless smaller fish that tried desperately to hide in the twisted metal and burst-open hatches of the disaster.

And then she saw the predators.

Just as her mother had suggested, and her brother had so far neglected to notice, slowly and methodically circling above the jumble of life surrounding the wreck were slender, thin, wide-finned phantoms with unblinking large eyes.

Jan had to agree that the Blues were indeed impressive and yes beautiful. But their beauty also masked a ruthless efficiency and unwavering methodical cleansing of anything that showed weakness or inattention to the facts of the sea.

Jan managed to get Jonathon's attention but he passed off the warning with a shrug.

In growing concern, she tried to picture what her mother was going through and how dangerous it might be for her. But for the present she followed her brother reluctantly back to the surface for precious air.

Marie had stoically pressed herself to the job at hand; however unpleasant that was.

She was not unaccustomed to the task; far from it. Only, this water was not what she was used to.

The immediate cold was a danger in itself. Her body could accommodate, but it needed more time than the fish that normally inhabited this clime. She did not have that time.

On the descent, she had gratefully passed through a layer that was more oxygenated and had passed as much enriched water over her gills as possible before what she knew lay below.

Wrecks were a common thing to her people. They had long ceased, too many years before her time, to be an amusement and in fact held simple truths. Danger, death, and decay…all amid the new birth of struggling life and the constant circle of it. Make a mistake and you were part of the food chain.

She entered the shattered wheelhouse as she had planned given the layout of the ship. There were no surprises here as any of the doomed crew had been washed away or fed upon. It looked like so many others she had encountered in her native tropical waters where sudden calamity had snuffed out human life trusting on technology; whatever the time period.

Only here, the coldness had stunted the sea's reclamation process.

As delicately as she could, aware that her tail movements would stir up sediment, she progressed down the open passageway into the lower decks. She ignored the thought of a tasty cold snack of the Cod she shooed away. No need to invite others looking for scraps of a meal.

Passing through several corridors she noted the telltale signs of several deceased crewmen. Unlike movies or supposed land-dwellers' ideas of the scene, these were not de-fleshed skeletons clad in their fishermen's' attire but were rather lumps arranged helter-skelter in varying degrees of decomposition. Dark piles suggested synthetic clothing that so far were not digestible to the clean-up crews of the deep.

Some of these wriggled with what she feared and found most detestable of cold, deep waters.

Hagfish.

The eel-like, jawless, slime producing living fossils of nightmares; they were repugnant to her more than any other creature alive. Still, they served their purpose.

She pressed-on past the display and found her way down a passageway that was slightly littered with unrecognizable objects in varying degrees of organic reclamation until she found the split, left or right, that would take her to her prize.

Left she went, and gingerly now, for the rusting metal walls were at such a state that a sudden powerful movement, like from her strong tail, could cause a cloud of debris to be released. Such a cloud would get passed over her gills and could spell untold troubles to her system.

The door to the cabin was in view. The listings of the ship put all the weight of the door onto the knob and lock side, but she tried the handle in hopeful attempt.

No such luck.

What could have compelled a man, she thought, except blind panic, to lock a ship's door when the likelihood of a wreck was impending?

Maybe, she further mused, it was the item that the man was guarding inside the cabin.

She holstered the shark-tooth weapon and retrieved a long, slim, pry-bar. This she forced into the space between door and lock and jamb. With a strong push-and-lever motion the door swung inward silently.

Here Marie waited a painful, protracted while to allow the water from outside the cabin to mingle with the stagnant volume within to again save her from passing over her gills an oxygen-depleted soup of microorganisms and stuff that had not been replenished for a while.

Satisfied that at least some settling had taken place, she cautiously moved in.

Once again, movies and fictitious books whose writers never experienced true unromantic nature would have this scene all wrong.

A jumble of the contents that the occupant of the cabin had assembled for the voyage lay in more piles of green and powder-white lumps strewn askew to the degree of the listing wreck.

Marie sought out, as she had before, the largest and longest of these humps.

Slowly and methodically, yet with a growing sense of urgency as the cabin was positively stifling to her ever-increasingly starved gills, she regarded the once living body. It lay on its side, right side, with what used to be arms outstretched in the common final resolution of giving-in to drowning.

Moving to the corner of the cabin she found the object she was looking for.

The case lay on the floor of the cabin. It was aluminum or the like with a handle and lock mechanism. No dents or damage was evident and she reached for it.

The sound was more felt all the way through her than heard. She drew her webbed hand back in more prudence than shock.

Deep bass in tone, the wave of sound repeated itself. She felt it came from within the case but could not be sure. It seemed the case wanted to be found. She touched the handle and the noise stopped.

Making no long protracted gesture in either symbolic reverence or the lack of the same, she prudently left the cabin to the eventuality of the sea.

Marie's retracing of her venture was speeded by both the need for oxygenated water and her concern for her children. As she burst out of the wheelhouse into the openness she spied her twins rather frolicking much too closely to the hulk than she had remembered ordering them to. But, she passed this off as the three made a swirling, spinning, and happy reunion.

Then they were off to the surface.

Jonathon broke water first, ahead of the ship, and caught Dearg's searching eyes in signal to stop the props.

Marie insisted that she go first, changed, drew a towel around her for modesty, and then aided her son and daughter in their transformations. The case was not spoken of. Only when the three were staggering back across the ship's deck, now pitching again with the motors roaring to life, did they stop to share a collective hug of 'victory'.

Fin met them as they made their way back into the sheltered corridors leading to the galley.

"Everyone alright, I see?" he almost shouted over the engines.

Marie nodded but also noted he was intently interested in the success of the mission.

"Can we look?" Jan asked, pointing to the case.

"I think that is a bad idea," her mother said emphatically. "This thing has some magic in it and I don't care to know what it is or expose any of you to it."

"You did good," Fin winked at Marie. "We just have a few finer points to go over and you and yours are richer than you may have ever imagined."

"We'll talk those particulars later," Marie said stoically. "I want to be with you when the exchange is made. I just feel that I am not to pass this off to anybody else."

Fin tried to shoo-away the thought.

"I mean it," she continued, "But I want to drop off Jan and Jonathon."

Before either sibling could mount a complaint, Fin nodded solemnly.

"Right-so, Missy," he conceded.

The return trip was long and uneventful. Sleep was fitful and not restful at all.

During one of the few times when the twins did doze off with their heads on their arms at the galley table, Marie sought out Fin and they formed a loose plan.

After the youngsters were dropped off, they would rendezvous just off Massachusetts waters at a predetermined GPS point. Both parties had made it clear that if any other ships were sighted the deal was off. Fin did not distrust the buyers but still was serious enough to be cautious. The subject arose of just where to electronically send their money.

"If you trust me," Marie suggested, "I have an idea. You said you wanted to avoid detection and, ah, taxes. Well, here goes..."

"You know something of my family," she continued, "But not everything. My mother's people, the Sea-People, her 'Pod' as we say; they own islands in the Caribbean. It's like your holdings in that nobody outside the family knows we own them, but we do. We are sovereign islands and our banks are, well, used by a lot of very wealthy people."

"I see," Fin nodded, raising his bushy eyebrows.

Marie continued.

"My mother never wanted me to be a part of it, I never touched any of the money set aside for me until..."

"Until after Manny disappeared," Fin continued.

"I just wanted to find out if we, that is, the kids and me, were going to be alright. That's when I found the extent of the family's holdings. I was shocked. I haven't touched any of the money yet, so it just grows, but I did contact my relatives a few years ago and conceded to having a passport made for me and the twins there. Just in case..."

"Wise," Fin agreed.

"So, we could wire the money to my account there. I can then either send yours anywhere you want or start an account for you."

"Interesting," the older man mused. "I like it. It's settled."

"I'll get my computer from below and write down the pertinent information."

"Finest kind!" Fin smiled.

"And," Marie added, "I'll just bet you have some sort of firepower hidden away on this boat. They need to be stowed very much where they are. Any hint of such would not go well for the group that we are about to encounter."

She held her hand up sternly to stop the protest.

"You'll find that I'm familiar with just about any firearm you might produce. I'm best with something automatic. I won't go into how I've learned this, but let's just say I learned at an early age. The 'sponge fishing' business is dangerous and sometimes lethal. But as I said, any even unintended show of force and this character would be disastrous. Trust me."

"You never cease to amaze!" the smiling man chuckled.

15

It was nearly noon when the seldom seen larger boat that everyone knew belonged to old Fin MacLeer cut thought the somewhat rough waves past the Light and rounded the curve at Fort Popham.

The two men piloting the craft were not very happy about making such a show in broad daylight. They had tried to even avoid the numerous lobster boats that they had passed on the way in. But they were on a timetable and as such everything else could just get hanged.

Even as the ship slowed in the small bay a skiff was headed out to meet it. A woman with dark, not-so-wild now but still windblown hair was at the stern motor.

If there were prying eyes they would have seen a hasty disembarking of two younger forms and a quick departure. As the smaller boat headed in, the larger one roared around and back out the mouth of the Kennebec as fast as possible.

Waiting on the dock at Fin's was the stoic strong male figure of Hunter looking dutifully to help with the landing. The other figure there was an uncontrollable fair young female who almost jumped into the small craft to get her arms around Jonathon.

Jan rolled her eyes at the display but Shere actually smiled and chuckled a bit.

Back inside the walls of the house, Jan and Jonathon began a quick retelling of the events. Shere had hot tea ready and did her best to warm up the two. Jonathon did not need as much of this as his sister since Celia smothered him. Eventually, Shere and Hunter pried her off the lad and Shere ordered the twins upstairs to a hot shower or bath and a change of clothes.

The afternoon then passed quietly with Jan opting to write her adventures in her tablet upstairs and her brother finally sleeping on the sofa in the parlor with Celia doting over him and dreamily watching him snooze.

Sometime around twilight Shere managed to get Celia to come into the kitchen and help her with a small supper. She also called to Jan that they would eat in 15 minutes.

Neither Shere nor Celia heard the shaky knock on the front door; the front door no one ever used. That was a 'Maine thing'. Front doors were hardly ever used.

The knock repeated a bit louder but still rather unsure.

Jonathon had been in between sleep and dream for some time. He didn't actually know if he was getting up in his dreams or if he was awake. He simply groggily moved to the door that was just a few steps from the couch and undid the deadbolt and opened it.

He vaguely recognized the figure standing there but before he could utter a sound a cloud of fine mist enveloped his face. He breathed in and everything went dark.

Some short time later Hunter entered the parlor expecting to rouse his cousin for food.

Instead, he found the young man standing stock still in front of the open door.

Jonathon stood with eyes partially open staring at nothing. He bore a dumbfounded look on his statue-like face. His arms fell loosely to his side and his shoulders were drooped.

Hunter peered outside and saw nothing. When he could not get a response from his cousin, he spread the alarm to the whole house.

"There they are," Fin noted as he pointed ahead and starboard. The other two in the wheelhouse followed his thick finger.

"She's not anything that I would have expected, can't make out the lines, and she does not appear on radar," he mused. "Smart and scary. Never seen the likes."

Marie and Dearg looked hard to make out the craft. It appeared to be a sleek, black, tri-hulled thing without masts and close to a hundred feet in length.

A series of short light bursts emitted from what was obviously their low wheelhouse.

"Right as rain," Fin mumbled again, and produced a hand-held, powerful torch of his own and flashed back the predetermined response.

"Right-so!" Dearg sighed. "I'm not keen of staying at the helm, but I'll do as you say."

Fin nodded.

"We'll let them close and come alongside," he reminded. "Remember what I said, Missy!"

Marie frowned but nodded as well.

"Fine," she said coldly, "But I'm telling you this; both of you. I won't take up a weapon on board as you heard me warn, but that doesn't mean I'll be defenseless. If anything starts to happen, I'm going to use my voice...the one I normally use underwater to stun prey. You saw what happened before. Only, be warned. When it happens out of the water its worse. There's no medium to tone it down. It will disable everybody and probably cause irreparable ear damage to anybody but me. But we'll have some time to fix things."

"Fine," Fin gave-in, "But only in emergency. I can't say why, but I trust these people."

The strange ship closed and then silently the center hull

detached and slid forward as a separate vessel. This impossible craft maneuvered alongside. Only dark, swept-back curved windshields suggested anybody inside.

Marie and Fin were there to catch heavy lines on the opposing boat to secure the vessels together but that was not needed. Some sort of magnets from the futuristic craft locked onto the side of Fin's ship.

Dropping the mooring lines, Fin and Marie watched as a small hatch slid open on the sharp bow of the craft and a figure emerged. Another low sound was heard as an automatic ladder slipped up to secure it to the gunnels of Fin's much taller side.

Another figure appeared on the sleek deck and the two nimbly ascended the ladder.

The first figure stepped to confront Fin and Marie. It was surprisingly female, very strongly built, in a dark jumpsuit or uniform. The most striking feature was a mass of brightly orange-red hair. The face seemed serious but remarkably handsome and smiling slightly.

"Name's MacAllister," she said clearly over the din of Fin's boat. "Would you be so kind as to tell your helmsman to cut the engines and join us? We can stay attached. And our sensors say he is the only other on board, aye?"

Marie could just guess that the voice held a distinctive Scottish lilt but not one she had come across before.

Fin quickly went to do as requested. The 'sensor' part had both he and Marie a bit puzzled. Fin returned with an obviously quizzical Dearg.

The second figure from the black ship now hopped spryly on deck.

This rather short but massively powerful looking man wore a white loose shirt and black calf-length pants. Marie decided he was clad positively piratical. The hair was curly, black as the night around them, and wild as well.

"O'Neill," he stated with bright black eyes and a face much weathered but jovial as if hiding mirth and who knew what other mischief.

Fin nodded a salute and gave his name.

"Dearg," the wide-eyed Irishman said, "County Connemara."

"Ulsterman, meself!" O'Neill beamed. "Family, anyway!"

MacAllister had scanned the scene and noted the case on the deck beside Marie and spoke again.

" And you must be our benefactor," she indicated Marie. "Marie, is it? Your people speak highly of you. You seem to be in the most opportune place in our time of need. Never expected it."

Marie shrugged slightly.

"Meant to be, I guess," she said lowly.

"Indeed," MacAllister continued. "And now, well, Himself..."

A third figure had somehow appeared at the gunnels.

Marie would forever more try to describe this personage. Try as she might, to herself especially, words would fail.

Clad in a black leather vest, white shirt, and dark pants what stood on the deck now was the epitome of a painting of a timeless seafarer. Dark brown almost black hair was pulled back and fashioned into a ponytail. The face sported an equally dark mustache that drooped and almost hid the mouth. The nose was prominent and, she found the word, regal in appearance.

The eyes would haunt her dreams from this time on.

Despite the low light, they shone with an eerie cold blue hue. She very briefly made the mistake of looking into them. She could only hold the gaze for a moment. They were disturbing and mysterious and dangerous.

Dearg and Fin were equally silent for the time.

"Dovarchu," he said. "Just Dovarchu."

The sound of the voice was the most chilling thing of all. It shot through the soul and seemed to demand either respect or flight in terror.

Everything Marie had heard from her family concerning this enigma paled in the actual meeting.

Dearg broke the silence.

"An honor to, to be in yer presence," he stammered uncharacteristically.

"I mean," he tried to recover, "All of you, of course."

MacAllister and O'Neill smiled slightly while Dovarchu remained unchanged.

"The honor is all ours," the dark voice remarked. "Your people are well know to us in the Old Country."

He motioned to Dearg and Fin.

"You, Milady," he returned to Marie, "And your kin are friends and collogues of ours from long ago to the present. My gratitude for this undertaking."

He stepped closer to Marie and it was all she could do to not step back.

"This is the prize?" he pointed to the case unnecessarily. "You have not opened it. I feel that you should know what you have risked so much to recover."

He took the case and Marie heard the low, bass sound again as if the case had found it's rightful master. Placing it on a table-like stanchion, he waited for all on deck to move closer. As close as they dared to him. Even MacAllister and O'Neill loomed nearer.

Opening the case Dovarchu stepped to the side to reveal the object. Nestled in a purple velvet molded interior was a sword. The blade was mirror bright and had the classic leaf design of antiquity where the middle of the weapon was wider than the point or near the hilt. Marie immediately recognized the Celtic, or older, craftsmanship. The handle and hilt were of the 'Antenna' type that actually was meant to convey the human body form. She decided that it must be of untold age but that had not put a mark on the metal.

"This," Dovarchu explained, "Has presented itself to members of my family when needed for before time was counted. Then, it hides until it is needed again. You did well not to open it. In the wrong hands it means certain demise. It has a terrible mind of it's own and when wielded in battle it destroys as it sees fit. Not even allies are safe."

Dovarchu glanced to MacAllister and O'Neill.

"We can only try to surmise why it has surfaced now," he mused. "We shall see."

"My gratitude, and now to business. MacAllister?"

The stunning woman produced a laptop and she and Marie set up the transfer of funds. When all was confirmed, in the entire incredible amount, Marie nodded to Fin.

"Thus concluded," Dovarchu said emphatically, "We shall retire."

Before she could stop herself Marie blurted, "You didn't ask after the courier."

It was a statement rather then a question and she immediately regretted it.

Sheepishly she looked into the cold blue eyes but could not bear it for more than a second and cast her own eyes to the deck.

The protracted pause almost caused Marie to panic.

"The custodian," Dovarchu stated in that voice that was so unsettling, "Was not a member of my crew. They were acting on... other orders."

Another pause ensued as Marie felt the gaze upon her again.

"I am certain that you, Milady, and I will see each other again. I am never wrong on such matters."

And then the three were off to their strange ship leaving Marie more than concerned about the cryptic remarks.

As the two ships went their separate ways in the now darkness of the Atlantic three people spoke in one of the wheelhouses over the drone of the motors.

"Glad it's all done, then," Dearg heaved as he was relieved of his arduous task and allowed the auto-pilot to return them home.

"Finest-kind," Fin agreed. "What's up with you?"

He addressed Marie, who was studying her cell phone.

"Can I make a call now?" she asked seriously.

Fin studied the GPS.

"Should be fine now, why?"

"Something's wrong," she returned. "Got a text from Shere via Jan. It says 'get back fast...trouble'..."

"Make the call," Fin said with a furrowed brow. "She don't say things like that lightly."

Dearg looked at Marie for a moment. His black eyes flashed red and then he buried the power levers forward.

16

The old doctor peered through his thick glasses at Jonathon's face for the umpteenth time. His thick, white, bushy eyebrows and thick, white, bushy mustache moved in independent but serious fashion. He reached without looking into the weathered black bag on the floor at his side and produced a modern sterile plastic wrapped specimen kit. He opened this and used the swab to gather something around the boy's nose and upper lip.

Jonathon never moved during the examination.

The youth was sitting on the sofa in the parlor. The old doctor was kneeling in front of him. Marie was standing behind her son with her hands on his drooped shoulders and a serious but not frantic look on her hard but still handsome face.

Beside Jonathon on the sofa was his sister who looked on stoically.

Dearg had just come in after hastily mooring the large ship that now no one cared about who saw it. Shere had fetched him on her second trip in the skiff as she wanted Marie to get to her son as soon as possible. Fin had been there on the first trip as well.

On the skiff Shere had tried to explain what had happened but everything was still unclear. When they arrived at the house the old doctor, a family friend and confidant for years was just arriving in his rusty 70's Jeep Wagoneer. Shere had prudently called him immediately after Marie learned of the situation.

Hunter had recounted everything he could but the mystery was too new and obviously too serious to be understood.

In the parlor Shere left Dearg's concerned side and strode purposefully over to a crumpled form on the floor in the corner.

The dark haired woman knelt gingerly but forced Celia's tear streaked face up from the knees she had her head buried in.

"Look at me!" Shere ordered. Jan turned her head as it was the most forceful thing she had ever heard Shere say.

"Look at me, girl!" she implored again. "Keening like a bloody banshee won't do anything to help him, you get me!"

Celia's large eyes regarded Shere in sudden wide shock. Her entire beautiful young face was red and grief stricken.

"You want to help? Do you?" Shere asked forcefully. She put her strong hands on either side of the girl's trembling head.

"Then pull yourself together and go upstairs and get some washcloths. Run hot water over them and then bring them down here! Go!"

Shere helped Celia to her feet and the youth tottered off as directed.

The doctor looked up from his patient.

"I know it won't help," Shere said for everyone to hear. "But it won't hurt and it'll give her something to do! I can't stand the caterwauling!"

Jan turned back to her brother while thinking that Shere was certainly changing since they had met and was now much more vocal and indeed decisive. It suited her, Jan nodded to herself.

The doctor bent back to his task, and after returning the swab to its sheath he looked up and found Fin's lowered head. The patriarch had been standing quietly near the front door.

"Well," the old physician proclaimed, "I'm going to send this sample down to Portland. Lord knows what they'll come up with and it will take some time to analyze. Something is here that the boy inhaled. I don't know what it is. Nothing else makes any sense, you can gather that."

Everyone in the room waited for the next words.

"Fin," the doctor continued, "You know me and I know you. I think this has more to do with your people than mere science. I won't ask any more questions, I know better. We've known each other far too long for that. I'll do what I can, on my end, and I'll let you know what I find, if anything. But I expect you'll get more answers on your own."

He straightened his untold-years form and scratched his wild tuft of balding white hair.

"See to it he eats. Lots of fluids, get him to go to the bathroom as needed. He seems to follow instructions well. Do anything else you would expect an old country doctor to tell you to do until I get more results."

Fin walked the old man to the kitchen door. He tried to press folded money into the doc's hand but it was refused.

"You've taken care of me plenty in the past and I didn't do nothing right now. Let's wait and see."

As the two parted at the door, the old doctor said one parting thing.

"As I said, this is more of your people and I figure you'll handle it. Call me if anything changes."

When the old man was gone, Fin returned to the parlor with a sad, lowered head posture.

"I'm so sorry," he said to Marie, without raising his head. "I'm so very sorry, Missy. I never should have brought you here. Now, it's the old curse come back on my family. I'm so sorry."

"What are you talking about?" Shere spoke up. "Don't tell me you're going to repeat that stuff! Didn't you hear the Doc? Something's been done and we have to figure out what!"

"It's the curse," Fin sighed. "It's come back. That's all."

"Now you look here," Marie shot back. Her eyes were flashing and her face took on the hard look that she exhibited when she was her other self.

"Shere's right," she continued, still holding her son's shoulders. "This is not just supernatural garbage! We all know that whatever 'supernatural' may mean to anybody else, but we here deal in cold hard facts! You all are Selchies! I'm of the Sea People! But whatever has happed to my son has all to do with something tangible and not some 'curse' that can't be explained away! I, no, we, are going to get to the bottom of this and if there's anyone to blame, which I believe there is, we are going to do something about it!"

"Right-so!" Dearg spoke up. "I can't quite wrap me head around this yet but something is familiar here! Is this what it was like for your other family members, Fin?"

"Yes," the tired man sighed again. "This is how it started. Then..."

Everyone was suddenly startled as Celia came back into the room with an armload of steaming towels and washcloths.

She dropped the lot and pointed in horror at the seated Jonathon. Her tears sprang forth again in renewed earnest.

All eyes returned to the catatonic boy. All his features remained lifeless except for his left hand and forearm. A peculiar twitching, writhing movement was taking place.

"He's convulsing!" Marie breathed. She ran around the sofa to kneel in front of him.

Strangely, Jonathon's left hand was flopping about in a wild motion. The fingers snapped loudly and quickly, making a hollow and haunting sound in the room.

Then, the hand made unmistakable gestures as if it was writing. Or, more to the point, as if it wanted to.

"What the..." Dearg started and Shere struck him on the arm to stop him.

"He wants to write something?" Jan offered.

"Quick," Shere took control again, "Dearg, go to the kitchen and get a pencil and pad! Now!"

She pushed the man into action. Sounds of him rifling through drawers were heard and then he returned with the objects. He handed them to Jan.

She put the stubby pencil into her brother's fingers and the jerky movements stopped a bit. Then she put the pad of paper under the pencil and the hand started to write.

It scrawled something and then dropped the pencil and tossed the pad across the room where it landed on the floor.

Then the hand started snapping fingers again.

During this entire scene Jonathon had not moved another muscle. His face was still a statue and he seemed oblivious to the entire process.

Shere rushed over and retrieved the pad and looked at it strangely and then held it up for everyone to see.

In large, irregular letters was an odd word.

"BEFUDDLED"

Dearg was quick to almost shout.

"By all the Powers! What an eedgit of me not to remember! I'm such a dolt! Why I..."

"What are you talking about, man?" Shere grabbed his shoulders. "If you know something, say!"

Dearg turned his shaggy head up to the ceiling and barked a curt laugh. He broke away from Shere and bounded over to Fin.

"Befuddled!" he shouted, "Don't you know the term! You should, I mean maybe you don't, but you must have heard of it!"

Fin looked blankly at the excited man.

"By all the goats in Kerry!" he implored to the rest of room. "Am I the only one?!"

"Please," Marie said through gritted teeth, "Get on with it!"

Dearg stepped back and lowered his head. He ran the fingers of both hands through his black locks. Then he tried to quiet his demeanor and addressed the room.

"It's like this," he started, rather somber-like, "It's an Anglicized word, 'be-fuddled'...there's older words but it doesn't matter. It's something that is a very, very, very closely guarded secret with our People. It's for chieftains alone. It's a thing that can be done to humans who find out about us and can't be trusted. It confuses them. They can't tell anybody else. It's only rarely used to protect us!"

"And you know about it," Shere said rather testily, crossing her arms and narrowing her gaze.

"Well, yes, that is, I, ah...found out about it...because, I, ah..."

"Because you've been around," Shere said icily. Her foot tapped the floor.

"It doesn't matter," Dearg pressed on. "Only, surely, Fin, your mother or your brother knew about this? How could they not?"

Fin was looking somewhat flushed and his mind seemed to be calculating.

"My grandfather must have been too caught up in his grief over his wife," the old man said slowly.

"Still, anyway, I can't believe it got left out. It's a powerful tool," Dearg mused.

"So," Marie caught up the thread, "Who would have knowledge of it now?"

Dearg was silent for a moment.

Jan had a thought and voiced it.

"Jonathon is not left-handed," she said flatly.

Another silence filled the room.

"No," Fin said thoughtfully, "But 'Lucky' was."

The idea sank in to the collected somberly.

"He's sent us a message," Shere concluded. "He's part of poor Jonathon now."

"Who would know about this?" Marie continued.

"Well," Dearg fumbled, "Chieftains and the like. The recipe is passed down and all."

"I'll kill him," Fin said softly. He raised his head to look at everybody and nobody in the parlor.

"I'll wring his fat neck. It's his witch-of-a-mother's doing. I know that now."

Before anyone else could speak he continued the soliloquy.

"Somehow she stole the secret. She and he are responsible for two deaths in my family and now he is trying for another. They used it to turn the Tribe against us and even had me believing in a 'curse'. They stole my family's property and our honor. I swear I will..."

"Maybe my father could help," Hunter offered-up. "Maybe he can undo it?"

"Good thinking," Dearg added, "But it's different with every Tribe. The recipe is tweaked and made so that only the one who set it has the antidote. That's so another Tribe may not interfere. And so that it can be reversed if wanted to."

"Fin," Dearg said softly but sternly, "It's high time you sought help. Don't argue with me. I know how proud you are and how ready you are for blood and action. But listen to me..."

The dark man tried to get in front of Fin but the cold eyes were somewhere else at the moment.

"Listen to me! You have to make a call! You have to ask...you know...Himself. It's time for justice and the way is to do it the old way. Do you hear me? I can't make the petition. Your blood-line will demand attention."

The gist of the conversation was above everyone else's head.

"You know I'm right," Dearg pleaded. "Don't do this alone. You've never asked before. None of your family ever has. It's time. He'll see the reason in your plight. There's so much here that may be righted. You know what I mean! Make...the...call."

Fin turned his narrowed eyes at the dark man in front of him.

"You will?" Dearg demanded.

Four days had come and gone and Jan was in the middle of a nightmare.

Her brother's condition had not improved and the entire household was trying to deal with it. She and her mother were doing everything they could to care for Jonathon. He remained zombie-like and had to be watched constantly.

Celia insisted on feeding him, which meant spooning food into his drooping mouth and wiping away most of it when it fell out. Dearg had been a trooper in assisting with the toilet duties as Jonathon had to be led into doing the most basic of functions.

Marie was holding up but growing more concerned as the days past. She had voiced ideas of taking her son to Boston for specialists but Shere had continued to promise, wisely, that this was nothing modern science could combat. Strangely, Marie had agreed given what she knew or thought she knew.

Jan found Celia, in her now constant weeping form, in the hallway near their rooms. The two simply embraced and Celia sobbed uncontrollably.

"Hey," Jan had a thought, "Jonathon told me about the two of you going up the roof. I need some sunshine. So do you. Let's go?"

The taller girl wiped the tears away and agreed. She led Jan up the close stairs and out onto the Widow's Walk. Jan thought about the title but let it go for the moment.

Celia brightened a bit at the view. Jan had not been so far privy to it and as such was marveling at the vista.

"I kissed him here," Celia finally said wistfully. "He's the first I ever kissed. He's the only one I want to kiss."

Jan stiffened but didn't give in to the awkwardness of the moment.

"I'm sure he enjoyed it," she said back rather flippantly.

"Yes he did!" Celia giggled.

Now Jan blushed for real. She was about to say something about TMI when something else caught her eye.

A black speck far up in the sky seemed to wheel about and spiral closer. She could make out long wings and a body and she realized it was a bird of some sort. Only, as the thing descended it started to grow in size and she suddenly realized it was no sea gull or even bald eagle. This was something else...

The dark-haired Asian girl broke into the office on Sequin Light in a near panic.

"Get out here, Dave!" she shouted to her collogue. "You gotta see this!"

She wildly opened drawers and searched frantically for another camera.

"What is it?" the balding scientist asked, looking up from his logbooks.

"You tell me!!" Kim shouted. "I need another camera! I was taking pictures as usual when it showed up and now the dang thing won't work!!"

"What do you mean?" Dave asked.

"Just get out here and see if you see what I see!!" she hollered back as she bolted out with another device.

He whipped on his jacket and tried to follow his female counterpart. Once on the rocks, he watched her cursing the new camera in a scathing tone.

"Look at that!!" she screamed. "Is that what I think it is?"

Dave got a cold shock down his spine as he regarded the huge bird sailing overhead. The form lazily rode the inbound currents and gracefully spun in downward circles.

"That can't be!" he shouted as well. "I never, I mean, not here, it's a..."

"A Steller's sea-eagle!!" Kim screamed back.

She tried again to click a photo but the camera did nothing.

"Not here!" Dave said incredulously. "That's a Pacific bird! Russia, maybe, sometimes China and rarely Japan..."

The massive creature seemed to lower its huge orange beak and regard the humans far below. The body of one of the largest birds of prey in the world was dark brown and black and stunning white feathers shone on its shoulders, tail, and legs.

"Why won't this camera work?!" Kim yelled. "I've tried three different ones and none work!"

She changed her aim and clicked off several rapid shots of the sea birds close by. When she returned to the impressive creature overhead, nothing happened.

"Ahhhhhhh!" she cried in frustration. "Nobody's gonna believe this!"

"I'm not sure I do!" Dave muttered back. "It looks like it's heading for...Parkers Head!"

Jan and Celia stood transfixed as the massive bird grew closer and closer. It finally came in with an impressive flutter of the eight-feet or more wingspan and grasped the railing of the roof with huge, powerful talons.

Strangely, neither of the girls moved except to take a slight step back to give the creature room.

Regally, the sea-eagle rustled its wings into folded shape and with the menacing looking sharp beak preened some feathers.

Then, it perked its large head to one side and cast its large eye at the bewildered humans.

The beak opened partially and the black tongue inside clicked.

"A very good day to you fine young ladies," it said.

Jan was not surprised at the obvious Irish accent. Both girls stood stock-still.

"May I inquire," The eagle continued politely, "As to whether or not I have found the house of one Finley MacLir?"

"You have, Sir," Jan answered back. She thought the 'Sir' was suited.

Celia just gawked.

"Ah, right-so, so I have, then," the bird nodded.

"Then, my fair Lady," the eagle continued, "Would you further be so kind as to inform the master of the house that he has company? From a-far, as it were?"

"At once," Jan responded, feeling like she was in a storybook. To further the dream, she curtsied, not knowing why, and grabbed Celia by the hand and beat a hasty retreat downstairs.

"There's a good Lass!" the bird concluded, and flapped the massive wings again to flutter down to the kitchen door below.

17

Jan had roused the house and the jumble of them now stood in front of the back door leading to the mud room and the outer door beyond.

Jonathon had been left, for the first time in days, alone on the parlor sofa.

"I'll handle this," Fin announced. He had to push through Shere and Dearg and Marie who looked on intently. Celia stood back from the rest but Jan craned to catch a glimpse over Fin's shoulder of the new guest. She wanted to catch everyone's face when they saw the huge bird. And she equally wanted to see what their reaction would be when it spoke.

Fin opened the outer door. He bowed swiftly and spoke in a voice very clear and steady.

"I am Finley Roin Magnus Og Brian MacLir," he said proudly. "This is my house, and I offer you the Scared Rights of Hospitality here. Enter, honored personage..."

Jan expected to see wide eyes as a huge bird strode into the room. What she saw instead was the massive form of an enormous dark shaggy dog.

The creature carefully wiped all four huge paws on the threshold rug and moved through the mud room into the kitchen.

Everybody else moved back in silent awe until Fin had also closed the outer door and moved to stand in front of the impressive animal. It sat down on its haunches and waited attentively.

Jan recognized the breed immediately as her mother had taken the twins to many Irish/Celtic events in Boston. This was the largest dog on the planet; the darker version of the Irish wolfhound.

When Fin had settled to stand next to Shere and Dearg the hound opened its long muzzle and spoke very clearly.

"If you will, please move a step or two to the rear. I need some space. Forgive me, but Himself likes it this way…"

All did as asked.

In a blink of the eye and an impossible to follow flow of features, the wolfhound transformed into a great, tawny male lion.

The great beast shook the full mane to fluff it to full effect.

Jan was overcome not by the sheer magic of the moment, but by the *smell*.

The room was filled with the *smell* of a lion…the musty aroma she remembered so vividly at the zoo.

The lion opened its gaping maw to reveal the sharp teeth and yawned before continuing.

"Greetings from Himself the Ancient and Forever High Chieftain of the Seal-People. I am to act as his emissary in this matter until such time as Himself the afore mentioned party may deem necessary. Are we clear?"

As no one moved a muscle, the lion continued.

"I accept the gracious offer of Hospitality and will do my personal best to treat such with appreciative actions."

The lion changed quickly back into the wolfhound.

"How was that?" he asked the assembled. "Not too formal or stuffy, I hope. It's just that Himself likes all the pomp and circumstance, you know…"

The large dog rolled large eyes at this remark.

"Nicely done," Jan offered up.

"Bit over the top," the hound mouthed, "But t'anks for the lie, anyway!"

"Now to the Par-tic-ulars..." the wolfhound yawned.

"Right," he said, moving to face Fin. "You have admitted to being the Man-of-the-House and I right-sociably put forward my highest regards as to your Blood-Line. I have known many of your ancestors and might I say that the entire lot has been rather fun. They enjoy life, and I enjoy that above all other human attributes."

"You," the hound took a few steps towards Shere, "Are his daughter. Quite a beauty, I must say, and lest you forget, my taste is impeccable."

Dearg had reeled back on his heels and was staring at the newcomer with wide, red-black eyes.

"Master Pooka!" He breathed. "Never thought I'd live to see..."

"Ah, so, and you have," the hound passed-off lightly. "Good to have that name out in the open, as it were. Not so fond of it, but you'd be amazed as to how many times my kind has seen you!"

Dearg looked quite quizzical.

"You are a loose-cannon!" the dog said rather side-wise. "I always got a kick out of seeing what trouble you'd be into next! And how you would get out of it!"

Shere punched him in the arm again to remind of past transgressions.

Jan tried to register the name given to the newcomer. She recognized the pronunciation from an ancient Irish mythological creature. A true shape-shifter of legend and renown also said to be a bit of a trickster. But why not, she shrugged. Hadn't her brother asked 'what next'? Anything seemed possible now.

"And so to the troubles at the present," the hound continued. "Indulge me, Sir MacLir?"

Fin matter-of-factly led the way into the parlor. Everyone else filed in after.

"And this is the pitiful afflicted," the hound pointed a muzzle at the seated unmoving figure of Jonathon.

The huge dog carefully approached the boy and gingerly sniffed the area around his nose and mouth.

"Aaaaragh!" the hound sneezed. "You've washed him, so you have! Been better if you hadn't, but there's still an unmistakable trace! He's been befuddled, all-right-so!"

"Then," the dog turned to Fin, "Let's have the whole story! History and all! Leave nothing out!"

Fin spent the next fifteen minutes recounting all that he knew. He went over his grandfather's demise after the death of his wife, the problems with his brother not wishing to take on the role of chieftain, the deaths attributed to 'the curse' and the whole business of his brother and 'King' and his mother.

The wolfhound listened with twitching and independently attentive ears in solemn silence. After Fin had finished and a somewhat dramatic pause had fallen over the room he lay down on the floor and closed his large eyes for a moment.

He lifted his head slowly and looked around at all the peering eyes in the room.

"Sorry to say," he started, "But shame on your grandfather, Fin, for not di-vulg-ing the secret of the befuddlement. I take it that whilst your kith and kin were out taking your grandfather to his final place there was no one watching his property?"

"No," Fin said thoughtfully. "Everyone was busy..."

"Ah!" the Pooka nodded.

"I'm beginning to see," Fin muttered.

"I believe you were burgled," the hound said with narrowed eyes, "By someone who had designs on things that were not theirs to have!"

"Back to the present," Marie spoke up for the first time. "Is there anything to be done for my son now?"

The wolfhound stood up and only had to stretch slightly over Jonathon's still form to bring his long muzzle close to Marie's concerned face.

"You, Madam," he said quietly, "Are one that I should like to speak to at length, at another stage, as it were. I find you most...curious."

"You see," He continued for all to hear now, "My kind shares a long history with all you Seal- Folk. Cousins, as it were. It is the same for the Sea-People as this Fair Lady represents, unless I miss my guess. Oh yes, hints and slyly-whispered questions from the Fey Folk, to be sure! Yours is quite the secretive and may I say dangerous part of the family!"

Jan shot a quick thought to the reference of 'Fey', meaning the 'Faerie-Folk' of legend.

"But for the present, to your question," the hound continued.

"Fin?" he asked quickly, turning to face the patriarch. "Do you have any of your grandfather or grandmother's things saved, as it were?"

"Yes!" Fin answered back. "I think I do! Everything was bundled-up and placed in a trunk. I have it somewhere upstairs in the attic, I think. Everything except their skins of course... those are in the vault..."

"The trunk will do," the hound nodded. "Lead the way..."

With Fin in the lead the entire entourage followed, except for Marie and Celia who found they could not leave Jonathon.

At the top of the first set of stairs the hound looked back and barked a short remark.

"Didn't figure on a parade, but give us room, will ye?"

Entering the musty attic, Fin pushed aside some cardboard boxes and other clutter until he came to a section well hidden amid the jumble.

He looked back at the shaggy dog and then the assembled and brushed the dust from an old sea chest. It was not locked and he started to open it.

"One minute," the hound asked. "Need a bit of a change."

With a fast motion the wolfhound transformed into a bloodhound. The dog shook its form and settled back.

"Sorry for the slobber," the bloodhound said with sorrowful, droopy eyes. "Can't be helped, but the nose knows…"

Fin opened the old trunk and stepped back.

The bloodhound snooped around inside at the contents and suddenly let out a yelp that startled everybody in the attic.

"Sorry again," it said, "But that box there is what we're looking for."

Fin fished out a decorative small arched container and held it up. Gingerly, he opened it.

Everyone wanted to see what was inside but Fin simply looked puzzled and reached in and held out a small cut-crystal squat bottle with an atomizing bulb and gold nozzle atop. There was a small amount of amber liquid inside.

"Careful with that!" the bloodhound warned. It very gently sniffed at the thing.

"And nothing else inside?" the dog asked.

Fin shook his head and offered the empty box as proof.

"What a terrible thing…" the dog started, then transformed back into the wolfhound. "Fin, that there is the antidote for your tribe's recipe. What is missing is the thing itself. That means that whoever stole the befuddlement juice didn't even bother to take the thing that would reverse the event! What a bunch of rat's knackers!!"

"Evil," Fin pronounced.

"Let's get downstairs!" the Pooka suggested. He let out a sharp, deep, resounding bark to clear the way.

Back in the parlor, the now again wolfhound sat down in front of

Jonathon. Marie had her arms cradling her son's drooped shoulders from behind the sofa. Fin and the rest entered as well to form a semi-circle around the young man. Hunter stood with crossed arms out of the way like he had for days.

"Please to back away," the wolfhound ordered. "Now, Fin, you spray a small puff into the boy's nose. As soon as he does, you, the mother, Madam; you nudge him sharply so he inhales! This is important, now!"

Fin came around in front of Jonathon and did as bid. Marie took the cue and shook her son's shoulders until he drew in breath at the rousing.

Fin backed away and there was another tense, silent moment in the room.

Jonathon sat bolt upright. His face, which had been hitherto a mask, seemed to light up and flush red. He opened his eyes very widely, shook his head, and then looked at everybody in the room strangely.

"What's going on?" he half-laughed. "Why is everybody staring at me?"

An explosion of sorts erupted. Marie hugged him tightly, even though he tried to protest, Fin sighed in huge relief, Shere and Dearg hugged each other, and Celia wailed-away in her tears of joy and fell down to hug Jonathon's knees.

Jan didn't exactly know what to do but she moved to give the shaggy wolfhound a great hug around its thick neck.

"And aren't you the sweet colleen?" the hound muttered to her.

After the bedlam had subsided into laughs Fin began to seriously tell Jonathon what had happened, how much time had elapsed, and more importantly questioned him as to what he remembered of events.

Everyone fell silent at this.

Jan started to stop hugging the hound. It looked her right in the eyes with the closest of its large, bright, brown ones.

"Ah, and you can keep-on with the headlock," the Pooka almost whispered. "I likes it, so I do!"

Jonathon perceived he was the center of attention. He looked around again and cleared his throat.

"Weird," he started, "I heard a knock at the door. Didn't think anything of it, so I undid the bolt and opened it. There was this woman there. She looked scared or something like that. Then she sprayed something in my face. I don't remember anything else until just now, when, you know..."

"What did the woman look like?" Fin asked solemnly.

"You know her!" Jonathon answered back. "The strange lady at the grocery store! Sort of old, I mean older, sorry, with white-blonde hair and bracelets jingling all over the place!"

Fin's face once again changed into a mirror image of the cold, dark rocks along the shoreline.

He nodded firmly and turned on his heels and strode off into the kitchen.

"Wait a minute!" Dearg almost yelled after him. "Stop and think a bit, Fin!"

The hound broke gently but quickly away from Jan's embrace. It followed behind Shere and Dearg.

Fin was trying to put on his old plaid jacket with Dearg attempting to stop him.

"Shear-off!" the older man growled at the younger looking one. "I'm going to end this once and for all!"

The deep, sharp, bass bark from the hound startled everyone.

"Prudence, my dear man, prudence!" the Pooka said now softly.

"I understand completely," it continued, "And I see that rightfully so your blood is high. But the young scallywag here has a point! Let us talk this through!"

"Two deaths of my kin and they try for a third!" Fin seethed, still fighting with the jacket and Dearg. "I will see justice…"

"Yes, yes you will!" the hound nodded. "But right now we need a battle plan as it were. And may I humbly remind you Sir, that I am a master in the art and that Himself will be here shortly? Let us talk with cooler heads, may we?"

Fin stopped his attempt to leave but his face was still a hard, determined thing to behold.

The hound spoke again.

"Shall we retire again into the parlor? Fin, your daughter, and the wild one, please? I need some more information, as it were."

Hunter walked away, silent still, and Marie took Jonathon towards his father's room. Celia was still attached.

"How about a movie?" Marie suggested.

Jan didn't know what else to do so she shuffled upstairs to write everything down in her journal.

Sometime later, Jan heard Dearg call for her mother. He said that 'she was requested' in the Pow-wow in the parlor.

Later still, since her door was partially open, Jan could hear the clicking sounds of the hound's claws on the stairs. She paused in her writing.

A large black nose poked into the cracked door.

The shaggy head followed.

"Ah, and may I come in?" the dog asked politely.

"Sure!" Jan said, and got up off the small bed to put her tablet away.

"I'm just nosing about…" the Pooka started.

Jan giggled.

"Glad you got the joke," the hound said.

It loped into the room and seemed to sniff the air in the way dogs do.

"Just wanted to get to know you better," it almost sighed.

"If you don't mind," Jan asked, "Exactly what is it I can call you? A name or..."

"So many names, so many times," the hound said with closed eyes.

Jan stood waiting.

"Bob," the Pooka said with wide eyes.

Jan laughed out loud.

"I fancy that!" the hound said with smiling eyes. "Same backwards as forward... what?"

"That's just funny!" Jan admitted.

"Thought you'd find it that way," was the reply.

"Ah, could I be so bold?" it asked seriously. "I mean, I'm a bit weary after the flight in and all and I could use a lie-in?"

It indicated her bed.

"Sure!" Jan offered, stepping out of the way.

The huge animal gently got up on the bed, yawned with a slight yip, and nestled down.

"Nice!" it exhaled. "Fin has too much on his agenda to offer me a place just yet, but again if you don't mind?"

"Not at all!" Jan said, and sat down on the bed next to the dark, shaggy form. It closed its eyes for a moment and then opened them to stare straight at her.

"Come on!" it said, "You know you want to! I could use the cuddle! I won't bite!"

Jan laughed at the jest and then slowly settled down next to the hound and started stroking its big head.

"Mind if I ask you some questions?" she ventured.

"Not as long as you keep that up!" 'Bob' said of the petting. He closed his eyes again.

"I've done a little research," she started, "But I want to hear your side of it. Your story, I mean..."

"Sure," 'Bob' yawned, "Figured you would."

"It's like this," he said, keeping his eyes closed, "I won't go into how long ago I came into this world. Doesn't matter, really. Your in-ter-net has probably recounted the auld tale. My kind was happy as larks, which I don't care to change into because of miniscule size, in Eire co-existing with the People of the Lady."

"DeDanaan," Jan suggested.

"Right-so," 'Bob' continued. "How were we to know we were being played when a certain group, which I will not mention by name, tricked the tricksters? They suggested we become great eagles, bigger than the one I arrived as, and carry a lot of them to go and spy on The Lady's ladies who were bathing in a stream? We thought it great sport! Never would pass up a chance to see beautiful ladies in the nip..."

He opened his big eyes.

"Sorry," he admitted.

Jan just giggled again.

"How were we to know," he started again, closing his eyes, "That it was a ruse and a plan to attack to do them bodily harm. You probably read the rest. The Lady's people prevailed but they judged us harshly for our part. More than you possibly can imagine, my dear...ah, scratch just behind the ear? That's the spot!"

"So, our punishment was this," he sighed, "Never more to be allowed to transform into any creature that has hands. You can't fathom what a cruel thing that was...opposable thumbs no more! Not even monkeys or raccoons or opossums! What a fate! And it's held on! Can't break the magic!"

"So many of my kind just couldn't take it," he spouted. "After a few hundred years or so they just chose to fade away or end it all. We weren't even allowed to leave with the DeDanaan when they passed into another realm of existence when the Irish came! So, the ones of us like me just tried to take sport where we could find it! Again, you must have read the folk stories. Scaring some poor farmer out of his wits with talking horses or better still taking some young man on a reckless bare-back race all over the island...that's our only solace!"

Jan lay her head down on the hound's side and nuzzled closer.

"Not nice at all," she whispered.

"No, not a bit." 'Bob' resigned. "We have to find some way to fill our days, which seem to be never ending. Part of the curse, I suppose. Why, think of it, just ninety-or-so years ago me own brother, the only one I had left, was having some sport up in the cold regions as a polar bear. In what you call Alaska. One minute he's just hunting, minding his own business, and the next you know he's shot and killed entirely. To make matters worse, so I'm told, they stuffed him and to this very day he stands in a musty corner of some Yukon bar. They put funny hats and lights on him as the season demands. And all because that par-tic-ular season he simply had a craving for seal and..."

He opened his eyes and stared at Jan.

"Sorry!" he said, embarrassed. "I totally forgot and..."

Jan just laughed again and buried her face in the warm, wooly side.

She tried another line of questioning.

"Have you seen much of the world?"

"Yes, yes I have," 'Bob' sighed again. "All of it, I suppose. Under the waters, too. I've learned to try meself at changing into every creature I can. Elephants and whales and great snakes and the lot. Only, the one thing they left us with was something you probably read about. I, that is we, the few left, get great sport out of being able to mix the species, as it were. Half horse, half cow, part pig, part goat...whatever! We did that before the curse. Why, surely you have read about your ancestor, Mannanan MacLir? We bounded his sea chariot all over the place with upper parts like white stallions and lower parts like dolphins! It to this day also gives us a sort of comical place with the Fey Folk from time to time."

"The Faerie Folk under the hills?" Jan asked.

"Aye and you are a keen student but listen to me," the Pooka said seriously. "I understand that you are young to your kind and just learning. If you ever run across any of them, beware, my new friend. They did not choose to leave with the DeDanaan and now they can't. They are not to be trusted. They are kin to me and so it keeps me coming back to Eire, but they can be deadly wicked and pernicious and finicky."

"Do you have a favorite shape?" Jan quizzed as she continued to stroke the large dog's head.

"Right now it's as I am and if you would, there's a spot... just down a bit...ah, and that's it!"

18

Jan awoke after a wonderfully restful night. She was still snuggled up to the peacefully slightly snoring shaggy wolfhound.

By the time she visited the bathroom and prepared for the day and returned to her room Bob was gone.

She went downstairs.

Fin was visibly not at the now crowded breakfast table.

Hunter was himself and looked sharply to devour what Shere and Dearg offered. Celia was as usual fawning over the suddenly ravenous Jonathon. Marie drank coffee and seemed light and jovial.

The newcomer at the table was the star of the show.

Seated just beside Jan, as casual as could be, a beautiful black panther sniffed and lapped-up eggs and kippered herring and bacon. It seemed totally at home and indeed the moment was further punctuated by nobody at the table being concerned at the jungle animal amongst their midst.

Just as the meal was nearing a close the mud room door swung open and Fin appeared hooded in one of the black robes.

Everyone knew what that meant. He had uncharacteristically been out as a seal.

He spoke to no one but went down cellar to the skins vault and soon returned dressed as everybody expected him to look. He shot a quick glance to Shere and something silent passed between father and daughter. He filled a coffee cup and went back outside.

The morning passed very pleasantly as Bob entertained everyone in the parlor with what he had spoken to Jan about the night before.

With a delighted Celia as childlike as ever, the Pooka took requests and had everyone in stitches with his antics. First a creature with donkey ears and goat's body with an elephant's tail, then a hyena's head with a small poodles' frame ...he solicited ever-increasingly impossible animal combinations with hilarious results. The grand finale was a dizzying spectacle of a thing with Great Kudu antlers, a Hippo's head, a Zebra's body, alligator legs and a large Platypus beaver flat tail.

As the laughter subsided, Marie asked a question.

"Is there nothing you can't do?"

"Ah, then, as I told your wonderful daughter," Bob admitted, "Nothing with hands or fingers or the like. Oh, and nothing mythological. Pity, that. Also, no species that has gone extinct; there's times I could have used a T-Rex or something, but sadly, not allowed."

Fin entered the room and somewhat deflated the moment.

"I need to speak to all of you," he said flatly.

Bob transformed into a gorgeous golden retriever and lay down with perked ears.

Jan stifled a giggle at the mirth and caught a wink from the Pooka.

"Things are in place," Fin continued. "Each of you has a part in what's coming. You will be notified as to what that part is. We are a family, with honored friends, and we will prevail. Please do not ask more than what is asked of you. All will work out if the pieces fall in place."

Then he was gone again. That left everyone with an uncomfortable but important feeling.

A rather large male seal swam around the island that had a single, impressive house on it. Satisfied as to the inactivity, it sought out a secretive opening under the rocks and surfaced into an enclosed room above. Shedding the seal skin, the male figure stood before a heavy door and pushed the button on the intercom system.

After a paused moment, a voice crackled back.

"What do you want?"

"I wish to communicate with the Chieftain. Now."

"What is this about?"

"Just get him. I won't talk to the likes of you. If I have to, I'll break this door down and you won't like what comes next."

Another protracted pause ensued until finally the door opened and 'King' stood red faced and silk-robed.

"What do you…" he started.

"Shut-up!" the naked and muscled human form barked back.

The figure was not young and not old; impossible to gauge the age. A thick gray-dappled beard and very long silver hair flowed around thick, stocky shoulders. The strong arms held a folded skin under one but the other raised a powerful hand to point an index finger at the fat form behind the doorjamb.

"How dare to speak to me…" 'King' started to blubber.

"I have a message for you," the man continued. "The Gathering is to take place in three day's time, at the high tide and risen moon. The place is to be the auld one, Malaga, in the ring of the trees."

"What insolence!" 'King' started. "This has to be that old coot Fin…"

The strong silvered-haired figure shot out the free hand and pushed the fat one, in the center of chest, backwards to stumble.

"In case you've forgotten," the long haired man continued, "Fin has used his contacts to protect us for years. You have no conception of the satellites that loom overhead! He has knowledge through contacts you don't care about of when and where they look down on us! Seal Island is exposed and even if you keep breaking the cameras of the bird-watching people, any passing boat could discover us! I personally think you use this to keep the meetings short. Everyone's nervous. You have occupied this dwelling that was built to keep us secret, denying us that respite, but hear me now!"

'King' had regained his feet, if not his dignity, and two other male faces appeared behind him.

"I'm not afraid of you!" the figure barked menacingly. "You know who I am! I've been silent these many years because I thought it didn't concern me! I know different now! I'm telling you this! You show up to Seal Island and there won't be a soul there. You show up to Malaga and face us, the Tribe that you have treated like chattel for far too long! You are elected, might I remind again, and you have some explaining to do!"

'King' tried to regain composure and puffed through his mustaches.

"I'll see you there..." he tried.

"Yes you will!" the powerful form seethed back. "Myself and more!"

He bowed in an obvious mocking fashion.

"Until then, *Chieftain*" he spat, the intending slight well voiced.

With a fast motion, he slipped into his seal skin and was gone with a resounding splash.

Jan felt like a prisoner again as the entire household was busy and secretive about the coming Gathering. Fin spent much of his time down on the dock communicating with the bobbing heads of what she perceived to be members of The Tribe. She also supposed that he had contacted his brother, her grandfather, and that this was to be a serious affair.

Her mother had outlined in a brief way what the two of them were being asked to accomplish. Many questions lay unanswered, but Jan was stoic in not asking them and instead reveled in seeing the dangerous and at the same time exciting plan. She felt as though her mother had placed a trust and a confidence in her that had never transpired before.

She felt like an adult.

Something was indeed brewing, like a storm over the Kennebec mouth, and even her dreams reiterated the fact.

Maggie-Shannon figured prominently in the nightly ventures. Her tinkling, warm, soothing 'voice' had a new and somber seriousness about it. Yes, it would be alright, it reassured her, but also warned in unintelligible ways about clear and present dangers.

The one thing Jan missed most about her days was the total absence of Bob. He had changed back into her favorite wolfhound just after Fin's announcement and bid her have a moment alone away from other ears.

"Got me duty to attend to," he had said. "I will see you soon, and I fancy that a great deal. I'm growing fond of you, Miss, and I know you will perform brilliantly."

Jan hugged his thick, furry neck.

The animal sat down and presented a great paw like a trained domesticated pet wanting to 'shake'.

Before she could take the outstretched offering, he surprised her entirely by making a lightning move and licking the side of her face.

"EEEUUWW!" She laughed, pretending to wipe her cheek.

"Ah, you love it, and you know you do!" the Pooka chuckled back. "See you soon, colleen..."

Hunter seemed only present at meal time and was repeatedly told that it was too dangerous to enter the water. He voiced all the young peoples' yearnings but took it in stride.

Celia and Jonathon remained inseparable in their not-so-secret blooming romance. They spent time up on the widow's walk and watching what was left of his father's video collection. Jan chided herself in her rising jealously and thought of calling Red numerous times. She never did, bowing to the severity of the situation at hand at present.

'What good would it do?' she wrote in her diary. 'I don't even know if he feels the way I do. I don't know what that means.'

Shere seemed a dominant figure. She went about her days conferring with Dearg and her father in private. Jan liked the new role she saw. Shere's set face made her even more beautiful and proud and strongly-feminine.

A good moment presented itself on the day before the Gathering was supposed to take place. Jan observed Shere beginning to haul seemingly all the black robes from their holding place.

"Could you give me a hand with these?" Shere asked.

"Sure!" Jan jumped; glad to have something to do.

They loaded the lot into the old fishing boat and stowed them with Shere carefully counting.

"We have to have enough," she explained.

Jan wondered silently what that meant.

Later that night, Jan was about to turn in when she realized she had not spoken to her mother for most of the day. She knocked at the closed door.

"It's me," she called.

"Come on in," her mother called.

Marie was reclining on her bed and obviously on her own computer and this she put aside as she warmly greeted her daughter. She motioned for a well-sought-after hug.

"Mom?" Jan started. "Is this all real?"

Marie stroked her daughters' head and cooed a soothing response.

"It is, if you believe it, Darling."

"I do," Jan said, putting her head on her mother's chest. "I don't know why, but I do…"

Jonathon lay on his bed on his back and stared at the ceiling in the diminished light. Sleep seemed impossible with all the thoughts running through his head. The nagging fact that he 'needed' sleep was the nocturnal curse of insomnia.

"What do I do?" he said out loud.

The short cough sounded like it was just across the room. Then he smelled the cigar smoke.

"You need to quit that," Jonathan scolded.

"Not going to do me any harm now," Loki's voice chuckled. "Anyway, YOU need to get off your keister and go find the girl. Now!"

"What's wrong?" Jonathon almost yelled. He sat bolt upright and stared across the room at nothing.

"Just go," Loki said.

Jonathon swung his legs off the bed and reached for his crumpled trousers.

"Fresh ones!" Loki sighed. "And a clean shirt! Sheesh!" Jonathon switched on the bedside lamp, but he still could not see a form to go along with the voice. He quickly went through drawers until he had the required items.

"I don't know how to tie a bowtie," he muttered as he threw the clothes on.

"Yeah you do, now, but don't be a wisenheimer," Loki returned. "And she's not in her room, no need to try and 'quietly' knock so as not to raise suspicion. You know where she is."

Jonathon slipped shoes on and headed for the door. He stopped for a moment.

"Thanks," he said over his shoulder.

"What are partners for?" came the reply.

Just as he opened the door Jonathon had a thought.

"McLeer and Larson," he said.

"Get out of here, already!" Loki laughed, coughed, and the cigar smoke was gone.

The moon was bright enough, almost full, so Jonathon had no problem seeing on the widow's walk. He stepped slowly towards the figure seated in the folding chair. Her head was lowered, and she didn't try to stop the sobs even though he knew she knew he was there.

"Want some company?" he asked shyly.

"Sure," Celia said blandly. She didn't look at him.

He sat down in the empty chair and noticed that it was not as close to Celia as it had been the last few times they were up there. He didn't try to move it.

After a long pause Celia seemed to control her tears but still did not look at Jonathon.

"What are we supposed to do?" she said suddenly without moving. "We are about to go into something that quite frankly scares me. Dangerous characters, Pookas, Sea People, I mean, just what are we supposed to be?"

"I guess," Jonathon shrugged, "We can only be ourselves."

Celia barked a curt laugh, stood up quickly, and walked to the left-hand end of the walk and stood at the railing. She didn't even attempt to look at Jonathon.

"Right," she said as she threw her head back. "Right, and that's just the problem, isn't it? My problem, my doing, no way to fix it."

Jonathon sat stock still.

"I mean," she continued to the open dark sky, "You may be new to this, but I know my skin's pasts and they talk to me all the time. Sometimes I wish they didn't. So, I then know that your skin, as powerful as it is, has figured me out as not the best actress to tread the boards. As they say."

Jonathon sat forward slowly and put his forearms on his knees.

"He told me just a little while ago to come find you," he said slowly, "And that was all he needed to say."

He couldn't see her eyes, but Celia finally looked his way.

"How long have you known?" she asked flatly.

"Oh, pretty much all along," he admitted.

"Then why didn't you say something?!" she nearly shouted.

Jonathon sat back and reclined as best he could in the folding wooden chair.

"At first," he started, "I was simply so stunned by the impossible thought that such a beautiful lady would be remotely interested in me."

Celia made a move as if to rush at him, but Jonathon held a hand up and stopped her.

"Hear me out," he continued. "The more I got to know you the more it was crystal clear that, for whatever reason you have, you felt it was necessary to play down your obvious amazing intellect. I figured, or really hoped, that you would eventually feel safe enough with me to be the real you. I mean, drop the act and just enjoy each other's company."

Now Celia did move towards him slowly. The tears returned.

"You have to understand!" she implored. "That has nothing to do with how I feel about you!"

She stopped and put both her hands to the sides of her slim face.

"And that's just it! Why would you believe anything I say now! I don't know why I did it! My mother, some of my skin's past lives, they all told me to act the blushing, demure, bubblehead. Keep my thoughts to myself. Be disarming. Then, when I first saw you, I got screams in my head saying that even after they had warned me about not getting involved so soon you were the one. My thoughts, no, deep feelings, told me. Why go through heartbreaks and incompatibles and years of disappointments when the right one for me was right in front of me! And now you can't trust a thing I say or do! Great."

Jonathon stood up slowly.

"I love you," Celia muttered.

"That's a good thing," Jonathon shrugged. "Because I love you. And, I didn't let my oft times low self-esteem convince me any otherwise that in that aspect you are genuine. Now let's look forward to a very exciting future. Together."

Celia let his words sink in and then flung herself on him, almost knocking him over.

Between sobs she kissed him like there was no tomorrow.

19

The woman with the wild, platinum hair pulled the expensive car to its normal place by the dock. She fumbled for the key fob that released the trunk lock and then struggled to transfer the cases of coffee brandy to the waiting motorboat.

A strange sound made her pause.

It was a pitiful whimpering.

She looked around and finally spotted a small form in the bushes just off of the side of clearing. She walked over, tentatively.

"What's this?!" she exclaimed. "Who are you?"

A shivering, pathetic and at the same time adorable miniscule dog eyed her with sorrowful and soul-melting eyes.

"Oh, my goodness!" the woman said through red-lipped pursed mouth. "Are you lost, Snook'ems?"

She spoke as if talking to a baby.

The tea-cup Pomeranian shivered and whimpered again. It raised a feeble little paw.

The woman looked around. She knew no one lived anywhere in the vicinity of the nearly hidden dock.

"Where did you come from?" she cooed. "You are sooooo cute!!"

The dog shivered and whimpered again, flailing the tiny lifted paw.

"Oh, you come to Mamma!" she doted, scooping up the shaking animal.

The dog lapped a tiny tongue to the make-up covered cheek.

There was more heavy covering cake make-up than usual. It was supposed to hide the bruises there but did a failing job of it.

"Oh, aren't you sweet," she continued in the fawning. "No collar or tag? I can't leave you out here all by your precious self, no I can't!"

A sudden thought crossed her mind.

"I don't care what the big brute will say," she decided. "You're coming home with me, yes you are, Snook'ems!"

The little dog licked even more at this news, producing further babying and cuddling.

As darkness descended on the old house, Jan felt an inescapable tenseness. It was as if every timber and hand-cut board was bracing for the coming storm. She had heard and read of old dwellings taking on an indescribable life of their own and now she knew what that meant.

Supper had not been served, much to Hunter's disapproval.

"Grab a snack on the way," Dearg had suggested as he passed, busy with his own orders. "Only, don't dawdle. Much to do tonight..."

Jan had caught the impossible joke and passed it off as 'normal' under the circumstances.

Shere was obviously about to leave when Fin appeared.

Jan was looking on with no one appearing to notice.

"Get them there and moor the boat on Horse Island," Fin said softly. "Are you ready for this?"

Shere straightened up and simply looked straight into her father's eyes.

"Good," the older man nodded.

Marie called for her daughter from upstairs. Jan obeyed and left the scene.

"It's time," Marie said, when she caught her daughter's eyes. "Ready for this?"

She had her hair tightly braided and had the murderous shark-toothed stick in its holster and belt by her side. She had a simple towel wrapped around her shapely form. The bag containing what must be her tail was on the bed next to her.

"Let's go," Jan answered back, with her own towel in hand. She started to quickly strip off her clothes.

"Of all the stupid, impossible, stupid things you have ever done!" the robed and ranting fat man shouted.

"Don't you listen to him," the woman with the platinum hair said into the small dog's ear. "The big old scary man won't harm a hair on your pwccious-widdle-head!"

"If I find even a spot on the carpet," 'King' continued his bellowing, "I'll skin that thing alive and have it for breakfast!"

"You won't do nothing of the sort!" the woman shot back. "This little bundle is the nicest thing to come into this house in forever!"

As if to accentuate the point, the Pomeranian nuzzled closer to the woman's neck and buried its small head in apparent hiding.

"I don't have time for this!" 'King' blustered. "I'll deal with it later, you hag!"

Two other male figures stood close by at the apparent ready.

"Let's get out of this madhouse!" the boss shouted. "I've got a score to settle tonight and I may have to break some heads!"

"You mean the two of us might have to," one of the figures noted.

"You shut up!" 'King' pointed. "You do as you're told! Let's go!"

He stormed off with the other two in tow.

The door to the secret changing room closed and the woman placed the tiny dog on the expensive sofa and gave its face a good tousling.

She was about to turn and fix herself a drink.

"I thought he'd never leave," the dog said.

The woman stared with ever widening cheap green painted eyelids and ridiculous arched brows.

Her mouth dropped open. If not for the over-done make-up her color would have been seen to turn a sickly shade.

"Right-so," the Pomeranian continued. "Now, down to business. Oh, and thanks for the snacks. Greatly appreciated, I must admit."

The woman took a few unsteady steps backwards. She gawked at the dog on the sofa in disbelief. Her bangles jingled in her nervousness.

"How shall we do this?" the dog continued. "You've been so kind and I'd rather not be showy, but..."

She fell to the floor in a near faint.

"In a few minutes," the pet continued, "There's going to be visitors, as it were; to the room you keep over the water. The very same that the oaf and his lackeys just exited from. I would greatly appreciate it if you would be so kind as to gain them admittance. If you would..."

The woman started to scramble and make a hasty retreat.

"Ah, and if it's to be that way, then," the dog resigned.

He sprang from the couch and in mid-air transformed into a massive white Siberian tiger. He growled lowly and cut off the woman's frantic escape.

A terrifying roar came next. What few pictures hung on the walls rattled and threatened to fall.

The hapless and petrified woman fell to her knees.

"Don't hurt me!" she sobbed.

"Now then," the tiger rumbled in a more civilized tone. "To the doorway?"

He gracefully licked a raised, sharp-clawed paw.

The woman crawled towards the secret room and somehow managed to gain her feet. She kept looking over her shoulders at the impossible feline following. Surely it had to a hallucination...

"There's a good girl," the tiger purred back.

She fumbled with the door latch, which was recessed and hidden. The entire door was built to be indistinguishable from the rest of the rich panels on the wall.

She swung the portal back, not knowing what else she might find behind it.

Her eyes indeed grew wider still.

Facing her was a serious but very attractive woman with tightly braided hair. Beside her was a younger version of the same only with unbraided hair.

Except for the strange object slung around the woman's muscular waist, both figures were stark naked.

"Ahem," the tiger said pointedly. "Might you get them robes?"

As if to play the gallant, he put one large paw over his eyes.

Jan tried not to laugh as she saw him sheepishly peeking between claws.

She tried instead to continue the severity of the moment.

The platinum haired one reached to gather some white terry robes. She offered them to the newcomers.

"Smells like men," Marie said with upturned nose.

"And not good ones," Jan offered.

"I'm so sorry," the frazzled woman stated, looking back to see if she had displeased the tiger.

Marie and Jan stepped out of the room and quickly went to work.

"Take us to his office," Marie ordered.

"Right away!" the older woman conceded, "Down the hall!"

When she turned to lead the way, the tiger had been replaced with a 12 foot King Cobra. The snake raised its wide hood to eye level.

"Time isssss of the essss-ence," it hissed.

"Ahhhh!" the woman howled. "I hate snakes!!!"

"Thought you might," the snake noted aloud.

As the mortified woman hurried to show the way, Marie followed but Jan held back a bit.

"Bit much with the hissing," she whispered to Bob.

"Effect is everything, my Dear," he said back, then transformed into a snarling hyena.

The older woman led the group down the carpeted passageway into a wing of the house that more resembled an expensive hotel. Jan noted the many doors on either side.

"Here it is!" the make-up-covered woman indicated. She pointed to a closed door by itself at the end of the corridor.

"Cipher lock," Marie muttered. "What's the password?"

The dazed and confused woman wrung her hands and the bangles made a dreadfully annoying sound.

"I don't know!" she pleaded, "So help me...!"

"Right-so," Bob said flatly. "You Ladies back up. It's el-e-phant time!"

"Wait," Jan said, having an idea.

She punched some letters and figures on the keypad. A green light replaced the red one and she tried the handle and opened the door.

"King#1," she announced. "What a sleaze!"

"In a word," Bob the hyena agreed.

They all entered the room.

As beforehand prescribed, Jan set about rummaging the large desk and Marie went to the vault. It was stupidly open.

"My, my," Bob observed with peering hyena beady eyes. "Look at the cash, will ya?"

"More than that," Marie said out loud. "Deeds and contracts and everything we need. Did you find it, Jan?"

"Here it is!" she said proudly, raising a small black-leather-bound notebook for all to see, "All the passwords and all the bank accounts. How did this guy walk around without bumping into walls?"

Her mother simply took the book and sat down in front of the somewhat archaic computer.

The keyboard was greasy and the chair smelled like stale fried chicken.

"Password?" she muttered.

"Try the same," Jan suggested.

Marie laughed out loud at the unbelievably predictable blunder.

"Got it," she muttered. Her fingers flashed on the keyboard. "Transferring now"

The woman with the platinum hair could not keep her ridiculously painted eyes off the hyena in the room.

"What are you?" she managed to shake.

"Yer not of Irish extract, are you then?" the Pooka asked back.

"No," the woman continued, "German and Austrian…"

The hyena became a snarling silver wolf with bristling hair along the powerful neck-line.

"I'm the one who ate Grandma," he growled. "I'm the eyes in the Black Forest that you know are there but can't see. I'm the thing under the bridge…the one you don't dare cross without, ah…"

He looked over to Jan who was standing with crossed arms and a look of consternation.

"I think she's had enough?" she admonished.

The wolf shrugged the powerful shoulders and looked somewhat dejected.

He changed into the form of a 20-foot salt water crocodile.

"I'm yer worse nightmare," he snapped convincingly.

"That's done," Marie announced. "I've changed the passwords as well. We need to get going. Only one loose end left…"

The older woman knew she was the now the center of attention.

"I only did what he made me do!" she blurted. "I'm so sorry! Don't hurt me!"

"Don't hurt you?!" Marie shouted, jumping up from the chair.

"You tried to kill my son! You've been a pathetic part of everything this monster has perpetrated for as many years as anybody can remember! For all I know, you know what happened to my husband! I know this fat excuse had something to do with his disappearance! No one would blame me if..."

She whipped the shark-toothed stick from under the shabby robe and pointed it at the trembling woman across the desk.

"Please!" the woman cried, sinking to her knees and putting her flabby arms up in supplication. "I didn't have a choice!"

The now silly silver bracelets jangled on trembling wrists.

"Ah, point of fact" Bob noted to diffuse the moment. "She does bare signs of abuse, I'll own to that."

"That coming from a crocodile?" Marie observed.

Bob changed back to a Golden Retriever and lay down.

Marie stepped from around her seat and continued to point the weapon at the woman's turkey neck.

"Mom," Jan said softly, "Is there another way?"

Marie seemed to listen and made a rough inspection of the cowering woman's painted face.

"He hurt you," she said, "A lot. Didn't you have any chance to leave or to get away from him? You had a choice!"

"No I didn't!" the woman cried back, real tears streaming down her caked face. "Well, maybe I did. I don't know! I wanted to! I..."

"You are to be pitied," Marie decided. "You don't and never will have a clear conscience. What would you do if we let you go?"

The woman rolled her eyes and thought frantically.

"I...I have a sister," she tried. "Older and she knows nothing about all this! In the Mid-West! Small town; I could..."

"Maybe you could," Marie softened. "What's to stop you from telling anybody about all this or..."

"Nobody would believe it!" the woman pleaded. "I swear I wouldn't say a word!"

"Not good enough," Marie decided, raising the stick again.

The Pooka interrupted the scene by changing into a sparrow and flitted around the room. Then he became a common house cat and rubbed up to the woman on her knees.

Changing again to a mongrel dog of mixed breed he addressed the one on trial for her life.

"I'll be watching," he said, "Me and my kind. You won't know we're there. But we will be. You best be kind to animals; you won't know if it's us or not. And should you falter..."

He transformed into a coiled rattlesnake.

"We'll know."

"Yes, yes!" the woman groveled, "I won't say a word! Only, I might need..."

"Saw that coming," Marie said, lowering her weapon. "Get whatever you can carry of that blood-money in the vault. Only, you won't receive another dime! If you try and want to bilk us for..."

"No!" the woman almost screamed, "You'll never hear from me again! I swear!"

"Get out of here," Marie ordered. "Take the money; get in your boat, into your car, and leave. You have just five minutes to get any personal belongings. Clothes you can buy later. Do I make myself clear?"

"Yes, yes, thank-you!" the reprieved blubbered. "I'm going! I'm out of here!"

"Start now," Bob offered, and changed into a squealing tusk-wielding Russian Blue Boar.

The woman grabbed handfuls of bundled money from the safe and made a hasty retreat.

"That went nicely," Bob said pleasantly, changing yet again into a white Shetland pony.

Jonathon came downstairs with Celia close behind. They had been yet again up on the widow's walk watching the darkness unfold.

He found Fin who seemed to be looking for him.

"There's a new ship in the bay," Jonathon noted. "It's a well-weathered sort of rusty large thing. It's flying an Irish flag off the stern and I think I could make out 'The Rover' as a name."

"Ah-yuh," Fin answered back. "I saw it. Don't concern yourself with it. I'll tell you more later."

"Right now," the white-haired man continued, "We have to get going. You remember what we talked about?"

Jonathon snapped to attention and saluted.

The comic antic was somehow lost.

"Young lady?" Fin looked at Celia. "Dearg and Hunter and Jonathon and I will change first, and then you follow us. Got me?"

Celia nodded her head and her now well-shaped brown hair tousled in the movement. Her doe-like eyes suggested understanding.

"I know it's a bit of a stretch wanting you and your brother to be there tonight," Fin admitted, "But there are reasons for you to do so. Tide's coming up, the moon is rising; let's get ready." The venerable man turned and headed for the boathouse.

Celia kissed Jonathon strongly on the lips and then sped upstairs.

"Gonna be a night to remember," he said in the Bogart lisp. "Bet your bottom dollar on that, Sweetheart!"

He heard Lucky's smoky laughter in his head.

Jonathon followed the other three male seals in a mad, determined, silent swim. Celia stuck close to his side. He noted that he had never seen Fin as a seal and that his great uncle appeared strong and resolved; not at all giving away his land years.

They all surfaced nearly together to catch air in the race. Past the mouth of the river, over the white sand shoal, they passed rocky islands and did not slow until the looming view of Malaga was seen.

As he followed the others, Jonathon saw below them the still present buttons that littered the small approach to a beach. It reminded him of the old times and sad history that he knew would still hang about the place.

Fin and Dearg changed quickly and donned the black robes. Hunter did as well. There was no time for abashment and Jonathon changed and took the offered robe Dearg held out. He placed his skin in the pocket inside and was a bit surprised as the three men turned their backs, still close-by and waiting.

He understood.

Celia surface and with no hesitation shed her skin gracefully. She gave him a coy, beguiling look as he tried desperately not to stare and offered a robe like a gentleman.

It seemed not to matter much as a line of dark seals' heads had appeared in wait of the same transformation. As Jonathon and Celia followed the now serious and silent members of his group, he looked over his shoulder to see many forms, male and female, making the magical change. Small piles of neatly folded robes awaited them.

Passing across the rough sand beach, a strand of gently rustling trees came into view. Fin led the way as they found a very old path into the interior of the island.

More dark forms of robed figures had already assembled. They formed a deathly quiet ring.

A lithe figure approached and Jonathon knew without peering outside of the heavy hood that it was Shere. No signs of endearment passed. This was all business, Jonathon decided.

No words were spoken and the only sound that could be heard was the haunting wind in the trees; the trees that had witnessed all the atrocities on this island and perhaps more of these meetings in antiquity.

In small groups of two's and three's more Selchies filed in. Jonathon placed the running count at near twenty or more.

As the near sanctimonious scene enacted itself, finally a group of three large forms came from the opposite side of the ring of tress.

The most portly of the three detached itself and moved into the center of the robed, head lowered assembled.

"I have issues!" 'King' shouted, breaking the sacred silence. "I demand to know why this place has been chosen again! Who is responsible?!"

His words faded on the night air with no response. All robed heads continued to be lowered.

"I am your Chieftain!" he bellowed. "What's all this about?!"

No response was given.

"What are you waiting for?!" he further ranted. "Answer me!"

A strong, bass, male voice came from somewhere just behind the trees to 'King's' right.

"They were waiting for me."

'King', his hood now thrown back, glared to see from whence the voice came.

"They were waiting for me," the clear, booming voice rang out. "Me...and my honored entourage."

'King' and his two accomplices were the only heads that turned.

Four figures strode proudly into the ring.

The lead figure was the most impressive, by far.

The black robes worn by everyone else was tied casually around the muscle-rippled waist to form a sort of kilt. The rising moon shone brightly on the massive, broad, powerful shoulders. These precluded being covered by the otherwise ample robe.

Jonathon tried to keep his head down, as ordered by Fin, but he could not help but wonder at the sight.

The man had every appearance of something out of a myth. Or perhaps a graphic-novel depiction of one, Jonathon thought.

Huge arms bulged with muscles and the chest was like something off a statue. Red-gold hair flowed down the equally ripped back in a mane fashion. The face was stern and regal and sported a mustache that covered the concealed mouth.

In a single moment, all the Selchies fell to one knee.

Jonathon followed suit.

Only a staring, wide-eyed 'King' did not. Even his goons shakily genuflected.

The three that accompanied the impressive figure did the same.

Striding to tower over 'King', the figure did not hesitate to bring a smashing blow down on the fat ones' right shoulder.

This crumpled him to the ground.

"Insolence!" the figure said lightly. "Know you not who I am?"

"You are..." 'King' started.

Another blow sent him lower to the sand.

"Speak-up!" the man above ordered.

"You are the High Chieftain of the Seal-People! From the Old Country! Your Highness!" 'King' managed to blubber.

The large figure placed the massive arms on hips and swelled even larger with pride.

"I am!" he said sternly. Then he turned from the cowering form and addressed the assembled.

"Rise, my good people... let us greet each other."

All did as commanded. The hoods were slowly removed and the Selchies silently nodded greetings to each other.

"On your feet!" he seethed at 'King'.

Jonathon recognized his grandparents but none others save Fin's household.

Two other figures approached from behind Shere. Jonathon saw his mother and sister. That came as a relief and he realized all had gone well.

The Pooka followed close behind as a midnight-black sleek stallion with red, flashing eyes.

The High Chieftain did his best to catch the faces of everyone there.

Jonathon thought he heard Celia gasp a bit but then she was

silent. She seemed to be diverting her eyes from one of the three that had arrived with the High Chieftain. The young man looked to this figure with interest.

"Thank you," the High Chieftain said with a flourish of his great right arm, "For your most honored invitation, by way of the venerable Finley MacLir, to this most hallowed event. I wish to introduce my equally honored guests for the evening's proceedings."

"Most of you of course know the respected Chieftain of the Northern Tribe..."

The tall, regal-looking man nodded his head slightly without losing any of his commanding composure.

Jonathon studied the countenance of Hunter's and Celia's father. His hair was their color and must have fallen far down his back. It was held in place by the robe. The face had Hunter's features only with a slightly more pronounced sharp-set thin nose. Again, nobility was written in the strangely light eyes and serious visage.

"And, if I may continue," the High Chieftain indicated the other two, "These are my trusted kerns."

Jan recognized the word as a Celtic one meaning the ancient weapons bearers and shield-men who protected a legendary warrior. The term was similar to that of 'squire' but with a much deeper allegiance-to-death.

The men certainly looked the part, she decided. Just as in the artful pictures in books on ancient Celtic lore, their hair was cut in a bowl fashion and the mustaches were again of the type only allowed to be worn by the warrior-caste. Their mouths were completely hidden by the bushy things. They crossed strong arms and the heavy robes seemed to want to burst stitching.

'King' suddenly pointed a chubby index finger in the direction of Jonathon, his sister, and mother.

"Outsiders!!" he screeched. "Fin has broken the unforgivable rule of bringing outsiders and..."

"Silence!" the High Chieftain barked at the bulging eyed, red faced puffing character. "I allowed it! It seems there are some grievances with you, 'Chieftain'!"

The word was spoken with obvious distain.

'King' tried to regain some particle of fortitude.

"Grievances?!" he huffed." They have no right..."

The High Chieftain raised his hand in a blur of motion. 'King' cowered again expecting another blow.

"You will stand," he said very slowly and powerfully, "And for once at least act the part of your sacred, *elected* title."

"But that one," 'King' continued, risking further punishment and pointing to Marie, "Is not even of our people! She is..."

Marie cut him off.

"I am your *first* accuser!" she said with rising ire in her clear voice.

She strode into the circle and marched up to face 'King'.

"May I?" she tactfully asked of the High Chieftain.

"Proceed," he allowed, sweeping his arm again, "And well-met, Lady of the Sea-People. It has been far too long since I have been graced by your race's interesting company. We are cousins, you know!"

Marie bowed slightly and then raised an arm to point at 'King's' ever-reddening face.

"You attacked my children!" she said, "No 'Chieftain' treats ones who are related to such a clan as their father's as such. So, I protected them!"

She cocked her head to the side and eyed the long, not-healed slice on King's cheek and jaw line. The stitches looked angry and possibly infected.

"Nice scar!" she almost purred.

'King' started forward but the point of the same weapon that had given him the mark suddenly appeared in front of his bulbous nose. He froze immediately.

"Do you know why I didn't kill you?" Marie asked icily.

'King' made no motion and only trembled at the lethality threatening him.

"So I could do this," she smiled.

Lowering the weapon, she slapped 'King' extremely sharply on the wound.

He fell back and, howling, put both meaty hands to cover his sobs.

"I have other issues with you," she said lightly. "But others will address that. No matter what else takes place tonight, just know that I have exacted my revenge. You'll find my people are famous for that. You'll find out soon enough..."

She turned to go back to her place.

"Thank you," she said softly to the High Chieftain as she passed.

"Well-met, indeed!" he said so that no one else might hear. His sharp eyes twinkled in approval.

Jan watched with pride as her mother stalked back. She also noted Hunter's father nod his head slightly as he watched. His slight smile was a bit wolfish, she thought.

Fin now moved a few paces forward but came no closer than that to 'King'. He raised his white head and began to speak.

"People of my Tribe and our honored guests...I hereby accuse the one who has abused his title given to him by us...of using a 'befuddlement' charm on members of my clan."

He let the words sink in. There were many slight murmurings around the circle.

"This magic," he continued, "Was meant to stop ones of the land-people from exposing us to disclosure or harm. But in fact it was used first on my mother and then on my sister. You were told it was a 'curse'. It was not. It was the deliberate misuse of things to keep you in line."

"My mother..." 'King' started, but was silenced by Fin's rising voice.

"Oh, she might have ordered the dirty deeds," he almost shouted now, "And she didn't have the courage to put a knife in their backs, but they died just the same! And just this week you tried the same thing on my grand nephew!"

Jonathon stepped forward at this.

He walked, like his mother, right up to the shaking hulk of 'King'. Leaning his face in close, he opened his eyes wide.

"Boo!" he shouted, making King flinch. "Didn't work, did it, blubber-head!"

He snapped his fingers in front of 'King's' blinking eyes and turned and walked back.

'King's' eyes bulged further. He started to take a fumbling step backwards.

As one, the two kerns brushed 'King's men aside and stopped his retreat.

The High Chieftain shook his mane of hair in consternation.

"Serious charges," he said solemnly. "The MacLirs' word is without reproach. How do you answer to this?"

'King' looked back at the kerns worriedly. He seemed to be grasping for words.

Fin spoke again.

"You can't even now face the truth, can you?"

A tense moment ensued with the wind rising to rustle the trees all about the assembled.

Fin now walked to stand and face the accused.

"Hear me now," he said to his Tribe, "I demand the rights of single combat with this pathetic excuse. I will end this tonight!"

"Hold," the High Chieftain interjected tactfully. "You have every right, Finley, but a point of order must first be enacted."

"Tribe!" he asked loudly. "Will any of you stand to retain this person as your Chieftain?"

The silence was punctuated by another gust of haunting wind.

'King' looked for his men. They looked at each other. Finally one of them tried a chance at pardon, seeing their lost plight.

"We didn't go along with it!" the one with the close-cropped red hair and beard pleaded. "His mother did the two women, and he sent his consort to do something to the MacLirs! It was only by accident the young one opened the door! We even refused to help when he..."

"What else?" the High Chieftain pressed, a strong hand placed on 'King's' shoulder to stop him from spinning around at the presumed treason.

"Well, when he..." the man continued, "When he used the charm...on his mother..."

A now serious muttering erupted from the Tribe.

The other goon chimed-in.

"We wouldn't help him!" he spouted, "When he chained her to the rocks and all! We said we wouldn't do it!"

"Oh," the High Chieftain closed his eyes and lowered his head. "But sure enough, you two have done your share of misdeeds, I'll own to that!"

"Matricide!" Fin further accused. "Add that to the list! And you two have forever soiled your names by trying to intimidate your own Tribe! Some of them kith and kin! And for what? I ask you...for what?!"

"Further point of order," the High Chieftain reminded, "If you are to depose this one, then who will take his place?"

Another complete silence filled the clearing.

"I will stand," the clear voice stated.

Jan's heart rate raced as Shere stepped forward.

Her wild features were now completely composed in the

moonlight. Her dark eyes were sharp and focused. Her mouth was set in a serious thin line.

"My people, you know me," she said proudly. "You know my family, you are aware of my lineage."

Nods began to come from the assembled.

"I will swear to you," she continued, her beautiful head thrown back in pride, "That I will make us what we once were. I will release you from the mindless restrictions of fishing grounds. I will do my utmost to restore relations with our northern brethren."

Here Celia's father smiled his somewhat wicked grin and nodded again.

"I will reopen the house intended for our collective use." Shere continued, "It will be a haven for us to reconnect as a Tribe of trust, not fear."

'King' started to open his mouth at this.

Marie interrupted his attempt.

"Just so you will know," she stated, "Tonight I have entered the house that was stolen from the Tribe to be turned into a sin-palace and diverted all the accounts and funds where no one else can touch them. I will turn over all of this to whoever is elected."

'King's' deflated slumped shoulders suggested a near final defeat.

The High Chieftain regarded the Tribe.

"If there are any more candidates?"

"Very well," he conceded, "Any opposing member may take a step forward?"

None moved.

'King's' men stood with bowed heads, not wishing to cloud their accepted guilt.

"Hail!" the High Chieftain said loudly. "You have made your choice! Please join me, Chieftain MacLir of the Southern Tribe!"

Sharon stepped proudly to stand next to the impressive figure.

Fin tried not to beam. Dearg's smile was somewhat tempered at what he knew his life was to now become at the right hand of the Chieftain and his love.

Jan could not help giving-in to the approving, tinkling sound of Maggie-Shannon.

Jonathon heard the smoky, chortling laugh he now knew all-too-well.

"Chieftain," the tall, muscular figure asked very seriously, "There is a matter before you. I trust you will act in the best interest of the Tribe, as I feel you will."

Shere nodded seriously and gazed at 'King'.

"Before you," the High Chieftain indicated, "Are members of your Tribe that have been justly accused of high crimes. How do you wish to proceed?"

Fin stepped up again.

"I remain fast in my challenge of single combat. My family's revered dead and attempted victim demands satisfaction. Blood for blood… it is our way."

Jan noticed Hunter's father smiling again at the thought. Despite his regal bearing, she thought it cold.

Shere locked her dark eyes with 'King's' bleary, darting ones. She never broke her steady, narrowed gaze as she addressed the High Chieftain.

"I bow to your wisdom, most Honored One" she conceded. "What is your verdict?"

"I find the deposed guilty," he shrugged his strong shoulders. "By admission of his own trusted he has betrayed both your Tribe and our people. The request for sacred combat is more than justified. However, my new Chieftain, your family's honor not to be dismissed lightly, has to be tempered by your now-not-to-be swayed loyalty to your charges. May I elucidate?"

"Nice choice of words," the black stallion mumbled into Jan's ear. "See why I likes Himself?"

Jan nodded thoughtfully. She passed off the fact that the comment had come from a talking horse.

"Finley," the High Chieftain continued, "I myself have been on this earth longer than even I could have imagined. There are things in this world worse than death, quickly administered, as I feel confidant you might dispatch."

'King' cringed again at the thought.

"I have at my disposal," he mused aloud, "A fate more in suiting in keeping with the severity of the crimes."

Fin waited as so ordered.

"My magic is old and far-reaching," he thoughtfully said out loud, "And I have skins for just this sort of purpose. I can place this vermin into one of these. He would not be able to converse with any of our kind nor the seal population except for me. I would order his every move. I know of several places, undisclosed to preclude chiding, where the land-people hold seals in captivity...to be gawked-at and viewed as artifacts. There-by exuding further..."

"I have questions," Marie spoke-up. "I feel he has some knowledge as to what happened to my husband...the father of my children..."

"Answer to the charges?" the High Chieftain again queried.

'King' said nothing and shut his mouth in guilty defiance.

"Right-so," the High Chieftain resolved. "This is what I meant. Untold years in restrictions in a tank might loosen lips."

'King's' right eye threatened to positively pop out of his skull. The other one was still half closed in wincing pain. His mouth dropped opened and he was finally the buffoon for all to see.

"No!!" he pleaded. "Not a cage! You can't do this to me!!"

"Very well," the High Chieftain shrugged again, "Then my kerns will lead you out to meet your challenger. They will see to it you don't skulk away as I presume you would..."

"No!!" 'King' tried again, understanding the consequences of that scenario.

The kerns again as one grabbed his arms in an obviously painful vise-grip.

Shere looked to her father.

"I accept your terms." she nodded.

Fin locked his face in resolve.

Jan took notice of Celia's father making a move to regard King.

"What a pity," he said, the voice sounding like black velvet cloth lightly dragged across a cutting razor's edge. "If Finley had not, I would have relished killing you ever-so painfully for your affront to my family."

The strangely sinister smile was only tempered by another odd look shot to Marie.

He moved to pose next to the High Chieftain.

Jan thought he looked like a heart-throb star on the red carpet at The Oscars.

"Take this filth out of my sight," the High Chieftain ordered. The kerns dragged 'King' off despite his sobbing and moaning.

"Chieftain MacLir," the High Chieftain called, "There remains the plight of these...lap dogs!"

Shere moved solidly to confront them.

"You have done much wrong," she said after the long pause, "To my family, to my Tribe, to the very name of the Seal-People. You have no home now as before. You have no stolen money to pamper your vices with. You have nothing to protect you, as all here know of your bullying. I decide that you be given a chance...the chance you would never give another. If at this time next Gathering you have redeemed yourselves, then you will be welcomed back into the Tribe. Until that time, you are banished from the Meeting House. Reconnect with your Tribe in any other way you wish, but be mindful of my wrath should you continue your ways. Understood?"

The two backed away, rather groveling at the Chieftain in

thanks. They turned and disappeared into the trees from whence they had come.

The Tribe nodded approval at the generous act of their new leader.

The High Chieftain again addressed the throng of black-robed figures.

"You have chosen well!" he said. "I see a great future ahead for you all! I must take my leave now, but first I wish to greet each of you in turn. Good hunting, good living, Southern Tribe!"

Still rather silently, the Tribe began to mingle and talk quietly. Some embraced family and friends with human arms for first time since the last Gathering.

Everyone paid their respects to Shere and congratulated her. She smiled ever so slightly but remained the epitome of a leader. She told many that she needed time to 'fumigate the stench' from the Meeting House but that soon all would be welcomed to come and go as they pleased. She would stock the place with victuals and comforts and no locks would preclude them.

Just as the High Chieftain had begun his rounds to meet and greet the Tribe warmly, Bob whinnied into Jan's ear.

"Ah, me Darling, I must attend to some business," he whispered.

Jan pretended to pout and stroked the devilishly handsome horse's muzzle.

"Cush, cush now!" he snorted back, "I'll see ya again before I depart for parts-unknown, as it were! I couldn't stay away!"

With that he bolted away and blended into the night as the large sea eagle again. His flapping wings made no sound as he soared out over the island and across the dark water.

Jan was about to walk up to her brother and admire his tenacity in the night's encounters, but she halted as she saw Celia sobbing uncontrollably into his arms. The scene might have been comical: her taller than he and having to bend to bury her pretty head into

Jonathon's chest but her heaving shoulders spoke to the severity of the moment.

Not wanting to interrupt, she instead caught up with her mother.

The High Chieftain had already paid his compliments on Marie and now more of the Tribe was engaging her in light conversation. Tactfully absent was any mention or line of questioning of her people and the history of the same.

Suddenly the group parted in hushed tones as Hunter followed his father to part the small crowd with not even a glance left or right.

The thin smile of the Chieftain of the Northern Tribe played across his sharp features. He had released his long hair from the robe and it now flowed down his back and around his shoulders in stunning effect. His eyes, which were shockingly gray, seemed bent on being locked with Marie's. She instead simply nodded politely.

"My most sincere thanks," he began silkily; "For your protection of my son and daughter. Hunter has told a small bit of your...gifts?"

Marie dodged the compliments deftly.

"Fin offered his house and his wise protection," she said. " He was the one who suggested we all come up. I feel it has been good for your children to interact with young people near their same age. I think they have learned a lot."

She expected Hunter to say something to that effect, but he had transformed into a mirror image of his father's aloof, regal statue.

"I imagine they have," the Chieftain mused, in passing. "I will thank the MacLirs as well. Only, it is more paramount for me to learn more about *you*, My Lady. I have not been so fortunate as to have met a member of your people before tonight, and if I may say, if you are to be in any way indicative of them, then they must indeed be a fetching lot."

Marie was grateful as Jan sidled-up to stand even closer to her. It allowed her to not make eye contact with the Chieftain and instead to gaze down at her child.

"May I introduce my daughter?" she asked, without looking up.

The Chieftain's smile faded slightly but he regarded Jan briefly.

"You have your mother's beauty," he started again. "Don't you think so, my son?"

The remark was said over his shoulder to Hunter without a hint of head movement.

"Yes, father," he answered rather automatically.

"Well then!" the Chieftain said, switching tactics. "I will return tonight as I arrived, via the conveyances of the High Chieftain. Decorum, you must understand. But if it is suitable, Hunter and Celia will return to the MacLirs and I will collect them in a day or so? I am due to purchase a new land vehicle and the taxes here in your country are much more agreeable than in mine, not that it matters much..."

He swept an arm to his chest in parting and then wheeled and was gone with Hunter in tow.

Jan looked up to her silent mother.

"Was that the biggest come-on you've ever seen?" she said quietly so no one else would hear. "And did you notice he never looked for his daughter? She's over there..."

Jan started to turn and point to where Jonathon had been trying to console Celia. She was somewhat shocked to find both of them suddenly standing very close by.

Celia was still shaking, her head ever buried in Jonathon's collarbone.

Marie walked to them in slight alarm. Jan followed as well and they were detached from the small group that had been talking to them.

"Mom," Jonathon said strongly, "I know this has been a crazy night... a crazy, crazy night! But as soon as we can, maybe when we get to Fin's, I have to talk to you. It is urgent."

"Of course!" his mother offered, noting that her little man did not sound so little anymore. "Everything alright?"

"It will be," he said back in a voice that cut through Marie's soul as it sounded much too much like his father's.

The next hour passed painfully slowly for Jan, her brother, and their mother. When it was clear that the evening was drawing to a close, Marie found herself face to brawny chest with the High Chieftain.

He spoke directly to her and there was no one else near enough to hear.

"My dear Lady," he offered softly but strongly, "I am impressed with your entire character and representation of your people. I remind you that we are cousins from far, far back in time. I wish that this could be a storybook ending...that I could produce your husband in a last minute Faerie-Tale wonderment. Alas, it cannot be."

Marie did her best to not shed the tears that welled-up in her eyes.

"I vow this," he continued, a massive arm clasp to his muscled chest. "I will use all my powers, which are great, to uncover this mystery. My word is the ultimate bond. Do you understand this?"

Marie breached protocol and hugged the rippled breast, at least as far as her arms could reach around.

"I will have contact with you and yours when I can," he finished, somewhat flushed, and gently broke away.

The High Chieftain made a grand exit with many flourished well-wishing.

More confidence and compliments were passed to Shere as the new and welcomed Chieftain. Embraces were imparted from all the members of the Tribe as they said farewells and slowly trickled to get back to the water's edge and change back into seals and dissolve into the night's dark waters.

Fin and Dearg helped collect the discarded robes and arrange them into neat piles to be picked-up at a later stage.

Finally, Fin and his daughter and her lover changed and were gone.

Hunter had not waited for his sister and instead followed Dearg.

Jonathon had waited patiently, eyes again diverted, as Celia changed and then he went to escort and further comfort her.

Mother and daughter were left alone on the island that, if it could speak, could spin a tale of happiness and woe.

Marie and her daughter changed together and swam back to the house that had figured so prominently in the summer's unfolding.

The two male seals conversed tersely as they swam.

"This was your idea," one said to the other. "I told you it wasn't a good one!"

"Leave-off!" the other muttered. "It was a good run; we got a good life, so what if it came to a bad end!"

"Just saying," the first shot back. "Now what? Thank the powers my cousin left the place for us to go to! Otherwise…"

The two surfaced on a rocky shoal of the mainland away from prying eyes and shuffled up the bank.

They both froze in absolute fear at the sight that confronted them.

A tremendous polar bear stared at them. The beady eyes of the beast caught theirs and locked them in a trance of terror.

"Good evening, gentlemen," the bear spoke lightly.

"I have been around a very, very, very long time," the bear continued. "I have come to be a keen gauge of character. In you two I foresee no good at all."

The white behemoth let the words sink-in.

"In fact," it continued, "I might very well see into the future!

Oh, you will placate yourselves and do whatever you feel necessary to gain a pardon from your Tribe. I heard what your new Chieftain said. But you will, at some stage, seek a way to exact your revenge and in so doing may jolly-well hurt some of those I have taken a liking-to. You must see I cannot allow this?"

The two sets of bewildered and mortified eyes stared in disbelief.

The bear casually sat back down on its haunches.

"Have I used too many big words?" the bear asked rather sorrowfully. "Anyway, more to the point..."

Two massive, powerful blows from first the left giant claw-set paw and then the right smashed seal skulls and sent the bodies airborne for a brief moment in opposite directions. The bodies then crashed down on the pebbled shore in instant death.

"Sorry about the skins, Fin," the bear said woefully. "But then, you wouldn't want them anyway...tainted, as they were."

"Right-so!" the polar bear sighed. "Never waste a meal, I says...let's find out why you were so bent on this, me brother...wherever you are! And a pox on those drinking tonight looking at your stuffed-self!"

20

As Marie and Jan reached the house, in the garb they left in the boathouse, lights were on despite the late hour.

In the kitchen everything seemed just as it had been before the night's happenings. Dearg sat close at the table holding hands with Shere and beaming. She had her hair composed and she seemed comfortable in gray sweat pants and shirt. His dark eyes shone a lighter shade of the twinkling red. He had on the skin-tight black shirt and jeans.

Fin was seated across from the two, smiling as well, in his plaid.

The compliments and congratulations were not needed here in this home. As surprised as the newcomers might have been, this seemed to have been well thought-out and executed perfectly.

Hunter was opening cabinets yet again in forage.

"Mom?" Jonathon called from the parlor. "Can we talk now? Just you, please. I'll talk to you later, Sis, OK?"

Shere looked up and caught Marie's eyes. "Go...let me know if there's anything I can do?"

About what, Marie wondered. She walked into the adjoining room strangely worried in some way.

Jan shrugged and went upstairs to catch up with the events in her journal while they were still fresh.

Jonathon was seated on the couch with one arm around a much more composed but still obviously upset Celia. He nodded for his mother to take a seat in the chair nearest them; the one normally reserved for Fin it seemed.

She did so, placing the bag with her weapon and tail on the floor next to her.

"Mom, please, don't say anything until you've heard me out, OK?"

Marie nodded but she knew something important was about to take place.

"I've been doing a lot of thinking these last few days, oh, maybe the whole time here. I know your first response is going to be, and rightfully so, that I'm too young to be thinking like this. But hear me out..."

"For the first time in my life I see a clear way to go. Not maybes or might be or 'I'll have time to think about it later'. I know what I want to with my life."

Marie tried not to smile or admonish or show any emotion other than her full attention to what he was saying. A knot in her throat started to grow.

"I am supposed to pick-up where Dad left off. I want to learn to help Fin and Dearg in their salvage. I've thought this through. I want to spend as much time as I can up here. I need my education, I know. You can help me back home set up the course of study; only, I don't want to go back to my school."

Marie started to speak now, disobeying her own wishes.

"Wait," her son cut her off, "You have to listen to me. You said now we got a lot more money. I want to accelerate classes and in some other school in Boston and get what I need from tutors; whatever. I don't have to pretend anymore to you, Mom, you're too smart. I don't fit in to my school and I never will and I haven't told you near the truth about the conditions with bullies and inept teachers. But I want to come back up here as often as I can to get my real schooling from the guys at the heart of the biz..."

Now Marie raised her hand and demanded a word.

"I understand this," she said solemnly, "But I have to ask, as a mother and concerned party here. Does this have anything to do with Miss Celia here seeing her father tonight and realizing she has to return home tomorrow or the next day?"

Fin had told Shere and Dearg that he was going down to the dock to 'clear his head a bit'. When he was gone, Dearg had cast a long, romantic, comical glance to his love when Marie popped her head from around the parlor doorjamb.

"Shere," she called softly but with an urgent twinge, "Or should I say Chieftain? Might we have an audience, alone with you, for just a while?"

"Of course," Shere said, rising immediately and heading in that direction. She made no excuse or even looked back at Dearg.

"And so it begins!" he muttered, drumming his fingers on the table.

Shere found her father gazing out over the black expanse of water at the far end of the dock. He didn't turn around. He knew her footsteps, as light as they were.

"Father," she almost whispered, her voice matching the lapping small waves, "I need to speak to you about a matter."

"Oh?" he asked now, and turned to smile at his daughter.

She noted the moistness of his venerable eyes.

"But first..."

She flung her strong arms around him. He didn't resist. His hug back was as much a flood of unsaid words that needed no voice. It was his way. It was the way of his people and all those along this rocky, sometimes inhospitable shoreline.

"Thank you," she almost sobbed. "Thank you for everything. I don't tell you what I feel often enough. You are my rock. You are my father and my friend and my teacher. When that thing happened with those men..."

"Hush!" Fin soothed back. "It's me who should be thanking you. Your mother, our family, our people are so proud of you. And I am proud of you."

They embraced for a long moment that didn't seem so long.

"Ah-yuh," he finally said, holding her at arm's length, "So what's this thing we need to talk about?"

A brand new Jaguar car gracefully pulled to a stop at the end of Fin's driveway path. It was silver in color and seemingly not suited for the somewhat rough passage.

Even before the purring, strong motor was switched off, Marie and Shere were outside to greet the new arrival.

The driver stepped out lithely and deliberately showy.

The Chieftain of the Northern Tribe was dressed in a white silk shirt, open at the neck, and gray twill trousers with a thin alligator belt. His rich hair flowed more than halfway down his back.

He regarded the two women and then slowly removed his expensive sunglasses and tossed them haphazardly back into the car.

"I am grateful for the welcoming committee!" he smiled, closing the car's door.

"What do you think?" he asked without expecting an answer. "I visited the hamlet of Scarborough and whilst they thought to sell me a Range Rover for the clime of my haunts, I found this more...sleek...and in keeping with my character, what?"

The two women didn't fall for the play.

Hunter exited the house with the backpack that contained his newly gotten clothes.

"Ah, good," his father noted, "Punctual as ever, my son. Well done...now to your sister?"

Celia came out of the house, her head down, with Jonathon at her side.

"Are we ready?" her father asked rather distractedly. "I must say my thanks to Finley, and of course, the new Chieftain, to you as well."

Celia lifted her pretty head and looked right into her father's disarming and to most women's alluring gray eyes.

"I'm not going, father," she said quietly.

"What's this?" he almost chuckled. "Of course you are! Now..."

"I'm not going, father!" she said back more strongly. "I want to stay here!"

There was a protracted silence.

"Well, well," the Chieftain of the Northern Tribe said, the smile straightening to a thin line. "What have we here?"

Shere spoke up.

"I will take her as my charge," she explained. "I know this is not what you expected so quickly as to my vow to reunite our tribes, but I have entertained her request."

The man with the long hair regarded his daughter as if for the first time.

"Do you remotely expect me to...?"

She in turn spoke to him as she had never dared.

"I am of the age!" she reminded. "Back home you expect me to choose who I am to be with. I have made that decision. He is here."

Her father now scrutinized Jonathon for the first time.

His face showed consternation for a brief flash before he regained the nobility mask.

And another wolfish smile returned.

He looked at Marie.

"My Lady," he started, "It seems we have a budding romance here! I have heard of your son's legendary skin and how it chose him. I am also somewhat intrigued as to a merger of his father's revered bloodline and mine; then add to that your own..."

"Wait a minute!" Marie shot. "Let's get this straight! Your tribe might find Celia 'of age' but I certainly do not intend for my son to get into any of that right now...that's the way we do it... for some time to come! I'm only saying..."

"What are you saying?" Celia's father further almost grinned. "What is to become of my daughter in this...arrangement?"

Shere took up the thread.

"As I said," she reiterated, "I would take your honored daughter into my house. I will instruct her in ways that one day may lead her to Chieftainship. Our tribes would have something new in common. I will swear to her safety!"

"It seems," Celia's father mused, "That she has decided she can take care of herself! And make decisions. That is testament to my bloodline! But on this other front..."

"Listen," Marie chimed in, "You know who and what I am. If Celia wishes to spend time in my house, there is no one who could offer her better safety. She could grow visiting the city. I could show and teach her things no one in either of your two communities could. And, I might add, despite what we adults banter about here, I will insist on strict, straight rules until such time as we all feel confident in anything further. Young people may change their minds."

"So," the man with the long hair almost laughed, "I have yet to hear from you, young sir..."

He looked at Jonathon with what could otherwise be called a withering gaze.

Without hesitation, he spoke clearly, taking Celia's hand in his.

"Sir, I know everyone here thinks me young and possibly brash. But look me in the eyes. I see my future clearly and it includes your precious daughter. I will not harm her, I will honor her, and I will protect her. I will prove to you the love I have for her. And when the time comes, well, you know the rest."

"Most interesting," her father noted. "What an unexpected turn of events. What do think of this, my son?"

He asked the question again without looking at Hunter.

The young man appeared briefly to be at a loss. Was his father actually asking for his true thoughts on something?

"My sister is of the age," he said, empowered, "I, of course, wish to return with you. But I have a good opinion of Jonathon, as well as his family. They have offered us nothing but pure hospitality. I say she has chosen well."

Another pause filled the still air.

Hunter's father switched to another mode and lightly walked to stand much too closely in front of Marie.

"I will again," he said to her alone, with all others clearly listening, "Say that I find this...most fortuitous. It will cause the two of us to spend some time getting to know one another."

"I hope to meet your wife as well," Marie stated blankly. "Shame she's not here?"

The face of the Chieftain of the Northern Tribe made a protracted attempt at not feeling the blow.

"She is seeing to her duties," he remarked matter-of-factly, "As she should."

Shere broke the tension.

"If you would, Chieftain, honor us by stepping into our house for a brief moment? We need to get some particulars down. My father's contacts can produce a passport and even a dual citizenship birth certificate can be obtained. Most of our Tribe has had such documentation rendered to reinvent ourselves for time's sake."

"As you say," he removed himself from Marie's personal space and lifted a white-sleeved arm as if to follow. "Hunter, this will not take long, I trust."

He nodded and followed his father and Shere.

This left Jonathon and his mother alone with Celia.

She threw her arms around Marie and hugged her tightly.

"Thank you!" she cried. "You are going to be the mother I want and miss!"

Marie hugged the girl back but looked to her son.

He shrugged and gave her the comic look she remembered from his father and that he had used since he was small.

"I told her you were the best!" he said smiling. "Oh, and remember, we have to make a trip soon down to the islands. I promised her I'd show her those funny, bright fish! Not to mention our family that I want to meet!"

Marie closed her eyes and laughed as Celia refused to let go.

Jan wandered out onto the scene.

"What did I just miss?" she asked.

21

The sun was just about to set and a welcomed breeze wafted in from off the bay through the open window of the room Jan had grown to love.

The day had been hotter than she supposed Maine summers could produce. She had just finished writing in her electronic journal and was wondering where the story would end for the present.

Without a doubt, she thought, the past few weeks had been the best of her young life.

Spending as much time as she could as a seal could not be fully captured in words. Shere and Dearg had taken Jonathon and Celia and her on several multi-day excursions to the far-flung islands to the north. They had visited the borders of the Northern Tribe and witnessed firsthand, or first-flipper, 'The Old Sow' whirlpools. Days had passed peacefully sunning on rocks and the nights had been magical sleeping under the stars.

There was no fear now; no boundaries it seemed. The word 'freedom' had taken on a new meaning. As before she had always regarded the ocean as something formidable and dangerous; it was now her second home and indeed the more preferred.

Jan's only regret had been that her mother had chosen to not accompany them. She had instead trusted Shere and gone back to

Boston to see to the business and inquire as to the legalities and steps needed to 'home school' her brother and at certain times Celia who was sure to not to want too many days away from him.

Oddly, she did not feel but only a hint of jealousy at their constant, happy inseparability. He was her twin, she often reminded herself, and they had shared everything else in their lives together. Even the still-sometimes-remembered impossibility of their Selchie sides and the improbable fact of their mother's magic. Yet none of this could allow her to deny him the unbridle joy he was enjoying.

She thought back on the recent times when they had visited the Tribal House, as it was now referred to. Shere had made good on her promise and it had become a place filled with laughter and good times. Jan had met so many more of the Tribe and spent valuable hours with her grandparents. That bridge had been firmly built now.

Her thoughts strayed back to the sea again. She knew it would be difficult to ever again keep her mind far from it. The looming idea of returning to school seemed like a prison sentence about to be enacted. How could she possibly see the faces of her acquaintances and classmates and enter into the same old post-summer-break questions?

'How was your summer?'

'Oh, I went to camp and met these gorgeous boys!'

'I hung out at the mall and got these killer outfits, how do like them?'

'Jan, what did you do?'

'Found out I was a Selchie and spent most of my time as a seal. I met a shape-shifting Pooka, foiled a bad guy, and oh, by the way, my mom's a mermaid!'

She imagined the blank stares.

'And I met this cute guy...'

That would register.

On that subject she was...a bit jumbled.

After she had returned to the house last week Fin had slyly mentioned that Red had inquired about her whilst getting his father's fish needs. Fin had told him when she was to return and the very next morning his truck had appeared in the driveway.

He had asked Jan sheepishly if her mother was about and then Shere had overheard and stepped in.

"I'm taking care of her," she had said rather inquisitively. "Is there something you wish to ask?"

"Yes, Ma'am, I mean, would it be alright," he had stammered, "If I take Janet to go get a bite down to Popham?"

Shere had considered this and in a Chieftain sort of way agreed.

"I trust you will act as a gentleman in keeping with your family's name?" she had grilled.

Red had nodded and as Jan started to get into the truck Shere had gotten very close to her ear and loosed a shockingly uncharacteristic low growl for her alone.

Jan had looked at her and caught a cat-like witty smile.

It was not until they were seated in the café by the beach that Jan realized she was on her first real date.

The meal went by with small talk and she felt very, very grown up.

They had walked on the beach then for a wonderful time. They again spoke of their likes, their dislikes, their differences and pleasantly their many shared things in common.

Red had her back in a sensible time and Shere had noted their arrival through the window but had chosen to leave them alone.

"Guess you'll be going back to Bean Town soon?" Red had finally said through the awkward pause.

"Yeah," Jan had actually sighed. "And you'll be working on the boat?"

"Ay-yuh," he answered back. "Not very interesting, is it?"

"Hey," Jan said back, and placed her left hand on his strong chin to make him face her.

"*You* are interesting," she said, locking his eyes with hers.

He hadn't moved to stop her from holding his face.

"I have to tell you," he had said slowly. "My family, me, well, we know about your family and I'm guessing you are one of them too. We have respected your people for many years, my father taught me, and..."

She had stretched from her seat and kissed him firmly for longer than she thought she could or should.

When she had settled back, she almost laughed at his blushing.

"Red Sanders," she said, "I'm going to be back to spend a lot of time here...as much as I can. See you again?"

He had nodded somewhat handsomely dumbfounded as she laughed and got out of the truck and went into the house.

She had not been sure, but she wanted to believe she had heard him shouting a "Whooo...Yes...Finest kind!!!!" as he drove away.

The sun was fading and Jan thought she might go to turn on the light in the room when a puffin with a brightly colored billed fluttered its short wings to land on the open window sill.

"Good day, me Darling," the bird said. "Plans for the evening?"

"Why, no!" Jan chuckled back. "What do have in mind?"

"Ah, well, you see," the Pooka clacked through the short bill, "I've taken the liberty to speak to Master Fin. He is waiting downstairs to drive you to the beach. I thought we might spend some time before I'm off again?"

"I'm there!" Jan nearly shouted, flinging her tablet aside and heading for the door.

Fin was quiet and smiling for the ride. He only mentioned casually that she was not to be too smitten with the Pooka's company.

Jan had nodded but was giddy with excitement.

Fin parked the old truck in a secluded spot near the open

expanse of sand shoreline. It wasn't long until a dark, large, red-eyed horse approached.

"My compliments, Master Fin," it said. "Just a wee bit of galloping in the night; you know the sort of stuff we are famous for?"

"You hold on tight, Missy," Fin grinned to Jan. "Your mother would probably disapprove of this..."

"Until she tried it," Bob shot back.

"Now, up you go!" he ordered Jan. "As Fin said, hang-on, girl! Grab my mane. Doesn't hurt much...there's the way!"

Jan swung up to straddle the horse barebacked. She didn't have time to thank Fin as they were off like a shot.

Down the beach they raced faster than Jan knew a mortal horse could muster. The salt wind in her hair and the sand flying up behind them were incredible.

It didn't take her long to learn to bend and match the movements of the muscled shoulders. Bob encouraged her all the while.

"Ah, and you're doing grand!" he said back to her. "A veritable steeple-jockey, you are, right-so, me pretty!"

Jan laughed, cried, and screamed in delight and exhilaration until she noticed that they were heading at break-neck speed towards the water. As he showed no sign of letting up, she had to bend close and shout into his perked ear.

"What are you doing?" she nearly screamed.

"Remember," the Pooka turned his horse's head and shouted back, "When I told you I couldn't change into anything myth-o-logical?"

"Yes!" Jan yelled back, her hands clutching the long mane and her eyes intent on the impending surf.

"I lied!"

Two massive feathered wings erupted from the heaving shoulders of the dark horse, just under Jan's clamped knees. They spread out and caught the stiff wind. The rising feeling made her believe she might fall and be lost entirely. She buried her face in the thick mane and heard her voice scream in a detached way.

Then, she looked down and beheld the strand of white beach far below them.

She was born aloft and the view was ever so much more than stunning.

The huge wings flapped and they wheeled around. The sea was a black velvet blanket below and the sky, with the shimmering stars, was an endless ceiling above.

"Wanted to show you my world," the Pooka called back. "You are worthy of it, with your gentile spirit."

"Thank you!" Jan cried and hugged the thick neck. "It's beautiful! You are so beautiful!"

"I'll take 'handsome', if you don't mind!" Bob answered back. "I have to tell you that the magic prevails. Anyone seeing us would only perceive a large black eagle. No photos work. It's the thing. We're alone, as it were!"

Time stood still as the two soared over the vista. Whenever Jan thought she might have the hang of it, the Pooka dropped or rose to give her an exciting change.

Presently they spiraled down and Jan felt her stomach drop again in a pleasing way now.

They circled a rocky outcrop she had come to know well.

Seal Island was indeed covered with sleeping forms. Most of them were just that; seals, but she detected some of her own kind. Some of the males of the animal species woke and started a barking at the overhead disturbance.

"Been quite the season?" Bob asked over the huge wings. "New things and all. What do you think of it?"

Jan simply hugged the strong neck tighter and let herself fall into the bliss. She lifted her right hand to tousle the rough hair between the alert ears lovingly.

The Pooka sealed the moment.
"Guess I'll give a name to it," he muttered back. "Summer of the Seals…"

Printed in the USA
CPSIA information can be obtained
at www.ICGtesting.com
CBHW071518180824
13255CB00044B/1188